Ray Connolly first becam[e] interviews in the *Evening* [...] later he wrote the Atticus [...] and, most recently, had weekly interviews in *The Times* on childhood. As a screenwriter he wrote the films *That'll be the Day*, *Stardust* and *Forever Young*, while for television he wrote *Lytton's Diary*, *Defrosting The Fridge*, *Honky Tonk Heroes* and the first series of *Perfect Scoundrels*, as well as writing and directing the documentary *James Dean, The First American Teenager*. His novels include *A Girl Who Came to Stay*, *Trick or Treat?*, *Newsdeath*, *A Sunday Kind of Woman* and *The Sun Place*. He is married, has three children and lives in London.

'A quality read – well-researched, stylishly written' *Daily Telegraph*

'Connolly has produced a book that keeps you reading to the last page . . . one not to be missed' *Evening Telegraph*

'This book is aiming for a large readership and it thoroughly deserves one . . . A feeling man's Jeffrey Archer would be a fair description' *Sunday Telegraph*

'Compulsive holiday reading' *Today*

'Murder, ambition, love and jealousy: it's all here, and the writing's good as well . . . I found it completely absorbing' *Good Housekeeping*

'One of the best books I have read in a long time' Barbara Taylor Bradford, *Mail on Sunday*

SUNDAY MORNING

Ray Connolly

CORGI BOOKS

SUNDAY MORNING
A CORGI BOOK 0 552 13947 5

Originally published in Great Britain by Bantam Press,
a division of Transworld Publishers Ltd

PRINTING HISTORY
Bantam Press edition published 1992
Corgi edition published 1993

Set in 10/11 pt Linotype Sabon by
Falcon Graphic Art Ltd, Wallington, Surrey

Corgi Books are published by Transworld Publishers Ltd,
61–63 Uxbridge Road, Ealing, London W5 5SA,
in Australia by Transworld Publishers (Australia) Pty Ltd,
15–25 Helles Avenue, Moorebank, NSW 2170,
and in New Zealand by Transworld Publishers (NZ) Ltd,
3 William Pickering Drive, Albany, Auckland.

Printed and bound in Great Britain by
Cox & Wyman Ltd, Reading, Berks.

For Charles Wintour

Acknowledgements

The foundations for this novel were laid in 1989 when my son, Dominic Connolly, went to teach in a small Zimbabwean village in his year between school and university. I wish therefore to acknowledge his unwitting help in preparing the background for *Sunday Morning* and reintroducing me to the Shona, as well as the help of the many pupils and teachers of Materera Secondary School, Marondera, Zimbabwe, who were so kind to him; to Naomi Buch, for her accounts of growing up in Rhodesia, and to Bruce Moore-King whose book *White Man, Black War* (Baobab Books, Harare) was invaluable source material.

I also owe a debt to Ilze Sissons and Cameron Brown for their generous assistance in providing general background information and to Robert Fisk for his account of the Lebanon at war contained in his book, *Pity The Nation* (André Deutsch).

Lastly, I would like to thank my wife, Elaine Connolly, for the many hours she spent preparing the manuscript for publication.

Ray Connolly
August 1991

SUNDAY MORNING

PART ONE

April 1978

Chapter One

He almost missed seeing it, the house, white and shuttered, caught in a sudden filter of sunlight up there above
the line of mist: a forlorn place now, under siege from
the encroachments of the forest. War did that to places.
It must have been a corner of paradise once.

He had been half-asleep, day-dreaming, when, as they
rounded the waist of the mountain, a sudden, noisy
movement in the maize at the edge of the dirt road had
startled him. Alongside him in the back bench-seat of the
Land-Rover, a young black constable in blue uniform had
smiled and clicked his tongue as a baboon had stared
insolently up at them from the field. 'Very bad, very
bad,' the constable had said, contemplating the damage
the baboon and his family would do to the crops. Then,
seeing the expression on the animal's face, he had joked:
'He wants you to take a card of him.' Embarrassed by his
sudden start the photographer had raised his camera to
his eye and pressed the shutter. 'I'll send him one when
the war's over . . .' he had begun to murmur, but his
voice had died in surprise as the curtains of mist on the
mountain above them had momentarily parted and the
house had stolen through.

It wasn't that it was an exceptionally grand house,
not by European standards, although even from a mile
or more he could see that it was elegantly proportioned,
with a wide, columned verandah and tall, stately windows. Rather it was its remoteness which surprised him,
this relic of late colonial Britain perched on the edge of
the old empire, a ghost, trapped between tropical forests,
looking west across the valley, its back turned resolutely
on Mozambique, Marxism and the mountains. One for

3

the archives, he thought, as he focused his camera and pressed. And then the house was gone, back into the fog and Rhodesian history.

All morning they had been driving, out with the frost at daybreak from base camp in Mungwingwi and then south and east, up through the pine plantations and into the hills. How many villages had there been, seven, eight . . . nine? The photographer had lost count. This was a routine patrol for routine interrogation: 'Have the terrorists been this way?' 'No, sir.' 'Had any of the young men left to join the terrorists?' 'No.' 'You wouldn't be lying, would you?' 'No, boss.' 'You know what happens to people who lie to the security forces, don't you?' Always silence then. They knew. And they knew what happened to people who talked to the security forces, too. So, to please the village children, the photographer had taken their pictures and climbed back into the Land-Rover. And on they had moved through the mist, just another day patrol seeking a phantom enemy who always came by night. 'You know we're only here to protect you from the terrorists, don't you?' Silence.

According to regulations the photographer should not have been there at all. Press were not encouraged in operational zones and were banned from joining patrols without written permission from Salisbury. In the end it had taken a dozen rolls of colour film, four bottles of Johnny Walker, and a promise not to photograph anything incriminating ('not that there will be anything incriminating to photograph') to buy the offer of a lift.

The Land-Rover bounced clumsily on through the ruts of the dirt road, a red cloud of dust rising heavily into the mist. So far it had not been worth the film let alone the whisky. But six days kicking his heels around Meikles Hotel in Salisbury, waiting for proper accreditation and drinking too much sanction-busting gin with foreign correspondents happily content to keep the war at arm's length, had left him restless. At twenty-three he was impatient. There was a reputation waiting to be won with a newspaper about to be born.

In the front passenger seat the fat, pallid-skinned sergeant in charge of the patrol, and now the new possessor of a duty-free supply of Johnny Walker, was rewriting the history of the Vietnam War for the benefit of the young Rhodesian soldier who was driving. He was the only man in the vehicle over thirty, an American mercenary, with 'Leader of the Pack' tattooed on his arm, a peaked blue football cap on his head, and God in his epaulette. Recently born again, he was there to tell anyone who would listen that he was ready to fight Ho Chi Minh's whole goddamned ('excuse me') army all over again right here in the goddamned ('pardon') Southern African bush if necessary. 'Way to go,' he incanted to himself, 'way to go.' The young driver nodded politely. They were nearly there. Soon they could turn around and go home again. *Show me the way to go home . . .* he whistled to amuse himself.

The field radio, tucked beneath the dashboard of the Land-Rover, crackled for attention as it had done intermittently all morning. Laconically, the sergeant pushed a headphone to his ear, listened and then began to speak quietly into the small microphone. 'When? Where? How many?' No one else paid much attention. In the middle row of the vehicle three white boy soldiers, the oldest no more than nineteen, were sharing a joke, something vulgar about a girl with one leg who gets married without telling her husband of her handicap and then on the first night of the honeymoon puts her wooden leg on the mantelpiece before going to bed.

'. . . the husband comes out of the bathroom and there's the bride waiting in bed . . .' The storyteller was a friendly, big-boned farmer's boy from a large spread down south. His elder brother had brought the joke back from Johannesburg at Easter. 'So he climbs into bed and begins to kiss her. Great. Then he runs his hand down her shoulder to her right bosom and strokes

5

it. Terrific. Then he feels the left bosom. Lovely. So he kisses her again and begins to slide his hand down across her naked body . . .'

'OK, we're on our way!' The loud extended vowels of the American broke into the clipped Rhodesian syllables of the soldier. 'Special Branch want us to check unconfirmed reports of possible activity in some place called Mupangare. Not far from here, they say. Is that right? Mupangare . . . ?'

This was louder and sterner to the black constables. Immediately both indicated with their hands, up and east. 'That way.'

'Is it far?' Already the boy soldiers were poring over the map.

'No, no. Close. Not far. Four k, maybe five,' came back one of the Africans.

'He probably means ten,' the farmer's boy murmured to the white corporal holding the machine-gun on his right. The African heard but said nothing.

'Got it,' came in the map-reader, seventeen years of age and seven weeks ago a trainee carpet salesman in a Bulawayo department store. He passed the map across to the sergeant indicating the place. 'It's just over this hill here.'

The photographer watched the sudden flurry of excitement among the soldiers, their joke now put aside. The patrol through the mountain mist was no longer routine. The possibility of action had sent a scribble of nervous electricity through the occupants of the Land-Rover. Opening the Billingham fishing bag he used to carry his equipment, the photographer checked once again the lenses on his two Nikon cameras, the wide angle 28mm on one, a telephoto on the other.

The drive to Mupangare took twenty minutes. As the Land-Rover pulled up on the neatly swept, sandy surface between the thatched huts a woman beating maize in a pen stood up. With her were three small children; a baby was on her back. Two of the children moved closer to

6

her for reassurance. The other, a three year old in a ragged yellow T-shirt with a faded-to-near-invisible Donald Duck on the front, stood apart watching keenly.

The boy soldiers, glancing nervously around, quickly spread out across the village as they had been trained to do. The black constables, rifles in hands, looked suitably stern. Gradually a small gathering of villagers formed a semicircle a few yards from the Land-Rover. Unlike some of the settlements visited earlier in the day Mupangare was not typical of an overgrazed, deforested Tribal Trust Land community. Situated in front of a wooded, rounded hill and in a dip off the road, this gathering of perhaps twenty huts, some painted white, not unlike a traditional wattle-and-daub English village, looked to the photographer almost cosy. Relatively speaking the people of Mupangare were well off.

'Who's the head man here?' The Leader of the Pack stared firmly at the villagers. The photographer's camera moved to his eye. Nothing incriminating, he had promised. Away to one side the child in the yellow T-shirt left his mother and approached, looking at the camera in fascination.

An old man with white hair and a checked shirt stepped forward. He was the head man, he said, and the only grown man left in the village. All the other men had gone to Salisbury and Umtali to work. Some of these ladies, he explained carefully, were his wives and daughters. Certainly all were relations. He indicated the children. And these were his grandchildren. Some of the women nodded. A baby started to cry. Tension is its own transmitter.

Twenty-five yards away where the village goats grazed something caught the photographer's eye. A slight figure in long trousers and a blue sweater buttoned to the neck was standing watching from behind a post, hidden almost beneath the wide brim of a red canvas hat, the sort of hat used for beach holidays in other places. A hand went up to the hat to protect the wearer's eyes from the slight glare

7

of the afternoon. It was a white hand. The photographer shifted his ground to get a better view. Now as the figure straightened and stood away from the post he saw a shy, shamed, bleached face beneath the hat, pink eyes screwed for protection against the light. It was an African face, full lips and a broad nose. But it was white: the face of a young albino boy.

'We've been told you've been helping the terrorists. Giving them food. Is that right?' The sergeant's voice drew the photographer's attention back to the other villagers.

The old man shook his head, surprised by the American's accent. 'Oh no, sir. We have had no terrorists here. I think they are further north. That is where they come. Not here. Perhaps in Inyanga.'

'We heard they came over the border here from Mozambique. Last week. Ten of them. And that you helped them, gave them food and shelter and a lot of information.'

The photographer wondered whether Special Branch had been so specific, or what possible information these people might have been able to give.

'Oh no.' The old man tried to laugh off such preposterous charges, as some of the women shook their heads and murmured indignant denials among themselves in English and Shona.

'What's that they're saying?' The Leader of the Pack looked towards the boy soldiers, who turned towards the black policemen.

'They say no terrorists have been here in Mupangare,' a constable translated. 'That they are very loyal people in this village. Perhaps in another village there are some bad people. Not here.'

'It's always somewhere else, isn't it?' The sergeant shook his head in stagey sarcasm. 'Always the same. All over the world. Seems like nobody ever sees or hears or helps these terrorists, but still they get food, still they come.' He turned to the patrol. 'OK, I want

8

the contents of every hut out here in a pile. Every stick and every stone. We're gonna take this place apart. If these people here have been divvying out some of their porridge to Mugabe's men they're going to be sorry. Let's go to work.'

'Oh no, we are telling you the truth . . .' the old man began to protest, but, emboldened by their combat uniforms and the weight of their FN rifles, the boy soldiers shouldered him aside.

'OK, you heard the sergeant. Everything out in a pile here,' shouted the former apprentice carpet salesman, now a lion of confidence. The villagers exchanged unhappy, worried expressions and then turned to do as they had been ordered.

Not interested in the soldiers the child in the yellow T-shirt watched the photographer who worked swiftly and quietly, his camera now recording everything, scatter-gun technique. Nothing incriminating. But what was incriminating? In the background the blue-and-red shadow of the albino boy flitted silently between the huts, accepted by the villagers, a source of slight embarrassment to some of the soldiers, a disquiet undisguised by dull attempts at humour. 'Looks like that one's not baked properly yet.'

Now for the camera the boy soldiers swaggered like seasoned troopers as they combed the village, sifting through the heaps of belongings which began to grow outside each hut – piles of inexpensive clothing, blankets, furniture, pots and pans, a kettle, an old torch; two batteries; here was a copy of *Far From The Madding Crowd*, an alarm clock, a wind-up gramophone ('you don't see those around much any more. My grandad said he had one once') and four seventy-eight r.p.m. records; there were magazines with knitting patterns, woollen hats, a mirror, clay pipes, a framed photograph of the Queen, a postcard from somebody in Victoria Falls; all the trivial household possessions that made up a lifetime in Mupangare. The boy soldiers were not polite, but neither were they bullying as older men might have been. Mainly they were confused as to their new adult role, having to demand that these women empty their homes: not very long ago some of them had had nannies like these ladies themselves. The two black constables kept their eyes cast down, occasionally mumbling questions of the villagers in Shona. Embarrassment speaks in hushed tones.

All the time the photographer's cameras clicked and whirred, motor-driven to the next frame, while the child in Donald Duck yellow followed, watching, giggling now, excited. Nothing incriminating. That had been the condition. A simple life being spread out on the ground for strangers to inspect, to peer at, to prod with the muzzle of a rifle and to mock. 'Look at this, Brucie, that big enough for you?' And the corporal with the machine-gun clinked his boot against an old, large, cracked chamber-pot. Nothing incriminating.

Quickly it became apparent that if there had been guerrillas hiding in Mupangare they were no longer there. And gradually as the mounds of belongings grew the photographer found himself observing the attitudes of the villagers: the old man sitting in a wicker chair fretting with a quaint formality 'that some valuable items can easily be broken', the long-suffering women, cowed even by soldiers as young as these, and the children, timid of the soldiers but increasingly fascinated by the photographer.

'He is Wonderful.'

The photographer stared down his lens at the child in yellow who seemed to have been playing a private game of grandmother's footsteps with him, following at a distance, but then freezing whenever he turned. He was gap-toothed, dirty, cheeky and grinning and was trying to coax the albino boy closer, pulling him impishly by the hand to join in the fun. The shutter opened and closed on him. 'He's wonderful all right,' he replied to the girl who had come across to watch, no doubt hoping that her picture might be taken, too. 'He's a little treasure.'

10

'No. His *name* is Wonderful,' came the reply. 'They are cousins.'

'Wonderful? He's called Wonderful? Perfect,' the photographer laughed and took another picture, this time of the albino as well. Wonderful giggled with delight. The albino's hand went up to hide his face, pleased but embarrassed. He was, the photographer reckoned, about ten years old.

'Better brew up,' the corporal suggested at last, with everything out of the huts and nothing found. The Leader of the Pack was talking on his radio, seeking further orders. Quietly the photographer reloaded his cameras. Everyone relaxed.

Around the fire the farmer's son had a story to finish: '. . . so anyway the bride's in bed waiting and the bridegroom's there with her,' he began again. The other boys moved closer. 'First night of the honeymoon it was. Desperate for it. So, first one tit then the other, then he slides his hand down across her stomach to her right thigh and runs his hand up and down the inside. Lovely, like velvet. Then he puts his hand out to feel the other thigh. But . . . what's this? Something's wrong . . . he can't find it . . .'

By the Land-Rover the American was asking for an order to be repeated.

'So the fella says to his wife, "Eh, girl, where's your other leg?" "It's on the mantelpiece," she says. "On the mantelpiece?" he says, "On the mantelpiece? Jeez, girl, you can't half spread 'em . . ."'

The young men guffawed. Even one of the black policemen who had not heard all the joke smiled. The children watching the photographer laughed when he laughed, particularly the one called Wonderful.

'"You can't half spread 'em . . ."' repeated the corporal. 'Jeez, who makes up jokes like that . . . ?' Then again as he poured the boiling water on to the tea in his mug, '". . . you can't half spread 'em."'

'OK, we're gonna burn the village.' The Leader of

the Pack had returned from the Land-Rover carrying his football cap. The laughing stopped abruptly. 'They want everybody moved out of here into a collective village. They'll be safer there, anyway.'

'But we didn't find anything,' the farmer's son protested.

'You tell *them* that.' The American indicated the radio in the vehicle. 'They want it burning. So let's burn it.' With that he strutted away to the old man sitting in his chair.

The corporal now noticed the photographer. 'You'd better put that away, mate.' He indicated the camera, but before the photographer could reply there came a bitter wail from the old man.

'No, no, no . . .' he moaned, shuffling urgently to his feet.

The Leader of the Pack walked back towards the soldiers, the old man in noisy pursuit. 'Hell, it isn't as though we're burning their belongings – goddamn grass huts, that's all. They can make another in a day. Let's go to work.'

'Please, sir, please. This is our home. Please. You must not do this thing.'

The young soldiers looked from one to the other uncertainly.

The sergeant's face reddened. 'Hey, come on. You heard me. Let's go to work.' His voice was now loud and angry, unhappy in his work. He was not a bad man.

Ignoring the photographer and the sudden protesting of the villagers the soldiers obediently began to move through the small village. Symbolically the Leader of the Pack took a burning stick from the camp-fire and strode across to the old man's hut. Behind him the photographer's camera went to his eye. As the flame reached up and licked into the straw of the thatch the shutter opened; then another shot and another as the boy soldiers took cigarette lighters and matches from their pockets, and one by one set alight the dry grass of the roofs. 'Nothing incriminating,' he had agreed. But that was before he had seen people lose their homes.

Heavy black smoke was rising from the village now, the vacuums of the empty huts sucking the flames inwards before suddenly exploding with a cascading bonfire of sparks high into the late-afternoon air. The black constables stood by the Land-Rover, awkward in their complicity. Weeping women, desperate to protect their belongings, pulled bundles of clothes and pieces of furniture away from the fires that had been their homes but where now clay and dung walls began to blacken and crack and central poles to tumble. The old man stared in dismay. The children cried. And the photographer shot everything.

With all the huts alight, and the separate columns of smoke drifting together into a red-and-black cloud above the village, the soldiers returned to the Land-Rover. Only then did they remember the photographer. 'Didn't I tell him, didn't that bastard promise . . . ?' The Leader of the Pack glared across the village at the young man with the camera.

'Oh Christ!' the corporal spat in irritation. 'Shall we get him?'

The Leader of the Pack shook his head. 'No. Let him be. But when he's through I want every piece of film on him. You understand? We'll strip-search him if necessary. The two-faced bastard.'

The corporal nodded. Unhappily, the troupe of young soldiers watched the fires of the village.

Over among the huts the photographer still worked, darting, spinning, crouching, shooting. He wanted everything. The fires, the soldiers, the old man, the weeping children and frantic women, the albino boy. The child in Donald Duck yellow had been left behind now: halfway between the photographer and the Land-Rover he stared in bewilderment at his burning home, rooted in non-comprehension, and wailed. Behind him the soldiers began climbing into the Land-Rover. The photographer

13

raised his camera again, found the soldiers in his view-finder and pressed.

He did not hear the mortar until afterwards. He knew only the force of the blast, the physical blow, followed by a confusion as his body seemed to rise and momentarily to hover weightlessly before falling heavily on to the sand.

It was some moments before he understood what had happened, lying face down in the earth in a thick cloud of swirling red dust, winded and gasping for breath. There was now no sobbing, no scrambling women, just fragments of belongings. Close by lay a bundle wrapped in yellow: the child called Wonderful.

The photographer rolled on to his side. A fragment of glass fell from the lens shield of one of his cameras, but he hardly saw it as the rattle of a machine-gun drove his head back down. In front of him he could hear the bullets puncturing the panels and shattered windscreen of the Land-Rover. It now lay on its side in the maize pen, a tyre smouldering, its radiator steaming, the steel broken and twisted; it had suffered a direct hit. In the back seat the embarrassment of the two black constables was now in the demeanour of their death, one sitting propped up, his rifle still between his knees as though awaiting an instruction, the other hanging across the back rail, blown there by the blast of the mortar, his head taken half away. In front the boy soldiers had died climbing into their seats or been blown among the beaten husks of maize, torn into parts by the accuracy of the blast, then raked with bullets by the follow-fire of the machine-gun. Only the American sergeant was still moving, the pale mercenary, the whisky soldier with the gut and the baby face. But now he was only two-thirds a man, a heap of disconnected and dysfunctioning parts, one leg of which seemed to be cycling by motor reaction through a spreading puddle of blood and urine and torn fragments of meat-red flesh.

Another drill of machine-gun fire strafed the compound. The bundle that had been Wonderful twitched from the impact. Two new holes appeared in the shrunken T-shirt; one in the beak for the faded Donald Duck. The Leader of the Pack stopped his one-legged cycling. The photographer closed his eyes: 'Please God, don't let me die. Please God.'

With a crack, followed by a roar of combustion, the Land-Rover's petrol tank exploded. The smell of burning petrol filled the air. 'Now. Go now,' the photographer told himself. 'Now, before they come to finish you, too.'

Crawling, gasping, his cameras bouncing on his chest, the fishing bag hanging from his shoulder, he pulled himself along the ground towards the burning huts, closer to the flames and the curtains of smoke. Behind him in the village he heard a woman begin to scream, and then another as children started to cry. Dragging himself to his feet, he pushed into the smoke around the side of the hut, and hurled himself away, down into the maize field, tumbling and falling against and between the body-high stalks. 'Please God, don't let me die.'

It was dark when he reached the house and bitterly cold. The mist still clung around the mountains, and as he came out of the trees the house seemed suddenly to rear up in front of him, white and shapeless.

From the maize field he had headed into the forest for cover. It had been dense and difficult, and he had not noticed the loss of the wide-angled camera. Sometimes it had been impossible and he had had to reverse his steps and seek another route, but eventually he had found a way, up and over the mountain. Soon the smell of the burning thatches and the screaming of the villagers had been behind him. He had wondered who would tend to the wounded. Three times he had stopped and crumpled up, not in pain but in fear, hiding deep in a thicket and sobbing until the cramp of despair had passed. He had not known there could be so much blood. Boy photographers of twenty-three covering their first war do not know these things. Why the attack on the Land-Rover had come

15

when it was still in the village was just another mystery of war, as incomprehensible as the decision to set fire to the huts. Had the guerrillas been watching all the time? Had they thought they were being betrayed? Were they now following him? Desperately he had pushed on into the tropical evergreen mountain forest.

Just before night fell he had heard the sound of a helicopter hovering, but it had not landed, could not land in the increasing mist. Another hour and it would have been impossible to aim the mortar.

He would wonder later in his delirium if perhaps the house had drawn him to her sanctuary, because, although consciously he had not sought it, it was not with any surprise that hours later he had found himself stumbling out of the forest and on to the dirt road which led around to the front and the side of the house. Now it was deep into the long African night. His only thought was sleep.

Above him a thin moonlight, spraying suddenly through the mist, washed the house, closed and shuttered, with a faint translucence as he approached. Cautiously he moved around to the verandah. It was large, overhung by a pergola, long overgrown, where something rustled and fled from his arrival. In the forest he had not feared the wild, but the scampering of some animal which scavenged off domesticity startled him. Moving on he edged across a paved rose garden, and turned a corner towards some outbuildings built around a small courtyard. Cautiously he tried the doors and windows. Everywhere was locked. A grey glint led him towards a greenhouse. The heavy scent of orchids, feminine and stifling as an old lady, drew him inside. In the grey gloom he could just make out neat rows of plants, some in flower; just inside the door he found what he had been seeking.

The peeling wood of the shutters surrendered easily to the garden fork. It was not even necessary to break the glass of the windows, the frames having at some time warped, making them impossible to lock. With a second manoeuvre they swung open. Lifting himself on to his elbows the photographer crawled over the wooden sill, into the house and on to a desk. Dropping down he quickly closed the window, then stood and waited, listening hard. The only sound was his own breath.

The interior of the house was darker than the forest. Afraid even to light a match he moved forward, feeling his way across the room. Beneath his feet was the hard, springy surface of a wooden floor. A door opened to his touch and led him into a large open area he guessed to be a hall. His footsteps echoed. Occasionally he bumped into items of furniture, a rocking-chair which fell away at his touch then came back and surprised him, a table. Alongside him a vase tumbled and shattered on the wooden floor. He froze, but there was no other sound. From the shuttered exterior he had expected the house to be bare: that it was furnished and that he was trespassing in someone's home made him feel like a thief. By the foot of the wide stairs his hand brushed against a telephone. Picking it up he put the receiver to his ear. It was dead.

Now sleep was pressing him. He climbed the bare wooden staircase. Floorboards creaked under his weight. At the top of the flight his hand took him around a corner and along a landing. A door opened. Under his feet he could feel a rug. He moved forward across the room until his knees came across an object in his path: the softness of a mattress. He stepped to one side, his hands feeling the contours of a bed. There were blankets but no sheets. Pulling back the counterpane he climbed fully clothed into the envelope of the bed. His eyes were already closing. Behind him, scattered through the house, was the trail of his arrival: splinters on the window-sill, the fishing bag abandoned in the study and the telephoto lens dropped on the bedroom carpet. But all that mattered now was to escape into sleep.

Chapter Two

(i)

They had begun arriving early, before eight, the secretaries and tele-ad girls and some of the more junior contributors, turning up in couples and foursomes, unsure of the place and uncertain of their place, the girls unrecognizably more glamorous than their weekday appearance. The main guests would not arrive before nine, when they could make an entrance befitting their status, and the big guns not until ten, when they would bring with them copies of the first edition. But the hoi polloi got there early, anxious not to miss a minute. This, then, was the phoney party, the time of nerves, of neck craning and anticipation, of champagne glasses too quickly emptied and refilled, of introductions unheeded, conversation unheard.

Emily Blake had volunteered to get there early, too, to hold the fort until they arrived, Richard and Hudson and the rest of them. Now here, a rake-like siren from the Hudson International publicity department at her side, she realized she recognized hardly anybody. *En masse* they seemed so much younger and more noisily, aggressively, attractive than she had expected. How sophisticated was this new generation of newspaper people, she thought, and then, in a tiny moment of uncertainty, wondered again whether the suit she had bought was smart enough for the wife of the editor? The children had told her how pretty she looked: but then, of course, they would. Thirty-five years old and behind her quiet and dignified front Emily Blake was nervous.

Making the excuse that she ought to see how dinner

18

preparations were progressing she left the publicist and picked her way through the crowded vestibule into Middle Temple Hall, the place, it was said, where Elizabeth I had seen the first performance of *Twelfth Night*, and now laid out as a vast, oak-panelled banqueting room. This night was a first night, too, and she prayed that everything would go well.

There were five long, end-to-end, candle-lit refectory tables and, judging by the names on the place cards, it appeared that virtually everybody she knew, and many more she had only read about in gossip columns, had been invited. There were bankers, of course, not just the Fiskes from Fiske-Forrester, but people with brittle German names which sounded as though they should only be uttered in cool bank vaults, and young Wall Street warriors over with their pretty assistants and wives. Then there were old-money aristos who revelled in glitz, and pushy new millionaires seeking respectability by association. From the West End there was James Cleary whose one-man show had closed earlier than expected in spite of his best supporting actor Academy Award nomination in March, and Diana Balmforth who had lost her sense of smell after being bitten by her dog. There was a place, too, for Sir Samuel Spoon, said to be the best Falstaff since some other actor whose name Emily could not recollect, and another for his boy-friend, Lennie Dangerfield, the chap who kept getting arrested. Naturally, television personalities being ten a penny were there ten a penny, but more glamorous was Mark Pinhorn, the boy-wonder director from Hollywood, working at Elstree this spring on an English language remake of *Jules et Jim*. *Jules et Jim*! Ah, happy memories. From the Government were two Cabinet ministers and a junior minister, while David Donoghue and wife were turning out for the Opposition. There were movie stars, too, or at least actors who had appeared in films, and sportsmen (Emily recognized the names of at least two footballers and a golfer), a musical librettist, two novelists, a well-known wildlife film-maker, a Russian dissident who was notoriously right-wing and religious, an ebullient economist frequently heard on radio programmes, a celebrated criminal and his brother, three editors of national daily newspapers, a squadron of television producers and current affairs presenters, and legions of journalists. Whichever way one looked at it the list was impressive. Hudson had always liked to impress.

It took her several minutes to reach her own name on the top table, not, as she had expected, as an appendage alongside Richard, but immediately across from Hudson. That was nice: a person in her own right again, just like in the old days when couples would be separated at editorial dinners: a house rule. Slowly she went along the top table. They were all coming, those bright boys and girls who had seen and taken the opportunity all those years ago. Nearly fifteen years on and how well they had all done. The cream always rises, Richard had said so often. Well, perhaps not quite always. The failures, the bit-part players, would not be there because they would not wish to face the shame of their failure being displayed in public. And she pondered whether Hudson or Richard would have remembered to invite them.

She moved on. Hudson's place was, of course, in the centre of the table, with a view down the middle two of the facing tables: Hudson, always at the centre, now, as then, always the leader, chairman and publisher-in-chief. She took another step. Alongside Hudson's name was that of Richard Blake, his oldest and best friend: Richard Blake, the editor, her husband.

'If I didn't know you better, Emily, I'd think you were plotting to change the name places.' A good-looking, prematurely grey, boyish man in a white dinner jacket was approaching carrying a gaily wrapped parcel.

Emily smiled. 'Why change when I've got pride of place? See here, right next to you. "Charles Latymer." days Ce Ah, pity, they've spelled it with an "i" instead of a "y".

It's embossed, though. And gilt edged. You've got me on one side and . . .'

Latymer peered over her shoulder. '. . . Penny Chilston on the other. Oh God, she'll be looking deeply into my eyes all night and telling me what a wonderful man Hudson is.' Leaning forward he kissed her modestly on the cheek. 'How are we?'

'Nervous. What's that?' She indicated the parcel he was carrying.

'D'you know I haven't the foggiest idea. It's supposed to be some sort of christening present, I think. Dominique insisted we give it to Hudson. She found it in South America or some god-forsaken place. They've got her in Rome tonight looking for Aldo Moro.'

Emily displayed what she hoped was an appropriately impressed response. These days Dominique was usually somewhere else when they saw Charles Latymer. Too beautiful, too bright and too French was how Richard had described her. But in the new European climate in Britain Dominique Fayence, with her husky, Gallic delivery, was the coming woman of television.

Latymer was busy walking away from talk of Dominique. 'My, my, we're all out tonight, aren't we?' He was leaning across the table peering at the names on the cards. 'Gimmelmann and Mrs, Willie Simmonds and his latest . . . the Tarlos, of course, the Adam Smiths . . . yawn.' Suddenly he stopped in mock surprise. 'Yuk! Even Berridge and the Mascara! I feel dirty already.'

Emily looked over his shoulder. The gossip columnist Peter Berridge and his gruesome, klaxon-voiced wife, the much eye-shadowed Celia McCabe, had been placed at the end of the table. These days Celia, or the Mascara as she was universally known, was fish-wifing it as woman's editor at one shabby end of Fleet Street while Berridge, who resembled nothing so much as a pink and polished skull, was vituperating an odious way with Federated British Newspapers at the other.

'Come on, Berridge isn't that bad,' she said unconvincingly.

Latymer wagged his head. 'Oh, but I think he is. Worse actually. I wasn't certain in the old days when I only loathed him. Now I am. He's appalling. I looked him up in *Who's Who* the other day. D'you know what it said under hobbies? "Peeling the skin off babies and underwater swimming down the sewers of inference, suggestion and character vilification."' He changed the subject. 'How's Richard been? Frantic?'

'I don't know. We've hardly seen him for the past three months. The children have begun to call him The Invisible Man. He and Hudson were on television last night talking about the launch and Benedict said, "Isn't that someone we used to know?" Then Catherine said, "No, the person we knew was a lot younger and married to Mum." They're furious they can't be here.'

'Really . . .'

Had Latymer at that moment suppressed a yawn Emily would have been unsurprised. Domesticity bored him. She didn't mind. She felt slightly sorry for him. These days while Latymer was reduced to fronting the low-grade television show, *News Quest*, his wife travelled the world seeking out those who actually were the news.

Together they moved back towards the early-comers who were beginning to spill into the great hall. As the wife of a newspaperman Emily had become used to going to places alone, a newspaper widow, to be joined at midnight by an exhausted husband, the first edition in his coat pocket, his hands grubby with ink; now as the wife of an editor she would have to learn the role of gracious consort; she only hoped she would have the right temperament for it. She turned to Latymer as they approached a glitter of guests. 'Give us a hand, will you, Charlie? This is more your caper than mine.'

'I'd love to,' he beamed. He meant it. To a minor television celebrity an excuse to meet people is an opportunity for one's very existence to be flattered. And together they weaved their way through the crowd, hands out like bayonets, smiles fixed. 'Thank you for coming. How are you? Thank you. How are you? How are you?'

(ii)

Just as in Thirties movies about newspapers, Richard Blake, the editor, put the first edition of *Sunday Morning* to bed himself. By eight twenty-five, he was satisfied, sleeves rolled up, waiting in the machine room, as around him overmanned television news crews exchanged bad jokes about overmanning in newspapers. He took it good-naturedly, although this night was too important for jokes. There had been dummy runs with varying degrees of success half a dozen times over the past month but on tonight's work rested everyone's future.

In fire buckets stuffed with melting ice, gratefully cadged from Smithfield Market around the corner, bottles of champagne waited. Outside in the street the distributor's vans stood ready for the dash to the railway stations, their drivers already reading the first editions of the *News of the World* and *The People*; on the ground floor linotype machines rested, having cranked and rattled all day as their operators had turned molten metal into words, a system of printing archaic fifteen years earlier but still practised in the Fleet Street of the late Seventies; while way above in the top floor of the building reporters joked away the moments until the launch, scanning the first editions of *The Sunday Times* and the *Observer*, as sub-editors perfected the news and sports pages for the main London edition which would not go to press until ten.

Mainly, though, everyone waited. The rush was over. Sunday newspapers change little after seven o'clock on Saturday evening.

At the far side of the editorial floor in a small,

23

partitioned loose box for writers, a very pretty young woman of twenty-three, her shiny, black, straight hair tied back off her oval face, pulled the cover on to her typewriter. There was no real reason for her to be there: her piece on Cabinet wives, witty and wicked, as was her style, had been written and set by Thursday. But the launching of a new Sunday newspaper was history of a sort, and she wanted to share in it.

The editor, Richard Blake, had liked her piece. He had told her, and for that alone it had been worth coming in. They had met, almost, if not quite, by accident, on the stairs that afternoon. As usual he had been shy with her. With the sub-editors and heads of department he could be fierce or friendly. She had seen all that. But with her he never knew what to say. Clover Merrifield, this year's holder of the Nicola Reynolds Award For Young Journalists, the girl most determined to win, found such reticence in a man, in this man, not unencouraging.

The first-night preparations had been perfect. The print unions had been on their best behaviour: the paper was ready to roll. In the machine room Richard Blake sipped pale coffee and checked his watch again. One of his three deputy editors, Stephen Symes, tugged anxiously at his bright red braces. They waited. Five minutes to go and still no sign of Hudson. Richard looked again at the vast, gun-metal printing presses, rented for this one night a week from the Federated British Newspapers chain whose spare offices and weekend printing capacity Hudson had relentlessly pursued and surprisingly won. The word on Fleet Street had been that Federated British would rather their presses rusted over than open up the field to any new rival. Yet here was Hudson International on the brink of breaking into the Sunday market. Hudson had a way of getting what he wanted.

'All right, sir, we're ready when you are.' Sholes, the machine-room overseer, generously moustached and militarily erect, indicated the presses. Every operator in this room was on triple time for working Saturday night and he saw no reason why they should not start earning their pay as quickly as possible. He didn't trust casual labour. Over in Gray's Inn Road it was bleeding *The Sunday Times* dry.

Already the hand-held television news cameras were turning over, recording the moment. 'Well, in that case . . .' Richard paused and stared down the thirty yards of rotary presses. Where could Hudson be? He was always there for the big moment, relishing, nursing, manipulating, orchestrating. Barney Flowers, the chief sub-editor, who had hurried down from the top floor with three young shirt-sleeved lions especially for this moment, was already wrestling with the wire on a bottle of Bollinger, a baton of stacked paper cups under his arm. Everyone was waiting. 'Well, in that case, why not . . . ?'

'Yes, why not?'

He swung around. Hudson was standing just six feet away alongside the nearest machine, already in his dinner suit, a six foot three, grinning, head boy of forty, his thick fair hair flopping loosely across his forehead. At his side was a girl of about half his age dressed in an identical man's evening suit, a pretty girl as always, the darkness of her eyes accentuated by charcoal satin stains.

'We came in the back way, through the fire escape,' Hudson explained, embarrassed almost, it seemed, by the eyes upon him. 'This is Anna, by the way. Well, are we ready?' He smiled around at the cameras, journalists and print workers who had assembled for the big moment.

Smoothly the cameras panned and zoomed closer to take in the youthful publisher and his mystery girl.

Where did he find them? Richard wondered to himself, as he nodded a welcome to Anna. 'We're ready,' he said.

Sholes dragged his attention from the girl and put up one military arm in signal to an assistant. Somewhere above them an alarm sounded.

'Go on then, Richard, start them rolling.' Hudson

indicated the button which would roll the presses.

Richard was surprised. He had assumed that Hudson would want to start the machines himself. 'Are you sure you don't . . . ?'

'No. It's your night. Come on. We've waited a long time for this.'

Even after all these years Richard never ceased to be surprised by Hudson. After being an interfering presence through all the months of preparation he had stayed away when it came to the real thing, dropped out of sight and left him to get on with producing the paper. Richard pressed the button.

For a second there was silence and he wondered crazily whether there had been a power failure tonight of all nights. But then, with the slightest of hums, the drums started to turn. The machine minder nearest to them adjusted a dial slightly. Hudson was now laughing. The girl, the accessory, too young to understand the significance of the moment, stood by, temporarily forgotten. Quickly the hum graduated to a whine and then a roar, as more and more machines began to turn, geared together down the length of this long, subterranean news mill. Above them a ribbon of newsprint began to move through the presses, gathering acceleration all the time as in and out of the matrixes it sped, folding this way, that, and then back, as it was cut, refolded and assembled. To the people who work in newspapers, each night seems like a minor miracle of production and distribution. By that token, thought Richard as his chief sub-editor passed him a paper cup of lukewarm champagne, and Symes and the other expensively recruited boys from the editorial floor turned to toast him, the launch of a brand-new newspaper must stand comparison with the loaves and fishes.

By the time they reached the warehouse the paper was already shunting from the rolling distributor belts, coming off in quires, staggered collections of twenty-four copies, only the masthead visible. *Sunday Morning. Sunday Morning. Sunday Morning.* Twenty-four *Sunday*

Mornings. Without time for sentiment a warehouseman in a nylon shirt, trainers and new black jeans, snatched aside a bundle, heaved it on to a table, and, withdrawing one, began to go quickly through every page examining the quality of the print. On some nights the machines might be stopped half a dozen times for minor adjustments before it was right. Tonight the paper was perfect. Another miracle. Almost embarrassed to touch, as though he were shoplifting, Richard stooped and helped himself to two copies of the warm, new newspaper.

'May our Sunday mornings never be the same again,' he said, and passed a copy to Hudson.

Hudson didn't reply. He simply stared at the newspaper as though in silent wonder. Both TV cameras lingered on him: close-ups of the man who was challenging the system.

'To *Sunday Morning*,' murmured Barney, the chief sub-editor, and emptied his paper cup.

It was nearly eleven when Hudson managed to drag his editor away from last-minute changes to the London edition. The ether of self-congratulations was everywhere. 'I think it's fantastic,' Clover Merrifield had said as her editor had thrown a casual, 'What do you think then?' in her direction. She had meant it, too. But Richard had just smiled, embarrassed by her enthusiasm, and moved on to thank the sports editor, while Clover had hurried downstairs to the fashion department, now a make shift changing room for those on their way to the party. She had brought black. Black flattered her slightly burnished skin: black made her look older.

The short drive in Hudson's Mercedes across a rain-polished, windy London EC4 would stay with Richard for ever. Tonight he and Hudson were like brothers, as close as ever, as silly as boys. Anna, the beautiful accessory, sat between them, warm and scented, as Josh, Hudson's driver, steered swiftly around vans still loading outside other newspaper offices in the south-running alleyways off Fleet Street.

'Terrific, terrific, terrific . . .' Hardly reading the headlines Hudson leafed happily through the pages. Every time he said 'Terrific' he sounded more American.

'We were going to lead on Carter Plans Middle-East Peace Talks until five o'clock, but then Harry Quirke suddenly came on from Teheran with the Shah's torture chamber.' Richard had changed into his dinner suit in the office and was still fastening his shoe-laces.

'And no one else has this?'

'Not in their first editions. They may scrabble something together by the London runs.'

Hudson beamed. 'And look at sport. At last a quality paper that has the nerve to put the national sport on the back page.'

'Lucky again. There were goals everywhere.'

'I don't think so. We make our own luck. You make it.'

'Well, we might have done better with the arts coverage. Too many bland reviews, not enough . . . I don't know, individual wit. We have to instigate . . .'

Hudson cut him off. He didn't want to hear any nit-picking. 'Who'd ever have dreamed it . . . ?' Then, turning to Anna, he said: 'What do you think? Do we stand a chance?'

'I don't understand,' she faltered. 'Can you speak slower?'

'*Te gusta nuestro nuevo periódico? Un día sera el periódico mas famoso del mundo. Este señor lo ha hecho posible. Este es un viejo amigo.*' He smiled towards an astonished Richard.

'*Este periódico es mui bueno.*' A bored, polite reply. The accessory had already begun to pout, cross at being ignored.

'I don't believe it. What did you tell her? And why didn't I know you could speak Spanish?'

'You never asked me. I told her you were a lazy son of a bitch who eats seaweed on toast and beats

28

up on his secretary alternate Thursdays . . .' He was smiling, but suddenly his voice faded as an item on the front page caught his eye. 'What's this in Rhodesia?' He was looking at a short paragraph which had only just managed to make the edition: *Eleven die in Rhodesia attack. Smith condemns killers.*

'That's all we have. Guerrilla attack on a patrol. We've been trying to raise a young chap we have there doing pictures for the magazine but no luck so far. He's probably boogying the night away in some Salisbury disco.'

Hudson read the brief details. Apart from the fact that a patrol and several villagers had been killed by mortar attack in the Eastern Highlands there was little else. Richard said nothing further, peering over Josh's shoulder as the Mercedes slipped through the gates which separated the tabloid backwater of Tudor Street from the legal dignity of Temple Gardens. Rhodesia held too many bad memories for them both. Tonight was not the time to be reminded.

At last Hudson quietly dropped the newspaper on to the car floor. 'Difficult times there,' he murmured, then abruptly changed the conversation. 'You know, I expected to see Emily's by-line . . . a column or something, or have I missed it?'

Another surprise. 'No, we . . .' This was slightly irritating. Of course Hudson hadn't missed it. 'Neither of us really liked the idea of the wife of the editor taking space . . .'

'Which others could fill less well. Come on, Richard, what is this? Where's your sense of nepotism? You're a Fleet Street editor now. One of the last of a dying breed of tyrant. You can do anything you want.'

(*iii*)

They devoured it, all of them, first-editioning party-goers in this small moment of publishing history: cover to cover they went, from the Japanese Red Army Faction to

Brezhnev and the neutron bomb, from Menachem Begin and the Lebanon to the blue-eyed blonde with the flower in her hair who had been accused of kidnapping and sexually abusing a plump Mormon missionary. Everything was discussed, bisected and dissected, as copies were passed down the tables, the review sections separated and perused and the magazine complimented on its verve. Younger guests wondered why the magazine was called *Witness*. Older ones, the ones at the top table, would never want to forget. *Witness* had been the best part of most of their lives.

The intention had been that copies of the paper would be left in the outer hall and distributed like going-home presents at the end of the party. But once the journalists began to arrive, carrying their souvenir copies and guffawing with pride as they crossed Temple Gardens, and it became known that a vanload of newspapers had already been despatched from Smithfield, every group sent out its own raiding party. And so the first edition of *Sunday Morning* was read with a late Saturday dinner.

Emily had never seen her husband in the role of central attraction before. Journalists are rarely celebrated, especially not those who put paper before personality. But on this night everyone wanted to shake his hand. Even accounting for the exaggeration of fawning, delusion and plain, freeload lying which greets the launch of anything sufficiently hyped, there was no doubt that *Sunday Morning* surprised everyone. It was good. Even Tim Gimmelmann, out with his wife, Jenny, for once, was almost moved to murmur clenched-jawed praise about the magazine cover, a nude with an oboe alongside a sleeping London tramp.

'Very tasty that, Richard. It's Honey Lascelles, isn't it? We tested her for Sweetheart but the magic was missing.' Then a little grin. 'Lovely girl, though,' followed by a barely disguised wink.

In three deft sentences he had congratulated, displayed his knowledge of the current nude model form and then put himself one up. Jenny, the porcelain doll from Canonbury he had married and then regularly and habitually broken, bit miserably into her lip gloss, as she had been doing for the past ten years.

How Gimmelmann had changed, thought Emily. What had happened to the sullen Cockney boy photographer who had been too nervous to speak in case he used the wrong words. And what about Holly Carter? Gimmelmann and Holly Carter. They had made a famous double act in the old days. Holly, the Face of 1965. For sure no one would have thought to invite Holly Carter tonight, wherever she was.

'And what about you?' Richard's quiet voice was in Emily's ear amid the hurrahs and verbal bunting. 'Give me an honest answer.'

'I'm very proud of you. More follows . . .'

He smiled at her. Reporters wrote 'mf', short for 'more follows', at the bottom of each sheet of copy paper. 'And me of you,' he said.

'You recognize me?'

'Only just. More follows . . .' And with that Richard kissed her gently on the head and turned to his father who was already pumping his hand proudly. Alongside, Emily noticed, his mother was gazing up at Hudson devotedly. She had always revered Hudson. Perhaps now they would concede that Richard had followed a serious career.

Emily returned to her seat by way of the family table, where her own mother sat with Daniel, her brother, and his new girl-friend, another blonde, leggy girl.

Gradually everyone found their places and settled down. At the centre of the top table Hudson was standing, totem straight, one foot on his chair. He was undoubtedly very handsome, still the most dashing man Emily had ever known. Still the leader. A man to admire from afar. Quietly Richard slipped in alongside him. There was a better man.

She looked along the top table. Just as he had feared, Charlie Latymer was on the end of a particularly intense

31

gaze from the formidable Penelope Chilston, who, in a bright red dress, red hairband and gold earrings, looked not unlike a fortune-teller. Alongside her Tim Gimmelmann was passing a card to the dark-haired beauty who had arrived with Hudson, while further down, past the porridge-complexioned Mascara, and loyal, unadventurous Adam Smith, Peter Berridge was dribbling acid through crooked teeth into the ear of Willie Simmonds, whose third wife, Ginny, was showing rather a large amount of bosom to Ben Tarlo. How little they had aged, Emily thought. Stammering Willie, now a playwright himself, no more the merry critic, and Ben, back from New York and on the team as managing director of Hudson Publications. Fourteen years on and, with the exception of Gimmelmann, they all looked and behaved in exactly the same way.

'Thank you very much. Thank you.' Finally Hudson had his guests' attention. From somewhere down at the bottom of the hall came the sound of two solitary hands clapping. Then more, and more, a sweeping tattoo of handclaps, until the ancient hall reverberated to the sharp rhythms of hundreds of beating palms.

'Thank you . . . thank you . . .' Hudson shone his smile down the tables and waited for a break in the storm. 'Now it seems to me there's nothing worse than speeches at a party . . .' Cries of 'nonsense' interrupted, but Hudson's hand went up again, '. . . but I wouldn't be doing my job if I didn't thank you all for coming to celebrate the birth of *Sunday Morning* with us here tonight . . .' Another shower of applause, '. . . and if I didn't ask you to join me in thanking the man responsible.' Putting one hand under Richard's arm he hauled him to his feet. Richard looked out shyly from behind his horn-rimmed glasses. 'Friends . . . Richard Blake . . . the best editor and the best friend a man ever had.'

Sitting on a bench with two colleagues from the Diary page, her back against the panelled wall, Clover Merrifield clapped so loudly that people turned to see who was making all the noise. 'Hear, hear,' she called. 'Hear, hear.' Her companions exchanged glances. Launches had that effect on people: the aphrodisiac effect.

Emily was tired. Three o'clock in the morning and still they would not let this night end. Celebrations spent, the old gang had adjourned almost *en masse* to a new red-eye hole in the wall where, even now, a Chinese pianist played from her Jerome Kern songbook and young waiters with American accents and red and white checked dish-cloths tied around their waists polished glasses and consulted their watches.

'Is it my imagination or is D..ominique Fayence beginning to put a d..istance between herself and the d..ubious d..elights of the Latymer marriage bed?'

With the exception of the 'd' in *Dominique* and to a lesser extent those in *distance* and *dubious delights*, Willie Simmonds more or less got through the whole sentence without stammering. Emily noted the progress. When she had first met Willie it had been virtually impossible to follow what he was saying.

'Charlie should have known when he married her that he was just a staging post. The best he can do is hang on as long as possible and enjoy a very nice ride.' Tim Gimmelmann spoke with the air of a man who knew a lot about very nice rides. At his side Jenny, his doll-wife, looked miserable.

'If he ever gets a ride,' guffawed the Mascara, over-loud from too much champagne.

Everybody ignored her, embarrassed now as always.

'I'm sure Charlie and Dominique are very happily married,' came in American Jessica Tarlo. Alongside her Ben Tarlo nodded, proud of her lack of malice.

Peter Berridge, his bald head reflecting the light from the table, sucked thoughtfully on his crooked teeth but said nothing.

The Delancey Street Bar had been Willie's idea, throwing out an invitation to the gang as they had left Middle Temple Hall, and, heady on the spirit of old times, they had, with the exception of Hudson, gone off for one last drink. Somehow, however, in the half-mile between Temple Gardens and Covent Garden, Charlie Latymer had slipped away. As always, the absent had become the target for the snipers.

'It's the shop windows I blame. You know he can never get past a mirror unassisted,' Gimmelmann mocked.

'The word is they're dropping him from *News Quest* as soon as they can find a replacement,' Ginny, Willie Simmonds' latest wife, a ripe demi-aristocrat with a tiny nose and a large forehead, floated a rumour on the gathering. Occasionally employed in public relations she knew the value of negative hearsay.

'I'm s..ure he'll find some s..inecure s..omewhere.' It was the letter 's' this time which broke Willie's flow.

'It would have to be a sinecure in television,' volunteered Penelope Chilston, thankful that she had not been the one to get lost.

'P'raps he could be a television critic then,' said Jenny Gimmelmann seriously. There was an awkward moment. Her husband looked scornfully away. Whatever Jenny said always came out sounding half-baked. For a moment it seemed that the porcelain was about to crack, but then Jenny sank deeper into the cushion of her seat and returned to biting her lip gloss.

Emily looked at her husband. He was haggard with exhaustion but had not offered that as an excuse to slope off home. Perhaps he wanted the night to go on for ever, too. Then she thought about Hudson and pictured him as he had headed towards his Mercedes, his arm around the girl, just another in a long succession of beautiful women. It was unlikely they would ever see her again. She had been too sulky, too petulant to last very long with Hudson. Still, he had gone off with her, happy for the night at least, deaf to Richard's suggestion that he join them.

Laying her head back on the leather of the banquette Emily listened as the conversation divided. Alongside her Richard, Adam Smith and Ben Tarlo were discussing newspaper advertising: 'Hudson's convinced it will explode in the next ten years,' Richard was saying quietly. 'Hudson usually has a sixth sense about these things . . .' came back Adam. Ben nodded, but did not commit himself, cautious as ever; at the next table Gimmelmann was trying fruitlessly to impress the quite unimpressible Jessica Tarlo: '. . . I told him, I said, "It's all right for you, Hudson, you've got half the banks in London wanting to lend you money . . ." You know what he said? "Let me be your bank, Tim. I'll back you and we'll build the best facilities house in the world . . . cutting rooms, off-line, viewing theatres, everything".' Willie Simmonds, playwright, had another angle for Penelope Chilston: 'He came. I d..idn't expect it, but he was there on the f..irst night. "Hudson," I said. "What a n..ice surprise. Are you enjoying it?" "To hell with en..joyment," he said. "How's the house?" He'd never s..aid, you see, but he was the mystery investor in *Toffee Ration*, Hudson himself.'

Emily closed her eyes. Hudson, Hudson, Hudson. It had always been this way. All talk led to Hudson.

Chapter Three

The photographer had woken once in the night with a scream, immediately stifled. A soaking sweat defied the cold.

When he heard the tractors the room was grey with shuttered light. He lay for some moments listening for voices. There were none, just the sound of the distant diesel engines across the valley. Pushing aside the counterpane he crossed to the window and, screwing up eyes now accustomed only to dark, peered through the crack where the shutters had not quite closed.

The tractors were far away on the dirt road he had travelled the previous day. One was an old, dilapidated vehicle and pulled behind it a cart crowded to overflowing with women and children, a human harvest of bright-coloured wools and cottons. Behind it was another, a larger vehicle towing two more trailers: one stacked high with household possessions; the other carried the village goats.

Suddenly from behind the mountain came the loud mechanical rattle of a helicopter and a shadow flitted momentarily across the overgrown paddock in front of the house. The photographer strained his eyes upwards, then hurriedly pulling open the windows and snapping back the shutters, he pushed out a hand and waved. He was too late. Already the sound was retreating back behind the house and over the mountain. When he looked back to the dirt road the tractors and carts were disappearing down the valley.

Turning from the window he now saw the bedroom fully for the first time. It was large, square and sparsely furnished: probably a guest room, he thought. Over the window was a patch of damp, where the floral wallpaper was peeling. He was aware of the mustiness of abandonment. Next to the door was a heavy mahogany wardrobe: on the other side a set of drawers. He slid one open. A sand-coloured spider ran out and darted across his hand, startling him. Otherwise the drawer was empty.

Opening the bedroom door he stepped out on to a wide landing. It was a substantial home and though, he estimated, unoccupied for some time, had been kept in good order. In a bathroom he found that the water ran brown with rust. His reflection in the mirror, the torn, sweat-smeared skin, and hollow, ringed eyes, shocked him.

Curiosity drew him to the other bedrooms. In the largest, immediately over the verandah which ran along the front of the house, he found no clothes but sets of leather-bound volumes of Thomas Hardy and Dickens and assorted issues of *Punch*, the most recent of which was eleven years old. On one wall was a painting of Wells Cathedral in Somerset, on another were two watercolours of grazing impala. Over a heavy dressing table was a black-and-white photograph in a silver frame of a fair girl on a pony, two plaits hanging down in front of her shoulders: a very pretty girl.

He found her room at the end of the landing: a girl's room from another time. Here the mood of the house changed with the mementoes of a youth enjoyed the generation before his own, a place of crammed, chaotic bookshelves, of orange-backed Penguins and dark green detective stories, more photographs of the girl and her pony, an expensive Victorian doll's house, a collection of fossils, a miniature Globe puppet theatre on hinges, a record player, and faded album covers of sulking American singing heroes with greasy hair. Where the other rooms were almost devoid of personal details this one was rich, as though all the ephemera of a childhood had been stored away at the end of this long landing. On a wall behind the head of a spindly four-poster bed was a framed school photograph: Highfield House School, 1960, showing a toothy, lumpy collection of sixth-form girls in blouses and skirts. He found her at once, the slight but healthy-looking girl on the end, laughing into the camera. Next to the school photograph hung a child's black ink drawing on yellowing paper and the neatly scrawled title in big letters: *Two giraffes. Nicola, aged six, at Mana Pools, May 1949.*

Nicola. She was everywhere. In the hall a formal portrait, almost chocolate box, painted at about the age of twenty, a beautiful, flaxen-haired girl in a pale blue evening dress, and in the dining room a photograph of a slim young fourteen year old in a one-piece bathing costume sitting by a swimming-pool with a sheepdog.

He wandered on around the house. The ground-floor rooms were wide and gloomy behind the shutters, with heavy pieces of dark, solid English furniture on wooden floors and deeply patterned Indian rugs: a colonial mansion with few signs of the trivia of everyday existence. At the back of the house he discovered the kitchen, a big old-fashioned, red-tiled room. The refrigerator door was open, its contents gone. One by one he opened each cupboard and peered inside. There was everything a kitchen needed except food. When the house had been left every morsel had been taken. Again the water was brown and unfit to drink. He was hungry and very thirsty.

Climbing out of the house the way he had broken in, he crossed the small courtyard, skirted the empty garages, stables and outbuildings and explored the gardens. They were extensive, once ornate but now overgrown. At the end of a long, wide lawn, directly behind the back of the house, stood an ancient, giant msasa tree, in which, half-hidden by the leaves, was a treehouse. He gazed up. Two monkeys chattered among the branches. He walked on past a small, empty swimming-pool to a round log summer house. Peering through the lattice window he could see croquet mallets and hoops and an old tennis net.

Behind the greenhouses he found a kitchen garden, and a surprise. This was not neglected. Here there were neatly kept patches of carrots, potatoes and turnips, as well as a somewhat larger area of maize. Sinking to his knees he picked a malshaped late tomato off a vine and, rubbing the dirt on to his trousers, he sucked hungrily.

It was at that moment he realized that he was not alone. Standing at the edge of the garden, half-hidden by a bush, someone was watching him, the face obscured by a branch. Very slowly the branches of the bush parted. A red canvas hat appeared and then a white blistered face. The albino boy he had seen in the village gazed at him. In his hands he held one of the photographer's cameras.

The photographer felt the violence of his heartbeat as he gazed at the pale, screwed-up face of the boy, standing as before with one hand up to protect his eyes from the sun.

For some moments they stared at one another. Perhaps there were others watching, too, the photographer thought, perhaps guerrillas were at that moment surrounding him, aiming their Kalashnikov rifles. Cautiously he bent down and, looking around, took another tomato.

Slowly the albino stepped from the bushes. Moving forward he very shyly offered the camera. 'I do not think it is broken,' he said in dignified, good English.

The photographer did not reply immediately.

'I am not a thief.' The boy had misinterpreted the silence. 'I am not trespassing. I can use this garden. It is permitted.'

The photographer continued to stare. 'Yes. Yes, of course,' he said at last. His voice cracked in relief as he spoke. He cleared his throat. 'I'm sorry. You gave me a shock. I didn't know anyone else was here.'

'No. No one lives at Wildwood now,' the boy replied.

'Wildwood?'

'This is Wildwood.' He indicated the house.

The photographer crossed carefully between the rows

of tomato plants towards the boy and took the camera from him.

'You dropped it in the forest,' said the boy. 'I think it will still take cards.'

Now close the photographer could see the tormented skin of the albino and the pale eyes, ringed red from rubbing, bare of eyelashes. 'How did you know I was here?' he asked.

'You left spoor. I followed. Everyone has gone. You must go, too. It is not safe for you here now.' Then, suddenly, without warning, the boy began to sob.

The photographer watched, ashamed now of his panic of the previous night. He should have done something, though he had no idea what that might have been. 'What happened?' he asked at last.

Words came in eddies between the spasms of grief. 'It was very bad ... All the soldiers are dead. My cousin, Wonderful, he is dead, too. And some women. Many people. Children were injured very badly.' He breathed hard, fighting for control. 'Today more soldiers came.'

He broke down again. On his forehead was a large lump and cut. His eyes were bruised.

The guerrillas, he said at last, had not come back to the village to see what they had done. He had not seen them again. They had arrived two days earlier and then left after they had eaten and slept. No one in the village had known that they had been watching. Now they had gone, probably back to Mozambique. After the fire and the killing some of the village children had been sent running to the next village seven miles away to fetch help, but the women had stayed with the dead and injured and their burnt-out huts. Because of the fog, the helicopters had not been able to land to take away the dead soldiers until that morning.

'The soldiers were very angry. They said we must be a bad village and they took my grandfather away with them. They beat me, too.' He pointed to the bruises on his face. 'When they released me I ran away.' There was a long pause. Finally he said: 'And then I came here . . .'

'Did anyone tell the soldiers about me?'

'No. I don't think so.'

The photographer nodded. Why should they have mentioned him? Information was dangerous here whatever you did with it. He turned back to the garden and collected two more tomatoes, one of which he offered to the boy. 'Are you hungry?'

'Very hungry. Yes, sir.' The boy ate the tomato and wiped his eyes and mouth on his sleeve. The photographer watched, struck now by the divine injustice of the boy's albino state. At last the boy spoke again: 'There is *sadza* here.'

'*Sadza?*'

The boy brightened. 'Yes, a great deal of *sadza*. We are very fortunate,' he said in his old-fashioned way.

Then indicating that the photographer should follow he led the way back to the greenhouse.

'It is for the women who work in the gardens, but they have gone away now,' he explained, as he opened a bin just inside the door, and lifted out a bag of mealie meal, a bucket, a pan, a box of matches, a mug and a dish. 'Please wait here.' And taking the bucket he trotted out of the greenhouse and off across the garden.

The photographer watched in admiration at such resilience. Then he looked at the camera. The boy was right. It would still 'take cards'.

They ate on the lawn, sitting in the long grass by a stone barbecue, to the side of the disused swimming-pool. There would have been more sophisticated meals there but few more welcome. While the photographer had collected sticks for the fire the boy had mixed the mealie meal in a pan with water from a stream, before providing a sauce of tomatoes and onions. When the *sadza* was ready he had shown the photographer how to knead it and eat it with his fingers, though his expression revealed astonishment that he did not already know how

41

to do it. 'We do not have *sadza* where I come from,' the photographer said, which the boy found very puzzling.

The food relaxed them and they began to talk. The boy's name was Michael Mavangwe. He had, he said, lived in Mupangare all his life, and had been to Wildwood before because his mother had once been employed there. She was now living with her husband and her other children in Mozambique. He lived with his grandparents.

'Not with your father?' asked the photographer.

The boy hesitated: 'My father is dead.'

'I'm sorry.'

The boy returned thoughtfully to dunking his handful of *sadza* into the relish. Around his mouth he had crumbs of white mealie meal.

'Where will you go now?'

'They have taken the people to a collective village beyond Umtali. I can go there. They will perhaps release my grandfather. It is safe there. Not too far. One day's walk.'

They continued to eat. 'Do you know the man who owns this place?' the photographer asked, looking across the lawn towards the house.

The boy shook his head. He had gone away, he said. He did not know if he would ever come back. The people from Mupangare were allowed to use the garden to grow vegetables but most did not like to come here. 'Only the brave ones.'

'Only the brave ones? Why is that?'

The boy did not answer.

'Does that make you a brave one?'

Again the boy did not answer. After this they lapsed into silence as the events of the previous day resurfaced and demanded reflection. Occasionally the boy would sniff to himself, but there was nothing the photographer could do to comfort him. Wonderful had been buried that morning before the soldiers had arrived in the helicopter. 'His mother cried all night over his body,' the boy said.

To try to take the boy's mind off the killing the

photographer began to talk about himself, of Australia, of his childhood in Sydney, of the first camera his father had given him, of his work as a photographer in London and of how he had come to Rhodesia to photograph the war for a brand-new newspaper. He even mentioned his girl-friend – Clover, Clover Merrifield. It comforted him just to say her name. But, though the boy's eyes widened with recognition when London was mentioned, the photographer knew that he had only the vaguest notion of life outside Mupangare, and would scarcely be able to imagine why anyone would put himself in danger to 'take cards' of a war.

Hoping that perhaps an army Land-Rover or helicopter might return for further surveillance the photographer returned to the village in the afternoon, the boy subdued and silent, head down at his side. Nothing even smouldered there now. Rings of ashes, inches deep, lay on the red earth. A couple of chickens, overlooked in the haste to leave, pecked at the maize pen where the Land-Rover lay crippled on its side. The bodies had been removed, but the dried blood remained. A division of ants was breaking it up and carrying it off. A hundred yards away on the side of a hill were five freshly dug graves for the villagers. The camera captured everything.

It was after seven when they arrived back at Wildwood and already dark. 'We'll have an early night and walk to Umtali tomorrow,' the photographer said as they made their way slowly up the long drive from the dirt road.

The boy did not answer, but walked on staring above them at the house.

'At least you'll be able to sleep in a bed,' he went on. Then thinking that might have sounded patronizing, he added, 'I mean, have a roof over your head.'

Still there was no reply.

Reaching the house they walked around to the back of the building. The shutter was slightly ajar as the photographer had left it. 'I'll go first and then you. All right?' The photographer eased himself through the window and then turned to help the boy. 'Now you. Give me your hand.'

'No, sir.'

'What?'

'I will sleep out here. It is better.'

'Don't be silly. It's freezing. Don't worry. I'll explain that you were keeping me company if anybody says anything.'

'No, sir. Please. Not in this house. You can stay out here with me, too. In the greenhouse. It is very warm in there.'

'Not at night, it isn't.'

'Please, sir . . .'

'I don't understand, what is it?'

The boy did not answer. His albino face was almost luminous in the slight glow from the moon. The photographer looked over his shoulder into the dark house. It was as silent as ever. Sighing, he climbed out again.

'Come on, tell me, what is it? What's the trouble? Aren't you tired? Don't you want to sleep in a nice bed?'

The boy stared at him. 'There are ghosts.'

The photographer smiled. 'Don't be silly. There are no such things as ghosts. Tell you what, you can sleep in my room with me and if any ghosts come we'll take photographs of them and get rich. All right? Come on.'

The boy backed away, unsmiling. 'No. It is a bad place. A bad house. No one ever sleeps here now.' There was no doubt he was terrified of something.

'I don't understand. Why is it bad? Who are the ghosts supposed to be? Do you know?'

'Oh yes. Everyone knows.'

'So, who are they?'

The boy bit his lip. He was a slight child and suddenly looked very young, his pink eyes ghostly almost themselves. He was trembling.

'Come on, who are these ghosts, Michael?' the photographer prodded gently. 'Tell me.'

For a long moment the boy was silent. Then very quietly, as though afraid that he might be heard, he began to whisper: 'They are ... they are ... Miss Nicola ...'

'Miss Nicola?'

'Yes, boss ... the ghosts are Miss Nicola Reynolds and ...'

'Yes? ... and who else?'

'Miss Nicola Reynolds and ... my father.'

Chapter Four

(i)

'Hudson wondered why there was no column by Emily Robinson.' A Sunday morning in bed: a newspaper-littered duvet and empty teacups sitting on precariously balanced columns of books on two bedside tables. Emily was getting dressed: Richard lolled back on the pillow and watched. This morning, this Sunday morning, was virtually the first private waking moment they had had together in weeks. They had even had to make love from memory, Emily had joked. Or had it been a joke? The fondnesses suggested by 'more follows' the previous evening had been put off when, shredded by tiredness, they had crept into bed just before five o'clock, passion postponed. Nature can be perverse. Too exhausted and excited to sleep Richard had then lain awake until nine, when with church bells ringing distantly further up the hill, Emily had turned to him, still full of sleep, and smiled. Married love on a Sunday morning, followed by tea and the newspapers thudding on to the doormat as the paperboy scraped his bicycle on the garden wall; this week an extra newspaper for him to deliver.

'Hudson was just making mischief,' Emily replied without altering the measured pace of her dressing. Richard continued to watch her. He felt guilty. They had not discussed the possibility of her working for *Sunday Morning* because he had never suggested it. He didn't even know whether she wanted a job.

Emily was now slipping into her shoes. She looked tired after the party but, as always, wanted to be down before the children. They lived in a five-storey, white, Victorian terraced house just to the north of Holland Park, a once dilapidated place they had bought cheaply in the early Seventies just before the property boom, and into which they had poured every available hour and penny. Now it was a light, colourful and comfortable family home, a place of too many books, family photographs, framed children's paintings, toys, bicycles, some antique pieces of furniture gathered inexpensively over the years, and, in the style of the moment, rugs on Ronsealed floors and stripped pine woodwork.

Their bedroom was on the second floor. Already the children were awake, and as usual there were sounds of conflicting cultures from above. From Catherine's room came the loud squeaking of a counter-tenor singing raspingly at the top of his range, against the heartbeats of a vibrating bass. Catherine was just ten and had made her first musical decision in life: she liked them loud and emasculated, her mind filled with lyrics of a banal metaphorical carnality, not properly understood, and, to Richard's mind, not always understandable. From the back of the house came another equally remorseless sound, the electronic whirring of two Scalextric cars as they raced around Benedict's bedroom floor. Intended as a game for two, Benedict was happy playing alone, directing operations ambidexterously, a control gun in each hand. They were two children as different as people can be, the sounds of their lives spilling through the house. Only Tom, at five, was quiet. He was probably reading.

Emily was almost ready. Demure for a Sunday, she had dressed in a loose burgundy skirt and cream blouse. Most people dressed down on Sundays these days, but Emily, at home with the children most of the week, still liked to make something of a day which was now special only for its newspapers.

She noticed him watching. 'What's wrong? What are you looking at?'

'I was just thinking, perhaps you'd like to write some interviews. No one does them like you.'

47

She shook her head and, picking up the teacups, headed for the door. 'Lots of people do them every bit as well as I do, as you very well know. Don't think about it. I'm quite happy. And don't go back to sleep, you're due at the BBC at twelve.' With that she went out, closing the door behind her.

Picking up the front section of *The Sunday Times* Richard ran his eyes admiringly once again across the front page. *The Sunday Times* was the paper to beat. It had led with a story about the crisis facing the Italian government following the kidnapping of the Prime Minister, Aldo Moro, by Red Brigade terrorists. A photograph issued by the Red Brigade showed Moro holding a copy of the Italian newspaper *La Repubblica*, looking helplessly into the camera. All the papers had carried the picture, although *Sunday Morning* had moved it down the page when Quirke's story about Iran had come through. No one else had caught up on that, he reflected with satisfaction, although again *The Sunday Times* had a piece on page four about fundamentalist religious opposition to the Shah. Tucked away in bold in the News In Brief column down the left-hand side of page one were two late paragraphs on the massacre in Rhodesia. A strange place, Rhodesia, he thought, and remembered being told how it was like a massive English county of the nineteen twenties dropped in a time-warp in the middle of southern Africa. Things happened in Rhodesia.

The bedroom door opened. It was Tom, his blue dressing gown over his Tintin pyjamas, a children's encyclopedia under his arm. Pushing the newspapers off the bed he slipped under the duvet next to his father. 'Have you ever seen a shark?' he asked, and snuggling down in the warmth he waited for a Sunday morning story.

'Well,' said Richard, putting an arm around the slight, warm body, 'there was a time when I worked as a pearl fisherman in the South Sea Islands and I had to fight off three great whites armed only with a Swiss Army knife and a plastic fork. I was nearly a goner that time.'

'Tell me,' said Tom, and, closing his eyes, better to be able to imagine the pictures, he rested his head happily against his father's body. Sunday morning stories: another family ritual.

(*ii*)

Charlie Latymer stared miserably at the six hundred and twenty-five lines which made up the features of his wife, Dominique. Standing in bright Roman sunlight, wearing a powder blue, expensively functional shirt and skirt, a simple pink ribbon tied across her forehead, and with gold glinting at her lobes and on her wrists, she was the epitome of working media elegance. Alongside her a plump Italian cabinet minister preened in her presence, his eyes flicking between her face and the contour of her bosom as she spoke. Her English was perfect, her French accent adding a grave colouring to whatever she said. It was not surprising she received so much fan mail, Latymer thought, so much more than he did; and then he wondered how many of her admirers actually listened to what she said. Possibly the cabinet minister was now suffering from the same problem because, having been asked a direct question about whether his Government was prepared to stand by and see Aldo Moro die, he had gone into an exaggerated waffle. With a razor smile Dominique cut him short. 'So while the threat by the Red Brigade to murder Aldo Moro is being taken extremely seriously by the Italian government, Moro's letters begging them to negotiate with the terrorists and save his life have so far this Sunday morning met with no official response. This is Dominique Fayence in a Rome where time is now rapidly running out for Aldo Moro.'

As the image of his wife standing on the steps of the monument to Vittorio Emanuele faded from the screen, to be replaced by an advertisement for Corn Flakes, Latymer turned off the television; another Sunday morning alone in bed while his wife flew the world. Three years married and Dominique's career was at full canter, while his own had slowed to a walk. Reaching for the pad at his bedside he wrote down a question for *News Quest*: 'To which political party does/did Aldo Moro belong?', and he wondered which tense it would be.

Thirty minutes later as he was observing his reflection in the coffee percolator, sulking in his neat and shiny kitchen five floors above the trees of Queen's Gate, the telephone rang.

'Darling . . .'

'Very good,' he said at once, trying to sound enthusiastic. 'You kept after him all the way. Terrific actually.'

The steeper the trajectory of Dominique's success the greater her need for reassurance. This morning his job was to convince her that no one could have interviewed the Italian cabinet minister better. Scratch a television presenter and you find an actor. No one knew this better than he did.

'How was last night?' Dominique asked when finally satisfied that her husband had appreciated her every nuance.

'Not too bad.' Latymer knew already which question would follow.

There was the slightest pause. 'And Hudson, did he like our present?'

'He loved it,' Latymer said dully, recalling the expression of amusement as Hudson had unwrapped a rough Colombian woodcarving of a boy selling newspapers, something Dominique had picked up off a pavement craftsman in Bogota.

'He did?' she breathed, evidently well satisfied with her choice of gift.

'He said he was looking forward to your interview with him.' Latymer miserably recounted the conversation.

'Ah, really!' She was pleased.

'When will you be home, by the way?'

'Tomorrow. Lunchtime.'

'So perhaps we'll go out tomorrow night?'

'Perfect,' she whispered. 'I'll see you tomorrow. Good-bye, darling.'

'Take care.'

And with what sounded like the breath of a kiss she hung up.

Latymer contemplated the dial tone miserably. It was one thing to have a beautiful and dazzling wife, to be the envy of half the intelligent men in London, but Dominique was more than that. She was a figure of sexual fantasy. Men wrote to her, spelling out in carnal detail the specific ways in which she might gratify them, intelligent men with good, strong handwriting, careful punctuation, perfect syntax and extensive vocabularies. Television did what no other form of communication had ever done before. Electronically it made a flickering image into an intimately observed, close companion: a friend, a lover, not fifty feet high in a darkened cinema, but some-one familiar around the home, in the living room, in the kitchen, in the bedroom.

Was Dominique faithful to him? he wondered. He did not know. Was she in love with Hudson? Probably.

(*iii*)

Hudson was waiting at Broadcasting House in Portland Place when Richard arrived, late and just in time for the broadcast. Looking as fresh and as bright as ever, show-ing no sign that he had missed the best part of a night's sleep, and with the sulking Spanish infant apparently already forgotten, Hudson was chatting easily to the girl producer: 'Didn't we meet once in Glasgow when you were a reporter? We did, didn't we? You did a terrific job. I never forget a good interviewer. There aren't too many around.' And then the little smile, especially for her. The Hudson smile. Richard watched in quiet amusement. He had seen it so many times. Few were immune to Hudson's smiles. And he wondered which bright spark at Hudson

International had unearthed the Glasgow connection.

They were at the BBC for a four-way discussion with a bow-tied pundit-for-all-seasons and a venerated, trade-union Member of Parliament. The discussion had been programmed with the intention of provoking confrontation, but once in the studio Hudson went immediately for the potentially hostile politician's weakness for flattery, disarming him with not only a sympathetic knowledge of his background, but what appeared to be first-hand familiarity with his constituency. As with the producer, thrilled to be remembered from a moment years earlier in Glasgow, the hours and money invested in research and briefings over at Hudson International were not wasted. The interview, broadcast live after the Sunday lunchtime news, was inevitably smooth and polished, a carefully prepared soap-box for *Sunday Morning* and Hudson International.

Richard had half-promised Emily that he would be home for lunch but when Hudson said he had something to talk over, suggesting a working sandwich at his home, he did not protest. Emily would understand. This was their moment. Hudson's and his. *Sunday Morning* came before everything.

Dismissing his driver Hudson joined Richard in his car for the drive across London. Hudson lived in a large house in The Boltons, an oval estate of nineteenth-century stucco town mansions in South Kensington, which also served as the weekend headquarters of Hudson International. It was a bright day, pink and white with cherry and magnolia blossom, a day for a new start, and all the way Hudson recounted the glowing reports he had been receiving from the *Sunday Morning* distribution network. The launch had been perfect.

His house sat like a large wedge of wedding-cake facing west across private communal gardens, a solid, white, gleaming, Italianate palace, five storeys high, perfectly symmetrical, and with a large central and columned portico. Carefully Richard pulled his family Renault through the open gateway into the drive. There were three cars already parked there and he had to manoeuvre carefully. One of the cars, to the side of the house, stood outside a white mews cottage which had been turned into a garage. It was a gleaming red Alvis from the early Fifties, looking almost newer now than it would have done when it left the factory, the chrome lamps polished, the bank of cream leather seats shining in the sunlight. The hood was open, and a mechanic was peering inside at a spotless engine. Richard turned off his engine, climbed out of his car and gazed across at the Alvis. 'She gets more perfect every time I see her,' he joked.

'Yeah, maybe,' Hudson grinned and hurried on towards the front door.

Richard glanced up at the house. He had never told Hudson but he found its very proportions, with its neo-classical stucco decorations, just a little bit intimidating. Hudson had always liked the idea of a large London house, right from the beginning. 'I'm not ready for her yet,' he had once said while looking at houses like this. He was ready now all right.

Following Hudson into the stark, white marble hall, 'the ice rink', as Emily had christened it, Richard nodded as he passed the gardener who, even on a Sunday, was at work changing the plants in a stone tub in the porch. Already waiting inside were Hudson's private staff of four, the youth club, as they were known at *Sunday Morning*, all young, very bright and very eager: Rajah Dehwola, the blazered, economic wizard was in conversation on the stairs with the lawyer, Robin, while a general researcher could be seen talking on a telephone in her office at the back of the house. Annabel, Hudson's personal assistant, hurried to greet them. All the youth club pleasantly correct, thought Richard, as their smiles lit up like lanterns: nothing so human as a hangover among these people, though they had been the last to leave the party the previous night.

'Unless it's absolutely pressing I'd rather it waited,'

said Hudson, pre-empting the battery of messages on the approaching Annabel's clipboard. 'I'd like to see you all at four, and, in the meantime, could someone arrange some sandwiches.'

Then with a little smile, but without waiting for a reply, he trotted quickly up the broad staircase which curved through the centre of the house. Inwardly Richard grinned as the two young men flattened themselves against the wall to let the publisher pass. Hudson, friendly and familiar to everyone as he was, summoned subservient, ever-smiling loyalty in his personal staff. It had always been that way.

Leading the way into the large, first-floor sitting room Hudson closed the door. In the car he had rattled on about sales projections and targets, but Richard knew there would be more.

'Well, are you going to tell me or do I have to guess?' he asked.

Hudson smiled and, going across to a desk, searched in a pocket for his keys.

Richard looked around the room. It seemed bigger every time he came, but still only half-furnished. That was nothing new. Hudson never got around to finishing his homes. At the garden end of the room was a small, upright, white piano, with intertwining flowers painted on the front and sides. It belonged to another age. That it was still played when Hudson was alone, he did not doubt: it was one wedding present that had never been neglected.

Turning from his desk, holding a see-through plastic file, Hudson indicated that Richard sit on the sofa facing him. Then, very casually, he said: 'What would you say if I told you we're putting in a bid for Federated British?'

Richard did not say anything for a moment. 'You're kidding!' he breathed at last.

Hudson shook his head. 'They want a buyer. They want out. They've had enough. Last year's losses were over seven million.'

'Seven million in losses, and you want to buy them?'

'That's *why* I want to buy them. They'll never be so cheap again. Twenty million, lock, stock and barrel, and another five million needed in redundancy payments. Twenty-five million. The site alone must be worth almost that without printing a word. What do you think?'

Suddenly Richard felt very tired and strangely disappointed. It was all too soon. Last night *Sunday Morning* had been the pinnacle of Hudson's ambitions. For two years he had worked for little else. There were great and safe fortunes to be made in magazine publishing, this palace in The Boltons was evidence of that. But magazines had never been enough for Hudson: the glossy fashion, entertainment, travel, business, home, sport, car, teenage, living, children's and women's magazines of Hudson Publications, and the dozens of down-to-earth *Fun and Profit*, do-it-yourself, hobby, pet, career, health and gardening periodicals had never been anything more than a means to an end, a way of buying Hudson wealth, power and time. *Sunday Morning* was his real interest, he had said, when he had tempted Richard away from *The Sunday Times*. *Sunday Morning* was his future. But that had been until *Sunday Morning* had become his present.

This morning, this Sunday morning, he had his ambition lying in stacks in every newsagent in the country and already it was part of his past, just another step towards a much bigger business empire. Richard knew he should have guessed something was going on, would have done if he had not been so distracted. When Hudson had wooed Federated British for their spare printing capacity he had already been looking several moves ahead.

'You haven't said. What do you think?'

'I think you're mad, if you want to know. Crazy. Barking. Marbleless. Total and utter megalomania begins here. Xanadu in The Boltons. The Kubla Khan of South Kensington. They make movies about madmen like you, you know.'

'So in principle you like the idea,' Hudson chuckled.

'Jesus, Hudson. We haven't even started getting *Sunday Morning* going yet. Do you have any idea of the difficulties we face? We've only done one issue, one single issue, packed with things that aren't right, only half-staffed, with no idea whether the public will take to us, riding on a wing and a prayer that the unions don't sabotage us every Saturday night, and you're talking about taking on a company which lost seven million last year. And why Federated British, for crying out loud? *The Reporter*'s . . .'

'Terrible, I know. Think of the scope. Think of all the things we can do . . .'

'We? Not we, Hudson. You. I've got my hands full enough.'

Hudson grinned again and passed Richard the file. 'Take a look at this. Go on, open it.'

Richard opened the file. Inside were several sheets of paper, all covered in Hudson's tiny handwriting. The first page was the most interesting, an A4 sheet of writing-paper on which were drawn a series of figures and boxes, all interlinked with arrows and forming a series of satellites around a large central box. Inside the box were the words, 'Hudson International'.

'Go from the top in a clockwise direction. That's the game plan.' Hudson was watching him carefully.

Richard looked at the other boxes. They were a series of companies starting with *Sunday Morning*; then came Hudson Magazines and Hudson Business Publications, and next Federated British Newspapers, with the figure of twenty-five million pounds written in red ink alongside; something called *Night And Day* was next and below that a London television facilities house, followed by a group of six radio stations, a burgeoning American women's magazine group, a local newspaper chain, and then several empty boxes. Alongside, also in red, had been written the name, 'Peter Berridge'. This isn't a game plan, Richard thought, it's a journey of conquest. But he said: 'What goes in the empty boxes?'

'Who knows?' grinned Hudson. 'This is only the beginning. The industry is changing all the time and will change even faster in the future. In ten or twelve years from now, in the nineteen nineties, we'll have filled all of them and a lot more with things we haven't even dreamed about. At the moment the news and communications industry is like an open-cast gold field with nuggets of the stuff just lying around waiting to be picked up, shaped, packaged and sold by whoever comes along.'

Richard felt an old discussion re-emerging. 'News is news, Hudson . . .'

'News is news is news. I agree. But it's also money. And we're getting there at just the right moment. If we don't do it, somebody else will. A new Beaverbrook or Rothermere. Murdoch for sure. Maybe other guys we haven't heard about yet. It's bound to happen. It's already happening. We can either stay outside and be bit players all our lives or jump into the ring and do this thing properly, top to bottom.'

'This thing?' Richard wanted him to spell it out.

'Build a totally integrated, multi-media news-gathering and publishing industry.'

'And where does *Sunday Morning* fit into the grand scheme?'

'Right there at the top where it already is. The flagship. You get *Sunday Morning* right and keep it right, and I'll do the rest.'

Richard shook his head. 'Isn't this for the youth club to be working on? I'm not even sure why you're showing me.'

'Why?' Hudson looked surprised. 'Because you're going to be there, Richard. All the way. Just like before. I want you as editorial overlord on whatever we do. The two of us again. Just like it used to be in the beginning.'

'I've already got a job . . .'

'So you've got two, three, four, five jobs. Can you imagine the fun we're going to have again?'

Richard didn't even try to suppress his smile. 'Jesus! I've got a three-hundred-hour-a-week job with *Sunday Morning* and you want to turn me into some kind of media Mussolini. It's impossible. Never mind the nineteen nineties. In six months' time you'll probably be out of business, the banks will be pressing for repayment and I'll be lucky to get a job as a relief sub on the *Radio Times*.'

Hudson laughed. 'I don't believe that and neither do you. We're going to win. And win like nobody ever won before. What's wrong with you? Don't you want to be the most famous editor who ever lived?'

'To be honest, no. I don't. I do want to be the best editor of a successful *Sunday Morning*.' He glanced at the sheet of paper again. 'What's this *Night And Day* thing, anyway?'

Hudson didn't answer.

'And Peter Berridge? What's he done to deserve being in on the greatest game plan of the century? He's despicable.'

'Maybe.'

'*Completely*.' Richard shook his head: 'Are you sure Federated British will sell to you?'

'Absolutely.'

'And can you raise that much money? Twenty-five million . . .'

'Yes.' Hudson was certain. 'What do you think, editor-in-chief of all our titles?'

'God, I don't know. You can call me anything you like so long as *Sunday Morning* doesn't suffer.'

'That's a promise.'

They left it at that as, on a sudden impulse, Hudson picked up an internal phone and, after hurrying along the sandwiches, began to jot down a series of figures, the results of a consumer reaction opinion poll.

Richard watched him, still the young, vital man in slacks and open-necked, button-down shirt, still the dynamic, boyish American he had been when they first met.

He looked again at the game plan. This, then, was their future as Hudson saw it: Hudson the empire builder he had always wanted to be and himself as the editorial brains and loyal friend. Back together again. He gazed around the room while he waited for Hudson to finish on the phone. He would probably be there for the rest of the afternoon, making plans, sharing in Hudson's dreams, bringing the focus of realism on to some of the more extravagant schemes. The youth club downstairs were for background, for research, for financial and legal advice. But they were not friends: not equals. Hudson had surrounded himself with brilliant lieutenants, offices full of clever young people. But like many chiefs he was an isolated man. Richard knew that friendship was the real reason he had been poached back from *The Sunday Times*, the real purpose of this afternoon together.

At last, as always, his eyes lingered on the place above the piano and the black-and-white photograph of the young woman which hung there. She was still beautiful, he thought, as he gazed at the face, partly shaded as had been the style for portraits in those days: still beautiful, and still in their thoughts.

Chapter Five

The boy showed him the grave before they set off for Umtali. It had been just after dawn when they had awoken, huddled together for warmth in the greenhouse, covered by blankets taken from the house. It would have been unfair, the photographer had reasoned, to have left the boy alone outside all night when he had been so obviously terrified.

The climb to the grave took nearly half an hour, along a steep path which wound from the back of the house through the forest and upwards across the smooth shoulder of the hill. This was a magical place, the boy told him as they climbed. It had once been the place where the Shona gods lived. Now it was an empty, misty land of thin, dry grass and evergreen woods.

'This is the way Miss Nicola used to ride her pony,' he offered at one point, a tour guide on a scenic route almost. The photographer nodded. It must have made a spectacular morning ride, up here among the rounded heavens of southern Africa.

The grave was on the top of the mountain, a vantage point with views in all directions, east across the plain which led to Mozambique, west down over the distant red roof of Wildwood and on into the valley, then north or south along the continuing ridge of hills of the Eastern Highlands. No wonder the gods had chosen this place to live, he thought. They would have been safe here.

'Miss Nicola's nanny used to come every day with flowers. But she is too old to climb here now. She has gone away.' The boy had his hand up to protect his albino eyes from the morning sun. Or was it to hide behind?

The photographer looked at the grave and its plain stone cross. 'Nicola Reynolds, 1943–1967,' read the inscription.

'You said your father was also dead . . .' He floated a request for more information.

'I don't know where they buried him,' the boy replied, and turned away.

This was how it had been the previous night, questions being met with either silence or a blank, slow shake of the head. Whatever had been the circumstances of the father's death and why that man should be linked with a young woman called Nicola Reynolds in the afterlife remained a mystery. He stared at the gravestone. 1967. The photographer doubted that the boy would even have been born then: whatever the connection he did not know or would not say.

'So how about you show us the way to Umtali then,' he said after taking a couple of shots of the gravestone.

The boy brightened. He was glad to leave this place. 'Perhaps you will take me to London with you?' he suggested innocently as they walked together back down the mountain.

'I'm sorry. You'll need a passport for that, I'm afraid.' The photographer felt lame with his excuse.

'A passport?' said the boy uncertainly. 'Perhaps when the war is over I will get a passport.'

'Perhaps.'

They walked on in silence through the African morning. And it was only when they were passing the jacaranda tree to the side of the house that the photographer remembered where he had heard the name Nicola Reynolds before.

61

Chapter Six

(i)

Clover Merrifield awoke in the wrong man's bed on Tuesday morning but was then so distracted for the rest of the day she almost forgot to regret it. The bed belonged to a personality, as she would have said had she been writing about him, an older man – ancient actually, fifty at least, a well-known television raconteur, re-encountered at a publishing reception for a Tuscan cookbook, a witty and agreeable companion for dinner, attractive and presentable in his suit, but somewhat soft of skin in the night. He felt, she thought as she waited for daybreak, breathing in the new-paint fumes in his Belsize Park halfway home for the freshly divorced, as though he had been dealt a coat of skin a size too large, and she wondered whether all middle-aged men's bodies were so slackly covered. Certainly Richard Blake's would not be. But then, even to Clover Merrifield's generation, thirty-five was not quite middle-aged.

At six she could wait no longer and slipping quietly from the new bachelor sheets she collected her clothes from a new wicker armchair and dressed in a tiny, new, windowless bathroom. The personality slept on quietly in his new bed, looking older and somehow smaller than his television image. She had slept with him because he had been so confident, so celebrated, so easy in the restaurant and so flattering about her work. She had not realized then how insubstantial his life might be behind the bubbling *bonhomie*. She left a thank-you-for-dinner note and fled. He did not stir.

In England's Lane she bought a copy of the *Guardian* from a newsagent and stopped a taxi at the corner of Haverstock Hill. The driver, a taciturn, comb-over type, glanced with sniffing suspicion as she climbed into the cab, an expression which seemed simultaneously to suggest both disapproval and contemptuous desire. She didn't care. She wore, she knew, the slightly wanton look of after-sex, the hurried demeanour of the dawn fugitive. And so what?

Settling back in her seat she ignored the silent stares through the rear-view mirror. She hoped no one would hear of her night in Belsize Park (did middle-aged men brag about their sexual successes like boys?), but then banished what was only a tiny cloud, anyway, by turning to the newspaper to begin her day. The photographer's picture was the first thing she saw, a single column, one-and-a-half-inch block just below the fold. *Massacre survivor tells of ambush,* ran the headline. She blinked and read the words again.

His voice, long distance and breaking faintly, was waiting on her answering machine. 'Clover . . . it's me, Rob. Just to say I'm all right. Right as rain, actually. Not to worry, and, er . . . Well, I mean, I hope you're OK. Er . . . I'll see you soon. Er . . . Bye.' There was a moment of embarrassment and then a muffled, 'Love you.' Clover frowned. Why did he have to say that?

There were a further eight calls on the machine, recorded the previous evening. The first three were from various members of the *Sunday Morning* staff, repeating what she had now read in the *Guardian* and telling how the word from Associated Press in Salisbury was that the photographer had suddenly turned up at Umtali and was now being interviewed by the Rhodesian army. One call was from the Press Association newsdesk in Fleet Street asking her to call them, while another was from a slim-witted friend: 'I've just heard . . . on the news,' she prattled, over-excited and very loud. 'It is him, isn't it? God! How thrilling.'

Clover looked again at the *Guardian* as the remaining

messages, two dinner invitations and a second call from PA, played themselves out. This must all have been happening last night while she was at that asinine reception and dinner, massaging a semi-geriatric ego. She hadn't even enjoyed the sex particularly: come to think of it, she could scarcely remember the sex. She wanted to kick herself. She had missed all the excitement. She stared at the photographer's picture. She had never imagined him as a hero, he was too young for that, a bit worthy, too. Dull almost, if she was going to be honest with herself. And now he would be coming home to countless days of celebration, generous backslaps and people who would scarcely have recognized him yesterday saying how jolly pleased they were to see him back in one piece today. It would all be too much. Why ring me, anyway, she grumbled, half-aloud, as she ran her shower? I'm hardly his girl-friend.

She lived alone in a small basement flat in Moore Street, a wide road in a slightly run-down island of late-Victorian terraces between Harrods and Chelsea. At irregular, though frequent, intervals for all of the day and much of the night, the rumble of trains on the Circle Line approaching or leaving Sloane Square caused the room to vibrate slightly, a source now, when she noticed it, of comfort rather than annoyance. It was a light, attractive place. She was lucky to have it. Most girls of her age lived in pairs, but Clover had never seen herself as one of the girls.

At nine her telephone rang. It was Stephen Symes, one of *Sunday Morning*'s deputy editors, the oily one with red braces. 'Richard was wondering if you could help us out with Rob Barnes,' he said. 'We hear words aren't his strongest suit and may need some shaping when he gets back.'

'Well, yes, I'll help if I can. Is he really all right?'

'Apparently, hardly a scratch. The word is the Rhodesians will probably be showing him the door when they've got all they can . . . probably tomorrow, so if you could leave yourself available for upcoming fixtures, as they say . . .'

Clover groaned inwardly at the man's style. The red braces had said it all.

'Of course,' she said.

'Jolly good. Richard will give you more details. So if you could pop in to see him some time today . . .'

'Right!' She liked the sound of that. The editor was thinking of her. And she wondered whether she would be able to inveigle a moment alone with him.

After Symes had rung off she replayed the photographer's message. How absolutely typical of a photographer, she thought. In the right place at the right time and unable to put it down on paper. His pictures had better be something special.

(*ii*)

Three hours later in a Notting Hill Gate classroom Emily was applying herself to much the same problem as she struggled to encourage a generation nourished on television to delight in the written word. The word versus the picture: a battle of attrition for the minds and imaginations of thirty-four eight year olds, interrupted from time to time by the guerrilla assaults of an apprentice hooligan named Barnaby. Even with Barnaby's interruptions this part-time, unpaid job was usually quite the best part of Emily's week, certainly the most fun. But today as she moved around the classroom, ruffling hair, advising and encouraging, she was teaching on remote, her thoughts elsewhere.

Richard had received the call before he had left the office the previous evening. 'The line wasn't great, but apparently he'd walked about twenty miles and then been picked up by an army truck. The Army didn't even know he'd been in the village. No wonder the foreign desk couldn't raise him,' he had told her when he arrived home. 'He's lucky to be alive. He kept talking about the mortar exploding just in front of him . . . seeing them dying.' He had paused for a moment before adding quietly: 'And, you know, right at the end of the conversation, just as he was about to put the phone down, he asked me if I knew anything about Nicola Reynolds.'

A frozen frame in Emily's mind. Nicola on her pony, Mashona, climbing the path ahead of her, beating the way, as she used to say.

'It's amazing. An extraordinary coincidence of war or something. He said he was hiding out in her house, slept there. He saw her grave . . .'

Mashona cantering now across the rounded curve of the hill. Richard's voice had been suddenly hushed. 'He didn't seem to have much idea of who she was . . . just remembered the name . . . the Nicola Reynolds Award . . .'

Emily had nodded. The Nicola Reynolds Award. 'What do you think, Emily? Would she have approved?' Hudson had asked. For his sake she had lied. 'Of course,' she had said. 'Nicola always loved prizes, probably because she never won any.' And then the smile. The famous Hudson smile. And the Nicola Reynolds Award had been born.

'Apparently he's friendly with Clover Merrifield,' Richard had added by way of explanation. 'The photographer, I mean. Clover's this year's Nicola Reynolds Award winner, you know.'

She had known. At another time Emily might have looked quickly at her husband at the mention of Clover Merrifield. She had seen his bashfulness with her on the night of the launch, noticed the unconscious stiffening of his spine, the creases of pleasure as Clover had dusted him in flattery. But she had said nothing. It was not the time. For a few moments the presence and memory of Nicola had filled that shared area of unconsciousness which is the binding in a marriage. With Nicola in their minds, laughing, outrageous and beautiful, they were both novices again, starting out, drawn together by her and despite her.

Together they had watched the late news for further

details to emerge from Salisbury, but they had not talked much more. Sadness is a silent pain. For Richard there were the practical details to consider, phone calls to make to ensure that *Sunday Morning* made the most of its good fortune in having an eye-witness to a massacre. Good fortune? Eye-witness. Witness. *Witness.* The very word was a trip wire.

At lunchtime, with the gravy smell of school dinners stealing under the door, and Barnaby the hooligan using his ruler as a catapult, Emily thanked the children for their efforts and ended the class, slightly guilty that this morning they had not had her full concentration. Quickly they crowded out into the corridor chattering about what they had written, handing in their exercise books to be marked.

Soon she would go in search of Tom. But now, as two little girls dawdled, memory tyrannized her. Fifteen years earlier, two older girls, young women almost, in a library. The smell of damp grass cuttings in the air from a lawn being mowed somewhere outside the open, latticed window. Oxford in June. 'Do me a favour, Emmy, give mine in with yours, will you? It's three weeks late. I'll be two minutes. Thanks.' And Emily had waited while her friend had raced to finish a very short essay ('Has *Piers Plowman* an intelligible structure?') that she might deliver the two together. Emily's work was always prompt, steady, never brilliant; Nicola's, scatter-brained, frequently terrible, now and again startlingly good. And invariably late. It had been Nicola's twentieth birthday celebration that night (also weeks late) and they had been going out to The Bear at Woodstock for dinner. Nicola had been paying, of course. Emily had bought her the Beatles' first album as one of her presents. Nicola had always loved the Beatles.

Gradually the classroom emptied, the two gossiping little girls, one in ridiculous platform sandals, the last to leave, dilly-dallying together. Girls are so close, she thought, as she watched them talk their way down the

67

corridor. So mutually dependent. Friends for life. Again the tyranny. Friends for more than life. She still missed her . . . Nicola Reynolds. A note in her pigeon-hole. An upturned bicycle in the middle of a rug and an inner tube dunked in a bowl of water. A face looking up at her through the spokes of the bicycle wheel as she pushed open the door, a wonderfully pretty eighteen-year-old girl in a pale blue blouse, more tanned and alive than anyone she had ever known: light brown hair bleached creamy blond on top from the sun. 'Hello. You're Emily, aren't you? We've been paired for tutorials. You can't mend punctures, can you? I'm Nicola Reynolds, by the way.'

(*iii*)

Decisions and decisions. Fifteen-hour days, Richard Blake in shirt sleeves, dirty coffee in plastic cups, restlessly moving between departments, sampling and reading; an encouragement to the design team, a grumble towards sport, mollifying words to the City editor who wants two more columns, a bleak glare in the direction of arts which says, 'You'd better be more fun this week'; Symes in his red braces at his side demanding a decision on whether to buy the new Desmond Morris book for serialization ('too expensive'); Penelope Chilston wondering if she can go to Pakistan now that Bhutto has appealed against the death sentence ('you are sure you can get to him, aren't you, Penny?'); circulation coming on with the latest revised figures – four hundred and sixty-one thousand for the launch ('not much margin for error there, what's Hudson saying about that?'); sending back for rewriting a leader on the Lib-Lab pact, sampling and reading; a few words with the editor of *Witness* about future covers ('they're too show-bizzy, Peter. We aren't here as an extension of the PR business'); a management warning from Ben Tarlo about some threat of industrial action next weekend ('we'd better get the home and reviews pages away extra early, just in case'); Beckett in Washington coming on with the Patty Hearst/Supreme Court background ('nothing new here, when's the appeal verdict expected and how are we doing with the Carter interview? Well, ask again'); Hudson enthusing down the phone about the terrific figures for the launch ('dead on target'); fashion pictures of a girl in stripes on a moped on the Croisette; the background to a particularly unpleasant series of child sex murders ('very good, but I think we can live without the details of the internal injuries, don't you? Imagine they were your children'), sampling and reading; and now a story from Reuters about the first funerals of the massacre victims in Rhodesia . . . a moment's loss of concentration and Nicola Reynolds has stolen back into his life, laughing at him as the swing falls and then soars in front of him, a pretty girl suspended from an oak tree by two long ropes and a piece of board: a happy afternoon in a wooded Wimbledon garden. 'Of course I love you,' she said as she fell away, and then, tucking her feet underneath as she swung back up into the leaves of the rhododendron bushes, she suddenly kicked them out straight as down she came, forward, missing his face by inches . . . 'Of course I love you . . .'

'Clover Merrifield wonders if you have a moment, Mr Blake?' Irene, the secretary from Tasmania, neat as a privet hedge, a brittle, electric voice on the intercom, and the past recedes.

'Oh yes, thank you, Irene.'

Clover was into his office almost before he had finished speaking, tidily closing the door behind her. He gestured to one of the easy chairs. Her cream shirt was two buttons undone at the neck. On the corner of her collar bone was a tiny chocolate spot. 'I was told you wanted to see me.'

'Ah yes, Clover.' He came around the side of his desk, taking off his glasses. 'Rob Barnes in Rhodesia . . .'

'Yes?'

'He sounds in very good form but sometimes when

69

people see sudden violence they blot out some of the incidents they find most distressing. If you could perhaps prompt him a little bit, help him to shape his thoughts . . . to remember. It'll be a bit of a ghosting job, I'm afraid.'

She nodded. She understood what was wanted.

'An awful lot of war reporting sounds a bit bland and second-hand. Body counts issued by the security forces Press corps, usually wild exaggerations and accounts of battles dreamed up in the bar at headquarters. That sort of thing. The PR version of war. Reporters don't usually like to put themselves where the bullets are flying thickest, not like photographers. Those guys always take bigger risks. Rob was very resourceful to get himself into this village, so we want to get it absolutely right . . . the feel, the smells . . . just as he saw it all . . . what led up to the killing. The history of the patrol in as much detail as he can remember.'

Another nod.

He smiled. Clover smiled back. She made him feel slightly uneasy. She was very pretty. This Rob Barnes fellow was a lucky man to have a girl like her. 'If you need to know anything, I think you'll find that Stephen Symes generally has most of the answers. He's the chap to talk to.'

Again she smiled.

'Well, then . . .' The meeting was over. She did not move, remaining sitting there, perfectly poised, 'one quarter Thai,' someone had once told him, 'the best quarter,' someone else had lewdly said. Perhaps that accounted for the flawless skin and innocence around the eyes. For some reason, although he could hardly spare a moment of time, he allowed the meeting to continue; there had hardly been much reason to see her in the first place. 'What . . . er . . . what else are you working on at the moment?' he asked.

'Oh, well, mainly a couple of interviews for the magazine . . . François Truffaut . . . apparently he loves women with a sort of obessional devotion, and Francis Bacon . . . he's hard to get to, and I've been doing a sort of tongue-in-cheek piece for features about sex and the working girl. "Is there love outside office hours?" That sort of thing.'

'And is there?' A silly question about the silly kind of article intelligent readers read and intelligent newspapers publish despite themselves: a question silly enough to keep the conversation going a moment longer.

'I think when girl meets boy there's always the threat of sex eventually, don't you?' A long stare and then suddenly she smiled, brilliant, warm, conspiratorial and totally self-confident.

Surprised, Richard found himself agreeing. Twenty-three and so assured, he thought.

Clover got to her feet. 'Anyway, I'd better be getting back to it.' She moved towards the door, then stopped and looked back. 'Just one thing. I'm friendly with Rob Barnes, but he's not, you know, not a boy-friend or anything.'

'Oh, I'm sorry. I thought you and he . . .'

'We get on very well. I'm sure we'll be able to do a terrific job on the piece. He's a good friend, but that's all.' She smiled again. 'Bye.'

Richard watched her as she made her way past Irene and out on to the editorial floor. She would go far. Then he thought, she likes me, and was aware of a flush of pleasure.

It was four o'clock. He pulled on his jacket for the management meeting. So far he had avoided telling Hudson that one of their photographers was claiming to have spent the night in Nicola's old home. If it were true the information would only bring unhappiness. There was lots of time for that. Perhaps when he had spoken to the photographer again he would know what to say.

Nicola. He paused by the door as memories engulfed him. He had never known anyone so broken. 'Richard . . .

I've got some terrible news.' Hudson had been distant and faint down the telephone line. Then the line had crackled, Hudson's voice had become clearer and their youth had ended.

Chapter Seven

The albino boy was waiting a hundred yards down the road as the military car taking the photographer to Salisbury swept out of the camp gates. He was sitting impassively alone against the outer of the series of fences which bordered the military base, a small upright bundle almost hidden beneath his protective clothes and red hat. A few yards from him a haphazard roadside market of women, with their arsenals of melons and oranges, and blackened overripe, undersized clutches of bananas, also waited. Beyond them loafed three young women, their faces bright with make-up, their dresses gaudy, tight and flimsy.

'Can we stop?' the photographer asked as the car passed the boy. 'He's just a child. Ten years old. An orphan virtually. I'd like to see him before I go. He sort of took care of me.'

'Sorry. Our orders were to take you straight to Salisbury. It's a long drive.' His escort was a Scottish sergeant who had emigrated to Rhodesia after the Second World War.

'Please. It's important to me. Two minutes can't make any difference.'

The sergeant shrugged. He wasn't a difficult man. 'Two minutes. No more.'

'Thanks a lot. I appreciate it.'

The photographer had more than one reason for wanting to see the boy again. Reckoning, correctly, that the first thing the security forces would do would be to confiscate any exposed films, he had given the boy everything which showed the burning of the village. These he had put, at the boy's suggestion, into the loose lining of the boy's red hat.

'They do not like white Shona,' the boy had said. 'I make them feel uncomfortable. They will not want to touch me. It bothers them. Probably they will not look under my hat.'

They had both guessed right. The army truck which had picked them up had taken them straight to the barracks at Umtali. There the photographer's cameras had been emptied before being handed back to him, all the exposed film in his bags, innocent snaps taken before the patrol had reached Mupangare, being taken for examination.

'We'll send your film on to you in England when we've been through it,' a young major said stiffly. 'Security will want to look at it. It may help us trace those responsible for the attack.'

'I doubt it. I wasn't allowed to use my cameras in Mupangare. And anyway I would have thought the guerrillas would be safely over the border into Mozambique by now, wouldn't you?' the photographer had replied.

The young major had not answered. A captain, the side of his face torn with a recent, yellowing wound, had sat watching, taking notes. He was no more than thirty. Everyone in this war seemed young, the photographer thought. Perhaps they did in every war.

The truth was, he had begun to realize, they hated him for surviving; and they hated him for being Press, British Press, the country that had stabbed them in the back. Perhaps they even thought his presence on the patrol had brought it bad luck. Undoubtedly they were suspicious of his having survived.

His separation from the boy on the Monday night had been sudden and arbitrary. He had been hurried away to be interviewed at length, while the boy, after a brief questioning, had been told where the Mupangare villagers had been taken and ordered on his way. He had been right. He had not been searched.

'I thought I would not see you again,' the boy said

74

as the photographer ran to him in front of the bemused smiles and chatter of the fruit sellers.

The photographer took his hand. 'I've brought you a present, you need a hat. This will keep the sun out of your eyes better.' And he pulled from his pocket a wide-brimmed bush hat, brought from England but never worn.

The boy understood immediately. 'I will exchange with you,' he said. Carefully taking off his own hat he put it firmly on to the photographer's head. A whinny of amusement came from the fruit sellers as they observed this ritual. One lady selling mangoes clapped her hands loudly, ululating appreciatively. The photographer adjusted the red hat. In the lining he could feel the five rolls of film. The three young whores at the roadside giggled at him.

Turning away from the audience the photographer put a hand into his other pocket and pulled out an envelope which he had addressed to the manager of Barclays Bank in Umtali. Inside was a letter of explanation, almost a hundred Rhodesian dollars and a hundred and twenty English pounds, all the money he had on him. He pressed the envelope into the hands of the boy. 'Take great care of this, Michael. It contains some money for you. Don't tell anyone you have it. When you get the chance go to the bank and show them this letter. They will open an account for you, which is somewhere to keep the money safe. It is not a fortune, but it will help. It is yours.'

'Perhaps I will buy a passport and go to England.'

'You can't buy a passport, Michael. But when you get a little bit older it will help in some other way. Promise me you will go to the bank.'

The boy nodded. From the car came the pipping of the horn. One of the whores moved hopefully a couple of paces towards it but stopped when she saw the sergeant's expression.

'All right, then. Let's go,' the sergeant called, irritably shooing the girl away.

'Look after yourself, Michael. And thanks. I'll come back and find you one day.'

Suddenly unembarrassed tears flooded down the albino's cheeks. The lips, wide and fleshy but pink like those of a European, trembled with emotion.

The photographer put an arm around his shoulders. He seemed so young. 'Hey, come on now,' he said.

'I'm sorry. I have been telling you lies,' the boy said at last, the words tumbling out in a rush. 'My father, I know where he is buried. I know how he died. He was executed. They said he was a murderer and they hanged him in the prison. He is an unhappy ghost with Miss Nicola Reynolds now.'

The photographer stared at him. 'He was hanged . . . ?'

'OK, that's it. You said two minutes. We've got to go.' The sergeant had climbed out of the car and was approaching.

'Just coming.'

'Perhaps you will write to me from England.' Having made his confession the boy was now drying his eyes.

'Yes. Yes, of course. But you said they thought your father was a murderer . . .'

'He was innocent. He was not a murderer. I am telling you the truth. My mother told me.'

'Right. In the car.' The sergeant was striding forcefully towards them. He glowered at the boy. 'Hey you, on your way. Down the road, OK.'

'Yes, boss.' The boy turned to leave, then looked back at the photographer. 'Believe me, please,' he said.

'Of course I believe you.' In a moment's unanticipated emotion the photographer suddenly clasped the boy to his chest. 'Good luck, Michael,' he said, then turned and walked quickly to the car.

The fruit sellers and girls by the side of the road had gone quiet as the sergeant had approached. Now they watched this demonstration of affection with silent interest. The boy trotted a few paces down the road, as he had been ordered, then stopped to look back.

From inside the car the last the photographer saw of him was a hand raised in farewell, a slight figure in a new khaki hat at least three sizes too large for him, a little white boy with a negro face, a living example of some cynical whim of the Almighty.

'They cry easily, it doesn't mean anything,' the sergeant breezed as the car accelerated away. The photographer, now wearing his new bright red hat, did not reply: it meant a lot to him.

Chapter Eight

'All right now, fingers on the buttons as away we go for tonight's *News Quest*, '78. And, as the topics tumble in the barrel of luck, what is tonight's first subject going to be . . . ? Oh yes, Pot Luck. We have Pot Luck. So for five points, ready on your buttons, for five points who can name the president of Egypt?'

Worried frowns, mouths open, a tip of tongue pressed against the two rabbit teeth of the man on the left. It's coming. Nearly there. A buzzer squawks. Too late. He's been beaten to it.

'Is it Mr Begin?' Polly from Hull, liquorice allsorts for earrings, has got it in first. Charles Latymer, lightly tanned and white of tooth, smiles softly, sadly at her. So near yet so far, his eyes say sympathetically. His mind says bluntly and silently that it is an irrefutable law of popular television quiz shows that given the choice of two well-known and recently linked names the contestant will invariably choose the wrong one. He presses a foot pedal and sounds a soulful blue siren. 'No, I'm sorry, Polly, it is not Mr Begin.'

Immediately there is another buzzer. The nose is twitching merrily above the prominent teeth. 'Could it be Mr Sadat?'

Charles Latymer fills the studio with his smile. His hand comes down on a bell and up there on the flashing green-and-red electronic board the name of Donald from Luton lights up the first score of the evening. 'President Anwar Sadat it is,' he beams, and the studio audience applaud. Relief all around. Well done, Donald. The show is on the road. Charles Latymer smiles, Donald the airline clerk smiles, the three other contestants smile and the

78

audience smile. Everyone smiles. It's a smiling sort of programme. Cheap smiles, too.

'So that's the first five points to Donald from Luton who's off to a *flying* start. And now for ten points who can tell me the name of the artist whose painting of Sir Winston Churchill was destroyed by Lady Churchill because Sir Winston thought it made him look cruel?'

Nothing. An abyss. A black hole of ignorance. Totally empty faces. Stumped, the lot of them. Charles Latymer groans inwardly. The second question and jaws are already sagging. God help us, he wants to say.

The truth is, he tells himself, he hates all of them, the contestants, the studio audience, the production team and most of all the producer, Terry with the stubble, the over-grazed chin masquerading as the beginnings of a beard.

He sucks his breath through barely parted, ever-smiling teeth. They are all so unbelievably moronic. This Churchill story was in every newspaper in the country not three months ago. Front-page stuff. Letters to the editors. Questions in the House. Churchill the vandal. Minutes on end devoted to it on all the main television news programmes. How can they have forgotten so soon? Is no one taught to remember anything any more?

His smile fixed, he stares at the contestants, four nonentities in a row, dahlia brains, each one behind a mock-up of a television news reader's desk, and behind them a thirty-foot-high collage of blown-up newspaper headlines, background for the words '*News Quest*' set in a vulgar tabloid typeface. Latymer watches in silent glee. He knew they were a cretinous lot at the rehearsal, but Terry had fancied the hairdresser in pink whose ambition it was to interview John Travolta for the *Sunday Mirror*. And Terry knew best. Of course he did. He'd been on a producers' course to Southampton. They learnt how to pick contestants in Southampton. He had to know best. Personality was what they went for in Southampton. And bright colours. So here they were, with the racing certainty Pinner schoolteacher who knew everything, being thanked for coming and sitting out there in the audience wondering why girls who wear glasses and grey cardigans never get on television quiz shows when there is a thick blonde in pink with a cheeky giggle and neat little bottom instead.

'The name of the man whose painting of Sir Winston Churchill was destroyed . . . ?'

Donald from Luton is opening and shutting his mouth like a distressed hare. Alongside him Polly from Hull is smiling as though she knows the answer but wants to keep it a secret, while at the end of the row Harry from Basingstoke stares darkly at his hands, hunched up, and brooding, his one eyebrow stretching, give or take a centimetre or two at the edges, from ear to ear. He has the look of a man who has just murdered his wife, thinks Latymer. And what a lucky woman she must be.

'I'm afraid I'm going to have to hurry you . . .'

'Is it Picasso?' The hairdresser in pink has interrupted and buzzed all at once.

Contempt seeps from Latymer's pores. The corners of his mouth droop in derision. 'No Polly, not Picasso, not even in his blue period.'

Obedient laughter from the studio audience in response to a flashing light reading 'LAUGH'. 'If it said "BARK" no doubt they would oblige,' Latymer said ritually to someone before every show. No one responded any more. Sometimes he varied it to 'ROAR' or 'MIAOW' or 'HEE-HAW'. Still no one cared. Out of sight of any camera a floor manager is flapping his hands together in front of his fat waist like a goose at Easter. Applaud you bastards, applaud, his message reads. And applaud they do.

Smug in his creamy-white suit, blue button-down shirt especially cut in Jermyn Street, and Liberty tie, his greying hair layered, lacquered and thick around his ears in the fashionable style, Latymer gives up. 'No, the answer we wanted was Graham Sutherland. Of course you knew all

80

the time, didn't you?' On his monitor he can see a close-up of half a dozen ignoramuses in the audience nodding to themselves at that. Liars, he thinks, but says, 'And now for another ten points who knows the Christian name of the Russian diplomat who defected at the United Nations in New York last week?' This, someone must know. It was two inches high in every newspaper in the country.

A buzzer: it's the wife murderer. 'Was it Boris . . . ?'

I shouldn't laugh, this is how I make my living, Latymer is thinking. This is what happens to fellows who read modern history at Cambridge. Up here like a jerk surrounded by flashing bulbs of green and red while my musky wife telephones from the heaving beds of Europe to say, 'Sorry, darling, change of plan. They want a couple of days in Paris for me to talk to Raymond Barre. See you Thursday.' And so it goes on. Or so it went on until today. It's in my pocket. The letter. The heave ho. They couldn't even tell me in person. 'Falling audiences . . . time for a rethink . . . thanks for the sterling work . . . but your contract will not be renewed.' And what next, Charlie? Commercials for building societies and dog biscuits . . . ? What went wrong? At what point did you take the wrong turning? It all seemed so certain, so right . . .

'Arkady. His name was Arkady Shevchenko.' It's the hairdresser in pink. She's jumping up and down as though she's just redefined the special theory of relativity.

A moment of utter disbelief and then Latymer's hand goes down on his bell. 'Absolutely right. Arkady Shevchenko is the name of the Soviet diplomat who defected last week. Well done, well done. Ten points for Polly in pink and a haircut for the producer.'

The hairdresser's face falls. Got her! He was right. Terry had tipped her off. The little creep. What a way to get laid. A crooked *News Quest*. And what a way to get waylaid in your career: Charlie Latymer facing a dead end. And the audience applauds again.

*

Latymer did not arrive at The Boltons until nearly nine. He had been drinking alone in the flat in Queen's Gate and was by then fuzzy around the edges. He had never been a good drinker. Alcohol got in the way of sharpness of mind and was ruinous to the looks. In television vanity has a high premium.

That he should have gone to see Hudson at all had been Dominique's idea. 'You need a friend,' she had said down the phone. 'Hudson will know what to do. He will help.'

Latymer had resisted. Why should Hudson help him? Especially him. What had he ever done for Hudson? But Dominique had been certain. 'It doesn't matter what you did, or what you thought you did,' she had insisted. 'He will help you. I know.'

Perhaps she did know. She certainly knew he had been sacked before he told her. In the high-tech world of communications no sound travels more quickly than the satisfying thud of a knife being sunk into an expensively suited back.

'You might have lasted longer if you hadn't despised the contestants quite so much,' Terry, the producer, had sniped after making the usual insincere and regretful noises about the incompetence of management. He was furious because Polly in pink had made a hasty exit in the car of a floor manager from Teddington, and he blamed Latymer.

Latymer had not replied. Already the bilious Berridge had been on the phone sniffing blood. By the next day all the comics would be gloating at his dismissal, and noting the extreme youth and working-class street credibility of his replacement. Oh yes, Terry had already let that slip. There was to be a new series with a new host. The yobs were taking over everywhere.

Miserably Latymer had cleared his desk. Better to get it over now than to have to return in a few days' time and be the subject of everyone's embarrassment.

He would reflect later when he was alone that

Dominique might have shown more sympathy, but that was not her way. Dominique, moving only with the successful, saw failure as a contagion. 'Hang out with losers and you become a loser, darling,' she would say, and the moral for him was clear. Their marriage would not survive failure on his part. She needed someone to bolster her ego, that was true. But that someone had to be a somebody.

It had taken three large whiskies before he had plucked up the courage to call Hudson. He had expected to be fobbed off by a secretary, a five-minute meeting two weeks on Thursday would not have seemed unlikely and Annabel had indeed murmured something about Hudson being 'chock-a-block'. But then suddenly there was Hudson on the phone, breaking into whatever deal he was devising and inviting him over immediately. That might normally have puzzled Latymer. But alcohol is the great evaporator of doubts and, after a final session with the mirror, he had called a taxi.

He need not have worried. Hudson could not have looked more pleased to see him. If Latymer's little betrayal all those years ago still rankled, Hudson never showed it.

'Great to see you,' Hudson smiled as he led him inside. He had been in the act of saying goodbye to two Japanese bankers as Latymer had arrived, and, after introducing everyone, he led him across the ice rink to his office. The house was now still. At nine o'clock Latymer was the last appointment of the day.

'I thought we'd have a chat here and then perhaps go out for some dinner, if that's all right,' said Hudson, sitting on his desk.

Latymer was surprised. He had expected fifteen minutes at best. 'Well, if you're sure . . .' he murmured. Had Hudson cleared his diary just for him?

Hudson's office was at the back of the house. From it there was an open door to a large domed conservatory, a lush glass palace. This was the first time Latymer had been to the house and he was astonished. Hudson International must have done even better than he realized, and he tried to calculate just how many millions a home like this might be worth.

The cheap wooden paperboy carving that Dominique had sent as a present was sitting on a marble mantelpiece. Hudson saw him looking at it.

'I'm sorry I've been so busy I haven't had time to thank you both properly for that little fellow.'

'Well, it was Dominique's idea really . . .' Latymer's voice faded.

Hudson crossed to the fireplace and stared fondly at the figure. 'He reminds me of you and me and Richard when we first started out. D'you remember, that old van we used to hire to carry stacks of *Witness* into shops when no one wanted to stock it?'

Latymer had never actually delivered *Witness*, so he said: 'And those appalling printers who kept on letting us down.'

'J.W. Purley and Sons.'

'I thought you bought them out.'

Hudson nodded. 'Eventually, eventually.' He smiled at his memories. 'Happy days, Charlie.'

Latymer nodded. There was a second's silence. He felt uncomfortable on the subject of the past.

As though sensing it, Hudson replaced the carved paperboy and led the way into the conservatory. Discreet low-level lighting shone up through the leaves of the tropical plants.

'I'm glad you rang me tonight, Charlie,' he said. 'As a matter of fact I've been thinking of calling you for quite a while.'

'Really?'

'Mmm.' Hudson was hesitating. Whatever he had to say appeared to be troubling him slightly. 'Look, I don't know whether this will interest you, and if it doesn't, for whatever reason, don't be afraid to tell me, but I need a favour and I think you're the man who can do it for me.'

84

'That's funny, I was going to . . .' Latymer stopped. Perhaps he ought not to reveal the weakness of his position just yet. Instead he said: 'I mean . . . what is it, what can I do for you?'

Hudson turned to him. 'Basically, Charlie, Hudson International needs a public image maker, someone at my side who can take over the job of explaining our role. We know that what we're doing is for the general good, but we need someone who can get that message across.'

Latymer was disappointed. 'You mean, sort of public relations?'

Hudson shook his head. 'I mean a mastermind, a star, someone with intellect and a business brain, someone who is as at ease in front of the camera as running a press conference. I need someone to take care of all that. And there's only one person I know I can trust to do that for me. What do you say?'

Charlie Latymer did not know what to say. It was what he had always wanted at *Witness* all those years ago. Status. 'Well . . .' he began, but Hudson cut him off.

'No. Don't answer now. Let's have dinner and I'll outline our plans. Is that OK?'

'Well, yes, that might be an idea.' The one thing Latymer had always prided himself upon was that he was quick to size up a situation.

'Good man.' Hudson patted his arm and walked ahead back into the main house. Latymer paused a moment, catching sight of his reflection in the conservatory window. What would he tell Dominique? How would she ever believe him? Now she would know where the weight in their marriage really lay. All that remained was the deal, making sure that Hudson paid him what he was worth. A seat on the board was essential. There was absolutely no point in selling himself cheap when Hudson needed him so badly. No point at all.

At that moment the lights in the conservatory went

out. Suddenly it was night in this glass-domed jungle. Hudson looked out from his study. 'Well, Charlie, are you coming or aren't you?'

Latymer smiled to himself. At last he was being recognized for what he was.

Some hours later as they were driven home, Josh, Hudson's driver, offered them the next day's newspapers. Latymer was surprised to find a two-column photograph of himself on page three of the *Reporter* and stories on pages five and seven of the *Mirror* and the *Sun* respectively. The *Sun* put the state of affairs most succinctly. *News Quest star axed*, it read. Through bleary eyes Latymer stared at the papers. Hudson, as sober as ever, scanned *The Times* and the *Telegraph*. *News Quest*. It already seemed so distant now: another life had begun. The green-and-red flashing scoreboard, Polly in pink, the appalling Terry and his flock chin. What had he been doing wasting his talents on such pygmies? Then he remembered. He had never got around to telling Hudson why he had gone to see him: he hadn't even been asked.

'Isn't that just like the comics?' Hudson chuckled, looking at the tabloid headlines. 'Always getting everything back to front. How can you be sacked when you've already resigned?'

'Well, actually . . .'

Hudson cut him short.

'Leave it to me. By the time we're through those *News Quest* people will look like the biggest crowd of incompetents ever to be let loose in television for allowing you to slip through their fingers.'

The Mercedes was already sliding down Queen's Gate. 'You knew, didn't you?' said Latymer.

Hudson shrugged. 'I knew I had to be quick before somebody else snapped you up. I knew that. Now where do you want dropping off? What number did you say it was?'

A few moments later Charles Latymer, the latest recruit to Hudson International, stood at the edge of the kerb as the Mercedes drove quietly away through the electric wash of the London night. He was going to be rich and important: everything he had ever wanted.

Chapter Nine

(i)

On an impulse Emily went back to Oxford for the day, something she had not done in years. Tom and Benedict had been invited to a birthday party in West Kensington and would not be deposited home (by another mother whose turn it was to do the birthday run) until six, and Catherine did not get back much before five these days.

The train from Paddington was smoother and quicker than she remembered: the open-plan carriage sunnier. In her day there had been closed compartments smelling of smoke and soot, and dud bulbs in the lights as though reading were to be discouraged. But there had been excitement, too, the inevitable encountering of friends on the platform or struggling along the crammed swaying corridor. In those days she had rarely travelled up when it was light, arriving always on the last train, her fingers swollen and rutted under the weight of her suitcases.

At Reading the train stopped above a new housing estate and she watched a young woman leaning over a high, lightweight pram in a small back garden. She thought about her own children and tried to picture each one at school: Catherine, confident in a music lesson perhaps, Benedict, quieter, more like her, spellbound by the Vikings (at breakfast that morning he had been happy that they had history on Fridays), and Tom, excited and inevitably nervous at the prospect of this afternoon's party. In the sweet tyranny of motherhood they were never far from her thoughts.

As the train turned northwards through the western

fringes of the Chilterns an elderly German woman sitting opposite, who had studied a guide to Oxford all the way from London, began to confide in her. She was, she said, recovering from an operation and then went on to complain that England was too overcrowded with tourists these days, before demanding that Emily tell her the purpose of her journey to Oxford.

'Do you know,' said Emily honestly, 'I'm not at all sure.'

Who knows why any of us ever does anything? she thought as the woman sniffed and returned to her tourist guide, taking the reply for a rebuke. But it was true. In all the years since she came down Emily had visited Oxford on only half a dozen occasions, and now not for a very long time. Her home and family belonged to London; Richard, she sometimes thought, could scarcely place Oxford on a map. She had enjoyed her time there and done reasonably, but had never numbered herself among those to whom life after Oxford is an anticlimax. Quite the contrary: at the end of her final year the future had beckoned so strongly that she had rushed away with scarcely a backward glance.

'We'll never get everything in . . . it's impossible.' She heard herself worrying about the size of her trunk.

'Of course we will.' Hudson was smiling, lifting, manoeuvring, shifting. He had bought an old car for a hundred and twenty-five pounds, a red Alvis from the early Fifties, a smooth ballooning monster of an open roadster with large, rounded mudguards, and thick wedge-like doors which perversely opened backwards, the hinges at the sides of the cream, real leather seats.

And he had managed. He always did. The trunk had gone into the car boot although it had jutted out of the back, and her suitcases had been squeezed into the back seat. At the last minute Nicola had come running to see her off, dashing along the pavement, giggling and carrying in her arms a life-sized, hollow, brass piglet which she had just found in a junk shop.

89

'It's a going-down present,' she had laughed, pushing the pig into Emily's arms. 'We'll feed him on spiked copy and give him pornographic pictures for a treat on Sundays. See his mouth's open, already waiting. The poor thing's obviously starving.'

And then as Hudson had watched, amused at her beautiful eccentricity, she had suddenly kissed them both, reaching over to hug Emily farewell, although she would be following the next day to join her in the flat they would share near Sloane Square.

'You know she's crazy,' Hudson had said as the Alvis sped across Magdalen Bridge.

'She's wonderful,' Emily had replied, wondering why on earth anyone would want to buy a life-sized piglet.

'That, too.' Then, touching her face with his hand, he had added: 'And so are you.'

Hudson had done that so often in those days. The gentle affectionate touch, the favours, no kindness too much trouble. The perfect, no, better than perfect, boy-friend.

But what had happened to the piglet?

It had not changed, their place to the right of the arch in the east wall. The Botanic Garden where, protected from the wind, they would look out across the sheltered square and its eight rectangular strips of flower beds towards the yew tree in the centre, the vast Austrian pine in the left-hand corner, the mulberry and the juniper: a one-time physic garden of herbs where two young girls had once sought the cures to the growing pains of emotion, and had shared everything, especially their secrets. Nicola had found it first, their bench, against the seventeenth-century wall. Behind them, through the arch, beyond the greenhouses, the Cherwell meandered. Occasionally shouts from the punts or the hum of buses on the High would disturb the tranquillity. But rarely: and not on this day either.

This had been the purpose of Emily's visit, she knew

it now. To sit silently as they had once done, talking, reading together or silently watching the garden, content in each other's company. Today she was contented, too, although the day was chilly and the sun not high enough in the sky to properly warm the stone bench.

She had walked through the town to reach this place, but she had noticed little, hardly even the tourists. Now she remembered everything. It was here in this garden that Nicola had talked about Richard. For a moment a blade of jealousy cut sharply at the memory, but it was quickly gone. Their lives had been so intertwined, the currents of their moods and their loves so capricious and changing. They were four people who had loved each other and learned to share each other.

'Can you smell the garden, Emmy?' Nicola would say, greedily breathing in gulps of air as though unable to get enough. 'Can you really smell it? It reminds me of home.' And then off they would go through the arch, tapping on the door of the orchid house, while Nicola would tell stories of a gardener called Joseph who grew orchids better than anyone in the world.

Emily did not stay long, an hour, no more, and then began to make her way back along the Broad Walk as they had always done.

'The trouble with Richard,' Nicola had said that day just before finals as they had strolled past the cricket on Merton Fields, '. . . the trouble with Richard is his insecurity. He's convinced I'm going to leave him. And, I mean, I'm not . . . not ever. Not him, not you . . . not any of you . . .' So young then. A four-way love affair. Best friends and best lovers. And no one more loved than Nicola.

(ii)

Richard called in at Hudson International in Knightsbridge, the seven-storey chrome and glass headquarters from where Hudson administered the dominions of his

91

publishing businesses, on his way home. It was nearly half-past seven and he had finished early. The excuse was to discuss the several appointments he wished to make: some of the salary demands had been on the high side, raising eyebrows in the contracts department, and by going straight to Hudson he hoped to bypass looming management obstacles.

For two days Hudson had been locked in meetings with his lawyers and those acting for Federated British and now, close to success, he was glowing with excitement. He had caught the moment and was slightly giddy with his own energy. On seeing Richard he put a shirt-sleeved arm around his shoulder and led him into his inner office.

Quietly, as he sat down, Richard told him about the photographer's visit to Wildwood.

Hudson's welcome dimmed. 'In the house, you say? He stayed in Wildwood? How extraordinary.'

'I didn't want to mention it until we were quite sure . . .' A white lie for kindness. 'It's deserted now. Apparently some local boy mentioned Nicola's name.'

Hudson, his blue eyes so happy a few moments earlier, suddenly looked tired. They so rarely mentioned Nicola that it was difficult now to find the words.

'It was her birthday last week,' he said at last. 'She would have been thirty-five.'

Richard nodded. Emily had remembered the date, too. He tried to be practical. 'I suppose her uncle must have decided the house was too dangerous a place to live when there was a war on, and closed it down for the duration.'

Hudson shook his head. 'Not just the duration. I don't think he's ever lived there again. In fact he's hardly been back.'

'So what happened to . . . I mean, I understood from our photographer that the house was still furnished. Nicola's belongings are still there. Just as she left them . . .'

'He wanted everything leaving exactly as it was. Eventually the servants retired or moved on and the place was closed up. I suppose I could have insisted on having Nicola's things, but after everything that happened, and the way he was, the way they all were, it would have seemed heartless. I can wait.'

Richard understood that. 'He must be getting on a bit now.'

'At least eighty. We still talk occasionally. There was a lot of business to be . . . you know, sorted out. He's still very sharp, but not very well. He's been living down in Johannesburg a lot recently, near to some hospital . . .'

Suddenly he breathed out, a long, weary sigh. Going to the window he stared down across Knightsbridge. 'I still think of her, you know. Every single day. No, much more than that. Ten, twenty times a day. I still think of her, of the times we had. She was just so . . . wonderful. Wasn't she, Richard? Do you remember how wonderful she was? Do you?'

Richard nodded. How could he not remember?

(*iii*)

Three-thirty in the morning, thirty-six thousand feet above the Central African Empire and the photographer cried out in his sleep, unable to escape his dream, a fretful, broken, black-and-white mind-film of a gallows and a jigging black man on the end of a rope. But then the rope turned to a string and the black man became a marionette dancing to the pull of the Leader of the Pack, the American, whose paunch now threw a shadow above the gallows as it was transformed into a puppet theatre, a white-walled Globe high in the mountains of Africa, where a beautiful girl smiled down at the photographer from a box, garlanded and scented with orchids, jasmine and honeysuckle. Beautiful and fair, beautiful and fair, beautiful and fair . . . the words formed an endless loop in his mind. But, as he approached, the box became an

93

open window and the theatre a house and the girl's face changed from white to black, more lovely now than ever. Still she beckoned and welcomed him until virtually at the sill, able almost to reach up and take her open hand, the mist swept down from the mountains above, obscuring her. When he looked again the window had snapped closed and in the place of the girl was a large black bird which, seeing him, flew straight at the window pane, shattering the glass from within, screeching and clawing into his face, its pincered, yellow beak aiming for his eyes, embedding themselves into the lens of his shield, his camera, piercing and gouging, seeking out the film of his mind, which it tore from the spools of his memory like a struggling earthworm. And then, dangling the intestines of his thoughts, the creature flew high on to the roof of the house where frame by frame it devoured the ribbon of film, holding it down tight with one claw against the hip of the roof as it ripped with its beak into the flesh of the images. Now there came colour to the dream as the images began to bleed, the child Wonderful from the village, blood seeping through his Donald Duck T-shirt, the interrogating captain with the yellow tear in his face, the pink-and-fair boy soldiers still laughing at their one-legged honeymooner joke and the blue-uniformed, black policemen in the green Land-Rover. And as he looked again she was back at the window, staring out through the jagged shards of broken glass, the beautiful girl from the portrait, her arm now around Michael Mavangwe, the albino boy, who was so proud and happy to be safe and secure with one so lovely.

He awoke in tears, shouting and struggling for breath as the noose tightened on his neck, victim now himself, death smiling up from the mist below. A stewardess, plump and Scottish, was leaning over him. 'You're all right, you're all right,' she said softly, a hand on his brow, smoothing and cooling the furnace. 'You're quite safe. It was only a dream. We'll soon have you home.'

The photographer stared at her, but for the longest

moment all he saw was the face of Nicola Reynolds. 'I am not a thief. I can use this garden. It is permitted . . . I am not a thief, I can use this garden. It is permitted . . . It is permitted . . . It is permitted . . .' he heard the albino boy say again and again.

Now he understood. The ghost of Nicola Reynolds would have permitted this boy anything.

PART TWO

June 1963

Chapter Ten

He was reading a newspaper and eating cherries from a bag when the taxi drew up, sitting on the steps of the hostel with the sun on his face, taking his time, an end of finals treat to himself, time to kill and decisions to make.

At the kerb the taxi's diesel engine idled noisily as a passenger's face peered uncertainly through the window. After a moment the cab door opened and a very tall, fair young man climbed out and stared up at the peeling, stuccoed columns.

'Excuse me, is this the Lamborne Hotel?' The accent was American: the demeanour and the clothes, blue jeans, solid, expensive brown brogues, an open-necked, blue, Oxford button-down shirt and a light summer jacket, had the stamp of casual confidence.

'So they say. But it isn't a hotel. Not really.' The cherry-eater smiled. This fellow was in for an awful disappointment.

The American shrugged. He was handsome in an old-fashioned, blue-eyed, lean, even-featured way. 'Oh well, I guess I'm not really much of a hotel type, anyway,' he said easily, and, paying the cab driver, began to heave a vast, battered, beige trunk on to the pavement.

Putting the bag down the cherry-eater went to help, grabbing hold of one end of the trunk and backing up the steps and under the Lamborne's shabby portico. It was impossibly heavy.

'Thanks a lot,' the American gasped as they struggled into the narrow hall. 'It feels like I probably brought too much with me.'

Helping manoeuvre the trunk down by the stairs

the cherry-eater pointed to the back of the house where a narrow-faced, middle-aged woman in a chestnut coloured suit was watching the newcomer suspiciously through the open door of her office. 'Miss O'Casey,' he said quietly. 'You see her about your room. Don't be put off. She stops biting when you bleed.'

The American grinned and pushed out a hand, a formal gesture. 'James Hudson,' he said. 'I owe you one.'

'That's all right. I'm Richard Blake.' Then smiling his 'good luck' he returned to his cherries and his position on the steps.

London in June 1963. Ten o'clock, Sunday morning. Richard Blake, lightly built with a wide forehead, black hair and horn-rimmed glasses, sitting in his slacks and tennis shoes, had been an ex-student for just three days, and for the first time in his life the future was unknown. It was the strangest feeling.

He had lived at the four houses which made up the Lamborne Hotel for the final year of his degree. Part of a crumbling terrace in a Bayswater square, the Lamborne was a home for students from colleges all over London. While in no sense comfortable, and altogether short of bathrooms, it was cheap and it was central. Obviously position counted for a lot with this man Hudson.

Richard sucked a cherry pensively. Most of the other students in his year had already taken off for their last summer vacations, but he did not want a holiday: he wanted to begin his career. So much was happening and he was missing it.

It had been quite a week. The last of the finals had been on Wednesday, three bleak hours in the cool and polish of the University of London Examinations Hall in Bloomsbury; celebrations had begun that evening, continued throughout Thursday and ended with a solo hand-paddle down the Serpentine in a commandeered, stray, oarless rowing boat at dawn on Friday.

On Saturday morning the most recent rejection had

arrived. The BBC had not selected him for their general traineeship. It was not unexpected. Many applied but few were chosen. But put alongside the miserable interview at Independent Television News which had followed the blank, formal rejections from Fleet Street, and a new reality was dawning. The world of news could manage very well without him.

A wan, intense girl in a baggy, home-knitted, green sweater and black ski-trousers, trotted down the steps alongside him and hurried away up the street, a cloud of lavender accompanying her. He knew her vaguely, a typical Lamborne girl she was rumoured to have won first prize in her year for the best-kept virginity. Not only her. Young when he had gone up to university virginity was still, if only just, a reluctant part of Richard's own life.

Virginity, the unmentionable nine-letter word, an embarrassment worn like an outgrown school blazer. Somehow it had never happened: the last of the Bayswater virgins when suddenly everywhere he looked London was tumescent with talk of sex: of homosexual spies and kinky civil servants, of call girls and cabinet ministers, of a dirty duchess and a notorious divorce. And now two trollopy girls no older than himself were threatening to bring down the entire British government. In June 1963 sex had become the national sport, a sport at which he seemed condemned to remain forever a spectator.

But something else was happening. London was changing, growing younger with the year. Something was going on. Richard didn't know what it was but he did know that he wanted to be a part of it.

Finishing the cherries he stepped back into the hall where Miss O'Casey was explaining the rules of the house to the American boy. '. . . the room is let to you and you alone . . .' she was saying: 'Now do you understand that, Mr Hudson? Do you really understand that?' Richard watched in silent amusement. She had never recovered from discovering her two Austrian kitchen girls in bed with a plucky boy from Cardiff, the one they called the Welsh Dragon. Most new hostel members shuffled their feet and looked meek when being delivered the O'Casey Commandments, but the American did something quite unexpected. He smiled: the biggest, widest smile Kathleen O'Casey must have received in her entire life. A show-stopper of a smile. And it worked. She stopped, lost her place in her litany, tried to start again with something about 'parties in rooms must finish at twelve sharp', moved on to the dangers of standing on the balconies and then simply gave up.

Richard Blake watched in admiration. This chap Hudson had charm by the truck-load.

At midday he went home to Wimbledon for lunch with his parents and sister, Carol, who was sixteen. They lived in a large white house on a wooded, unmade road behind the Common, a well-off, protected green suburb of London from where men in suits would be driven to Wimbledon Station by their wives each morning and collected each evening after their day in the City. It was the ordered, sheltered rhythm with which he had grown up, a cautious father and a mother grateful that they had done so well in life. 'It's all right for you to criticize, Richard,' she would say, even when he wasn't criticizing anything, 'but your father has worked hard for all of us. And if you had any sense you'd go into the City, too.'

But he had other dreams. So, avoiding discussions of what he knew had been disastrous finals, he ate the roast lamb in the dining room, exchanged Profumo rumours with his father ('I hear that four High Court judges are involved' . . . 'I heard five'), discussed the forthcoming Wimbledon tennis fortnight with his mother, and then went outside into the garden, his father's reward for all those years. Though he had always hated mowing the lawns he liked the garden, too. Between two birches, deep among the azaleas, was the hammock he and his sister had played on as children.

Close by a long swing hung from the branch of an oak tree.

'What are you going to do?' asked Carol as she dallied backwards and forwards on the swing. 'About a job, I mean.'

He shifted in the hammock. 'I'll get something.'

'The careers adviser at school said the only way into newspapers is by joining one in Manchester or Newcastle or somewhere and . . .'

'I can't leave London. Not now. Not when it's all beginning to happen.'

'What's beginning to happen?'

He shook his head. 'I don't know.'

Carol contemplated this and then said: 'D'you think Christine Keeler is pretty?'

'Yes, of course,' he replied. 'Why?'

'Well, it said in the *Daily Express* that you can tell a lot about a man if you know which one he likes best, Christine Keeler or Mandy Rice-Davies.'

'Really? What can you tell?'

'I don't think it said,' she replied after a moment, and slipping from the swing went back into the house to telephone her friend.

A summer silence broken only by the distant drone of an aeroplane and the murmur of bees in the rhododendrons. The day was almost windless but still the thin birches on their shallow roots whispered and moved above him. The hammock, its webbing weakened from years of boisterous games, sagged deep into the ferns: a summer hiding-place. He watched a cabbage-white butterfly as it meandered through the trees, and then thought about a photograph of Christine Keeler he had seen in a Sunday newspaper. It had showed her apparently naked sitting back to front on an upright, modern, triangular-shaped chair, her thighs clutching its waist, her elbows and arms resting on its back, hiding her breasts and supporting her head. Christine Keeler and Mandy Rice-Davies. Sex again.

*

103

'Can I repay you now?'

Richard stopped and looked around. He was o[n] his way back to the Lamborne from an unsuccessfu[l] interview with *The Illustrated London News*, his hea[d] down, his thoughts casually vengeful.

The American boy was sitting under the canopy outsid[e] Luigi's, the local pavement café, drinking lemon tea fro[m] a glass cup and examining a street map of London.

'Repay me?'

'I told you. I owe you one. Do me a favour and I'[ll] repay you. Cheat me and I'll get even. So what do yo[u] want, tea or coffee or . . . well, whatever else they serv[e] here?' He smiled, but then, seeing Richard's expression[,] turned down the corners of his mouth in comic imitation[.] 'Come on, it can't be that bad, can it?'

Richard hesitated, then slumped down. 'Probably not,['] he answered. Alongside this tall, handsome, casual Ameri[-] can, he immediately felt pale and weedy. He had worn [a] jacket for his interview (his only jacket, Harris Tweed[)] and was feeling uncomfortably hot and constricted. A[s] he took it off, Luigi crept into view and he ordered [a] cappuccino. 'How are you finding the Lamborne?' h[e] asked when he had settled again. 'Sorry if it's not wha[t] you expected. There should be a health warning with th[e] place.'

'It's just fine,' Hudson shrugged away his apologies[.] 'I've stayed in worse places, I can tell you.'

'You're here to go to summer school, are you?' That was usually the reason young Americans came t[o] London.

Hudson nodded. 'There's a course in English busines[s] law at King's College that looked interesting. In fact I'[m] just trying to find King's College on the map. It's some[-] where on the Strand . . .'

'Look for Somerset House. It's next door. The Circl[e] Line's your best bet.'

'Oh yes. Right! I see.' Hudson stared at the map for [a]

moment, familiarizing himself with the lie of the streets and then closed the book. 'What about you?'

Richard paused. 'Well, I suppose you could say I'm just about to set out on the great adventure of life,' he said at last with grim facetiousness, 'but unfortunately they don't sell maps to where I want to go.'

The American grinned. 'So it's going to be all the more fun finding the way. Right?'

After that they spent the rest of the afternoon together, sitting in the shade and talking. Though at twenty-four James Hudson was only four years older than Richard, he had all the worldliness and dignity of a man of thirty. He was from California, where his parents owned land around Sacramento. College had been a first degree in law at Berkeley followed by a year at Columbia in New York doing business studies. Then there had been some travel in the States. This was his first visit to London.

When the pubs opened at five-thirty they went up the road to the Prince Albert and continued their conversation. Their friendship was immediate: Richard found that he could explain his frustrations, and Hudson was fascinated by his stock of current political rumour. When a newspaper vendor wandered into the pub with the final edition of the *Evening Standard* they bought a copy and read together an account of the sexual chain which led from a slum racketeer called Rachman, through a gun-toting West Indian dope-dealer to a Russian naval attaché spy, the former War Minister and on to naked men in masks at parties at Lord Astor's country estate. 'And I thought you British were sexually repressed,' said Hudson.

'We were. Now we're not,' Richard replied, hoping his virginity wasn't showing.

At seven they had dinner together in the Lamborne and then at Hudson's suggestion set off in search of adventure. 'This is your town, show me how to enjoy it,' he said as they made their way along Notting Hill Gate towards the Underground.

Given this responsibility Richard was uncertain. 'I dunno, James, what kind of thing are you looking for?'

'Hudson.'

'I'm sorry?'

'Call me Hudson. My friends call me Hudson, and whatever you want to do is fine with me.'

They met them outside the Hereford Arms, a pub in Gloucester Road, two Scandinavian girls in London to perfect their English. Solveig was a secretary at the Norwegian Embassy, pretty and healthy with her straight hair the colour of pale copper, cut in a fashionable bob, shorter at the back than the front so that her face appeared to be framed by the beginnings of two inverted question marks. Britt-Marie was her friend from Bergen, and was also a secretary, tall and cool and efficient-looking. They were obviously looking to be picked up, standing on the edge of the pavement so that they could see and be seen by all passing men, but, without Hudson, Richard would never have dared approach them. He had never considered girls as glamorous as these to be within his range. Hudson broke the ice, fixing both girls with his smile, buying them drinks, and listening intently to them as though he was fascinated by life in the trade department of the Norwegian Embassy. Solveig was the prettier, more vivacious of the two, but, seeing Richard's interest in her, Hudson went immediately for the older girl.

The girls were unlike any Richard had ever known. There were no intellectual points to be scored, no intense undergraduate conversations, no pretensions. They were carefree, enjoying the moment and their youth. A school-boy thought crossed Richard's mind and he smiled to himself.

'What's the joke?' Hudson asked as the girls lapsed into Norwegian, probably discussing the boys they had picked up.

'I was just thinking' – he indicated the two girls – 'Miss Health and Miss Efficiency . . .'

'What's that?'

'You know, *Health and Efficiency* . . .'

Hudson shook his head. He did not know.

Richard laughed. 'Look on any bookstall tomorrow. You'll get the idea.'

The Café des Artistes on the outskirts of Chelsea had been Britt-Marie's suggestion, the sort of place blue-eyed au pairs knew about almost before they had boarded the bus from the airport, but which university students only read about in magazine articles. By himself Richard would have been unsure how to behave among the nutmeg tans, matelot shirts and high-necked tab collars. But with Hudson it was impossible to feel awkward. While dubious Chelsea layabouts cast dismissive glances and the girls trod water in the latest dance steps, Hudson merely smiled and shuffled, one foot to the other, a giant of confidence in the knowledge that whatever he did was acceptable.

'*Our day will come*,' sang Ruby and the Romantics as Health and Efficiency, their handbags on the floor stating claim to their territory, moved backwards and forwards, first one shoulder then the other, in time with the backbeat. Was this it? thought Richard, valiantly trying to copy Solveig. Was this part of the change? He looked around the deep gloom at the flitting shadows, self-aware and narcissistic in styles which had barely reached the world he knew. A Tuesday evening and everyone was so casually elegant: dressing to be seen. Fashion had never been important to him, nor to many students and obviously not to Hudson. But to these people, moving like phantoms in and out of the ultra-violet beam which shone from the ceiling, style was everything. '*If there's anything that you want, if there's anything I can do* . . .' He looked at Solveig; she was mouthing the lyrics, a perfect, neat, young woman, so confident in her body. She caught him watching and smiled.

At one they followed Solveig and Britt-Marie back to their flat in Rosary Gardens, where with the minimum of embarrassment Britt-Marie and Hudson disappeared into one of the two bedrooms: Solveig, sensing Richard's shyness, asked him if he would like some coffee.

The answer was no, but he hesitated. 'Well . . . ah . . .'

Solveig smiled and, stretching up, kissed him. Her mouth was fresh, he thought, like a child's. Then, taking his hand, she led him into her room.

She was so practical, he would remember later: so certain. From the moment he entered her room there was never any question of how the evening would end. She had already decided that. But she neither hurried nor delayed him: no false protestations of innocence, and no urgent tugging at his clothes as he temporarily lost confidence or dawdled along the way. He had always had it in his mind that a man made love to a woman, subject, predicate and object, that he led the way and that she yielded. But if Solveig had heard such a rumour she had not believed it. To her they were equals in this endeavour, making love to each other, neither one the leader nor the led, as shoes clunked to the floor, straps were unhooked, clasps unfastened and zips undone. At first he worried because they had not turned off the light, convinced that she would read the anxiety in his eyes. But he did not dare disturb the mood by rising from the bed for even a moment, and soon he forgot as their clothes unpeeled from their bodies, his skin white and smooth, hers lightly tanned other than for the triangle of a bikini bottom and her small white breasts. When naked she was unembarrassed. From her breasts and arms he smelled the faintest trace of talcum powder. Her body was short, compact and deceptively muscular. The single bed creaked under their double weight and the broken old hammock at home came to his mind. Mandy Rice-Davies, he thought, I must be a Mandy Rice-Davies man. Christine Keeler represented the angst of sex, the neurotic desperation of aching, physical need. Her photographs told him that. Mandy Rice-Davies meant good times, and never looking back. Summer, 1963. After this he would never look back. He slid on top of Solveig, kissing her, increasingly aware of ripples in her body beneath him. That's what he was, the Mandy Rice-Davies type. Then, despite the moment, he smiled to himself. Perhaps he would write to the *Daily Express*. Perhaps they were giving prizes to Mandy Rice-Davies-type men.

Reaching up Solveig kissed away the silliness. She gave her own prizes.

The Beatles were playing on a small portable radio as dawn reached the slate roofs of South Kensington; a foreign station, an announcer who spoke a language Richard had never heard before and then George Harrison, *Do You Want To Know A Secret?* They were quiet now. How many times had they made love? He was uncertain. The sheets lay tangled, hanging down on the threadbare carpet. At some point Solveig must have turned out the light. He could not remember that, although he could remember Britt-Marie's soft moans coming from the adjacent room. Hudson had obviously not disappointed. Now the sun was creeping back into their lives through the sash windows. Solveig slept softly, her legs drawn up in front of her body, her face resting against his shoulder. So healthy and so practical. No terrors, no embarrassment and no guilt. At what point, and from where, had the contraceptives been introduced? He could not be sure: some time before they had made love for certain. She had had her own supply: taken no chances. They had talked occasionally during the night when, his passion momentarily sated, he had rested, waiting for the next inevitable rush of desire. It was then that he had fully realized the nature of these moments, that the relationship which had started in this room would end there.

'My fiancé is coming to London on Friday,' Solveig had said, quite matter of factly as she had caressed patterns on his skin with the backs of her fingernails.

'Fiancé?'

'He works for the electricity. Hydro-electricity in Norway. An engineer. He wants to go to Stonehenge for midsummer's night. Have you ever been to Stonehenge?'

Richard said that he had not. Fiancé? 'Do you love him?' he asked.

'Oh yes, of course,' she replied, as though he had asked a silly question.

He had left it at that. How strange that his first act of sex should involve a betrayal, and he wondered what other betrayals by him and against him lay ahead. Infidelity. He doubted if the thought had ever crossed Solveig's mind.

They had made love again after that, his body fired by the knowledge that she belonged to someone else. That their relationship had no future did not trouble him now. He would put this summer night into his pocket, the touches, the scents, the soft, breathy kisses and the smiles: he would put it away, this first time, to save and savour throughout his life.

'Do you think Hudson liked Britt-Marie?' Solveig asked later, as the sound of running water in the bathroom signalled the beginning of another day. Britt-Marie had to be at the embassy by eight-thirty.

'Oh yes, I think so,' he replied.

'He's a strange one,' said Solveig.

'What do you mean?'

She shook her head against the pillow. 'I don't know. Just strange. Alone.'

He thought about that. She was right. Hudson was strange, indefinably older than his years. Then he realized: Hudson had made all this possible. It was Hudson who had brought them all together. Hudson made things happen.

Alongside him Solveig reached out and retuned her radio in search of breakfast-time news. She found a brief summary on the BBC Light Programme. The first woman in space, Valentina Tereshkova, was fit and well after her return to earth, boxer Cassius Clay was going home to America after only just beating Britain's Henry Cooper, Church leaders were 'expressing grave doubts about the effects on moral standards caused by the introduction of the birth control pill, on sale for the first time in Britain this week', and President Kennedy was preparing for his forthcoming visit to Europe.

So much news, a runaway train of events that somehow Richard just had to jump on to. He would keep on trying. Whichever way you looked at it change was coming. And then for positively the last time he turned back to the smiling, healthy Solveig.

He found Hudson sitting in the window-seat of a local Italian café drinking coffee and reading the *New York Herald Tribune*. A message taped to Solveig's door had told him where to go.

'Glad you could make it,' Hudson said quietly as he entered the café. 'It was a great night last night.'

'Yes,' Richard agreed.

With that the subject was dismissed. That was the way Hudson was, discreet and tactful, never talking about sex.

Now he was moving on. 'I did what you told me,' he said, pushing aside the *Herald Tribune* to reveal two magazines. The first was small with a monotone cover of a naked girl holding a beach ball, her pubic hair painted out so that where her sex should have been there was simply a smooth, grey triangular plain.

'*Health and Efficiency*,' laughed Richard, and taking the magazine flicked it open at the centre spread where three similarly desexed girls were lying on a beach.

'No wonder some of your civil servants get a little confused about these things,' Hudson said. Then, still amused, he produced the latest edition of *Private Eye*, opening it at an enormous double-page Timothy Birdsall cartoon. 'But more important, did you see this?'

The cartoon, entitled *Britain Gets Wyth Itte, 1963*, showed a Rabelaisian, carnival London peopled by tarts, newspapermen with megaphones, homosexual-bashing judges, doubting clerics, touting royals, pantomime politicians, TV cameras and everywhere free, floating, give-away money. 'Yes, I saw it,' Richard said. 'Like I was saying, this year London's gone crazy.'

Hudson sipped his coffee. 'Seems like I got here just in time.'

That was the beginning. They were perfect friends, Hudson older and wiser, and determined never to accept that in the natural order some things simply could not be done. To him a man could do anything he wanted: 'It just takes belief and application, and maybe a little know-how along the way.'

'And money,' Richard would argue. 'It takes money.' Now that he was an ex-student money, and the lack of it, had suddenly begun to worry him.

'There are always ways of getting money if you really need it,' Hudson insisted.

'Maybe for you. Your parents are rich.'

'I don't mean parents. I mean here. London. The place is stuffed with money, old, new, straight, crooked . . . whatever. If you have the right idea you'll always find the money to make it work. Believe me.'

Two days later Richard took a job doing clerical work for a new insurance company in Oxford Street called The Fire, Auto and Marine. It was cripplingly boring but it paid the rent and left the evenings free for dreaming, writing uncommissioned, and evidently unwelcome (since none were accepted), articles for newspapers and magazines and, most important of all, rediscovering London in the company of Hudson.

There were no more double-dates with Solveig and

Britt-Marie, although he knew Hudson saw Britt-Marie alone occasionally. It didn't matter. In the summer of 1963 London was full of pretty girls. ,

Chapter Eleven

Emily saved Nicola's letter for a lunchtime treat. 'Here you are, one from Some Floozy Named Flo,' her father had joked, as, standing by the front door, he had sorted through the daily handful of bills. Shoving the letter inside her book Emily had humped her bicycle down the steps and hurriedly pedalled off towards Kensington High Street. The mere presence of the letter would be something to get her through the morning.

It was Monday, the start of another week of the fat and the foolish straining the stitches and zips of dresses they had hardly any intention of buying, a sunny morning on Pimlico Road, and a vacation job to help ends never likely to meet. She wondered what Nicola was doing now. Would she be sleeping? No. Rhodesia was ahead of Britain in time. Out riding perhaps? The Vumba. The way Nicola had described the hills of the Vumba made it seem very un-African. Perhaps she was reading Emily's last letter, the one hers must have crossed in the post. She hoped not. It would seem so dull. London was dull in the summer, her mother had always complained about that, and Irina Zaaloff's dress shop would certainly qualify if there were a prize for its dullest corner.

At least, busy with the Monday returns, the morning passed reasonably quickly, Emily earning the rare praise of her riotously rouged employer by selling a dress which had been hanging in the stockroom since 1959 to the wife of a Conservative Member of Parliament, a hideous royal-blue Bo-peep number in size forty-two with a bow between the bosoms. 'It will do very nicely for the conference in Blackpool,' the purchaser commented. 'The flak should have stopped flying by then all right.' Emily bit her lip.

At ten to two she managed to get away for twenty minutes and, as usual on fine days, cycled along to the Royal Hospital Gardens. It was always quiet there. Sitting on the grass, her feet aching from the unaccustomed shop assistant's standing, she slipped off her shoes, uncovered the cheese-and-tomato sandwich she had prepared the previous evening and carefully opened the letter. The opening words made her smile.

Darling Emmy,
Talk about whinge. It can't be that bad. I refuse to believe it. Think of the experience of life you're getting. Think of what the blacking factory did for Dickens, the glass works for Thingymebob and the truss with a spike for Gryptight-Thynne. Seriously it sounds grim, but if you can manage to purloin the odd bra mine's a 34B, easily undone in the dark.

Life down here staggers on with most people pretending the sun will never set. Way back up here among the evergreens (C.B. 1958, Chess, if you're interested), we're sheltered from the ostrich mentality they have down on the farms, but every time I come home I realize how out of step with the rest of the world Rhodesia has become. Mark my words, there'll be tears before bedtime. The trouble is no one wants to admit how unfair it all is because with half a brain and a white skin a person can live like a king/queen here, and I suppose that includes yours without the pith-helmet.

Not that one needs a pith-helmet at the moment. It's brass monkeys this winter, the hills as white as Norway, no snow of course, but frost until nine, and log fires every night. I do wish you'd been able to come with me. You'd love it, you really would and I'm missing you terribly. I'll get you here one of these days, Emily Robinson, by hook or by crook, although I'll have to put Mashona on a diet before you see him – he's so fat I can hardly get my legs around him. Sounds rude, doesn't it?

What news? I hope that drip from Teddy Hall isn't still pursuing you. He was absolutely dire and as thick as a brick. Did your brother buy his guitar? I'd ask him to teach me to play but I suspect I've got cloven hoofs for fingers. Here we have a new housegirl working in the kitchen. Her name's Fortunate, which will sound odd to you, but by Shona standards is pretty unextraordinary. She's sweet, pathologically timid and probably only about fifteen. I told her to use the pool the other day if she feels like a dip – something I don't suppose I'd have thought of doing a few years ago, I'm ashamed to say – but I know she'd never dare without me virtually pushing her in, which probably wouldn't be wise as I don't suppose she's ever learned how to swim. Alice says I shouldn't encourage her, which, I'm afraid, just shows how conservative Alice is. I suppose like everybody else she's terrified of change and is afraid she'll be sent back to her village if things become difficult here. (She won't if I have any say in it.)

What else? Well, the really big news is that Uncle Alec and the lawyers are finally settling on the details of my mother's will, ten years on, but never mind, and it means I get a bit when I'm twenty-one (so start planning the party now) and the big stuff when I'm thirty-five. Crumbs, can you imagine us at thirty-five, Emmy? Virtually in our dotage, me with a widow's hump, lots of dogs, mad as a hatter and living down the lane where the bats fly, and you . . . well, I suppose you'll be as lovely as ever, one of those cool beauties with dozens of children, and sophisticated men taking you to adulterous lunches in bijou Chelsea knocking-shops. Talking about knocking-shops I hope you're keeping every word on Jolly Jack and the Keel-Haul. The *Jungle Telegraph* does its best, but *Private Eye* it isn't.

Anyway, I must go. Uncle and I are driving into Umtali. He wants me to sign some papers at the lawyers. So I'll post this and hopefully you'll get it within the week. Love to your parents and a kiss for your father. I'm glad he's feeling a bit better. Tell him I hope his book is going well, and tell Daniel that if he plays his cards right I'll bring him an Ndebele drum back. They're Zulus and more warlike than the Shona, so I suppose their drums are louder. Please, please, please, write soon, if not soonest.

Love and kisses and the occasional non-sapphic hug,
                          Pith-Helmet and the Dandelions.

Pith-Helmet and the Dandelions! Scribbled sideways in the margin of the page was a cartoon showing a stick-like Nicola wearing a pith-helmet as a lead-singer in an all-girl group, the other girls being depicted as dandelions gone to seed, their hair out like puffballs. Then there were the inevitable three kisses.

Emily refolded the letter and put it into the envelope. A gardener who was watering the roses was watching her and she realized she had been smiling goofily to herself. She nodded towards him, took out her apple and polished it on her skirt.

Love and kisses, always love and kisses. She had never known anyone as affectionate as Nicola. That was partly why Emily's father liked her so much. Some Floozy Named Flo: he even had a pet name for her. Vaguely Emily wondered about the inheritance. It was almost certainly quite a large one. Nicola rarely talked about money, probably because she had never had to think about it. She wished she had been able to go out to Africa with her. Nicola had offered to pay, she always wanted to pay for everything and everyone, but that would have been too much like taking advantage of her generosity.

Emily finished her apple and lay back on the grass. The earth was warm beneath her head. 'A puncture . . . yes, of course,' she had replied, 'but are you sure it isn't the valve?' Their first week at Oxford. St Hilda's: all girls. She had been terrified, shying at shadows on the walls, and then there was Nicola from the next room pouring the burgundy while Emily set about sliding a new rubber valve on to the bicycle wheel, Nicola's expression quite comical as she watched. 'Shouldn't that little rubber thing be closed at the end?' she had asked. 'It looks terribly irresponsible to me.'

They had joined everything together, all the societies, a very catholic taste, and then after the first few weeks had hardly ever gone to the meetings. Half the men in Oxford had wanted to meet and/or make love to Nicola that first Michaelmas term and she had encouraged them wickedly, while Emily had watched, admiring yet fearful, 'resisting and arresting', always the would-be romantic.

Nicola provoked such passion. 'Thank you very much,' she had told the young don who had first seduced her, 'that's got rid of that,' and had then rushed home to report all to Emily. 'All I can say for certain is that it's definitely more fun than Middle English, somewhat shorter on this occasion than a sentence by Gabriel Henderson, perhaps not quite so rhythmical as Mystery Train and nothing like so romantic as Hardy's sonnets . . .'

Emily picked herself up off the grass. Next time Nicola went to Africa she would go with her. In the meantime Madame Zaaloff of Pimlico Road would be counting the minutes.

Chapter Twelve

By August Hudson's large, first-floor room overlooking
the square had become the centre of all that was exciting in the Lamborne. His was an easy grace. He drank
little, did not smoke, had time for everybody and was
quickly accepted as a leader and confidant. Summer
was the time for foreign students in London, and, while
serious-looking young men from Strasbourg and Milan
would seek his opinions, pretty Continental girls would
dawdle in his path on his way to and from King's College.

For Richard it was a time of watching and waiting,
a little in awe of the handsome American. Sometimes at
the weekends he would loaf in Hudson's room looking
through his books, while Hudson would play his blues
records on a Dansette borrowed for the summer from
the Scottish dancer in room nine. That Hudson should
have taken the trouble to bring these records three and a
half thousand miles surprised Richard. But so did much
of what had been packed into that massive trunk. The
old cracked mug, the steam iron, odd pieces of cutlery
and the reading lamp. Then there were the books. A
Serbo-Croat dictionary, several histories of the Second
World War, *An Actor Prepares* by Stanislavsky and a
dozen or more biographies of rich and famous men,
J.D. Rockefeller, Lindbergh, even Orson Welles. And
why had he brought that heavy Brooks Brothers winter overcoat, the evening suit and cummerbund, the
three-piece worsted suit and the heavy tweed sports
jacket? Did he really think England was so cold in the
summer? Hudson was a student like none Richard had
ever known.

A couple of nights a week the two of them would

venture out, sometimes to The Establishment in Soho, a satirical club of the time, and on other occasions to The Marquee in Oxford Street, where the music was loud and bluesy but the girls usually too young. Often, however, they would find themselves sitting out in the square opposite the Lamborne mulling over the events of the moment. One evening they discussed the suicide of Stephen Ward, the social fall-guy in the Profumo Affair who had withdrawn from his own trial the previous day by taking an overdose of sleeping pills. For once Hudson was not relaxed.

'How could he do that?' he worried. 'How could he kill himself? For Christ's sake, he didn't even wait for the verdict. He might have got off. And even if he hadn't, the worst they could have got him on was pimping. Pimping! So what? It isn't as though they would have put him in prison for life.'

'His friends had turned their backs on him. I suppose he felt his life was finished, the only part of his life he valued, anyway,' suggested Richard.

'I can't see that. I really can't. Nothing can be that bad. There always has to be some way out, something else to do. Some new place to visit. New people to meet. A new career. A new girl. Anything.'

Richard shrugged. 'Who can say? Perhaps you'd feel differently if something terrible happened to you.'

'No. I'd feel exactly the same,' Hudson insisted. After that Richard changed the subject. The subject of despair depressed Hudson. It did not fit in with his view of the world as an endless orchard of opportunity.

Five days later came the Great Train Robbery, provoking a quite different reaction. 'Can you imagine, over two and a half million pounds?' Hudson bubbled as they celebrated in the Prince Albert. 'That's over seven million dollars. Seven million. With seven million dollars you wouldn't have to look for a job on a newspaper, you could buy your own.'

Richard screwed up his nose. 'No. That's more your

line. Business. I just want to be a journalist and no one will let me.'

He had, in fact, been a journalist for much of the past three years, certainly more of a journalist than he had ever been a student of history, first with the university newspaper, then as editor of the college magazine. He had always assumed that it would be no more than a step and a jump into Fleet Street, but newspapers were closing and unions were nervous. For as long as he could remember Richard had been addicted to the gathering and dissemination of news. Now he was barred from that mysterious society of dealers which controlled the flow and marketed the substance of his addiction.

'So maybe you don't need seven million dollars.' Hudson was juggling impossible ideas.

'That's reassuring.'

'No. Maybe you don't need anything like that.'

Richard couldn't see where this conversation was heading.

'So?'

Hudson grinned and withdrew from the game. 'Hell, I don't know,' he said. 'You're the guy who wants to be a journalist.'

So the summer meandered on, dusty on the streets, sweltering in the insurance office. At the end of August the baleful news that Richard had been awarded the consolation prize of a third-class degree resulted in a particularly frosty Sunday lunch in Wimbledon, despite the presence of Hudson, whom both his parents regarded as only slightly less charismatic than John F. Kennedy.

Hudson had so much charm. He had only been in London for a couple of months but already he had a wider circle of friends than Richard. Everyone took to him, the good-looking American boy with the grown-up manners. There were dinner parties with Hampstead dons and their wives, invitations to lunch in the boardrooms of City banks and even salmon and Chablis at Lord's as the West Indies set about England.

Richard lived mainly for the uncommissioned articles he dreamed would lead him into newspapers. He wrote about everything he saw – a greyhound racing fraternity, an old Russian *émigré* fencing master who had become a virtual derelict, teenage prostitution, the kids of Amphetamine Alley and racial discrimination among slum landlords. But, every time, back came the articles.

Then one weekend, while Hudson took the train to Scotland at the invitation of a visiting lecturer on his course, Richard set out to talk to a group of gypsies who had settled illegally on a strip of waste land near Shepherd's Bush.

One look at the broken-down vans and the rusting caravans on the scrubland killed any romantic idea of the wandering Romany he might have just been harbouring. Everyone hated the gypsies and, in turn, the gypsies hated back.

Their apparent leader was a thin, muscular man with heavily tattooed forearms, thin grey hair, long sideboards and a mouthful of rotting, nicotine-stained teeth. Across his cheek was a slash mark and four white stitches. His name was Jack Carter. Everyone deferred to Carter, the three older boys changing a tyre, the old man drinking Australian sherry in the shade, the women, uniformly thin and knife-faced, one making a peg rug, another peeling potatoes, and the three ragamuffin children who were playing a kind of ruleless hockey with a plastic bottle and a couple of broken umbrellas.

'How do we know you aren't a spy from the child welfare?' Carter asked.

'I'm a journalist,' Richard said. 'I'd like to write an article about you. Putting your point of view.'

Jack Carter laughed coarsely and, clearing the morning's catarrh from his throat, spat into the dust. 'That's a good one,' he said.

After a moment he asked: 'How much are you paying?'

'I hadn't thought about that,' Richard said.

Carter shrugged and fetching a paraffin stove from

inside a caravan began to take it to pieces. Richard looked around at the broken glass and mangy, tethered ponies. He was about to learn a universal truth of professional journalism. From the gypsies' point of view there was no reason on earth why they should co-operate with him without being paid.

'If I sell the article I'll give you half of everything I get,' he said at last, 'provided you let me come back here tomorrow with a photographer.' Only a picture could do justice to the litter-blown waste land on which the gypsies scraped their living.

'Shake on it,' Carter said, offering a paraffin-fumed hand. Richard shook. In the back of his mind he knew he had made an important step. He had agreed to pay for information, and he hoped he had done the right thing. Somehow he felt sullied by the agreement, a first compromise in a career which hadn't even started.

That evening, his pockets heavy with pennies, he locked himself in the telephone cabin on the Lamborne's first-floor landing and began calling photographer contacts. It was not easy. Almost everyone he knew was away for the summer. Tim Gimmelmann was a last resort, a name and number given to him by the siren sister of a schoolfriend. 'Watch him. He's a bastard, but at least they'll be sharp,' she warned before adding somewhat forlornly, 'and remind him that I'm still alive, will you?'

He met Gimmelmann at Shepherd's Bush Underground station the following morning, a pretty, dark-haired lad with deep blue eyes. He was confident, semi-tough and working-class, a North London Lothario who had, he was quick to mention, just been sacked as an assistant with a West End fashion photographer.

'I mean, he's as bent as a boomerang so I dunno why he was complaining. He shouldn't have come back anyway. He told me to lock up and then there he is sneaking in when I'm giving it one on the divan. Know what I think? I think he was jealous.'

'I thought you said he was queer,' said Richard

as they hurried across the Green.

Gimmelmann looked pained as if this ought not to need an explanation. 'Not jealous of me. Jealous of her. I bet it really got him going seeing my little pink dimples bobbing up and down there. Lovely, too, she was. Helenecca Shaw? D'you know her?' He threw this out with a cool nonchalance.

Richard shook his head. Models belonged in another world. 'I don't think so.'

'*Vogue* use her a lot,' Gimmelmann said casually. 'She looks sort of stand-offish, but she goes like a train. Does anything you want. Anything. Know what I mean?'

Richard nodded, though, in fact, he had no idea what he meant. He changed the subject. 'They're a bit wary, these gypsies. Suspicious.'

Gimmelmann shrugged as if to say, 'Don't worry, I can handle them', which Richard did not doubt. He had a cocky street savvy, and was elegant in his way, in his newly washed blue jeans, Cuban-heeled boots, to give him an extra inch of height, and collarless leather jacket. He carried his one camera, a twin-reflex Rolleiflex, the sort that is held against the chest, over his shoulder. A city boy with little education he had grown up early and lived alone in a bed-sitter in Kentish Town. 'I had to get out when our mum fell for another. They needed the room,' he explained, matter-of-factly.

The gypsies were not suspicious of Gimmelmann. He was cheeky and familiar and they took to him immediately. Quickly, however, it became obvious that his photographs would not, as Richard had hoped, be the work of an observer so much as a series of carefully framed images, some posed, all directed to some extent: a would-be fashion photographer on a day out.

'The thing about photographs,' Gimmelmann explained as he reloaded his camera, 'is that anybody with a Brownie can get a picture these days. It's that easy. If these are going to get noticed they've got to be better than that.'

He looked around again for more angles. Alongside them two toddlers were playing with an empty and rusting sardine tin while their mother knitted, unconcerned. It would have made a good picture of squalor, but Gimmelmann wasn't interested.

Remembering a friend from his own childhood who had died of tetanus poisoning, Richard said quietly to the woman: 'Perhaps they shouldn't play with that.'

The mother, a thin woman with a broken, flattened nose, looked up from her knitting, challenged. 'What's that?'

Richard indicated the sardine tin. 'I mean it might be dangerous. It's very sharp.' He could feel Gimmelmann's smile on his back.

The woman shrugged. 'If they get cut they'll learn, won't they? Be a good lesson for them. They've got to learn some time.'

Richard looked again at the sardine tin. 'I just think it would be a shame if one of them got a septic finger,' he said.

'He's right, Mum. The fella's right. Come here, Lynette . . . give me that tin. Bring it here.' He looked around. A girl was standing at the top of the steps of the nearest caravan, a beaten-up, green-and-cream early Fifties tourer. She was, he reckoned, probably not much more than sixteen, if that, but with her ridiculous high heels, a black, tight skirt slit up the front, a much shrunk, small, dark green sweater and her lips bright pink, she was trying to look much older. Obediently the child trotted across to her with the sardine tin.

'Well, well, well . . .' Gimmelmann's voice was just audible. He was staring at the girl who, aware that she had caught his eye, was now lounging on the steps, pouting, the sardine tin in one hand, a cigarette in the other.

'You had to learn, Dolly,' whined the mother.

'Yeah, and I bleedin' cut myself, didn't I?' The girl smiled confidently at Gimmelmann. 'Gonna take my picture then?' she said, breathing out a whisper of smoke through full lips.

'Just warming it up for you, Dolly,' murmured Gimmelmann. 'Be with you in a minute.'

She smirked. This girl, with her dirty hands and stringy bleached hair, knew all about men.

Gimmelmann walked a few paces away and then turned to Richard. 'See. They're all the same, women. There's no elastic been invented that doesn't go all slack the minute a camera comes out. Doesn't matter who's wearing them, down they come.' Then with a smug little wink he turned back to Dolly. 'Over here then, girl, all right?' he said, positioning her alongside a large caravan cartwheel.

Richard watched in amazement. Without any encouragement or training the girl was coming on to the camera like a professional.

Two days later Richard was having coffee in Hudson's room when Gimmelmann arrived clutching a large - manilla envelope. On Richard's territory and in the - company of students he was nothing like so sure of himself, and even in his Annelo and Davide boots he looked quite petite alongside Hudson.

Quickly making the introductions Richard opened the envelope. He had worked at his typewriter all Sunday and Monday evening writing and rewriting his article, half-afraid that Gimmelmann's casual arrogance might indicate a carelessness about his photographs. He was wrong. Gimmelmann had produced a beautifully printed series of black-and-white portraits of life as a modern urban gypsy. 'These are wonderful, wonderful,' Richard murmured honestly, laying the pictures out on Hudson's bed. Gimmelmann smiled, casting shy glances towards Hudson who was looking over Richard's shoulder.

The photograph of Dolly was the last out of the envelope. 'Wow, who's she?' Hudson asked, picking it up.

'Just some gypsy girl,' said Richard.

'She looks kind of . . . well, wanton, I guess. Isn't that the word?'

Richard took the photograph from him. Wanton was exactly the word: wanton and mesmerizing. He gazed at it. 'You know, if I were editor of *The Sunday Times Magazine* this would be on the front,' he said at last.

'Why?' asked Hudson.

'Half a dozen reasons, but mainly because it was the one you picked up.'

Hudson thought about that for a moment and then turned to Gimmelmann. 'Congratulations,' he said. 'They're terrific.'

'Thanks,' said Gimmelmann softly. 'Thanks a lot.'

He's frightened of him, thought Richard in astonishment. This tough little Cockney swordsman is completely overawed. And in unconscious confirmation a shadow of a blush crossed Gimmelmann's cheeks.

Chapter Thirteen

The dog-days at Madame Zaaloff's came at the end of August, when not even white finger-painted Sale notices in the windows and 60 per cent reductions could entice shoppers along Pimlico Road. Business had never been so slack and one Friday afternoon, with a dry kiss and a free peach camisole as a gift (selected because it was unsellable), Emily was dismissed. 'Thank you, God. You're a pal,' she murmured as she undid the padlock which chained her bicycle to the railings.

That night, sitting up in bed, with her window open to keep her bedroom cool, her brother Daniel practising guitar chords in the room below, and her father coughing over his manuscript in his study, she wrote to Africa.

> I know I could, and probably should, have walked out weeks ago and found another job, but really she's so nice I didn't have the heart. Anyway, if you're coming back early that's done with work for the summer, unless I can get a couple of weeks before term begins in Blackwell's – I know, there's a warthog flying past you as you read.
>
> I told my father that you hoped it was going well and he says, 'thanks – that'll make all the difference'. He thinks the world of you, you know.
>
> I'm thrilled that you're coming back early. I telephoned about the flat and the man said we could move in as soon as we wanted, the sooner the better as far as he's concerned . . .

When she had finished, Emily read over what she had written. There were none of the lashings of affection with which Nicola laced her letters here. She was restrained. It was always Nicola who threw her arms around her, Nicola with the kisses, Nicola with the guts to say exactly what she felt. 'I love you, Emmy, you know. I really do. I always will, I know I will,' she had said one night in Oxford. Emily had turned towards the fire, holding the fork up to the flames, toasting a slice of bread. Nicola had rocked with laughter. 'It's all right. I'm not dykey or anything. Nothing like that. God, you should see your face. You could toast the bread on your cheeks. But I do love you. Really. That's all. Nothing kinky or physical or anything like that. You're the best friend I've ever had. Better than the best. Better than anybody. We're friends for life, and every day I think how lucky I was to meet you . . .'

Emily sat silently for some moments, warm from the memory. She hadn't said it, but she had thought it: she was the lucky one. Some people had networks of friends, glibly moving from one set to the next, but with Nicola she never felt she needed anyone else. Boys, yes, she had had boy-friends, but there had never been anyone wonderful: eventually romance would find her, and, please God, sex, sooner rather than later. But it would have to be right. In the meantime Nicola Reynolds, tucked up there on her mountain in Africa, was the spirit which fired her world, and soon she would go back to Oxford and wait for their life together to begin again in their final year.

She turned back to her letter.

Oh yes, I forgot to tell you, my father says the rumours are that the naked man in the mask is Harold Macmillan himself . . . but if you'll believe that . . .

Chapter Fourteen

(i)

It was just beginning to rain, an early September damp turning to drizzle, when the sound of Penelope Chilston in full rage split the London traffic.

'You ought to be ashamed of yourself. What d'you think you're doing exploiting the poor creature like this? How would you like to be chained to a stick and peddled up and down the street like a stuffed doll? Well? Well?'

In the shelter of Selfridges a young Amazon was laying into a weak-chinned street photographer who hardly came up to her shoulder, and who had made the mistake of suggesting that she might like to have her picture taken holding the monkey he had tied to a pole.

'All right, love,' the touter was saying as he tried to retrieve his monkey from Penelope's clutch. 'No need to get upset. You don't like the idea? Suit yourself. The monkey don't mind.'

'How can you possibly know whether the monkey minds or not? Did he tell you? I suppose you've taught him to talk as well as balance on his tail, have you? I suspect he minds very much . . . don't you, darling?' The monkey, cradled across her breast, fixed her with an expression which could have meant anything. Penelope took it as an affirmative. 'There you are, he does mind.'

'Do us a favour, love . . .'

Richard approached the two. Penelope Chilston was six feet tall, a plain, square-shouldered, big-thighed, fresh-faced girl, with a fringe and straight, dark brown hair. Perhaps she would have been less plain had she not been so obviously in search of a crusade, a task which dug a permanent furrow between her eyes. 'Yes, do us a favour, Penny. Shout any louder and you'll stop the buses.'

Penny sniffed imperiously, not at all surprised to see him. 'Typical of you, Richard Blake, to side with the oppressors. This man's a Fascist. I don't think he even feeds the poor thing.'

At this point, seeing her grip on the unfortunate monkey loosen, the street photographer jerked his stick. With a flying leap the monkey was out of Penny's grasp and on to the fellow's shoulder.

'Hey,' shouted Penny, but before she could protest further man and monkey had scampered away into the crowd.

'You're such a bully, Penny. The chap was only trying to make a living.'

Penny pushed a muscular arm through his and smiled. 'Do shut up, Richard. If you're very nice to me I may allow you to buy me a cup of tea. How are you, anyway?'

They had tea and scones in the Lyons Corner House at Marble Arch. Penny had been a fearsomely bright philosophy student at the all-girls Bedford College in Regent's Park when they had met nearly three years earlier on the university newspaper. He was not surprised now to hear that she had come away with a first.

'I suppose you heard that Luke Wilson went up to Liverpool on a graduate trainee course with the *Liverpool Daily Post*,' said Richard.

'Liverpool? Where the Beatles come from?'

'Well, yes. Obviously. He's there for three years. It has a very good reputation.'

'I always thought there was something odd about that boy,' she said. 'What about you?'

'Oh, you know . . .' He shrugged, as though to suggest it was just a matter of time. He wanted to tell her about the gypsies piece, but *The Sunday Times Magazine* was taking longer than he had expected to reply. 'What about you?'

She smiled sweetly. 'Same,' she said. Not many people could fool Penny Chilston. In the meantime she was scraping a living coding questionnaires for the Labour Party and sharing a basement flat in Hampstead with an Indian medical student called Vasco. 'After Vasco da Gama. He's a Portuguese Indian, my Indian, and very sweet. He covers himself in rose-water all the time so that the place smells like a funeral parlour. To be honest I think he has an over-active gland, always trying to inveigle his way into my bed. He even suggested we might share a bath the other day to save water in case of drought. He's very worried about drought and very enterprising. D'you know one night I woke up and found him praying at the end of my bed. He said he was asking the Virgin Mary to intercede on his behalf and put an end to his torment.'

'I thought the Virgin Mary wasn't keen on leg-overs.'

'Good for her. I rattled his ear with a copy of Karl Popper's *Poverty of Historicism* and suggested that he go back to his own room and look for the dirty bits. He'll look for ever.' She laughed.

Richard had always liked Penny, though she had terrified him when they first met. Chaps like Penny had once built empires. And as she had nothing better to do he suggested she join him and Hudson for dinner.

They ate in Luigi's. It was the final week of Hudson's course and he was in good spirits having been taken to lunch in the House of Commons dining room by two young Tory Members of Parliament.

'I felt like Goldilocks,' he said. 'You know, expecting Winston Churchill to come and tap me on the shoulder at any moment to tell me I was sitting in his chair. One of the MPs was talking about publishing, and the advantages of being in England now that English is the world language.'

'What does he publish?' asked Richard.

'Mainly scientific text books, I think.'

Penny pulled a face. 'No jobs there.'

'No,' Hudson agreed, 'but what he was saying about publishing was interesting.'

'Is that what you'll go into when you get back to the States?' asked Penny.

Hudson grinned. 'Maybe I won't go back.' He was answering Penny, but now he turned and looked directly at Richard.

'You'll stay here? In London?' Richard was surprised. 'What'll you do?'

Hudson shrugged. 'I don't know, but it seems to me there are opportunities here. I'll find something. Things are exciting here. You told me yourself, Richard, and it's true.'

'Aren't things exciting in the States? Kennedy's exciting,' said Penny.

'Maybe he is. I don't know. But right here I feel a groundswell of change that says to me this is where things are happening. Surely you sense it, too, don't you, Penny?'

He was staring at her, hard and bright. Slowly Penny nodded and then silently cast her eyes down to her plate.

Hudson turned to Richard. 'Maybe we can do something together,' he said.

'What sort of thing?'

'Hell, I don't know. We'll think of something.'

All of this called for a celebration so they ordered a third bottle of Soave, toasted each other and blessed the future. Richard had no doubt that Hudson would succeed. The only question was how and when. He looked towards Penny. She was listening in rapt attention as Hudson explained to her the art of corralling stray ponies up in the mountains of Colorado.

'The important thing is you never frighten them. You tempt and guide and direct, this way, that way, drawing the rein across your pony's neck to guide him. This way, that way, never hurrying. Patience is everything if you're to get him to do what you want. I guess it's the same with people.'

133

'I didn't know you'd been a cowboy,' said Richard.

'Wrangler, not cowboy. I worked as a wrangler in a place called Divide, that's up above Colorado Springs, near Cripple Creek. Beautiful country. There are worse lives, believe me.' He grinned at Penny.

She took another drink.

(ii)

From the next room the sound of a single cough reached through the plasterboard dividing wall. 5 a.m. Vasco smokes too much, Penny thought, grateful for the distraction, a momentary relief.

For three hours she had tried to analyse it away, her nerves sharpened, her skin alive with the sharp torment of physical arousal. He had not shown a special interest in her, had hardly been more than friendly, and was not a man so handsome and self-assured certain to be consumed by vanity? Perhaps, but it had not shown. Strangely she could scarcely remember anything he had said, nor, now in the darkness of her basement room, could she properly recall the contours of his face: was the white, serrated scar on the right side of his chin or on the left? What about his hair? Was it parted? The details of the evening, the chronology of conversation came in successive eddies of reflected delight and despair. Dinner in Luigi's, coffee and then later red wine in Hudson's large square room. She had been almost silent by then, only half-listening as Hudson and Richard joked and discussed a future together, her head back on the cushion on the spare bed, staring at the peeling cream cornice which ran around the edges of the ceiling, examining the cluster of Victorian plaster petals which made up the rose in the centre. She had had to do something to keep her eyes from him. She could not let him see.

She had come home by taxi, a luxury she could not afford. She had needed the solitude of the cab to consider, to re-endure: at one point he had leaned across her to put on a Muddy Waters record, and she had scented clean, scraped skin, and the warm balm of freshly ironed clothes.

He was powerful, she knew instinctively, though his manner was gentle. There was a certainty in everything he did, as though he had rehearsed his life and was familiar with his lines, confident in his moves. Later in the evening he had asked her questions about herself, her army upbringing and her ambitions. But, though his eyes had been kind, there was a barrier of formality between them, as though he knew how she might feel and did not wish to encourage her. But when he had smiled at her she had felt her stomach tighten in desire.

It would always be futile: she could see that, had known it on meeting him. 'This is Penny Chilston, Hudson,' Richard had said. 'She's intrepid.' Intrepid. He had intended it as a compliment. Intrepid? Was that what she was? Yes. Not beautiful or enchanting. Certainly not sexy. Not on the outside, anyway. Though the fibres of her body ached for sex: not sexy.

She watched as the lights of a passing car lit up her basement ceiling, contemplating the patterns it made. Her nightdress had ridden up around her waist. 'What do you think, Penny?' he had asked. 'Is it possible for a man and a woman to be close friends, best friends, without ever going to bed together?' Her mother's pretty face, concavely distorted in the glass she was holding, had confronted her. Her mother had best friends, lots of friends, men friends, in Aden, in Hong Kong, in Germany. Just friends, darling, just friends, while her father, big and lumpy and thoughtful, had nodded over his pipe and plotted manoeuvres in the American sector. Just friends, darling. Then one afternoon, a school holiday in Hanover when the tennis courts were suddenly, and without warning, closed for resurfacing, returning home to discover them. The sounds of ecstasy which she had mistaken for pain coming from her parents' bedroom. Pushing open the door, cautious from too many years away at school. They did not see her, lost in the utter concentration of sex. Her mother, her face gripped by approaching delirium, gasping, fingers pushed into a broad, pink, unfamiliar back. Just a friend, darling. Just a friend. Standing in the doorway watching, an officer's suit neatly folded on the dressing-table chair: watching as the rhythm increased, until, each of them swept in the single selfishness of release, the storm passed and tranquillity returned to the room. Watching.

'Penny?' Her mother's voice, in quiet, sleepy, uncomprehending surprise. A shuffling, then heaving bed, sheets billowing. 'Penny!' Her mother screaming, her face contorted with fear, shame, anger. 'Get out. Get out.' At thirteen it was too early to learn about these things.

She took her hand from between the sheets and held on to the pillow. His face was clear now, the dimple in the chin, the slight, white scar to the right, the fair hair, thick, wavy almost, parted high on the left, long at the back and sides. She pushed her head into the pillow. A desire so futile. 'What do you think, Penny? Is it possible for a man and a woman to be friends, best friends, without ever going to bed together?'

'No,' Richard had said. 'Not for ever. It isn't possible, not if the friendship is balanced.'

Yes, she had thought. When you're big and plain and intrepid everything is possible.

From the next room she heard the sound of another cough. When she had arrived home her flatmate had been asleep, and she had been glad. Such a sweet man: Vasco, who said he loved her, but didn't mean it. Vasco was a good friend.

'I'm glad we met, Penny. I know we're going to be friends,' Hudson had said, waiting with her on the Bayswater Road, while Richard waved down a cab.

'Yes, I hope so,' she had said.

At five twenty-five she climbed from the bed. Stretching, she pulled her nightdress up and over her head. In a dressing-table mirror she caught a moment's reflection of herself, pale in the glow of the street lamp: a young woman, broad hipped and bulky, milky blue-white skin and small breasts. Her nightdress fell to the floor as she reached the door.

He was asleep. His eyes closed, breathing steadily. The room smelled of rose-water. She looked down at him, at the dark, even features, the long eyelashes and the luxuriant black hair. Just friends, darling. I hope so. He stirred and awoke as she pulled back the covers. He whispered her name. She slid in alongside him, his skin smooth and warm, his body comforting. 'Just don't say anything, all right, Vasco,' she said quietly. 'Just don't speak. Promise. Not one word.'

In the darkness he nodded. His arms enclosed her.

That night, though he would never know it, Hudson made love to Penny Chilston, her lips clinging to his through the darkness, her eyes closed, her body alive only to him.

Just good friends. She hoped so.

Chapter Fifteen

(i)

Richard had seen it coming all year, everyone had. Like a weatherman he had noticed the beginning of the storm, charted the deepening of pressure and observed the attendant fronts as they arrived, fresh and boisterous. But nevertheless when at the end of summer the cyclone turned septic and *charged like a tornado through the heart of Britain* (as the *Daily Express* reported), he was surprised and excited. Beatlemania had arrived, and everywhere a gale of self-induced collective hysteria blew away the leaves of fuddy-duddy Britain. There had never been anything quite like it, or so people liked to say.

'It's like Nazi Germany,' said Hudson, as they watched television news film of a Beatles concert. 'A Nuremberg rally with guitar logos for swastikas. That was what it said in the *Herald Tribune*, anyway.'

'More singalong than Wagner, though,' said Richard.

'And harmless,' said Hudson. 'I'm a Lennon man, if you want to know. He doesn't give a damn.'

Richard stared hard at the insolence of John Lennon's long top lip. 'We should go and see them,' he said, 'before they become softened by fame.'

Hudson saw the sense in that. 'OK,' he said, 'let me see what I can do to cheer you up.' Richard had been subdued in recent days, his article and the photographs on the gypsies having finally come back from *The Sunday Times Magazine* with a printed compliments slip and no explanation. It had been returned by the *Observer*, too, with a trite compliment, and the excuse that they were not taking any non-commissioned pieces at the moment, and by the *Guardian*. At first Tim Gimmelmann had telephoned almost daily asking for news but now, as disappointment bit, his calls had become less frequent. He hadn't said anything but Richard was sure Tim blamed him. The pictures had certainly been good enough.

Getting seats for Beatle concerts was already practically impossible, fans besieging box offices on the day the tours were announced, but, somehow, Hudson managed. He always did. 'A girl I know felt she owed me a favour,' was his only, slightly enigmatic, explanation. Richard did not press him further. Since his decision to stay in London Hudson's social life had become ever busier.

The tickets were for the first house at the Odeon, Hammersmith. They met on the forecourt where, standing almost a foot taller than most other concert-goers, Hudson was surveying the growing excitement. 'What about this?' he laughed, as a gust of screaming and flurry of feet greeted a black car making its way through the police cordon towards the back of the building.

Richard peered into the car. Whoever the occupants might be they were definitely not Beatles. All around adolescent children milled in anticipation: young hen's-legged girls in stockings too slack for them and skirts too skimpy, or provocative in school uniforms, two buttons of their blouses undone; and raw, acne-necked boys, hair universally now combed forward in fringes over their eyes, V-necked Marks & Spencer sweaters over gingham, tab-collared shirts.

'Special Beatles souvenir,' yelled the hawkers, peddling their twenty-four-page picture booklets. 'Half a crown. Beatles souvenir book.'

'Here you go,' said Hudson, producing the money and taking the magazine.

Together they glanced through the pages, a series of black-and-white publicity hand-out photographs, large headlines and tiny biographies on the four heroes. 'You don't get much for your money, do you?' said Richard as he reached the Beatle quiz inside the back cover.

'No, but the publishers do,' Hudson mused, scanning the questions. 'OK, here's one, "What do the Beatles have in common with Brigitte Bardot?"'

'They wash their hair every day,' answered Richard.

'Really?' Hudson was impressed. 'You know so many things, Richard.'

'I try to keep up.'

Together they moved towards the crush of fans. 'What do you think, will we wet our pants with excitement when they do *She Loves You*?'

Richard shook his head. 'Not grown men like us. We might on *Please, Please Me* though.'

They were good seats, halfway down the front stalls and in the middle of the row, a testimony to Hudson's influence, but they might just as well have been two chairs out in the street for anyone wanting actually to listen to the Beatles. No one did want that, of course, not even Hudson and Richard. Like everyone else they were there to witness an event of the time, to share in the act of communion between the four pale young men on the overlit stage and the three thousand young girls and boys in the audience. It would be untrue to have said it was impossible to hear the Beatles above the screaming. That was always an exaggeration. What could not be heard was the music of the Beatles. It did not matter. Everyone there knew every note, every gasp, every moment of every song well enough to let their memories do the singing for them. All the Beatles had to do was be there, four laughing, endlessly surprised high priests at the ritual: an adolescent initiation ceremony, nineteen sixty-three, girls and boys together, screaming longer and louder than the night before because that was the way to behave at Beatle concerts. It said so in the newspapers.

What the Beatles themselves must have been thinking of the pandemonium they generated Richard could not imagine. Throughout they appeared to be sharing some private joke. In person they looked somehow smaller than he had expected, less glamorous, certainly younger. Later he would be surprised at how insubstantial would be his memory of them, up there in the colliding haloes of spotlights, thumbs up to the audience, 'Hello Hammersmith', rushing from song to song; John Lennon, his jacket too short and tight, aggressively full faced, his guitar high across his chest, and Paul McCartney all eyebrows, bass on hip. Even at this stage in the legend the other two looked less substantial.

Turning from the stage Richard looked around at the audience: everywhere little tableaux of devotion were being enacted. '*She was just seventeen, You know what I mean . . .*' At the front of the cinema a herd of young policemen wrestled in good-natured embarrassment with lithe, wriggling fourteen-year-old assault troops as they tried to take the stage; down the right aisle two St John Ambulancemen were carrying a collapsed victim of hyperventilation out towards the Hammersmith traffic fumes; while behind them a rich little thing in an expensive coat trimmed at the collar and cuffs with velvet had sunk to her knees, sobbing hopelessly though she would never know why. '*Last night I said these words to my girl, you know you never even try, girl . . .*' The screaming grew louder, the heat intense: on the air drifted the faintest odour of urine. So it was true about the soaking of cinema seats. Just across the aisle from him a portly, dark-haired girl was almost doubled up, her eyes peering upwards at the stage, her expression desperate, her hand pushed deep down between the tops of her thick, corduroyed thighs. Richard looked away, embarrassed to have seen. '*Thank you, girl, for loving me the way that you do, Way that you do . . .*' The collective joy was overwhelming, hundreds of young faces, tear-smudged, vanilla make-up, fingers over ears and black-mascara-daubed eyes, hair shiny and shampooed for this night, this moment; while here and there sat the occasional parent, perplexed or amused to see such delight, and groups of striped-scarved students, too old and too self-conscious to scream, too young not to want to. '*Love, love me do, You know I love you . . .*'

141

He caught sight of her by chance as he gazed at the flood of devotion. She was standing at the side of the cinema, her head back against the wall, pushed there by the wave of hysteria which had lifted her from her seat, a surging tide of hot, pressed flesh as fans fought to get out into the aisles and down to the front of the cinema, there to be thrown up in waves against the blue uniforms of the Metropolitan Police. At that moment as he watched her buffeted by the currents he thought she was the most beautiful girl he had ever seen, her long, carelessly tumbling hair shining golden in the yellow glow of the cinema aisle lights, her eyes big and laughing. While all around the uncontrollable wash of frenzy was threatening to break the dam of authority and bear her away, she was simply giddy at the joy of it all. Perhaps she was unaware of the danger, because suddenly another girl, a little shorter, he thought, reached out from the seats and, grabbing hold of her coat, pulled her back into the aisle just as the river of excitement gathered momentum and swept down the aisle towards the stage. And in that moment she was gone, out of sight, submerged into the sea of euphoria, and he was left staring in vain for her through the screaming.

It was all over so quickly. Ten songs, twenty-five minutes, *Twist and Shout* and the curtain was coming down. 'Wow,' said Hudson, at his side. That was the only word for it. 'Wow!' And Richard wondered who on earth she could be.

(ii)

The Morris Minor picked up speed in the climb out of High Wycombe. There had been patchy, low-lying fog closer to London causing Nicola to lean forward in concentration for several miles, but up in the Chilterns the visibility cleared and she could relax and sing again. Whenever she was happy she would sing: tonight she was happy enough to sing all the way home.

142

'*I've got arms that long to hold you, and keep you by my side, I've got lips that long to kiss you, And keep you satisfied* . . . Wasn't it wonderful, Emmy? I mean they were fantastic, weren't they? I felt as though I'd been plugged into some massive explosive generator, didn't you?'

'Yes and no,' said Emily.

Nicola ignored her. Since they left Hammersmith she had hardly stopped chattering. She began to sing again. '*Last night I said these words to my girl. You know you never even try, girl. Come on, come on, come on, come on, Please, please me, oh yeah, like I please you.*'

Emily, muffled inside a dark green duffel coat, the hood up to protect her from the draughts which razored through the gaps between the canvas roof and the windows, contemplated the lyrics. 'It's about sex, isn't it?' she said finally as Nicola stopped singing to negotiate a potentially slippery, leaf-clad corner.

'Not specifically,' Nicola replied, accelerating back up into fourth gear.

'Oh, come on. *I do all the pleading with you, it's so hard to reason with you, oh yeah, why do you make me blue?*' she recited slowly. 'What else can it mean? When a boy pleads to a girl and finds it difficult to reason with her, there's only one thing on his mind. And that's sex.'

'On the other hand it could be the lament of a doting father, like yours, frustrated by a badly behaved daughter, unlike you.'

Emily shook her head. 'It's about sex.'

'All right. Probably,' Nicola conceded. 'What do you think? Is he asking her to go all the way with him?'

'Hard to say. P'raps he just wants a bit of mutual petting. *Please, please me, oh yeah* . . .'

'Oh yeah?' Nicola gurgled.

'*Like I please you* . . .'

'*Please, oh yeah, like I please you, please, oh yeah, like I please you* . . .' Nicola peeled the song away, joined for the final five imaginary guitar chords by

Emily. 'Clang . . . clang . . . clang . . . clang . . . clang.'

Emily edged her legs nearer to the heater. The fan was on fully but it was still cold. She glanced across at Nicola. As she never complained about the heat Nicola never appeared to feel the cold particularly either. She was beginning another song now, a happy smile turning up the corners of her mouth. Such good spirits. '*Love, love me do, you know I love you . . .*'

'Or alternatively, *Licence my roving hands, and let them go, Before, behind, between, above, below . . .*' Emily interrupted.

Nicola stopped singing: 'What?' she said, not having heard properly.

'Not me. John Donne.'

'Oh yes.'

'He's very sexy. Sexier than Lennon and McCartney.'

'But unfortunately dead. Three hundred years dead with a terrible haircut and a very rude-looking beard.'

'Really?' said Emily. She hadn't thought of this before. 'When does a beard look rude?'

'When it's triangular, very pointed and Venus shaped. All Elizabethan men had rude-looking beards. Have you never noticed? I thought everyone had noticed that. Think about it, Shakespeare, Marlowe, Raleigh. They had the most perfect V-shaped, pudenda-sculpted beards, every one of them. Very rude, if you ask me.'

Emily considered this for a moment. It was exactly the kind of thing Nicola always threw up when they were driving. She had probably only thought of it at that very second. 'P'raps it was because they were ruled by a very strong woman and subconsciously they wanted to look like one,' she suggested.

'Not unlike the Beatles who are very feminine looking, fluffy haired and clean shaven and, according to you, write songs about heavy petting.'

'Which John Donne did better. Can you imagine

lines in a song today about roving hands that go *Before, behind, between, above, below . . . ?'*

'God, Emmy, I'll crash the car if you don't stop going on about it.'

'Sorry,' said Emily and smiled in the darkness.

They drove on in silence for a few minutes before Nicola suddenly giggled: 'So what d'you think the Beatles mean when they sing *A Taste Of Honey?*'

The car rocked with laughter.

It had been such a terrific day. Emily had been reading in the Botanic Garden, enjoying the sunshine, when Nicola had come dashing down the path insisting they go to London. 'There's nothing else we can do. If the Beatles won't come to us, we'll have to go to them,' she had said, deaf to all excuses.

'What if we can't afford the touts' prices?' Emily had tried to protest.

Nicola had simply felt in her jacket pocket and produced a small wad of notes. 'We can afford.'

Even had Emily not wanted to go there would have been little point in arguing. Nicola would almost certainly have persuaded her, not because Emily was weak, but because Nicola usually wanted things so much more than Emily did not want them.

The Morris Minor sped on through the black, beech-rimmed tunnel of the A40. The car had been Nicola's treat to herself at the beginning of term, seventy-five pounds and a promise that everything was in full working order. When she was twenty-one she might buy an MGB or E-type Jaguar, she had threatened one night in their new flat, if Emily would promise not to describe it as a penis substitute. Emily had promised. 'I should have thought that's the last thing you're in need of,' she had said, and ducked as a cushion had hurtled her way.

It wasn't actually true, anyway, although this year more than any other, the sexual chase that was Oxford was in full cry. Already Nicola, ever impetuous, was outgrowing Oxford, and knocking back every overture to come her way. Suddenly it all seemed so small, so gossipy, so young, narrow, incestuous. An extension of school. Thank God it was their final year.

'You know, Emmy,' she said as the little car dropped back into the mist of the Vale of Aylesbury, 'what we need is some new blood . . . or at least some new bloodstock.'

Emily nodded: they could even read each other's thoughts.

Chapter Sixteen

(i)

Hudson would say later that *Witness* was conceived for the fun of it at about four o'clock one Sunday morning, 'just one of those crazy things you get up to in the middle of the night', but Richard would remember it differently. In one way or another Hudson had been preparing for *Witness* from the moment he set foot in England.

'There has to be something wrong,' Hudson said laconically the weekend following the Beatles' concert. He was wearing his dinner jacket, and lying back on Richard's narrow bed, his feet dangling off the end, precariously holding a glass of Macon in one hand and the photograph of Dolly Carter in the other. 'Either you're a lousy journalist who doesn't have an eye for a story, or London is full of lousy editors who can't see a natural talent when he's doing everything but breaking down the door. Am I right?'

Richard sat cross-legged on the threadbare carpet and stared into the flames of his gas fire. He had been working through the night, reworking his article on the gypsies, when Hudson had come clambering in from a party in Chelsea, a bottle of wine in his overcoat pocket and a smile that said the night was just beginning.

'I'm not a lousy journalist,' Richard said firmly, pouring himself a plastic tumbler of wine. As the guest Hudson had the only glass.

Hudson was silent for a moment as he stared at the photograph of Dolly Carter. 'It's all about identifying the market,' he said at last.

'Market for what?'

'For anything. Identifying the market and then getting the product to the market. That's what it's all about.'

'Well obviously.'

'Not so obvious. Not to most people. If it were so obvious everyone would be doing it and there'd be no room for us.'

'No room for us to do what?' Hudson was becoming tedious.

'To start our own magazine.'

Richard laughed. The drink was talking. How strange to see Hudson drunk. 'It's impossible,' he said.

'Why?'

'Why? . . .' He stopped. He wanted this conversation to continue. Just to say these things was exciting. 'What kind of magazine, anyway?'

'The kind you want to write for and to edit and I want to publish and to read. The kind of magazine that can see what's going on right here and now.'

It would be wonderful if it were so easy, thought Richard, but he said: 'We'd never do it, magazines take money, lots of money, distribution networks, advertising people, offices, secretaries . . . resources.'

Hudson shook his head. 'Most of all they take courage. People who aren't afraid to try.'

Richard wanted to believe, but Hudson was drunk and he wasn't. 'Before publishers launch magazines they do market research to find out what the readers want.'

'Which is why they always come up giving them more of what they already have. There's no point asking people what they want. They don't know what they want until they get it. You've got to ask yourself, "What do I want in a magazine?" We'll publish a magazine that we want to read, and that our friends want to read. People of our age. We'll attract everything that's new, from music to politics to movies to fashion to satire to . . . I don't know, cannibalism, if that's what excites you. It'll be a place where you can read something intelligent about the Beatles, something thoughtful about Kennedy, something honest

148

about the kids of Amphetamine Alley, and something funny, or at least entertaining, about who's screwing who in the Conservative Party. Pass me that bottle, will you?'

Was it just possible? 'What about money?'

'Don't worry about that. Leave it to me. There's a little family money I can find. Your job is to get together the best bunch of writers and photographers in London – all those people like you who can't get past the front office. People who are hungry for a shot. You edit and I'll publish, and, if you still think it's a good idea, I think the first issue should have this gypsy girl on the cover.'

Richard reached across and took the photograph from him. Dolly Carter had an extraordinary look, child/ woman, gaol bait, call it what you would. 'I thought you were drunk,' he said.

'I am drunk, a very rare sight, so study it while you can. But I'm also serious as hell. We're going to do it. You and me. We'll be the perfect team. I won't interfere with what goes in the editorial and you don't worry about the business side of things. You start tomorrow at twenty pounds a week.'

'Now you are joking.'

'You want more? How much?'

'Of course not. That's more than enough. But where . . . ?'

'I tell you. Don't worry. I'll find the money.'

'Five thousand pounds is the absolute minimum for a very basic . . .'

Hudson held up his hand. 'Do we have a deal or don't we?'

'What will we call it?'

'I don't know. Tell me.'

Richard paused for only a moment and then said, '*Witness*.' He never knew where the title came from.

'*Witness*.' Hudson rolled the word on his tongue. '*Witness*. Can I get a witness?'

'What's that?'

'Oh, just something they say in some of those churches

149

down south. *Witness*. You just made your first editorial decision.' He pushed his hand out. 'Shake on it.'

Feeling rather foolish, Richard offered his hand. Hudson grabbed it, then suddenly he leaned across and gave him a tight, brotherly American bear hug.

'You wait, Richard Blake, we're gonna cartwheel around the moon. Trust me.'

Although tired and a little drunk Richard did not sleep after Hudson staggered back to his own room just after five. He was too excited. After the wine had run out they had brewed coffee on the hob and planned their magazine. '*Witness*, a fortnightly look at the new, the news, and the popular arts', was their first slogan. Hudson had wanted the word 'young' there, too, but Richard had argued successfully that youth was an attitude rather than a state. They did not want to find themselves boxed into a youth ghetto.

At seven o'clock, impatient to begin his new life, he made his way down to the dining room for breakfast. Hudson was already there, sitting alone eating his Corn Flakes, doing some sums on a pad. By eight-thirty Penelope Chilston had been invited to join the venture as features editor. She didn't even ask about pay.

After breakfast, while Richard telephoned his farewell to the insurance company, Hudson went off to visit a bank, see a lawyer and view some offices. He had been doing his homework. He already had a folder full of estate agents' details of vacant premises.

By lunchtime *Witness* had its home, the top floor of a Hayward Mews house in nearby Notting Hill Gate. It was small, cheap and white walled, but best of all, it already had two telephones. There were three rooms, one large, obviously the editorial office, and two others which were immediately called advertising and distribution offices. Hudson, as publisher, would work from the distribution office, although it was dingy and badly lit. The editorial office was the best room in the building, with bare floorboards, a ceiling which had been opened up to steep wooden eaves and a skylight. Folded against one wall they found an abandoned decorator's trestle-table, which immediately became an all-purpose editorial bench. 'What do you think?' asked Hudson as he showed Richard around. Richard just smiled.

They spent the day cleaning, buying pencils, pads, biros and sticking paste from W.H. Smith, and, in the absence of anything to sit on, a wobbly collection of old dining chairs from a second-hand shop. Penelope Chilston joined them at four bearing a plastic bag containing rolls, pâté, cheese, fruit, coffee, milk and wine and three packets of digestive biscuits. In another bag she had a kettle and six mugs. She had wanted to come earlier but had diligently finished coding some questionnaires first. She was silly with excitement; if Richard had any doubts about the project Penny's euphoria dispelled them.

At twenty-past five when Tim Gimmelmann, summoned by a phone call, climbed the stairs, suspicious and surly, there was already a hand-painted *Witness* sign on the door, and a large calendar on one wall, the date of first publication ringed: Friday 22 November. They had given themselves just five weeks to prepare their first issue.

Gimmelmann hardly spoke that first day. Awkward in the company of Hudson and Penny, he simply sniffed and polished the cuff of his leather jacket on his neat, mod, herringbone trousers. But he took everything in. He would make his contribution, Richard was certain. Ambition was pancaked on his pretty face. At least he didn't push the question of pay too hard. It was taken for granted that for the first few months there wouldn't be very much.

That night Richard made a sudden trip home to Wimbledon. In his bedroom he had a collection of Roman coins. They were the only things of any value he possessed and had been bequeathed to him by his grandfather. When he returned to Bayswater the following morning, his parents' forebodings of failure ringing in his ears, the coins were hidden in his bag. By midday they had been sold for forty pounds, enough, he reckoned, to keep him at the Lamborne for just seven more weeks. He wouldn't take Hudson's offer of pay until they knew whether they had a success or not.

The following days hurried by. A lawyer was visited and a limited company was set up, Witness Magazines Ltd, with a nominal hundred shares, of which Richard was given 10 per cent. Then, while Hudson set off on a trawl of cheap printers, Richard moved his typewriter into the office and set about designing his magazine. The logo came first, plain and simple lettering, a contrast to the squeezed, condensed types which had recently become fashionable. If Richard had any theory about make-up it was that everything should be as uncluttered as possible.

On the third day an accountant was hired, following an advertisement in the *Evening Standard*. He arrived timid and early, wearing a cheap, grey suit, with a thin, wispy beard. His name was Adam Smith, a good name for an accountant, thought Richard, and he was as pale as blotting-paper. Since no one else had bothered to come for interview after being told by telephone what the job entailed and the size of the starting salary, Hudson was curious about what had attracted Adam Smith.

There was the briefest pause. 'I have no choices,' he replied. 'I've just come out of gaol. No one will take me on as an accountant but that's the only thing I can do.'

'Why were you in gaol?' Hudson asked.

'Embezzlement. But I won't do it again.'

Hudson hired Adam Smith and the pale young man took the office next to his, where he pinned a picture of Dolly Carter over his desk.

When Richard wasn't designing he was pursuing, talking to writers and photographers. Penny's contact book was encyclopedic. Willie Simmonds was her first suggestion, a broad, shambling young man with a thatch of blond hair and a very bad stammer. He would, he said, take care of film and theatre reviews as a job lot if he got free tickets. He was twenty-four, sexually voracious and a former actor from the Bristol Old Vic.

'Actor?' Richard couldn't disguise the surprise in his voice. They were meeting for the first time in a pub in Portobello Road and during the first few minutes of their conversation hardly a consonant had come from Simmonds without explosions, lock-jaws and tearaway repetition of syllables.

Simmonds grinned. 'It g..oes on st..age,' he said. 'It's m..e who st..amm..ers, not the ch..arac..ter, you see.'

'That's right,' said Penny. 'You can always tell when Willie's lying because he starts playing a part and doesn't stammer. It's only when he's being honest, playing himself, that he stammers.'

'Wh..en have I l..ied to y..ou?' said Willie.

'Every time you've tried to get me into bed. You come on like Richard Burton, all Welsh and fluent.'

Willie grinned wolfishly. 'That d..oesn't count.'

Quickly the team began to come together. Because it was necessary to have decently typed letters Hudson found a secretary called Sonia who moved into his office with her own typewriter, high heels, yoghurt and beehive hairdo, while a college friend of Richard's, Ben Tarlo, a smiling wide-necked boy from Manchester who worked for an advertising agency, was prevailed upon to be a cartoonist. Photographers were more difficult to find, not least because they expected to be paid, but by the end of the second week Richard had a promise from Bill McGough, a freelancer linked with the *Observer*, that *Witness* could have first sight of everything they didn't take. The *Observer* had turned down Gimmelmann's pictures of Dolly Carter, so what else were they rejecting?

Dolly Carter. That first picture was mesmerizing. Even Penny commented, holding it out at arm's length to get a better look. 'Who on earth is that?'

'A gypsy,' Richard told her. 'We thought we might put her on the first cover. What d'you think?'

Penny nodded. 'She's . . . extraordinary,' she said.

She kept on staring. 'Dark. She has a dark look, the bad girl child who will gobble you up.'

'Really?'

'I think so. In one way or another.'

'So you think she might be wrong for us?'

'Oh no,' she said. 'I think she's absolutely right. I think she's a star.'

(*ii*)

Tim Gimmelmann pulled the large zinc bath sideways through the door into his basement room. From outside in the passageway the sound of water bubbling and steaming on the old gas cooker could be heard. Dolly Carter, her legs splayed out and her tight black skirt ridden up to her mid-thighs, lounged on the mattress on the floor watching him. Her lips were vivid, blackcurrant-red against her powdered white face. Her eye make-up had been too generously applied and was smeared. Her blouse, with holes where the lace had become torn on the scrubbing board, was unbuttoned so that a dirty grey bra showed beneath.

'What are you doing?' she asked as Gimmelmann carried a large copper pan of boiling water and began pouring it carefully into the bath.

Gimmelmann did not answer. Emptying the pan he went outside into the dingy passageway and returned with a large saucepan of hot water.

'You taking a bath then?'

Next Gimmelmann emptied a steaming, large, black kettle. 'Not me. You,' he said at last.

'I don't think so.' Airily the girl looked around the little room, at the worn orange lino on the floor, the string from the curtain rail to a nail on the wall from which hung Gimmelmann's shirts, the old bread bin, the cracked cup and the faded curtains over traffic-grimed windows. Outside a bus roared into first gear, the smell of its exhaust ghosting through a crack in the window frame.

'Get undressed. You're dirty.'

'Dirty?'

'I'll go out if you like,' Gimmelmann said, lighting the gas fire.

'I'm not getting in that. You're just trying to get my clothes off. Why don't you come here and try, if that's what you want?' She was smiling at him from the bed.

He stared bleakly at her. 'How old are you?'

'Eighteen.'

'Liar.'

'All right. Seventeen.'

'No.'

'What does it matter how old I am? Nobody else ever bothered. The younger the better. Isn't that right?'

He looked at her for a moment and then crossed to the door. 'I'm going down the road to get some ciggies. I'll be fifteen minutes. If you want some cold water it's in the passage. There are some bath salts here you might like to use and some shampoo. And there's a new towel on the sideboard.'

'I'm not getting in that bath.'

'If you want me to take your photograph you will,' he said, and reaching for his leather jacket he left the room.

At the corner shop he deliberately dawdled, looking through the single copy of *Vogue* stocked there. There wasn't much demand for *Vogue* in his street. He was killing time. He thought of Dolly spreading herself carelessly across his mattress. She frightened him. He was sure she was no more than sixteen, possibly less. He hoped not. She was dangerous: but fascinating. She had a look, something more knowing than a street urchin. Her eyes challenged with a cool wisdom. There was something boyish and soiled about her.

The shopkeeper was preoccupied counting some change out on the counter. Expertly Gimmelmann slid the copy of *Vogue* inside his jacket and pulled up the zip. Then picking up a copy of the *New Musical Express* he turned back to buy his cigarettes, Marlboro. They made him feel tough.

He walked slowly back to the basement, nervous now. He wondered if he had done the right thing bringing her back to his place. Might it make him vulnerable? He had met her on Shepherd's Bush Green that morning, their third meeting since he and Richard had found her on the scrubland. The other times he had sat in a coffee bar with her and listened to the juke box. She liked her coffee sweet and sickly below a head of warm foam. They had hardly spoken. How had Hudson described her? 'Wanton.' That was the word. He wasn't sure what it meant. He checked his watch. Twenty-five minutes. If she had taken a bath she must surely have finished by now.

Going down the outside steps he entered the dark basement corridor and listened. Silence. He felt awkward. He tapped on the door to his room. 'Dolly?' No answer. 'Dolly.' From inside came the sound of a giggle. He opened the door.

Dolly was sitting in the zinc bath shampooing her hair. Brazen was the word his mother would have used. 'You took your time,' she said as he gazed at her body. He had seen girls naked before. Quite a few. But none like Dolly. She radiated an insolent sexuality. She was watching him.

'I brought you a present,' he said, taking the magazine from his jacket and dropping it down on to the mattress.

She didn't thank him.

He knelt at the side of the bath. The smell of bath salts was overpowering. She had used the whole packet. Through the water, dirty, scummy London hard water, he could see the details of her body. 'Shall I rinse your hair?' he asked.

She laughed, a dirty chuckle.

There was still some warm water in one of the pans. He lifted it. 'Close your eyes,' he said, and gently he allowed the water to run through her hair and down

156

across her shoulders and breasts. When he had finished he reached to the bed and taking the new bath towel put it around her shoulders. With a deliberate sullen absence of modesty she stood up and turned to him, the towel open. He gazed up at her. Then crossing the room he pulled three plastic bags from beneath the bed.

'What've you got there?' she demanded.

'Something for you to wear. Get dried and put these on and perhaps I'll take some photographs of you.'

She looked at him curiously. Then stepping from the bath on to the rug in front of the gas fire she began to dry herself. Very carefully he took the clothes from the bags: three pairs of pastel-coloured panties, a long-sleeved, cream, silk blouse, a navy-blue velvet shift with lace collar, a shiny PVC wrap-around skirt, a long, deep green scarf, a smoky-blue suede frock coat . . .

'Did you buy all those?' she asked.

'Some,' he replied. 'Some things I've borrowed from a friend. She's a buyer in the West End.'

He passed her a pair of pants. Those he had bought. She looked at them strangely, felt the texture of the material, drew them across her face and then bending over slipped into them.

He emptied the zinc bath while she examined the clothes. She took her time, feeling and smelling every single item. Her hands were small and her nails were bitten and short. He would have to hide those.

At last she made her decision. A black-and-white kilt, but with the top turned over so that it was hitched high above her knees, and a charcoal polo-neck sweater. Monochrome: a conservative choice, but on Dolly, with that bleak, puppy-dog face, there was no innocence. He gazed at her. She smirked. On the dresser was a leather cap with sheepskin flaps which he had worn while working on a building site the previous winter. Tucking her hair up she pulled it on. Then very deliberately she ran the pointed tip of her tongue around the rim of her lips.

He felt uncomfortable. 'Let's take some pictures, shall we?' he said.

(iii)

Everything Richard wanted was made available. He knew that Hudson was counting the pennies, the careful manager of his family's money, but every day as *Witness* needed something new, the extra typewriter, the blowing up of photographs, a part-time secretary, petty cash to hire Willie Simmonds a dinner jacket to attend a film première, Hudson was there, hand in pocket and doling out. If he was ever careful with money it was only for his own needs, giving up everything so that he might have more to invest in *Witness*. The printers he found, J.W. Purley and Sons of Cricklewood, were the cheapest available.

During those first few weeks Richard and Hudson were inseparable, racing with each other to get to the office in the mornings, arguing about who would lock the door at night. It's like being fourteen again, Richard would think: two young men with a shared obsession. Quickly Richard noticed that Penny would be quieter in Hudson's presence, although Hudson would go out of his way to be friendly towards her. He was friendly towards all the girls. Sometimes when they worked late into the night girl-friends would turn up and wait until he was ready to leave. On one occasion Britt-Marie came: on another, a red-headed lady lawyer. Women liked Hudson more than any man Richard had ever known. But men liked him, too. Adam Smith was devoted and Tim Gimmelmann was reduced to blushes in his presence.

News of *Witness* spread quickly and every day new, would-be journalists would arrive carrying their unpublished pieces and envelopes of cuttings from student magazines. Usually it was pretentious dross. But Richard would read it all, searching carefully, talking to anyone who had taken the trouble to come in. The days were never long enough.

At the beginning of November, in search of a political writer, he set out for Oxford, persuasion on his mind. A research student at Magdalen College had written a very sardonic piece for *Isis* and, when Richard had managed to get him to the telephone, had sounded guardedly interested. 'Why don't you come up and see me?' the student had said airily. 'Perhaps we can discuss it.'

There were three ways for the editor of *Witness* to get to Oxford. With a view to Hudson's family's funds Richard chose the cheapest.

October 1963

Chapter Seventeen

(i)

It was misty, a mid-autumn afternoon with the sun filtered through a thin layer of cloud when he saw the green Morris Minor approaching. Twenty-five minutes earlier the potato truck had dropped him at the Thame turn-off. Fifteen miles still to go and he was beginning to panic. He had agreed to be at Magdalen at four.

There was never any question that the car would stop. Almost as soon as his hand went out he was aware of gears changing down and brakes being applied.

'I'm going as far as Oxford if that's any use.'

'Oh yes . . . perfect . . . thanks very . . .' began Richard, but the words stuck on his lips. He knew immediately where he had seen this girl before.

'Jump in.' She released the passenger door for him. 'Sorry, I'll just move my notes.' Scooping up some files she chucked them carelessly on to the back seat, alongside several bulky brown paper envelopes.

He climbed in.

'Have you come from London?' she asked as the car began to pull away. He meant to say, 'Yes', but instead he said: 'I've seen you before.'

She looked faintly bored. 'Yes, if you're at Oxford you probably have. Sorry, I don't think . . .'

'No. I don't mean at Oxford. You were at the Beatles' concert in Hammersmith, leaning against the wall when the fans rushed the stage.'

Nicola Reynolds smiled. 'You were there, too? Wasn't it terrific?'

The twelve miles weren't long enough: the importance

of the appointment at Magdalen suddenly diminished. Close up she was no less pretty than he had remembered, the small, neat nose, the wide, curly mouth and straight jaw and the pale-honey tan. But he could see now that her hair was two-toned, lighter on top and at the front where it fell across her eyes and was brushed away by an impatient hand, but darker where the sun had never reached.

She was, she said, just returning from seeing some lawyers in Lincoln's Inn and due at a tutorial at four. 'Lawyers. They take so long. They're absolutely hopeless.' Then, after a slight hesitation, she murmured: 'You aren't doing law, are you?'

'I'm not doing anything any more. I mean I'm a . . . sort of journalist.' He hardly liked to say the word.

'Only a "sort" of journalist?'

Briefly he explained about *Witness*. 'In the sense that we're all witnesses to history in the making,' he said, and then wanted to bite off his tongue.

'Was that why you were at the Beatles' concert, to write about it? I mean that's history, I suppose, not them particularly, but the baby-boom hysteria.'

'Not really. We just wanted to see what it was all about, Hudson and me, I mean. He's my partner. I'm not quite sure how we're going to handle the Beatles. The thing is changing so quickly, growing so fast that whatever is written will seem out of date by the time we publish.'

'Mmm.' She was now concentrating on the traffic. They were already in Oxford. 'I'm just wondering if the Botanic Garden would do us both a very large favour and let us park in their forecourt for an hour.'

He liked the way she said that, the way she talked about 'us'.

They raced over Magdalen Bridge and she pulled off the road and manoeuvred up to the arch outside the Botanic Garden. A gatekeeper noticed and began to shake his head. 'If I were you I'd hop out now while you can,' Nicola said. 'It'll be easier for me to charm him if you aren't around.'

Richard opened the car door and climbed out. He couldn't leave just like this. 'Look . . . er . . . I wonder if we could perhaps meet . . . have a drink or something after your tutorial,' he said.

'Well . . . ah . . .' Nicola looked at him. For a moment he thought she was going to invent some excuse. Then she nodded. 'All right. The Kemp at five-thirty. In the Broad. Now, go on, scoot, he's coming.'

He slammed the door and hurried across the road. Looking back he saw that she was pleading with the gatekeeper, who continued to shake his head. But then, as the coaxing continued, the man began to look around, his resolve weakening. Finally, with a smile of resignation, he pointed to a gap between two parked cars. She had won the day.

He ought to have been furious with the fellow. At the very least he could have telephoned and explained that he'd been made a better offer. Richard would have understood. At this stage anything had to be better than *Witness*, even *Time and Tide*. But to allow him to go all the way to Oxford and then to airily dismiss the notion of writing for *Witness* over an arrowroot biscuit and a cup of weak tea was almost maddening. But only almost maddening. If he hadn't gone to Oxford he would not at five forty-two have been sitting in the Kemp Café gazing into the eyes of Nicola Reynolds.

'Of all the bloody cheek . . .' she sympathized.

'He was all right, really. Just an arrogant little toad. We can always find somebody else.'

'If he hops across my path I'll tread on him for you.'

Richard grinned. 'Thanks.' There was a silence between them. All around students were meeting and welcoming, several talking louder than was necessary, others leaning conspiratorially forward imparting details of the utmost intimacy. From time to time Nicola would acknowledge faces she knew, but she gave no indication that there were people to whom she would rather be talking. All the same Richard was aware that more than one young man cast admiring glances in her direction. With her navy-blue coat discarded now and hanging on the back of her chair and the sleeves of her polo-neck sweater rolled up, she breathed sunshine. 'I've been trying to work out your accent,' he said. 'Is there the slightest trace of a colonial childhood there somewhere?'

'Well spotted. Southern Rhodesia. Most people don't hear it. I went to school here from the age of ten when my mother died, but I've just come back from three months in Africa so perhaps there's more Rhodesian in me than usual this term.'

Southern Rhodesia, thought Richard, the third country of the Central African Federation, the one not heading towards independence.

She read his thoughts. 'I know. We're a bigoted, racist group of ox-cart reactionaries who don't know which way the wind's blowing. But some of us are also quite nice.'

'And always good for a lift,' Richard smiled.

'Not always. It depends on who wants one.' It was a flippant compliment, designed, though he could scarcely believe it, to encourage.

If there was any trace of frost that melted it. For some reason she had taken a liking to him. For every obvious reason he was head over heels for her. The notion of publishing one's own magazine intrigued her. 'It's just so brave,' she enthused.

'Did you ever do any journalism?'

'Perhaps a few bits and pieces in my first year, tongue sticking out of the corner of my mouth, trying to do joined-up writing and thinking I was making my name.'

'What sort of things?'

'Mainly things I knew nothing at all about but which sounded good. They seemed to like that.'

'What do you want to do when you finish?'

'Oh, I don't know. Emily . . . she's the girl I share a flat with, we've been together from the beginning, she's wonderful . . . we both talk vaguely about publishing, but to be honest I've hardly given it much thought. Books always seem such a civilized way to make a living. I suppose Emmy's keener than I am. It's in her blood, or something. Her father writes novels, though he's not very well and having rather a tough time at the moment.'

'What about your father, what does he do?'

'He doesn't. He was killed in the war.'

'In the Army or . . . ?'

'The Crazy Cow Saloon actually.'

'Sorry?'

'He was in the RAF on leave in London in a low dive in Soho called the Crazy Cow Saloon when it was hit by a bomb.' She smiled. 'Not exactly killed in action. I like to think that he died with a large gin and tonic in one hand and the other on the bottom of a very buxom tart.'

'Did you know him?'

'No. My uncle took over the job of bringing me up, particularly after my mother died. He's been very kind in his way. Wiser than God and twice as old.'

She chatted on, toying with a loose strand of hair, casual and self-deprecating, until at eight o'clock, having moved on to the King's Head, they exchanged telephone numbers, and she pointed him in the direction of the railway station.

'Look,' he said, as he dawdled on the pavement, 'the Beatles . . . I mean, we have to find a way of covering them . . . why don't you do something for us?' It was a crazy thing to suggest. He didn't even know whether she could write.

'Oh no. I'm not a journalist. What would I write about?'

'Whatever it was that made you stand in the aisle in front of all those fans. What it's like to be an intelligent

167

fan. Why the Beatles are different from anything that's happened before.'

'No, I couldn't, really. Sorry.'

'Just think about it. Will you?'

'Well . . .'

'And I'll telephone you. Perhaps when you come to London . . . we could meet and . . .'

'That would be nice,' she said quickly.

Her invisible presence accompanied him back to London. In the dismal station waiting-room he sensed the trace of perfume he had noticed when he climbed into the Morris Minor; and, in the sooty third-class carriage her face smiled at him from behind the No Smoking sign in the filth of the window, laughing as she had told him how her friend, Emily, was threatening to put John Donne to music. 'Can you imagine,' she had said, '"*Mark but this flea . . . it sucked me first and now sucks thee . . .*" in four-four time with a harmonica introduction and twelve-bar guitar break?' For the only time in their conversation the spectre of sex had watched them. Her smile had been faintly wicked, as though she had been wondering what might be his reaction. But then Emily had stolen her thoughts. Emily. She was the girl who had pulled her from the flood of fans in Hammersmith. 'She's everything I'm not,' Nicola had said. 'She's perfect, gentle, forgiving, kind, hard-working, without a malicious bone in her body. You must meet her. You'd love her.'

At Reading he had to change trains and wait half an hour for the express from Bristol but such was his distraction he scarcely noticed the inconvenience. He was a young man. Usually sex was never far from his mind but not on that night. Nicola Reynolds. He repeated the name to himself just to hear the sound of it. Nicola Reynolds. Undeniably beautiful, but quirky and disdainful of posturing. Nicola Reynolds. Her head forward, her chin resting on the bridge made by her bare elbows and hands, her face no more than eighteen inches from his, listening and nodding. A picture he would mentally frame and save. Nicola Reynolds, Nicola Reynolds, Nicola Reynolds . . . over and over in his mind it went, in rhythm with the spinning steel wheels on the track as the outskirts of West London slid by outside the window.

(ii)

Nicola was in bed, a cardigan over her nightdress and woolly socks poking from under the bottom of the sheet, when Emily arrived back at their second-floor South Park Road flat. Emily had been to La Scala to see *Last Year In Marienbad* with a randy theology student and had had a job shaking him off. 'God, did you miss a treat!' she groaned. 'I've seen more entertainment in a geometry set.' Then, noticing the inquest of legal documents scattered about Nicola's counterpane, she said: 'You look like a barrister preparing your brief.'

Nicola looked up from her documents. 'I have three things to say to you, Emily Robinson. One, it serves you right for pretending you like those boring arty films when you know very well you're a *Sound of Music* child at heart; two, bugger the brief, getting to the plot in these things is like swimming through blancmange . . .' She passed Emily a stack of papers.

Emily took them and dropped them further down the bed. She did not want to know about Nicola's money. If she were to discover for certain that Nicola was extremely rich it might affect their friendship. 'And what's the third thing?' she asked.

Nicola pulled her legs up under the bedclothes and hugged her knees. 'Ah, well now . . .'

Emily was surprised. She'd never seen Nicola being coy before. 'What's his name?' she asked.

'He's lovely, Emmy, he really is. You'll adore him.'

Chapter Eighteen

The fury of work was a distraction from the smiles and scents which trespassed on the edges of his mind. He had mentioned her name to Hudson, with a feigned and dishonest casualness, but Hudson, busy with the problems of the first-time publisher, had not enquired further. There was so much to do. The date they had set for publication was hopelessly unrealistic but it was written in stone in their minds. To miss the date would have represented failure. When they were more experienced they would wonder why they never attempted a pilot copy so that they might make all their mistakes in private.

While Richard toiled to build his editorial team Hudson was an engine of enterprise, flooding the advertising departments of banks, theatres, cinemas, galleries, bookshops and restaurants with begging letters and rate cards. He was a born salesman, just to hear him on the telephone was inspiring, his jaunty, persuasive American *bonhomie* setting about the most resistant of executives.

Quickly the character of *Witness* began to take shape. Penelope Chilston's friend, Willie Simmonds, was a true find. 'I th..ought I m..ight have a go at the Holly..wood way of r..ogering,' he announced one afternoon having returned from a Doris Day movie preview. 'You know, flood-lit con..fectionery col..oured, co-ed bed..rooms, Rock Hudson in b..aby blue py..jamas, Doris look..ing mutton-ish in cast-off, zipped-up b..baby dolls, sep..arate beds and I can only sup..pose hand jobs all round.' He was wittily vulgar, a clever critic and always fun to read, although his suggestion that his first

170

movie review should be headlined *Doris and Rock in the Land of Onan and the Blue Rinse* was appreciated but rejected.

Penny herself had begun by laying siege to a young, psychopathic landlord who owned freeholds in Westminster and was, in one way or another, encouraging tenants to leave in order that he might join the great Sixties redevelopment boom. She was more than intrepid now, she was indestructible, going from semi-derelict flat to basement squalor interviewing leaseholders, trying to convince them that right had more divisions than might. And because she didn't know any better she got away with it. When the enraged landlord cornered her on the stairs of an empty house, instead of fleeing she charged from above, her leather handbag sending him tumbling while she made good her escape.

'I never met anybody so brave,' Hudson congratulated as, sitting on the edge of the trestle-table, he read the copy coming off Penelope's typewriter. 'I hope you know when to duck and run, Penny. Some of these guys can do pretty desperate things when they see their plans being threatened.'

'No need to worry about me, I can take care of myself,' Penny said, reaching nervously for a paper cup of wine. Richard looked up from laying out a theatre review. Poor Penny.

Hudson patted her affectionately on the shoulder and turned to Richard. 'With any luck we'll have a London distribution deal by tonight. W.H. Smith have half-promised they'll take ten thousand on a sale or return basis.'

'Half-promised?'

'And half not promised.' A Hudson smile. 'Trust me.'

Each one of them trusted Hudson for everything. They were giving their time and their efforts: Hudson was giving his family's money.

Day by day the first edition, not a carefully planned venture but a hurriedly scrambled collection of pieces and pictures, came together. Richard and Penny Chilston were the major contributors, albeit under a variety of pseudonyms, all those rejected articles now finding a home. The gypsy picture of Dolly Carter for the first cover never had serious competition, not even when Tim Gimmelmann turned up with some fashion shots of her taken in the London streets. The girl had a startling, disquieting, almost destructive quality. But she looked absolutely of the moment.

Meanwhile Nicola ghosted through Richard's days and nights. On three occasions he had plucked up the courage to call her, but had never had a reply. Then, early one Friday evening, she telephoned him from a call-box in Holborn. He was alone in the office, Hudson having left early to go to a dinner party with a girl from the Chase Manhattan Bank.

'It's just that I have to virtually drive past your front door on my way back, and with the fog being so bad I thought I might look in for a while . . . until it clears a bit,' she said.

'Of course, of course . . .' Outside the window the familiar yellow haze was swirling around the street lamp. 'It's great to hear from you,' he said, his voice cracking with excitement.

'Right. See you in about twenty minutes.'

His smile was silly as he put down the telephone. Racing quickly around the office he pinned up posters which had been laid to one side since that first burst of home-making energy, washed Penny's coffee mugs in the washbasin on the stairs, where he also brushed his teeth and combed his hair, and laid a scattering of the better photographs out on the trestle desk. Then switching on the table lamp in Hudson's office he opened a bottle of red wine, rolled up his sleeves, and, returning to his desk, began to sub a short piece by Willie Simmonds on television satire. 'If one isn't inv . . ited to join them, dear b . . oy, one m . . ight as well ridi . . cule them,' Willie had explained, before launching a torrent of vitriol against David Frost and *That Was The Week That Was*.

Nicola took over an hour to crawl the three miles from Holborn, but suddenly she was with him. He hadn't heard her arrive.

'I'm sorry I didn't . . .'

'I parked down the road . . .'

They had both begun talking at once, then stopped together in nervous politeness. He gazed at the tiny drops of damp caught in the electric of her hair. She wiped her face with the back of her hand. She was prettier than he had remembered.

'I had to see some more lawyers. It's interminable. And as I was in town I thought . . .'

He wanted to kiss her. 'Would you like some wine? It's terrible, actually. But very cheap.' He filled a mug without waiting for her reply. 'Oh, sorry.' Tiny buoys of cork were floating on the surface.

She took the wine and, ignoring the cork, drank a little. 'I like it foul,' she laughed. She stared around. 'Everywhere looks so . . . professional,' she said at last.

'A week today we'll be on the news-stands.'

She moved across the room, looking at everything. 'It's so much bigger than I expected.'

That was good to hear: it meant he hadn't exaggerated too much. 'The Beatles . . .' he said, '. . . did you manage to write anything?'

'Well, yes and no . . .'

'Yes and no?'

'Well, yes really, I mean. But I'm not sure.'

He waited.

'It was a thought Emily had, actually. Lennon and McCartney lyrics. Are they about kissing, petting or going the whole hog, as one might say? I mean, *Thank you, girl, for loving me the way that you do*. What way does he mean exactly? Is it an officially recognized way, itemed and annotated in the *Kama Sutra*?' She was pulling a couple of sheets of paper from her coat pocket and he

173

suddenly realized that she was just as nervous as he was. She pushed the copy towards him. 'It's all nonsense really, but . . . I thought it might be vaguely amusing.'

It was amusing but very short. '*She was just seventeen, you know what I mean* . . . well, no, not exactly,' Nicola had worried. Was there perhaps something about being seventeen that we were missing? Some initiation ceremony perhaps or unspoken betrothal? Why did the Beatles sing, *Doo-doo do dooo, doo-doo do dooo*, after their taste of honey? A triumphant yodel, perhaps? 'After all, honey,' she had written, 'is, as everyone knows, a many yodelled thing . . . God willing.'

'You know what I wish,' he said as he finished reading.

'Go on.'

'I wish there were another ten songs to be analysed.'

She looked disappointed. 'Oh.'

'Not that this isn't terrific . . . it's just that it's such good fun I could read another eight hundred words.'

'D'you mean it? I mean, it made Emmy and me laugh, but that's what friends are for, and she did help write it.'

'It's marvellous. I love it . . .'

'Well, look there's a new Beatles' long player out any second . . . tons of new songs. If you can wait I could include those, too.'

He handed her back the article. 'Perfect,' he smiled. 'We'll do it as our cover story for the second edition. But there's one condition.'

'Yes?'

'That you stay a while and have something to eat with me.'

'Only if you let me pay,' she said, and then added, 'That's my condition.'

She treated him to a Greek restaurant off Queensway where they ate lamb which melted in the mouth and drank Retsina which didn't. It was a cramped place and noisy, despite the flock wallpaper and carpeted

174

floor ('like a Turkish tartorria,' Nicola reflected), and smelled slightly of cats, Richard thought, though he didn't say. Nicola talked most, gabbling on about the tedium of this final year at Oxford, how cold it was in the bedrooms of South Park Road, and the personification of virtue that was Emily. But mostly she talked about Southern Rhodesia and her home there, high in a place called the Vumba, a servant called Alice and the uncle who was her guardian. 'He's a cantankerous old Nazi, really. Africa does that to people – exaggerates any latent faults one way or the other. He's actually very kind to the people who work for us so long as they don't get any thoughts about equality, independence or answering back. I'm afraid that's the way most Rhodesians think.'

'But not you?'

'I suppose I would have done if I'd stayed and probably do a little bit, anyway, subconsciously, because I'm always desperately over-compensating, full of guilt.'

'Were both your parents from Rhodesia?'

'Only my father. He met my mother in London in the war. She was Polish, and in the Air Force, too. I remember she used to say to me that when she first went to the Vumba she thought she had stepped into the Garden of Eden. It's so beautiful. It really is. Vumba is a Shona word meaning mist. The mist gives the hills a sort of dreamy, only half-awake, fairyland quality.'

'It must have been very strange, from Poland to the middle of Africa in two jumps.'

'Mmm, I expect so. I think she was probably very lonely. There was no real family, you see. Nobody on her side. They disappeared into Russia in 1941, and my father only had his elder brother, Uncle Alec, who wouldn't exactly be among the ten most entertaining people I could name.'

'You don't like him?'

'Oh yes. I love him. He's sweet. When my mother got diphtheria and died he devoted himself to me. But I can imagine he takes some getting used to. You know

175

the sort: an old bachelor, gruff as an old bull elephant, always counting the pennies, although God knows he has enough. He spends a lot of his time in Salisbury these days. Wildwood's a bit remote.'

'Wildwood?'

'That's where I'm from. Wildwood, near Mupangare.'

'African names always make everywhere seem so exotic.'

'Not so much now, although I think my grandmother had a tough time. The story goes that my grandfather dragged her out kicking and screaming into the bush in a wagon pulled by oxen just before the First World War. He'd planned to go to Australia but had second thoughts on the dock at Southampton so took a boat to Beira in Portuguese Mozambique instead of Melbourne without bothering to tell her. When she arrived in Beira she's supposed to have said she never realized there were so many Aborigines in Melbourne.'

A Greek waiter, catching Richard's eye in the clatter of plates, bazooki and conversation, slid a dish of Turkish Delight on to the table.

Delicately Nicola took the wooden toothpick provided, speared one, and licked at the powdered sugar. 'Mmm, the reward for suffering the Retsina.'

'What did your family, were they farmers or . . . ?'

'Sort of, at first, anyway. Real Pilgrim Fathers' stuff, actually, stumping out the land, growing maize and all the time looking for gold. Don't laugh. The old boy found it. Copper, too, but that was up beyond the Zambezi, and not before the heat had finished off his poor wife. The Zambezi was no place for wilting English wives from Redcar. Rumour had it that he kept a couple of bush wives going after that, but Uncle Alec swears it's a "kaffir lie".'

Richard thought of his own suburban childhood just behind Wimbledon Common, and his parents' timid obsession with security. It seemed so dull by comparison. Everything about Nicola shone with vitality.

She was watching him. Without speaking she stuck the toothpick into another cube of Turkish Delight and, leaning across the table, put it to his lips. 'Let me tempt you,' she said.

When they left the restaurant the fog was thicker, a quiet muffled London, so they bought a bag of chestnuts from a man with a brazier outside Bayswater Underground station and walked the length of Queensway, first one side and then the other, using the lights from the shop windows to seek out roasted maggots.

They shared the last chestnut, their fingers black from the charcoal, and then, as they walked on and he told her about his family and sister and his guilt about selling the Roman coins, she unselfconsciously slipped her arm through his and snuggled close. Through his tweed jacket he felt her warmth.

They sauntered slowly back to the Morris Minor but she did not get into it. It was too foggy to drive anywhere now. Instead she said: 'Can I come home with you for a while?' He did not reply, but putting his arm around her they walked on through the strangely echoing streets of Bayswater towards the Lamborne.

There was no light under Hudson's door as they climbed the stairs. For once he was glad. In his attic room he drew the curtains, turned on the bedside light and lit the gas fire. Nicola sat in the one easy chair, still wearing her coat, her hands in her gloves as she toasted them over the fire. He knelt alongside at her feet, his elbow resting on her thigh. There was no hurry, so he waited, afraid to break the spell of the moment. Nicola Reynolds: above him, she took off a glove and ran a hand through his hair. He looked up at her. Her creamy hair fell across his face. She bent forward. Turning he undid the buttons of her coat and ran his hands inside and around her waist. Nicola Reynolds: so warm. Their lips grazed then parted, then momentarily joined again in the delicate dance of romance. He sank his face into her neck and held her close, her coat falling open. She babied his head. So soft, and all the night to play. Presently he turned and drew her towards him, their lips closing together. Parting, she smiled and brushed his hair from his face as he slid his hands under her sweater and caressed her skin. No hurry: no indecent haste. Outside the fog blanketed the tiny attic, a thick, grey blanket of splintered frost. Standing he drew her towards him and they moved together the few paces to the narrow bed. She slid under him and, putting her arms around his neck, pulled him down across her so that their bodies fitted in the contours of desire. Nicola Reynolds, as he had first seen her, laughing in the aisle as the flood of hysteria had borne down on her: and now beneath him, bearing upwards, drawing him to her. Nicola Reynolds, and all the night to come. Her coat slid from her shoulders and freed her arms as his hands traced her body, long and slender, and found her breasts; her skirt risen high now in the gentle capering. Nicola Reynolds: 'I'm going as far as Oxford . . .', hair tumbling down around her face. Nicola Reynolds and all the night was theirs. Two grown-up children slipping between the frosty sheets, cleaving together in the yellow and blue of burning gas, fitting together, toes trembling with cold, lips caressing and tasting secret flavours and scents, limbs intertwining, bodies joining. Nicola Reynolds. And all their lives to play.

'I love you,' he said, although he knew that she was sleeping, the smiling eyes now shuttered, her breath warm and regular on his face. A grey-quilted attic room in West London and a happiness he had never known could exist: the most perfect moment of his life. He dozed and Hudson appeared, happy for him. 'Nothing can stop us now, Richard,' he laughed. 'Nothing at all.' Then there was Nicola staring around the office: 'You're so brave . . . so brave . . .' 'Why?' he said. She smiled. 'Because don't forget, honey is, after all, a many yodelled thing . . . doo-doo-doodooo.' Nicola Reynolds from Wildwood.

When he awoke she was standing at the window staring down, her coat around her naked body. She heard him move. 'I must go soon. The fog's lifted. Emily will wonder where I am.'

'She'll be asleep. You could call first thing.'

She shook her head. 'We have a tutorial together at ten-thirty.'

'It's Saturday.'

'I know. We go to his home in North Oxford. He's very old but very good.' She slipped back into bed, her body now chilled from the window. The gas had gone out hours before from want of funds.

'I love you,' he said once more.

'Yes.'

They made love again. It was different in the morning, the sheets now crumpled, warm and scented with passion, their bodies familiar. He wanted to hold on to her, keep them safe in this attic, to hide inside her.

At half-past six and still dark they crept downstairs and out into the street. A thin rime covered the pavement and road, broken by the tracks of early-morning drivers. At the Morris Minor he used the backs of his gloves to clean the windscreen and windows, then waited while she turned the engine, hoping the car would not start, that they might creep back to bed. On the fourth attempt the spark caught and with a little roar the engine puffed into life, a cloud of smoke billowing from the exhaust. She wound down the driver's window.

'Just wait till I tell Emily about you. She'll be so jealous.'

He blushed. 'Next Friday, publication day, we're having a party, a celebration in the office. Perhaps you could come.'

'I'd love to.'

'Bring Emily, if you like . . . I mean if she'd like . . .'

'I'll ask her. See what she says . . .' She smiled. 'Well, anyway . . .'

Leaning into the car he kissed her again. He could taste his toothpaste on her lips. She had used his toothbrush. He liked that.

'Drive carefully,' he said, and then realized he sounded exactly like his mother.

'In this car it's difficult not to,' she laughed. And with coughs and revs the car pulled away into the wide street and turned up towards the Bayswater Road.

Richard watched it go. Nicola Reynolds. How could he exist for a week without her? Slowly he made his way back to the Lamborne. It was almost light. He imagined her driving down Holland Park Avenue, the little car chugging from too rich a mixture of petrol and air. Reaching the steps to the hostel he felt in his pocket for the key. Wondering if Hudson had ever returned he glanced casually upwards towards his window. Something moved. He would never be sure, but for a split second he fancied he saw Hudson watching him, lonely and lost. But then the figure was gone: and the window was empty.

Chapter Nineteen

Tim Gimmelmann never saw the blow coming. He hardly felt it, not the first, the one which put him down, nor the boot which ripped into his thigh and dug deep under his testicles. All he knew was the warm, sweet taste of blood and, somewhere close, the screaming of Dolly. 'Bastard . . . bastard . . . bastard.'

He had been awoken by a hammering on the basement door, and, pulling on a coat, he had padded down the linoleum of the passage, confused in the gloom and early morning cold. The attack had begun before the door was properly open.

'You want her, you pay for her,' he had heard as the leather knuckle caught his eye, sharp as a piston, and his knees buckled on the doormat.

'Bastard, bastard . . .'

'She don't give it away. Not to filth like you. D'you understand?' Another kick, an explosion in his head, and then darkness.

In the distance, the far distance, there seemed to be some kind of argument. 'All right, come on . . . he'll be all right.'

'You stinking pig.'

A sharp sound, perhaps a slap. A scream. 'Bastard.' A scuffle. 'Little slut.' Another slap, and another. Then silence.

When he awoke he was alone on the floor of his room. It was light. Consciousness had returned in little eddies of comprehension. He ached about the head and body. His groin was numb. He climbed painfully on to his mattress. He was surprised that his legs would bear him. He sank into his pillow, pulled at the bedcovers and shivered.

She came back in the late afternoon. He heard her steps in the passageway, heard the creak of the door. She leant over him. Her lipstick was smudged, her eyes black with mascara. She had a bruise across her forehead. She stared at him without speaking, examining the extent of the damage. Then, sitting in the chair by the window, she settled in to wait.

Chapter Twenty

(i)

Hudson was furious. The easy charm and smiles were gone, and with them went the boyishness. The expression was walnut hard: the eyes bleak. Richard had never seen him like this before and was slightly nervous. But Richard was angry, too. It was publication day, and already they were behind. Mr Purley himself, the elder son of printers J.W. Purley and Sons, had promised that copies would be available for delivery the previous afternoon. 'Thursday, one o'clock, no problem, you said,' Hudson said coldly.

It was eight o'clock on Friday morning. The van Hudson had hired to collect and deliver the first edition of *Witness* stood waiting to be filled, its rear doors open. In Richard's hand was a collection of loose pages.

'Yes, sorry about this, lads . . .' Harry Garstang, the overseer in the brown, ink-stained overall, did not look at all sorry. Two apprentices carrying galleys of print smirked to each other. 'We had a problem with the stapling equipment. Hopefully by tomorrow . . .'

'Tomorrow nothing. You've got two hours. Ten o'clock dead or you're in breach of contract. And you're in trouble, Garstang.'

Richard looked at Garstang. He was a small, self-important man who had made the mistake of treating Hudson like a boy.

'Now listen, sonny, don't come . . .' Garstang began, stung by Hudson's tone. Probably no one had called him by his surname since he was in the Army. The protest died in his throat.

'Ten o'clock or we scrap the whole goddamned

183

issue and take you to court for the return of our deposit and damages like you never heard. I mean it. D'you understand? So you'd better get on to your boss right now and tell him to get his ass out of neutral or hire himself one hell of a lawyer.' With that Hudson strode to the van and climbed in. Richard followed.

'Perhaps there is a problem with the stapler,' Richard suggested as they pulled into the road.

'And maybe there isn't. Maybe they got a rush job yesterday from some old pal and gave it priority. And maybe they took us for a couple of kids starting our first magazine who didn't know the rules. It's just a lousy, stupid way to begin and I'm not taking it. Now where the hell can we get some breakfast around here?'

They found a transport café on Kilburn High Road where, over a plastic-topped table smeared in grease, they drank coffee and ate toast in silence. The unexpected delay had made them both edgy.

'You never said how much of your family's money you've had to lay out,' said Richard, ordering more coffee.

'No, I didn't. But don't worry, we'll get it back. Every dollar. A million times.'

'D'you really believe that?'

'Yes.'

'What about your father? What does he think?'

'What?' For a moment Hudson was surprised.

'About the money. You did tell him?'

'Oh sure. But he's getting on. These things don't excite him too much any more. It had already been made over to me. It's no big deal.' Suddenly he smiled. 'Hey, come on. I worry about business. Right? What about this girl of yours? You didn't tell me.'

'I did, but you didn't listen.'

'Tell me again.'

Just to talk about her made Richard feel good. 'Well, I don't know. Let's see, she's called Nicola Reynolds and she says yodelling the honey is a many splendoured thing.'

Hudson stared at him seriously for a second and then laughed so loud a taxi driver looked up from his sausages and eggs. 'She said that? Hell, she can't be all bad.'

'She's all good. She's terrific. You'll see.'

'I hope so.' Hudson looked around the café. There were four other customers at various stages of breakfast, each one accompanied by a newspaper, a *Daily Express*, *Daily Mirror*, *Daily Sketch* and *Sporting Life*. 'Will you look at that. Newspapers. The perfect throwaway consumer product. Every day the people have to buy another one.'

Richard frowned. 'Jesus, Hudson. A throwaway product! If that's all you think newspapers are thank God you're only involved in the business side.'

And for the second time that morning Hudson guffawed, blowing away the tensions of the day.

(*ii*)

The party began at six with half a paper cup of champagne each for the early-comers, one of Hudson's well-earned extravagances. All day Richard, Penny, and her flat-mate Vasco, Willie Simmonds, Sonia, the bee-hive, photographer Bill McGough, Hudson's red-headed lawyer, Britt-Marie (taking a day off work) and Ben Tarlo's girl-friend, Jessica, had been hurrying around London helping deliver the gleaming fresh bundles of *Witness*. W.H.Smith had, in the end, not been tempted and without a distribution deal the only way was to do it themselves. For the time being *Witness* would be not only an exclusively London magazine, its sales would be heavily concentrated in the bed-sit acres of North and West London, plans for a print run of forty thousand copies having already been halved. But at least they were off and running.

Very quickly, as the helping hands arrived, the meagre supplies of champagne were transubstantiated into

185

cheap wine, but nobody appeared to notice. And when the Scottish dancer from room nine heaved up the stairs with the Dansette, a convivial Friday evening in Hayward Mews began to take shape. Only Gimmelmann and Dolly stayed away, which was a pity because every man there was keen to meet the cover girl.

'Didn't I tell you to trust me?' Hudson was leaning against the door to his tiny office.

Richard giggled, a little drunk, and polished his spectacles. He was proud of his magazine. There was much that was wrong, it was too worthy, too self-consciously clever and going in too many different directions at once. But it existed.

Nicola arrived at half-past seven, already carrying a copy, peering through the crowd, aware that men would look at her. Behind her came Emily.

Neatly introductions were made. Emily was pretty, too, but quite different from Nicola. Emily was serene, her dark hair held back at the temples with two butterfly clips.

'It really is terrific,' Emily said. 'You must be very pleased.'

'You actually bought a copy?' It seemed odd to Richard to think of *Witness* being sold in shops.

'Off the man with the Italian newspapers and dirty magazines in Notting Hill Gate,' Nicola said. 'It was a toss-up between *Playboy*, *Witness* and *Il Corriere dello Sport*. We couldn't afford *Playboy*.' She put a hand on his arm, almost proud, he thought. 'Very clever,' she said and kissed him. Over her shoulder Emily smiled.

'You must both meet Hudson,' he said, but seeing Hudson head to head with Ben Tarlo and surrounded by half a dozen well-wishers he introduced them to Penny and Jessica who were searching under the table for more wine.

'Don't tell them how well they've done or we'll never get paid,' Jessica laughed as she poured the drinks. She was a dark-haired, artistic girl from Philadelphia who genuinely liked giving. When the cry to help distribute *Witness* had gone out she had been the first to respond.

So the party drifted on, groups finding each other, merging and then subdividing to make other groups. It was a launch party for people launching themselves on the world. In one corner Willie Simmonds was stammering a rather blatant, and possibly illegal, proposition to one of the younger student helpers from the Lamborne who, deceptively mature in double-decker eyelashes, went almost white with shock before being rescued by Penny Chilston; by the table Ben Tarlo was discussing libel with Hudson's red-haired lady lawyer; while on the stairs Vasco, having cornered Sonia, was bleeding earnest romance into her ears. Britt-Marie, meanwhile, was efficiently helping Adam Smith file invoices in a corner of the advertising department, while Bill McGough was pleasing everyone by wandering through the crush taking photographs, something Tim Gimmelmann could never have been expected to do. Nicola and Emily stuck together and together they stuck to Richard, content to be a part of it all.

At last Hudson pushed his way through to Nicola and Emily. 'I'm sorry,' he said, 'I didn't see you arrive. You must be Nicola. How are you?' He put his hand out formally.

Nicola took it. Richard introduced Emily.

'Hi, Emily,' Hudson said, and smiled so warmly she dropped her eyes in surprise. 'I'm glad you could both make it. The support helps.' With that he was gone, shaking hands, thanking everyone, the busy host.

Two minutes later the party ended. 'Haven't you heard?' gasped one of the Lamborne helpers as he rushed up the stairs. 'Kennedy's been assassinated.'

The news blew across London, across the world, like a cold breeze. Someone said they knew a pub with a television and everyone rushed to find it, *Witness* forgotten. They were wrong and the group moved on through streets filled with fleeting shadows. 'Is it true?' people murmured. 'Is it really true?' Then there in the corner of a public bar, a place muted in shock, was the bleak face of the BBC telling and retelling the story of the shots, the grassy knoll, the secret serviceman who had jumped on to the moving limousine, Jackie in her pink suit and hat, the Texas Book Depository, the race to the hospital, Governor Connally's injuries and those crazy Texans and their guns. No one said very much: Ben Tarlo soon led Jessica home to telephone her mother in Philadelphia while two girls from Chicago sat sobbing quietly together in a corner by a coat-stand, holding on to each other in reassurance. At one point Richard noticed Hudson quietly murmuring to them, reassuring and sharing, before patting their heads, the healing touch. Then quietly he bought more drinks. At the back of the bar Nicola stood with her hand on Richard's arm, sharing the moment.

(iii)

Emily went back to Hayward Mews the following morning. Only Hudson was there, sitting on the trestle-table surrounded by the remains of the party, a copy of every morning newspaper spread out around him. Afraid to break into his isolation she watched in silence, embarrassed to be there.

They had stayed in the pub until closing time and then, because no one knew what to do, a group had followed a middle-aged woman, whose name no one ever caught, and who was, for some reason, wearing a black trilby, back to her flat. There they had again turned to the television while she had provided coffee. Only then had Emily realized that Hudson had not been amongst them, and she had wondered with which of the pretty girls she had seen around him he would spend the night. At one o'clock after everyone had said again how shocked they were, and wondered who on earth Lee Harvey Oswald

188

might be, the inquest had broken up and everyone had gone home.

'I'm sorry. I didn't see you there.' Hudson was looking at her, rising from the trestle-table.

'I . . . I was looking for Nicola.' Emily felt like a trespasser.

'Oh yes . . .'

That seemed to place her for him. He smiled. He was, she was certain, quite the most handsome man she had ever seen. Everything was perfect: the proportions, though he was tall, the style, the dignity. At a time when the boys she knew were growing their hair long and combing it forward in a fringe, or, in the case of the American boys at Oxford, growing beards, Hudson had one of those high side partings, a James Stewart haircut which acknowledged no fashion. He had grace. The previous night as a publisher he had worn a tweed jacket and tie: now he was in his jeans and a navy-blue sweater over a blue shirt. It was, she thought, like being in the presence of a film star and it made her nervous. She indicated the spread of newspapers and the screaming headlines: 'Seeing it in print . . . somehow it makes it more real.'

'It's a good day for newspapers all right,' Hudson said, then added: 'I'm sorry. Does that sound callous?'

'A bit.'

He nodded. 'I think so, too. Look, why don't we get some coffee around the corner? We can leave a note for the others.' Again the smile.

They went up the road to Notting Hill Gate where they found an Italian coffee bar with rubber plants and a juke box which, according to a hand-written sign, had been switched off, 'out of respect for President Kennedy'. She told him about herself, about her family and about Nicola. He was easy to talk to because he was such a good listener, inquisitive about how her family worked, amused by her stories of her guitar-playing little brother ('I always wished I had a brother or sister. It can be lonely

189

being an only child'), and sympathetic as she told him of her father's illness.

'And what about your family?' she asked. 'Are they Democrats? Will they be terribly upset over Kennedy?'

'My mother will be,' he said. 'They're dyed-in-the-wool Republicans from way back but she's always liked the way Kennedy looked. My father threatened to divorce her and cut her out of his will when she didn't vote for Richard Nixon. But she holds 50 per cent equity in the business so I don't think that worried her too much. I guess Dad will be sitting in front of the TV today, shaking his head and blaming the unions or the communists or both.'

'Did you speak to them?'

He shook his head. 'I tried to get through last night, but the international lines were all busy. I'll try later today. Seems like that's the thing to do. They're pretty old now, married for forty-five years. I always had the oldest parents in high school.'

'Forty-five years?'

He laughed. 'Sometimes I think I might have been a mistake. At best an afterthought.'

Richard and Nicola found them at ten-thirty, flushed and indignant, Nicola sliding into the bench seat alongside Emily as Richard got the coffees. 'Have we been up before God this morning, Emmy old girl,' Nicola said, eyes full of mischief.

'What's happened?'

'An Irish landlady called O'Casey, that's what. I'm a hussy, she said, which, I suppose, hasn't always been entirely untrue. She caught me creeping out of Richard's room this morning, knickers in pocket, so to speak, and refused to believe that I was his aunt from Epsom. The third degree it was, a lower second at the very best. Thumbscrews, the rack. Did you or did you not share a bed with the accused on the night of the assassination of President Kennedy? Can you believe it? I think she blamed us. Anyway Richard's been kicked out on to the street and

190

told to "go and fornicate somewhere else if fornicate he must".'

'And he must, he must . . .' Richard whispered from the counter.

'Crumbs,' said Emily. 'How embarrassing.'

'It was for her,' smiled Nicola. 'We could hardly keep our faces straight.'

Richard joined them with the coffees and sat down next to Hudson. 'She's a wonderful woman but I don't think Miss O'Casey is quite in tune with the times. I have a week to find a new home.'

'I'll be eternally guilty if they find you frozen to a park bench one morning,' Nicola said, cupping his hand in hers.

'And I'll be eternally cold.'

Hudson chuckled. 'What do you say we find ourselves an apartment together?'

For just a fraction of a second Emily thought she detected a hesitation before Richard grinned and said: 'Sounds like a great idea to me.'

It was the first time they had all been together: the four of them. For a while the conversation meandered, Richard wondering whether Aldous Huxley and John F. Kennedy had shared a fiery chariot to the Pearly Gates, since Huxley had also died on the previous day. But soon the talk returned to the shots, the swearing in of Lyndon Johnson on board the presidential jet, and Jackie in her bloodstained suit at his side.

'The thing that gets me,' said Hudson, 'is how sad everybody is. I mean, let's face it, none of us knew him, but everyone's going around feeling as though they've lost a best friend.'

'That was the way he was perceived,' said Richard.

'That was the way he was *sold*,' said Hudson. 'And we bought it. All of us. Maybe it was true, maybe he was a young knight on a white charger who was going out there to overcome the forces of darkness and prejudice. But maybe . . .' He stopped.

'Yes?'

'Well, I don't know, but maybe he was just one hell of a self-publicist who knew how to handle the newspapers and came across well on the seven o'clock TV news.'

'Does it matter, if there was some truth in what he stood for?'

'It might. Who knows what truth is? As sure as hell truth isn't news. News is just one interpretation of history. Control news and you control history. What about that? Isn't that an incredible thought?'

'Is that your philosophy?' asked Nicola.

Hudson laughed. 'Hell, I don't know. There are worse ones, I guess. Anyway, I've got to control our distribution people. I'll see you later, OK?' And getting up he went across to the bar, paid for the coffees, although they asked him not to, and left.

Although she knew Nicola was watching, Emily could not resist watching him go.

'Well, well, Emily Robinson,' Nicola murmured as the door closed.

Emily blushed.

(*iv*)

Richard had realized the moment he heard the news that the first edition of *Witness* could not have been published at a worse moment. The only magazines which would sell in the following week were those with a Kennedy on the cover.

'With the possible exception of the outbreak of the Second World War we probably chose the worst day in the twentieth century to launch,' he told Hudson later that Saturday afternoon, when the first of the student reps began to arrive back with their unplaced stacks of *Witness*. Nicola and Emily had both returned to Oxford and the boys were sitting on Hudson's desk surrounded by mountains of magazines.

192

Hudson nodded slowly. 'Yes. I see that. If we had the resources we'd be able to do a special Kennedy souvenir edition, get it out by Monday and clean up, wouldn't we? That's what everybody else will do.'

From the financial point of view he was right, but it would have been wrong for *Witness*. As editor Richard simply frowned.

Hudson laughed. 'Don't worry. I'm not suggesting we do anything like that. Not yet, anyway. And not with *Witness*.' Then, clapping Richard on the back, he said: 'Anyway, how are we doing for the next edition? We'll have to be twice as good next time.'

It was an aspect of Hudson that Richard would see again. The next project was always more exciting than the current one.

'We'll be going on Nicola's extended piece on the lyrics of Lennon and McCartney.'

Hudson's eyes lit up. 'The Beatles! That's better! Now you're talking, fella.'

Chapter Twenty-One

Gimmelmann watched as Dolly gazed, mesmerized by the cover. It had been difficult to find *Witness* in their neighbourhood but he had eventually found some in Hampstead, buying the newsagent's entire stock of six copies. Now Dolly was staring at herself as a very young or savage child might look into a mirror, examining the contours of her face, pouting her lips to copy the expression on the photograph.

'Too fat,' she said finally, very quietly to herself. 'Too bloody fat.'

Gimmelmann did not reply. Too fat, that was what all models said. But she wasn't too fat. She was perfect, not a rangy clothes-horse like the girls in *Vogue*, but a cheeky, voluptuous, wide-chested, sulky street kid with a tiny nose and big, brazen eyes. She had looked pretty and interesting in her pancaked make-up and tart's tat. Now, in her new clothes, she was stunning: a nothing person from a waste land whom nature had endowed with the most valuable of modern beauties: the camera loved her.

It was two weeks since the attack and Dolly and Gimmelmann had been together throughout, apart from her occasional excursions in the late afternoons after which she would return with pocket money, cigarettes and some new item of clothing. She had made little effort to take care of him when, too hurt to stand, he had lain on the mattress for three days eating only the canned tomato soup she had reluctantly prepared. But, though she was probably risking the renewed violence of her father, she had stayed.

Gradually Gimmelmann had recovered from the beating: the bruises around his face and body had faded to mauve and yellow stains, the stiffness in his shoulders had loosened and his testicles, though still tender and blue, were no longer swollen. He would have liked to have been present at the *Witness* launch party: Hudson himself had telephoned inviting him, but he did not want to be seen while his pretty face wore the traces of pummel marks. So instead he had stayed at home, read, with no particular feeling, of the murder of Kennedy, and dreamed revenge.

They were short, bleak November days, made even shorter by the gloom of the basement flat, days which matched his mood and which ran into each other as Dolly watched him with cool indifference. Before the attack there had been sex, lots of it, frightening, addictive rituals of desire when the scents and juices of the body intoxicated; games of dark communion played out in the blackness of the night. She tantalized him, stretching and twisting every sensual fibre of his body. But there was no affection. They needed each other. With her he saw a future, a dim, unshaped outline of possibility. He was, he knew, her road into the world, her route away from the squalor of the scrubland. But he could use her ambition to match his own.

Surprisingly, because he prided himself on his street wisdom, it had not occurred to him when they first met that she might have been selling herself, the furtive encounter in the parked car, the hurried ecstasy in the caravan. And when finally he realized where the new clothes came from he discovered something about himself. Lying on his mattress in the afternoons, listening to the traffic outside on the street and waiting for her to return, he would imagine her, teasing and flirting, a child-bride for fifteen minutes and ten pounds, and his body would grow tense with excitement.

Across the room Dolly was now carefully detaching the cover from the rest of the magazine. Climbing off his mattress Gimmelmann went to the top drawer of his dresser and took out a file. Inside were over a dozen large black-and-white photographs of Dolly in various street situations. He examined them one by one. Then dropping them back into the file he took his jacket off the nail behind the door. 'Come on,' he said. 'Let's get your hair cut.'

The wild young animal disappeared with the tangled hair as geometry set about re-creating Dolly in the shape of the moment, long at the sides, sculpted up the neck at the back. 'Who on earth cut this last then?' Terry, the muscular young hairdresser demanded witheringly as, T-shirted and arms bare, he strode around Dolly examining and measuring.

'Me mum,' Dolly spat back, nervous in the back room of the Mount Street salon.

'Well, she might be a wonderful mother,' the hairdresser joked, 'but a haircutter she isn't.'

'She's a cow,' Dolly replied, snatching her head away angrily.

Confused, the hairdresser looked towards Gimmelmann. 'You sure she wants her hair cutting?' he asked.

Gimmelmann nodded, and scowled at Dolly in the mirror. 'Do whatever you think is right, Terry. You're the expert.'

Sniffing to himself the hairdresser again picked up some loose strands of Dolly's hair, every piece a different length, different colour or texture as the home-applied perms and rinses had grown out. 'Well, don't expect miracles, all right?'

For Dolly to be even sitting in this place was a testimony to Gimmelmann's own cheek and connections. He had known Terry from playing Sunday morning football years earlier at Finsbury Park and had seen him on a couple of occasions watching Arsenal at Highbury. The North London old boy network was at work: in return for the haircut Gimmelmann had promised to take portrait photographs of Terry's models, the girls from the surrounding offices who allowed him to experiment with new styles on their hair. Gimmelmann looked around the marble emporium: it smelled rich. If those toffee-noses at *Witness* could see him now. London, his London, where back-street boys understood the currency of favour, was beginning to run for him, too.

It took two hours before Terry was satisfied: two hours to re-create Dolly Carter. At first he had set about his work reluctantly, but as the shape had begun to emerge and Dolly's scowl had dissolved through suspicion into appreciation, he had obviously felt the excitement of the occasion, the scissors shining, quicksilver sharp in his fingers. 'Nice, nice, very nice . . .' he muttered to himself as athletically he waltzed around the chair, examining Dolly from all angles. 'But do me a favour, will you? Don't try any more of those cheap rinses. You want hair a different colour you come and tell me, we'll talk about it and we'll do the job properly. Likewise the perm. Your hair looked like something the cat had killed when you came in here.'

Dolly stood up and pulled back the sheet from her neck, allowing the cut hair to fall around her feet. She looked quite different. Gone was the sensual adolescent: in its place was a startlingly attractive young woman, her eyes seeming bigger now, her cheek-bones firmer. Gimmelmann wished he had brought his camera to have captured the transformation.

For the second time that day Dolly examined herself. Hanging her head down and then throwing it back to see how her perfectly weighted hair hung from her head.

'All right, Tim?' the hairdresser asked, obviously pleased with himself.

'Not bad,' Gimmelmann muttered admiringly.

For the first time Dolly smiled. 'I've never had my hair cut before,' she said. 'Not professional like. Me mum always did it. It's lovely.' Then quite coolly she gave the hairdresser a long slow look, her hand catching his on the side of the chair against which he was leaning.

Embarrassed in front of Gimmelmann the hairdresser

stepped back. 'That's all right, Holly . . . Dolly . . . Sorry, Dolly.' In his awkwardness he had confused her name.

'Dolly,' said Gimmelmann flatly.

'Oh, I don't know,' Dolly said, still smiling at the hairdresser. 'Holly . . . That's a nice name, isn't it? What do you think, Tim? Holly . . . Holly Carter. Thanks, Terry.' Another smile. 'Holly Carter.'

Five minutes later Gimmelmann pulled the newly named Holly Carter into the dark doorway of a solicitor's office on Mount Street, his hand at her neck. 'Listen you little slag, don't ever, don't you ever start coming on to a bleeding hairdresser. All right?' And before she could answer he turned his fist around and struck her hard across one side of the head and then the other, catching her behind the back of both ears, somewhere it would never show. Holly Carter took the blows in silence. As Dolly Carter she had grown used to being beaten.

Inside Gimmelmann glowed: it was the first time he had hit a woman and he had enjoyed it.

Chapter Twenty-Two

(i)

As always Christmas came early to Oxford with end of term drinks almost before December was decently launched, carol services for those so inclined, parties for everybody else and everywhere that year black polo-neck sweaters and the second Beatles' album. When Emily and Nicola had first gone up just two years earlier traditional jazz had been the accepted form of popular music, middle-aged sounds borrowed from parents by a middle-aged youth. The Beatles had blown that away for ever, a short head in front of the Rolling Stones. Oxford was growing younger, too.

For Emily and Nicola in South Park Road life in those last weeks of term went into a prolonged canter: there was work, an Oxford Christmas social life and, for Nicola, London, Richard and *Witness*. Filling the Morris Minor with bundles of the first edition, she had scored minor victories as a distributor at Blackwell's and Parker's who took twelve copies each, found mixed fortune at Balliol and Brasenose where she attempted to recruit former and would-be boy-friends as salesmen, and came a complete cropper at the all-girls' colleges where she was not best liked. As a saleswoman Nicola had the sunny persistence of the door-stepping God peddler, always carrying a half-dozen copies around in her duffel bag that she might convert the benighted. And not wishing to appear disloyal Emily also carried with her a couple of spare copies, though she never had the heart actually to ask anyone to pay for one.

'In a world divided into buyers and sellers, Emily

199

Robinson . . .' Nicola scolded one lunchtime, 'you're absolutely too polite for your own good.'

'I like to think so,' Emily conceded happily.

It was a sudden mild day, almost warm, and the weather had tempted them out to loiter along the banks of the Cherwell, where the river, swollen with recent rain, was muddied and brown. Whenever possible Nicola liked to be outside for at least some time during the day.

On that particular day she had news from Richard. Although sales had been 'dismal to appalling', opinion had been very complimentary. The biggest surprise had been reaction to the cover, with calls from the picture desk of the *Daily Mirror* and another from a freelance photographer asking where they might find the gypsy cover girl. The big news, though, was that Richard and Hudson had moved into their new flat.

Emily liked to hear about Hudson, although she denied it. 'He's not my sort,' she would insist. 'Chaps like him should be off with cool blondes like Carol Lynley or that tall Swiss girl from St Clare's who's always sitting by the door in the Kemp.'

'Ursula, you mean.'

'Is that her name?'

'That's what they call her. Ursula Undress, because apparently she does at the drop of a title.'

'Yes then, Ursula . . . she's Hudson's sort, I should imagine.'

'He likes you. Richard told me.'

'Nonsense.' Emily didn't want to hear. All this talk about who fancied who was too silly, like Beatles' song lyrics, the stuff of day-dreams. And besides, Hudson was just too attractive to be seriously contemplated.

They sauntered on through a grove of loosely curtaining willows. At a bend in the river there was a wide, deep puddle to be negotiated, and, stepping back, Emily tried to stride to a firmer stretch of path. Neither of them had heard or seen the solitary runner until he was upon them, colliding with Emily and ending up standing ankle deep in water.

'Oh, I'm terribly sorry,' Emily said, hopping to dry land. Nicola was trying to hide a smile.

'For Christ's sake, you stupid cow, can't you look where you're going?' The runner was a man in his early twenties, a chinless, thin fellow, who was now absolutely livid as the muddy water ran down his legs and soaked his socks and running shoes. He looked like a man who took his running seriously.

'I really am terribly sorry . . .'

'Bloody, stupid, brainless . . .' The runner waded out of the water muttering under his breath.

Emily was embarrassed. It had been an honest mistake. There was no reason to make such a fuss. She put an arm out to help him, but he pushed her away. Now she noticed that Nicola was no longer smiling.

The boy stepped out of the puddle and began to take off his running shoes, still grumbling to himself.

Nicola stepped towards him. 'I suggest you apologize to my friend,' she said quietly.

'Get stuffed!'

Nicola stared at him.

'Let's go. It was an accident,' Emily said, turning away.

Nicola stood her ground. 'You bloody apologize to Emmy, you bastard.' She was standing in his way. She had gone quite white.

The runner tried to go past her, but she moved to prevent him, sending him crashing back into the puddle. 'Christ!' he swore.

Nicola blocked his way out of the water. 'You heard me, apologize. Come on . . . apologize. Bloody apologize. Bastard!'

The whole incident was out of control. Nicola was baiting him now, kicking water, her face contorted with anger. He watched her, half-astonished, half-afraid, unable to comprehend how he had become involved in this situation.

'Bloody apologize to Emmy!' Nicola screamed, so loud that other students on the path turned to see what the row was about.

'It's all right. Really it is . . .' Emily just wanted to get away.

Nicola did not move. Her reaction had been out of all proportion to the runner's miserable insults. It was a temper Emily had rarely seen, and all the more disturbing because of that.

The runner looked around. 'It's all right. Keep your hair on. I'm sorry. All right?' He looked worried. There was something unstable about Nicola's fury.

'You'd better be.' Nicola stared at him, and then deliberately kicking water into his shorts and shirt she grabbed hold of Emily, and, throwing her arm around her, marched her back towards the High.

'Was that really necessary?' Emily asked as they left the confused runner staring after them. 'I mean it was my mistake in the first place.'

'Yes, it was necessary,' Nicola said. 'No one is allowed to talk to you like that, Emmy. No one. Ever.'

They walked on. Sometimes Nicola's affection, her possessiveness, could be almost violent.

(*ii*)

Hudson had found the flat, a high-ceilinged, ground-floor place in Chepstow Villas which did not appear to have been decorated since the war. There were two small, cell-like bedrooms where a larger room had been divided, a bathroom, a kitchen and a large sitting room with an open fireplace, the marble of which had at some time been painted cream to match the walls. The furniture was minimal, cheap and old. 'Isn't it terrific?' Hudson had said. 'You choose which bedroom you want. I'll take the other. There's so much potential. By Christmas we'll be living in a palace.'

That was never likely, but eight gallon tins of Dulux

202

white emulsion later the place looked fresh and new; white walls upon which to write the beginnings of new lives. Together they decorated deep into the night, Hudson rolling paint across the ceiling with a wide distemper brush, his long legs balancing precariously on step-ladders hired from a do-it-yourself shop; while below Richard splashed away at the walls.

'What kind of Christmas did you have in California?' Richard asked at one point. He had been telling Hudson that his mother was insisting Hudson join them for Christmas Day in Wimbledon, an invitation which, to his surprise, Hudson instantly accepted.

'Oh well, quiet, I guess. Church, carols, stuff like that. *The Wizard of Oz* or maybe *It's A Wonderful Life* on TV. Turkey . . . Mother in the kitchen all morning. The same as everywhere. About a week before I'd help Dad put fairy lights on the tree out front. It was one of those tall pines. You could see it for miles. We were a regular tourist attraction. People would drive by just to see the Hudsons' lights.' He paused to add paint to his brush. 'You know, we should get a tree here . . . and lights.'

Richard was surprised. 'If you want to organize it.'

'It would make it cosy . . . festive . . .' Hudson left the sentence dangling as he stretched to reach a corner of the ceiling. 'This is my home now, I want it to look good, Richard. I'm here to stay. We're going to build an empire. What do you say to editing a national newspaper?'

Richard smiled but did not answer. It never seemed fair to allow reality to impinge upon Hudson's dreams. The unhappy launching had neither deterred him nor dented his enthusiasm.

Lessons had been learned, however, and the publication of the second edition went with absolute precision. Without delays from the printers the van was hired, filled and its contents distributed by six o'clock on the Thursday. Altogether it was a more professional, better-balanced magazine, with a greater emphasis on music and movies.

Nicola's piece on the Beatles' lyrics was given pride of place, not just because Richard was in love with her but because it was funny. It was headlined: *I Want To Hold Your Gland.*

With the second edition came a new tide of contributors. A girl called Beryl arrived straight from art school, offering to write about fashion and was welcomed despite her inability to spell, while a giant named Colin asked to find new ways of presenting sport. The following Monday Charles Latymer and Peter Berridge met on the narrow stairs. For reasons no one ever understood they hated each other on sight.

Latymer had arrived wearing a smart, double-vented suit, a good-looking, silver-tongued fellow who had been expensively educated and carried an umbrella with a shiny copper tip. Although no more than twenty-five, and indigant that he had been forced to spend two years in the Army, he already had a wash of grey in his hair. A snob to his toe-nails, he struck Richard as shrewd and ambitious, having already winkled interviews for the Cambridge student newspaper, *Varsity*, out of the two Harolds, Macmillan and Wilson. He wrote like a bricklayer, his words following each other as predictably as bricks in a wall, but he was already well connected in establishment terms.

Hudson was suspicious, judging him arrogant, vain, and, because he looked wan when the rates per thousand words were mentioned, greedy. 'What can he do for us?' he wanted to know.

'Open doors, I hope,' Richard replied. 'The least we can do is let him hang around the office and borrow his contact book now and again.'

Peter Berridge was altogether different. As thin as a whippet, his hair was already receding across a skull head and his fingernails were dirty. His suit looked as though it might have been second-hand, because although it was of an expensive cut in City navy-blue with the thinnest stripe, it was also two sizes too large. Physically most disturbing of all was his collection of jutting and crooked teeth. He had, he said, things to sell.

'We haven't any money to buy,' Richard replied honestly. 'We're all working for next to nothing at the moment. What have you got?'

Berridge looked around the office. 'Bits and pieces,' he said gnomically. 'Gossip.'

'So why don't you go to Fleet Street with it?'

'Because I want to make my name.' Berridge's teeth criss-crossed inside his skull.

That was why everyone went to *Witness*. It was the way in, the shop window. Again a place at the desk was offered. If Berridge could stand up his 'bits and pieces', *Witness* would print them.

Hudson took to Berridge straightaway. 'There's no pretence in the guy,' he would enthuse. 'He looks like Dr Death and that's exactly what he is. One hundred per cent bastard. Don't you think there's a kind of purity in that? I'll lay you any money you like that guy is totally incorruptible. Latymer you'll be able to buy and sell and maybe he'll be good for us and maybe he won't. But no money on earth will induce Berridge to do the decent thing.' Hudson could sometimes be quite perverse.

No sooner was the second edition on sale than the third and fourth were being planned. Suddenly the office was filled with reporters squabbling over telephones (no one ever knew how Hudson did it but in Christmas week he managed to get two new lines connected), and typing furiously at their portables. When they were there the newcomers Latymer and Berridge sniped at each other from opposite ends of the table, while fashion girl Beryl brought with her the names of new and outrageous designers and art-school nonchalance, despite Willie Simmonds' attentions as he hung around and stammered suggestions of a sexual nature.

Christmas 1963, and *Witness* was generating a momentum of its own as every day new faces emerged, fringed boy photographers offering pictures of the young and suddenly fashionable, working-class actors with flat accents, slumming debutantes, new fashions and new styles. Three years into the decade the Sixties had begun and *Witness* was watching.

(*iii*)

Penny Chilston was watching, too: everything he did, everything he said. Hudson obsessed her. As each day dawned his smile greeted her: his imaginary conversation accompanied her around her flat, on the Tube, on the streets. Vasco made love to her, but Hudson was her lover, even though he did not know it. In the office she would be quiet, getting on with her work, ready always for his kindly smile. Sometimes she would take him an apple or sandwich from home, worried that in putting all his money into *Witness* he did not get enough to eat. 'Thanks Penny,' he would murmur, an affectionate hand on her shoulder. Hudson's triumphs were hers. She could, she knew, have torn herself apart with jealousy for the girls who threw themselves at him, the red-haired lawyer, Britt-Marie, the bubbling blonde from the Chase Manhattan, and the others who came and went. But having relinquished any hope of ever sharing his bed she did not see the women in his life as rivals: not even as objects of envy. So she would watch as they came and went, friendly and helpful to them always, her face alight with a knowing smile. The man they slept with was not the Hudson of Penny's dreams. Those girls would never love Hudson the way she did. Confident in her love she was happy just to serve, to be close to him. And if Hudson was happy, Penny was happy, too, and would take a drink to celebrate her happiness. It was as simple as that. Big, plain, invincible girls like Penny took happiness where they could.

Chapter Twenty-Three

(i)

It was at the *Witness* Christmas dinner that Emily first encountered the chill of Holly Carter. Most of the guests had already sat down when Gimmelmann and Holly arrived, Gimmelmann obviously nervous. Perhaps it was a party likely to intimidate: the tall Christmas tree in the bay window, the old, sheet-covered decorator's table (especially transported from the office for this evening) buckling under the weight of food, the wine glasses glowing, the flames on red candles stuck into brass church candlesticks, and a fire which spat sparks from burning birch logs. At one end of the table Hudson, in a bow tie, like a proper American, stood carving crumbling slices of roast turkey: at the other Richard, in a new gingham shirt and waistcoat, served vegetables to the pretty girls of *Witness* with their long hair and loose, flowing dresses. Noticing Gimmelmann hovering by the door Emily's first thought was of how young and small he looked.

Hudson reacted first. 'Tim, where have you been hiding? How are you? We've been waiting for you. Come in, come in. Merry Christmas.'

Gimmelmann blinked around the table, nodding greetings to Richard and Penny. Then, as he stepped to one side, a shadow moved into the light. Framed in the doorway, a twig of mistletoe Sellotaped directly above her head, stood the first *Witness* cover girl, her hair now precision shaped, her eyes ringed with black. Wearing a deep burgundy smock, with lace at the cuffs and the collar, puffed at the shoulders and

207

chopped at the knee, she looked, thought Emily, like something from a different world. She was stunning, and the effect was immediate. Every person in the room fell silent, unnerved, as though a shadow had fallen across them. At last a plump, debby girl, who had arrived with Peter Berridge, giggled nervously and then pretended to cough into the holly motif of her paper napkin. Further down the table fashion editor Beryl murmured in nervous admiration: 'Oh yes. Yes.' At the top of the table Hudson was caught as if in a frozen frame, the fork and carving knife suspended over the turkey.

'I don't think most of you have met Holly, have you?' Gimmelmann said quietly.

'*Holly*?' Richard said, his voice trailing away in surprise.

'Holly Carter,' repeated Gimmelmann, staring Richard down. 'Holly.'

As though enjoying the eyes of the room Holly simply stood in the doorway, backlit from the hall, the light from the candles playing on her face: a street urchin in a little girl's dress. She looked at Richard. 'Hello again,' she said and, before he could answer, stepped forward into the room.

Immediately there was a shuffling of chairs and moving of plates and glasses as space was found to accommodate the two latecomers, a gap for Holly appearing between Ben and Willie.

'I h..ope you d..on't mind my say..ing, b..ut I think I'm in l..ove with you,' said Willie as Holly sat down. The Indian girl in a blue sari who was Willie's escort for the evening laughed. Willie's girls expected this kind of behaviour.

'Tim said he'd make a salad with my tits if I so much as look at another fella tonight,' Holly said, her eyes heavy.

Willie guffawed, not at all put out. 'How very in..ventive of him,' he said. 'I do hope he s..erves them with an indecent dress..ing.'

What a time, what a Christmas. All day Emily and Nicola had been either shopping or cooking, discovering how to stretch a little a long way. Based at Emily's parents' house in Kensington, they had foraged along Kensington High Street seeking bargain groceries, requisitioned her mother's kitchen in order that at least the turkey might be properly cooked, appropriated her second-best silver, then transported a meal for fourteen in trays and tinfoil by Morris Minor up to Chepstow Villas, where a stone-age oven would just about keep it warm until eight.

All day Richard and Hudson had been dressing the flat with tinsel, holly, mistletoe and streamers. Hudson wanted it to be an old-fashioned, traditional Christmas, 'just like home', and alone had carried a twelve-foot Christmas tree the mile and a half on foot from Earl's Court. Now fairy lights shone from top to bottom, with a cut-out picture of Dolly, now Holly, Carter on the top, while on every branch were presents from Hudson to each one of the guests. When Emily discovered this she felt guilty. So far as she knew no one had thought to buy him anything.

'I must say for an adolescent Venus fly-trap she's got tons of style,' Nicola said as, elbow to elbow, she and Emily stacked the plates in the tiny kitchen.

'She looks quite different from the cover photograph. Prettier. Her hair's amazing.'

Nicola nodded. 'Cut by set square and compass, I'd say.'

'Quite sweet really . . .'

'Oh, very sweet . . .' repeated Nicola.

'You don't mean that.'

'Neither do you. Sweet, she isn't. Disquieting, she may be, or even disturbing. But to describe her as sweet would be stretching it a bit, I think.'

There was a moment's silence before they both broke up giggling. 'God, what bitches! She's only a child,' Emily laughed.

'Of course she is. And I'm a blue-bottomed baboon with a penchant for bananas and tinned pilchards. Mark my word, Emily Robinson, that little girl is no one's child and is going to be deep trouble for some poor sod.'

It was the first time Emily had seen Nicola take such an instant aversion to another woman. 'Probably for Tim Gimmelmann,' she said. Gimmelmann hadn't uttered a word during dinner.

Nicola nodded. 'The poor thing looks terrified, doesn't he . . . "like a kaffir at a garden party", as my appallingly racist uncle likes to say. Did I tell you I got his Christmas card this morning and twenty Rhodesian pounds "to buy myself something"? Twenty pounds! The Reynolds certainly didn't get rich by chucking their money around. He's thrilled to pieces because of this hairy-backed Ian Smith cowboy who's promising he'll turn the clock back half a century if they vote for him. God knows what will happen if they do.'

'Don't you ever get drunk?' asked Emily. The candles and the fire had burned right down leaving the room in a deep glow. It was one-thirty in the morning, half the guests had left and Emily and Hudson were sitting together on the sofa.

Hudson shook his head. 'Not if I can avoid it. If I'm drunk I might make a mistake, and I can't afford that.'

It was a hint of vulnerability Emily had never seen before. Perhaps he was slightly drunk. 'What kind of mistake?' she asked.

Hudson had something specific in mind, she was sure, but he just shook his head. 'Have you had a good time, Emily?' he asked. 'Have you? This is going to be the best Christmas I've ever had.'

He had such a beautiful face she wanted to reach across and kiss him, but she didn't. Instead she put her hand on his and said: 'I'm having a lovely time and it's a terrific party.'

He smiled at her. 'Before I met you Richard once told me that you had a face like a Modigliani painting. I didn't know what he meant so I looked in an art history book in Foyles one day and now I know. But he's wrong. All the Modigliani women I found looked sad. Maybe Modigliani gave them a hard time, I don't know. But I've never seen you looking sad, Emily. You've never looked anything but beautiful and kind.'

And then quite unexpectedly he leaned behind her, found a sprig of mistletoe and imprinted a kiss delicately on her cheek. With any other man Emily would have considered this an opening gambit in a game of seduction, two people after a party looking for consolation in one another. But this was different: honest affection. She dared not hope for more.

In front of them three couples moved together in the space left when the trestle-table had been folded away, a pink balloon floating haphazardly at the feet of Ben Tarlo and Jessica. Beryl was limpet-stuck, groin to groin, with Colin from Sports, an unlikely coupling made out of desperation, while by the window Richard and Nicola rocked gently together, occasionally murmuring to each other, amused and happy. In a far corner Penny Chilston sat watching as always, Vasco asleep, his head in her lap: the residue of the first *Witness* Christmas party. Fondly Hudson put an arm around Emily's shoulder. She relaxed against him.

(*ii*)

Willie Simmonds' Indian girl-friend Sarojine gave Tim Gimmelmann and Holly a lift home to Kentish Town in her Ford Anglia. Willie sat in the front passenger seat, his hand inside Sarojine's sari, his head turned to the back throughout the entire journey as though he were afraid that Holly might disappear if he allowed himself to be distracted.

'What you really n..eed, Holly, is an a..gent,' Willie

stammered as the car turned north at Regent's Park.

'I don't think so. Not yet,' Gimmelmann said. 'What would be useful would be an introduction to some of the fashion editors, people at *Vogue* and *Queen*.'

'That shoul..dn't be too diffi..cult. Why don't I m..ake a few ph..one calls and s..ee if I can't help y..ou a li..ttle bit?'

Gimmelmann smiled. 'Would you mind, Willie? That would be really nice of you, really nice. Wouldn't it, Holly?'

'Very kind.' She looked at Willie, her lips slightly apart.

A few minutes later the car drew up and Gimmelmann and Holly climbed out, Holly's skirt riding up as she clambered through the open door, giving Willie a full, free moment's glimpse of upper thigh and black knicker.

As the car drove away Holly's smile faded. All evening she had appeared happy, chatting easily with the fashion girls, flirting with the boys. But now that they were alone the indifference returned. They went down the steps and let themselves into the flat. With his mind still full of the cosy, busy warmth of Chepstow Villas, Gimmelmann saw the reality of his own home for the first time. It was as bleak as a prison, a dirty cream cell. There was no relief, nothing beautiful, nothing interesting. No warmth. Chepstow Villas had been a poor person's flat, too, but there had been books, Hudson's records, Richard's *Private Eye* collection, posters stuck to walls, a red sheet thrown over a lamp to make the room more intimate. Gimmelmann's flat had no personality.

'Aren't you gonna see what he gave us then?' Holly asked, taking Hudson's gift from Gimmelmann's pocket.

'He said to wait until Christmas Day.'

'Jesus Christ,' she snorted, 'you're pathetic!' And tearing open the festive wrapping paper she pulled out a small book of photographs, *The Romance of the Romany*. It wasn't expensive, but had obviously been carefully chosen. Holly looked at it with disdain.

'Christ, more bleeding caravans,' she said, and tossed the gift to one side.

Later, when she was sleeping, her body curled up in her customary, defensive, angry knot, Gimmelmann climbed from the mattress, rewrapped the book and slipped it away into the bottom drawer of his dresser. Hudson's present to him would not be opened until Christmas Day.

(iii)

The party was over, with just the four of them left. Best friends. Hudson with Emily, Richard and Nicola. Richard closed his eyes, Nicola's face pressed into his shoulder, her creamy hair against his face, her body locked into his. He was glad that Hudson had found Emily. There had been so many girls in the few months he had known him. Girls who came to the flat late at night and departed early in the morning, who telephoned and left hopeful messages, who sought him out at *Witness* and offered to work for nothing and in any capacity. Hudson, the best friend he had ever had and still a mystery to him. There had not been one Christmas card from America for him. Nothing from his parents. 'I guess they're still mad because I didn't go home,' Hudson had murmured vaguely, as he turned on the fairy lights on the Christmas tree, his face creasing in the homely pleasure of it all.

Nicola moved her lips along Richard's neck and nuzzled his ear lobe delicately. Quietly they slipped from the room. Hudson and Emily danced on.

The first time they had made love the passion of the moment had sponsored and driven them in a race to speedy fulfilment. Now in the security of friendship they were two lovers absorbed in giving, their senses stretched, the musk of their interlocked bodies intoxicating their dreams. 'I love you, Nicola Reynolds,' he murmured as his passion bled into her. Beneath him in the dark of the pillow he could feel the shape of her face breaking into a smile.

213

They slept a little and then awoke and found each other again. Twenty and all of life to come. Let me remember this moment, Richard thought, as he lay in her: this perfect shelter of my sheets, this boat made by my pillows, the sanctity of this night when everything was perfect.

At four o'clock they emerged from the bedroom, Nicola holding his hand, Richard slightly abashed. There was no sign of Emily or Hudson. The fire had died and the Dansette had been switched off. 'Well!!!' said Nicola, her eyes wide with approval. She was wrong. The door to Hudson's bedroom, where earlier the coats had been stored, lay open. The bed had not been slept in. Nicola sighed and shook her head. 'Oh, Emily, what are we to do with you?'

(iv)

The walk home had revived them both, the frost on the air turning their breath white, their cheeks and noses pink. All the way Hudson, his arm around her, had talked excitedly of his plans, now sounding more American than ever. Outside Emily's parents' tall, narrow Victorian house he had kissed her, a moment's embrace, and had then strode away up the hill again, erect as a guardsman, hurrying off to get on with his life.

In her room she looked at his present, turning it over in her hands, examining his small, neat handwriting.

In her bed she heard her father's cough from her parents' bedroom on the floor below. Would he approve of Hudson? she wondered.

They met late the following afternoon as they had agreed. It was raining and he suggested the cinema. She wanted to impress and mentioned that she had never seen *Rocco and His Brothers*, which had come out a couple of years earlier and which was enjoying

214

a revival in Charing Cross Road. It was Christmas Eve. Nicola had gone down to Wimbledon with Richard for the evening. She would be back at midnight. Tomorrow it would be Hudson's turn.

The film was rather longer than she had expected and Hudson's concentration shorter and he snoozed through much of it. Out in the street afterwards they wandered around the corner into Leicester Square to see the Christmas lights. A choir of families, wrapped in woolly hats, overcoats and scarves, were singing carols by a crib. Emily wanted to join in but with Hudson alongside she was too shy. They each put money into a tin and moved on. A drunk approached to wish them a happy Christmas and Hudson gave him a pound note.

'Can you afford so much?' Emily asked. Even the drunk had been surprised by the size of the gift.

Hudson fixed her with such a smile that she instantly regretted the question. 'Probably not,' he said, 'but it is Christmas,' and taking her hand he led her into the Chicken Inn.

They arrived back at Chepstow Villas just before nine, shivering from the cold. In Hudson's Brooks Brothers coat pocket was a bottle of claret bought from an off-licence in the Bayswater Road. Emily sat in her coat while Hudson lit the fire. She was surprised at how tidy the flat was again. When she had left in the early hours of the morning the floor had been littered with cracker paper, decorations, bottles and glasses, and the kitchen crammed with dirty dishes. Now neatly piled on a sideboard were her mother's borrowed cooking trays, cutlery and plates. On top was a small gift wrapped in paper and an envelope.

'Just a little thank you for your mother,' Hudson said, indicating the gift. 'She doesn't need any of these things tonight, does she?'

Emily shook her head. Her mother had a kitchen full of plates.

Taking two glasses from the sideboard Hudson opened

the wine. He was careful in everything he did and very polite. He passed her one, then sank down at her side. A redundant copy of the first issue of *Witness* had been screwed up and used as a firelighter. Other copies stood in a small pile along with a carton of broken branches and twigs which he and Richard had carried home from Holland Park. The damp wood hissed steam. For a long moment they were silent while they sipped their wine and watched the yellow blades of fire cutting into the logs.

'I'm glad you came out with me tonight, Emily,' Hudson said at last. 'It's nice that we can spend Christmas Eve together like this.'

'I think so,' Emily said.

'It's like . . . family, being with you.'

'Family?' Hudson was not remotely like anyone in Emily's family.

He shrugged. 'I mean, it feels right. The four of us. We all get on so well. Like family. Richard and Nicola. He's crazy about her, you know.'

'I think she's pretty smitten, too.'

'She should be. He's a terrific guy. Dedicated. I knew as soon as I met him he was one person I was going to get along with. I've never known anyone work so hard.'

'What about Nicola? Is she right for him?' Emily had never seen Hudson show the usual interest in Nicola.

'Oh yes, of course. I think so. Don't you? To be honest I hardly know her. She's bright, and she's pretty . . .'

'She's beautiful.'

'So are you.'

'No.' Emily knew that she was attractive. Pretty girls always know that. But she had never regarded herself as beautiful.

'Oh yes you are. And you're surrounded by an aura of tranquillity. You make me comfortable just to be with you.'

Emily did not answer. The fire was struggling to stay alight so Hudson leaned across and threw on a

216

fresh ball of paper. Slowly the smoke increased before, with a tiny explosion, flames burst from beneath the screwed-up paper, gently unfolding it and smoothing out the creases as it burned. It was the front cover of that first edition of *Witness*. For a moment the girl who had been Dolly Carter stared out at them, before the flames licked upwards and consumed her.

Hers had been the generation of petting. So far but no further, panted breaths and sweated cotton in the warm, long grass of summer, and tugs and tussles on squeaking beds in gabled Oxford rooms. The everything-but generation. If there was any virtue in Emily's behaviour, and she had long doubted it, it had nothing to do with a sense of morality. If she had repelled all boarders it was only because none of them had ever been quite persuasive enough.

Surprisingly Hudson was nervous. Sitting on the carpet by the fire they had kissed and held each other and forgotten the wine. And presently, because she no longer wanted to wait for this new part of her life to begin, Emily had taken Hudson's hand and led him through to his bedroom. Words had been unnecessary. He had kissed her and she had tasted the red wine on his lips. It was cold in the bedroom and she had shivered and kneeling down he had plugged in a small electric fire. Then, as she had stood before him, he had sat on the edge of the bed and undressed her. She had begun to help, undoing a button of her blouse, but his hands had gone to hers. 'Let me,' he had said. Quickly the layers and outer skins had fallen around her feet or been tossed on to the bedside chair as she had watched the changing shape of her silhouette on the wall. In the darkness she could not see his expression, did not want to see it. Unlaced, unzipped, unpinned, unclipped, unrolled, unsaid, undone, she thought, and smiled to herself. His face was against her body, his head in her hands, his lips puckering the smoothness of her skin.

Into bed, crisp new sheets, pillow-slips smelling of a recent ironing. A smooth young man's body, more muscular than she had expected. How well they fitted, cuddling together to keep out the cold. How affectionate he was. Generous and protective in all things. Men were supposed to be *conquistadors*, selfish in their pleasures. That was what she had read. But not this one. Hudson, the beautiful; handsome Hudson with the long list of girl-friends was tentative, gentle and unhurried. She felt as though she were outside herself, an observer in this dark room. She had wondered, like every girl, like every boy, how she would feel at this moment. Now that it was happening to her, and the motor of her body was responding, she still wondered. The pleasure was urgent and exquisite. There was no sudden pain, not the way she had expected. In the darkness she sheltered him and hid him, the mighty Hudson, his head lost in the fold of her neck. She remembered when she had first seen him, his smile at the launch party which had brought blood surging to her cheeks. She had wondered before this night if she would know what to do, but the flesh dictated. Her body knew what to do though her mind soared and raced. It was, she thought, as though she had lost her body, given it up, and made it over to his that the two might be one. Two bodies joined: two minds apart. Her soul watched and congratulated her. Such short moments, then the saddest, sweetest of partings as the single body, exhausted from delight, divided. Two people, separate again, body and soul. And content. In the darkness Emily's fingers traced the contours of Hudson's face, the thick, fair hair, the beginnings of frown lines on his forehead, the tiny furrows between his eyes, the smooth cheeks and firm unfleshy jaw with its white scar, and the mouth, wide and smiling as she caressed his lips, which opened and closed around her fingers, playful and sensuous. Once she had been terrified of Hudson. But that had been before.

'We're going to be terrific together,' Hudson said later as they recharted the steps which had brought them to this bed.

Emily smiled. 'We already are.'

Chapter Twenty-Four

The following months capered by. For Richard and Hudson *Witness* dictated their lives: Emily and Nicola had June finals to concentrate their minds. In the week they worked in pairs, at the weekend they united as couples: and as a foursome they were inseparable. Two sets of best friends and two sets of lovers. Most Fridays Nicola and Emily would drive up to London in the Morris Minor, bringing their unfinished essays with them, and stay in Chepstow Villas. But occasionally Hudson and Richard would descend on Oxford with their stacks of the latest *Witness*, using South Park Road as their distribution base.

Against all expectations *Witness* blossomed with the new year, the self-confidence of the age acting as a locomotive and pulling the new magazine along in its train. Rapidly the circulation built, from ten to fifteen, to twenty thousand, and bit by bit Richard became used to spending his salary. By Easter thirty thousand had been reached and Hudson set a target of fifty thousand copies for the end of the summer. But more important was the advertising revenue *Witness* was attracting; Hudson had a gift for encouraging companies to take space who had never before thought of advertising. A quick learner and a creative entrepreneur, he was continually dreaming up new schemes to promote and enlarge the business. Soon he introduced classified advertisement columns aimed specifically at young people. From the back pages of *Witness* a person could find a room, a flatmate, a partner, a cheap meal, a fresh passion fruit, a new Fender bass, an amplifier, text books, a cheap ticket to New York, a narrow boat on the Regent's Park canal, Banjara mirror bangles from Hyderabad, Beatles' tickets and Beatle boots, a second-hand car, third-hand clothes and fourth-hand furniture, how to play barrelhouse piano, how to practise karate or give a massage, and where to get one's urine tested for pregnancy. The classified columns never stopped growing. By March the advertising department had outgrown its tiny offices and had spread to the floor below, where new, full-time circulation staff were also housed. People came and went with increasing rapidity, Sonia, the beehive, bringing three girl-friends in to help and then leaving when her boy-friend issued the ultimatum, '*Witness* or me?' It was a borderline decision.

Upstairs the editorial staff was also swelling. There was Belinda, a fashion assistant who could spell, to help Beryl, who could not; a girl called Carol who had a peaked face, a fringe and a manufactured Liverpool accent, who wrote about pop music; a fey little pal of Willie's called Harold, who wore a Hawaiian shirt and wrote film gossip; and all kinds of itinerant correspondents on everything from herbal remedies to kindergarten affairs. Not everyone stayed very long. The pay was poor and the hours were long. Before long Sporty Colin had moved to the *Daily Telegraph*, to be replaced by Gordon from Aberdeen. Around the same time photographer Bill McGough joined the *Observer* full-time, an Australian sub-editor came, had a brief tryst with Belinda on the office floor one night and left, while an occasional correspondent on comparative religious affairs had a nervous breakdown and went off to form a mime group.

The central players were, however, unchanging. Before long Berridge had his own column, a scurrilous ratbag of information, more amusing than illuminating, while Charles Latymer proved a solid feature writer, provided somebody else thought of the ideas. That was usually Nicola's job. She was good at ideas. The biggest surprise was Emily, who, when pressured into deputizing for a 'flu-ridden books editor in an interview with Norman Mailer, turned in a very funny account of their meeting.

She was, Richard told Nicola, born to be an interviewer: an intelligent listener, she made her subjects feel at ease. And in the next few months, when she had the time, all kinds of people confided in Emily – Albert Finney, Mick Jagger, Quintin Hogg, Lenny Bruce.

For Richard there were never enough pages to cover all that was happening. In January Mary Quant wore a mini-skirt and told the French fashion industry they were old-fashioned, while in the middle of a cold February night Richard and Hudson crouched around a radio burning the legs of a broken chair to keep warm as a hysterical young Cassius Clay became the world heavyweight boxing champion. They had been lucky. A planned cover piece on *Fanny Hill*, the book banned for obscenity, had not materialized and at the last minute Richard had put a picture of the wide-mouthed Clay on that week's cover. A new hero was born and they sold out.

But the big story of 1964 continued to be rock music, as the Beatles did to America what they had done to Britain the previous year. Again *Witness* was lucky. Unable to send one of his writers to tour the States with them Richard turned instead to a new and more accessible group. The edition of *Witness* featuring the Rolling Stones on the cover was also a sell-out. *Witness* could be serious, too. Charlie Latymer wrote a piece on an exchange of spies, Jessica Tarlo wrote a profile on Martin Luther King, and there was an angry outburst against Ian Smith and the new Rhodesian government by Nicola Reynolds. 'One pace behind, but always in step, the Rhodesian Front will now try to follow South Africa back into the nineteenth century,' she wrote, that week's cover showing a cartoon depicting Ian Smith driving an ox-cart entitled *Rhodesia* over black protestors out into the bush.

'Just wait until Uncle Alec gets this,' she grinned as she pushed a copy of the magazine into an envelope. 'He'll have me disinherited.'

'Can he do that?' Richard asked.

She shook her head: 'No, but I don't get the real money until I'm thirty-five, by which time I'll be too old to enjoy it. D'you think you'll still love me when I'm thirty-five?'

'If you're loaded I'll adore you.'

'Creep,' she said.

Richard was never sure what his parents thought of Nicola. After a difficult Christmas Eve, with his mother and sister snapping nervously at each other and his father thinking he was saying the right thing by picking the wrong side on the Rhodesian question, he had not taken her to Wimbledon again when they were there. With Hudson there were no such problems. He was always welcome, charming his mother and talking business with his father. And Carol adored him: Hudson and his women.

Tim Gimmelmann was only ever seen with one woman, but what a girl. Though no one ever heard them speak more than a couple of words to each other Gimmelmann and Holly were inseparable during those months, turning up at the *Witness* office once every couple of weeks so that Beryl and Belinda might try out new fashion ideas on them. By Easter they had moved out of Kentish Town to a two-floor flat just off Primrose Hill. The ground floor was for living, the basement being what Gimmelmann called his studio, a bare room with a roller he had picked up cheap when a photographer he knew got into difficulties with his tax. His lights were a couple of spotlamps on tripods which had somehow walked out of Pinewood Studios: and his only camera was his Rolleiflex.

It had only taken Willie Simmonds to make one introduction at *Queen* and Holly had been away and running. When asked who Holly's agent was Gimmelmann had replied that he was and she was not available for anyone else to photograph. And because his photographs were fresh and innovative the situation was, for the moment, accepted.

Holly was not the only model *Witness* used, but

it was to Holly they would always turn first when they had an idea. Holly's look, arrogant and wise beyond her years, captured, if only on film, the spirit of *Witness*, the burst-the-barricades energy of the early Sixties. And once a month Holly's dark sexuality would hang over the *Witness* dinners, when Hudson and the entire editorial staff would resort to an upstairs room at Mama Vecchi's in Westbourne Park Road, and the unattached boys would vie with each other to impress her. Naturally Gimmelmann guarded his asset jealously. 'Don't lean across Holly, she doesn't like it,' he hissed one night as Gordon, the lumbering prop forward of a sports writer, the worse for too much Valpolicella, trapped her in a corner of the restaurant.

'She hasn't complained to me, son.' Gordon was looking down at Gimmelmann derisively.

Gimmelmann stood his ground. 'I'm complaining for her. All right? Come on, Holly.'

'Don't you move, darling?' Gordon smirked and cupping Holly's bottom in his hands he kissed her fully on the lips. He realized his mistake at once. With a shout he pulled back his head, a hand going to his mouth. Blood was trickling from two deep cuts in his bottom lip. 'She bit me . . . she bloody bit me. You cow!' he sobbed, feeling for a handkerchief. 'Bloody cow.'

Holly did not answer, silently following Gimmelmann from the room.

'There's something very Muslim about that relationship,' said Richard back at Chepstow Villas that night. The foursome were drinking cocoa by the fire, Emily curled up on Hudson's lap, Richard lying on his back, his head on Nicola's knees as she sat on the carpet. 'I mean, he rules her life completely. How can he behave like that?'

'He can because she wants him to,' said Emily. 'It must suit her. What d'you think?' She turned to Hudson.

'I think he's made a deal with the devil,' Hudson said.

'Oh, come on!' Emily protested. 'That's a bit unfair.'

Nicola looked at Hudson. 'I know what you mean,' she said. 'There's something there. She frightens me. Do you fancy her, Richard?'

It was a casual question but Richard could sense the rigid tension in Nicola's body. 'No,' he said, not altogether truthfully. No normal man could be impervious to Holly Carter.

Apparently satisfied Nicola stroked his hair. 'What about you?' she asked Hudson.

Before he could answer Emily broke in. 'I don't think we're being very fair. I mean we hardly know the girl. She must have had a hell of a life growing up. I think it's amazing she's as normal as she is. And she really is wonderfully pretty.'

'Trust you to be the nice one, Emmy.' Nicola was laughing. 'I take it all back. And he's a little darling, Timmy Gimmelmann, with his built-up boots and bum-freezer jackets. A little darling.'

'He worships Hudson,' Richard said. 'Absolutely worships him.'

'Does he?' asked Emily. 'Really?'

Hudson didn't argue. 'He's easily impressed,' he said quietly.

So many evenings ended like this with the four of them sitting around mulling things over before the two couples would retire to bed. One night after they had finished making love and were lying listening to the sound of tyres on the road outside, Nicola asked Richard if Hudson saw other women during the week when Emily was in Oxford. 'No,' Richard could truthfully say. 'That side of him is quite finished now.'

'Good,' Nicola had murmured. 'It would kill Emmy if he were unfaithful to her.' She paused. Then she said: 'And I would kill you if you were ever unfaithful to me. Promise you won't be.'

She looked so strangely stern Richard was surprised: 'I promise.' And with the purity of the very young he wondered why anyone would ever want to be unfaithful.

PART THREE
April 1978

Chapter Twenty-Five

(i)

Clover Merrifield was waiting at Heathrow Airport at seven on the Friday morning to welcome the photographer home from Rhodesia. Arrangements had been made and, accompanied by a jug-eared driver from the taxi company, she was led by a junior member of British Airways ground staff past customs and out beyond the baggage carousels.

The flight was early and almost immediately she saw him, loping down the side of the moving walkway, noticeably more gaunt and suntanned than the youth who had left barely ten days earlier.

Automatically his arms went out in embrace, but almost as they touched there was a double flash of light. Clover swung around in surprise. She had not noticed the small group of airport agency Press who were laying out a semblance of a red carpet for one of their own. It was obviously a quiet morning.

'Come on, this way,' she snapped, suddenly aggravated, and, ignoring her fellow Press, she indicated the hand luggage to the driver, took the photographer's arm and hurried him through the crowd.

The three agency reporters, a girl of about her own age, a boy in an unpleasant brown suit with flared trousers, and an older man with 'booze' written in Pitman's shorthand in every vein of his face, fell professionally into step alongside them.

'Nice to see you back, Rob,' led the older man, instantly familiar. 'How does it feel to be home?' came in the girl, rather fatuously, thought Clover. 'We understand the Rhodesian authorities deported you.' This was the boy in brown. They were playing it like a rehearsed routine. 'Give her a kiss, Rob,' chipped in one of the photographers. Clover scowled, killing that idea. 'The word is that you were actually in the village when the massacre was taking place . . .' That was the man again. 'What about torture,' asked the boy, 'or mutilations?' 'Or rape?' demanded the girl.

Embarrassed to be the centre of this little posse the photographer could do little more than shake his head and answer in monosyllables. His face wore the silly expression of the subject of a surprise party. All we need now is a bloody kissogram, thought Clover savagely, but what she said, rather smugly, was: 'You can read it all in *Sunday Morning.*'

The wait for the suitcases was surprisingly short, probably no more than fifteen minutes, but to Clover it seemed interminable as a BBC News camera crew, called out too early to catch the Foreign Secretary flying home from Bahrain, decided to make good their enforced idleness.

'I never thought to see myself on the receiving end,' the photographer gasped in honest, colonial-boy astonishment as he caught sight of a hand-held TV camera focusing on him.

'Well, we know what Andy Warhol said about everyone in the future being famous for fifteen minutes,' replied Clover. Then, realizing how bitchy that sounded, she added: 'Are you all right?' She was looking at the scabs which had formed where his face had been ripped by the mortar blast and flight through the forest.

The photographer nodded. 'No problem,' he said, and shoving his hands into his pockets he pulled out two handfuls of film. 'I had to do a spot of smuggling to get these out. God knows what's on them, but . . .' He grinned, pleased with himself.

Clover was pleased, too. No one loves a photographer who comes home without his film.

'It's good to have you home, Rob,' she murmured. 'We were very worried.'

(ii)

It was the surprise in encountering death that the photograph captured so precisely. The war had come to Mupangare with the sudden lob of an exploding mortar shell at the moment that the shutter on the Nikon had been pressed, and now five thousand miles and six days away Richard Blake was experiencing that rush of adrenalin which is the fix of the professional newsman. The words 'horror', 'hell', 'disaster', 'nightmare', even 'massacre' are for the consumers of news. To the retailers, the editors, to Richard, there was only one word to describe the photograph which lay in his hands.

'It's fantastic!' he breathed. 'Fantastic!' A fleeting pity for the young, anonymous boy soldiers caught for ever at the second of their deaths momentarily gave pause to his excitement. 'Poor beggars,' he added.

Scattered across his desk were perhaps fifteen ten-by-eight prints and six contact sheets, strips of black-and-white photographs of the burning village and the desperate villagers, of the grinning Wonderful and weeping women standing by their mounds of household goods: and then the aftermath, the circles of ashes where the huts had collapsed inwards, the freshly dug graves on the hillside.

'We got the right man, all right,' said Andrew Kirby, young and balding and recruited from Associated Newspapers to stamp a hard-edged visual style on to *Sunday Morning*. It was he who had arranged for the collection and processing of the film.

'We did indeed,' said deputy editor Stephen Symes, fingers clasped behind his braces.

Richard kept silent, reflecting silently how, right man or not, Rob Barnes had paid his own flight out to Rhodesia, his career advancement at *Sunday Morning* dependent upon the quality of his pictures. Management would have to offer him a staff contract now.

With the aid of a magnifying glass Kirby was peering, one by one, at the contacts. 'God knows what this is,' he muttered as he examined a frame showing a white house high in the mist of forest-covered hills.

Richard looked over the top of his glasses at the picture. Despite the neglect and encroaching forest he recognized the house instantly, although he had never been there. 'I believe it's a place called Wildwood,' he said quietly.

'Of course I love you, silly boy,' she had said that afternoon in Wimbledon, as the swing had soared back into the trees. 'I'll always love you. For the rest of my life. Now do you believe me?' And with that Nicola had come hurtling from the bushes and fallen into his arms, sending them rolling, giggling down the lawn together.

'Hey, what's going on?' Hudson and Emily, who had been loafing together on the hammock, peered up through the waist-high ferns to see what was happening across the garden, all four of them a little drunk on picnic wine. A happy day.

Richard put the memory away. 'Any word on when we can expect copy?' he asked.

Symes grinned. 'We've locked him away with Clover Merrifield and a typewriter in a suite at the Savoy Hotel and told them not to come out until the piece is finished.'

'The Savoy? Not bad.'

'We thought we'd butter him up a bit, make him feel important. And the Savoy was handiest. There was no sense in sending him home. He'd have had all his Aussie pals calling around to buy him a drink.'

Richard nodded. 'Good thinking,' he said. He thought: lucky boy, a suite at the Savoy and Clover Merrifield. He won't complain about that.

The delicate porcelain features split two inches above the right eye as a fountain of blood arced out, a trajectory of sheer surprise at the force of the blow. Gimmelmann, his arm back, his fist clenched for another strike, stopped himself just as the first specs of blood reached his pale blue denim shirt. She did not scream out: not even a whimper. She simply crouched there in the corner of the kitchen, an arm feebly wrapped around her head in defence.

'Christ! Now look what you've made me do.' Gimmelmann, his pretty face puckered by rage and frustration, struck his hand viciously into the grooved pine of the kitchen wall. 'Stupid cow.'

His wife Jenny winced and put her wrist to her forehead. Blood soaked into the cuff of her blouse. It was cream silk.

Trying to control his breathing Gimmelmann looked at her with contempt. This was the first time he had drawn blood. If she hadn't moved at that moment as he had lunged at her . . . It was just a friendly clout, really. If she'd kept still the worst she would have suffered would have been a bruise, a black eye perhaps, easily disguised by make-up.

'I'm sorry, Tim, I didn't mean what I said. I don't know what I meant . . .'

She was being pathetic now, dabbing at the cut with her arm, tears and nose beginning to run. The blouse was ruined. A two hundred pound blouse written off because she couldn't keep her mouth shut. You can never get blood out of silk. Lucky he'd got it cost price, slightly soiled, after the shoot.

He made no attempt to comfort her.

'It's just that . . .' She stopped.

It's just that nothing. There was no need to carry on. The battle was over and lost.

Seeing that Gimmelmann was now under control she lowered her guard and reaching for a kitchen paper roll unwound several sheets, which she now dabbed against the wound.

Gimmelmann sighed as though at a loss to understand why his wife should have been so deliberately provocative, as though the inevitability of his violence had been her fault. 'I know I'm not perfect, Jen, but . . . you do all right, don't you? I mean you get everything you want. More. More than everything. More than anyone I know. I can't think what more you could get. It's very difficult at the moment. You've no idea. Hudson's being terrific. He's right behind me. One hundred per cent. If he wants to talk until five in the morning there's no way I'm going to say, "Sorry, Hudson, I've got to go now, it's past Jen's bedtime . . ." This is a big deal for him, too, you know. And he's a busy man. Very busy. You catch him when you catch him these days.'

Jenny opened the door of her fridge-freezer and took out the ice container. Then tapping it on the draining board she picked up a cube and pressed it against the wound.

Gimmelmann talked on. He did not know, did not care, if she believed him, nor even if she was listening. There was some truth in what he was saying. There always was. He had seen Hudson the previous night. They had met to discuss the film facilities house he was planning, and to look over a property in Great Marlborough Street. The building, a carpet wholesalers run by two Egyptians on their way out of business, was a mess, but the lease was long and the place had possibilities. He could see it now, lacquered pine floors, white walls, some of his awards on display in reception, upstairs the studios and changing rooms, and downstairs the plush little viewing theatre, the cutting rooms and video suites. His own little industry and Hudson in with 80 per cent of the backing. Hudson had been very impressed. He could tell that. He liked it when Hudson was impressed. Then off they'd gone for a quiet dinner to work out the deal. Hudson–Gimmelmann Film and Video. Hudson's name was going on everything these days. He was the moment. Everyone in London wanted to get to Hudson and there he was having a quiet dinner in Soho with Tim Gimmelmann. Gimmelmann liked the idea of that, too.

That Gimmelmann had not gone home immediately after dinner had been the cause of the morning's outburst. For years it had been unlike Jenny to notice, or at least to comment upon, what time he arrived home. If Emma hadn't woken up early to look for foxes and seen his car slide into the drive at six-thirty, the engine off for silence, there would have been none of this. That was what had made him so angry. Jenny didn't care whom he screwed. She just wanted to keep up appearances for the kids. They were growing up now and beginning to ask too many questions: the perfect family, as portrayed in soppy women's magazines and Sunday supplements. *Dishy former photographer, commercials director Tim Gimmelmann, with his stunning wife, lovely former model Jenny Quinn, and their two beautiful children.* It was all so bloody boring. Suburbia, school sports days, fondu with the Fosters, whoever they were, nibbles with the Normans. He knew what the Fosters and the Normans thought about them: Jenny with her Canonbury consonants trying to talk posh, while behind her back they mocked and mimicked, getting friendly with her to get to him because he was something different. Those wives, pampered and lazy, putting out, or worse, pretending to put out but keeping it locked up like the Crown Jewels, while their husbands blistered their brain cells in banks every day, paying for it. Jesus! No wonder he belted her one now and again. She'd dragged him to this.

He stared at her. She was silent now, other than for the occasional little shuddered intake of breath. Crossing the kitchen he took the ice cube from her, wrapped it in paper and pressed it to her forehead. 'You really shouldn't go upsetting me like that, Jen,' he murmured. 'I've got a lot on my mind.'

'I know, Tim. I'm sorry. I wasn't thinking. It gets a

bit lonely out here sometimes, you know. People aren't
very friendly.'

'Well, I did warn you, didn't I? It was your idea to
come to Richmond, wasn't it?' He didn't give an inch.
'There you are. The bleeding's stopping now. It looked
worse than it was. Just a scratch really.'

Jenny sniffed, clearing her nostrils.

At least it wouldn't need stitches, Gimmelmann told
himself. 'All right now, Jen?' He never apologized.

Jenny blew her nose.

He took that as an affirmative. Turning away he
filled the kettle with water. Thank God it was Tangiers
next week. Anything to get away from this. That Dee Dee
Jenkins they'd booked looked a bit tasty, too. Perhaps if
she'd been around last night . . .

Last night!

Desperately he tried to force his mind away, but the
mud and the caravan, and the smell of cats and drink and
flesh, and Holly's smirk flooded back, nauseating him.
Holly. God knows how or why, but she still tantalized
him, even now after everything that had happened. The
cold empty eyes had not changed: the face, half-hidden
by a hood, now wore a permanent grimace. 'Like a nun,
aren't I?' she had mocked. 'A nice juicy nun, eh?' She
was fat now, and filthy. Dirtier even than when he had
first known her. And last night she had been drunk. 'It
helps when I can't get anything better,' she had said bitterly. The inside of her elbow was blue and bruised, and
when she had caught him looking she had pulled down
her sleeve. She was a pudding of hatred.

He should have stayed away. He had not seen her
for three years, but meeting all the old gang again
had rekindled his curiosity. What she did to him, the
sweet taste of decadence, the black rites of sensuality
only she could perform: the secrets she whispered. She
knew.

He had thought he was free of her, that his disgust
armoured him against her. But sex without her was a

pale imitation. She knew what to say: she still knew what to say.

He looked back at Jenny. She was silent now. He lit a Gauloise and together they waited for the kettle to boil. They had never had much to talk about at the best of times.

(iv)

It was not what he had expected. Home-comings never are.

They had hardly spoken in the car from Heathrow, certainly not about anything that mattered. The presence of the jug-eared driver, whose eyes had followed every bend of Clover's body in the airport, had seen to that. So, while they had sat in the back of the Ford Granada and Clover had made polite conversation about the first-day success of *Sunday Morning* and Hudson's bid for Federated British, the photographer had thought about the albino boy. 'My father was not a murderer. I am telling you the truth.' But whose truth? Then again: 'Perhaps when the war is over I will buy a passport and go to England,' he had said, the cracked white face grasping at dreams he could not begin to imagine properly.

The England the photographer was now discovering was new to him, too. Being led up to a suite in the Savoy by a uniformed porter was not what he had grown up to expect.

'Is this really necessary?' he said, looking around at the small sitting room with its reproduction chairs, scattering of table lamps and gilt-edged mirrors, as the porter took Clover's tip and left.

Clover smiled. Lying waiting on a desk was a portable electric typewriter and a stack of copy paper. Everything was ready. She took her Sony tape recorder out of her bag and placed it down. Then, standing over the desk, she typed: 'Welcome home, Rob. It's good to see you.'

He watched her. Standing there, with her face and

237

black hair backlit by the spring sunlight, she was so pretty. He remembered telling Michael, the albino boy, about her, boasting about her beauty. Very gently, tentatively he put his hands on her shoulders. She stopped typing and turned to him.

'I dreamed about you, you know,' he said. 'When I was afraid and thought I was going to be found and killed . . .' He gazed at her. There was a moment's awkwardness.

She glanced at the typewriter. 'What do you think? Do you want to go through it all now so that I can be getting on with it while you get a few hours' sleep? You must be dead on your feet.'

He shook his head.

'It's an early page and they want two thousand words by tonight. So we'll have to get cracking before very long.' She glanced at her watch. She was absolutely professional.

Putting his arms around her he held her.

After a moment she got up. 'I think the bed is through here,' she said.

This was how she had always been: matter of fact, unemotional. When they had first met he had rejoiced in her spontaneity and directness. They had been sent to Brighton to do a pilot interview with an ageing ballerina, a day-out by the sea which they had stretched into two. Arriving at the station for the train back to London and discovering that they had just missed one, they had gone into the bar for a couple of drinks. It was there, out of the blue, that Clover had suggested sex.

'Whoever heard of going to Brighton if it wasn't for a dirty weekend?' she had teased as they wandered back down the front looking for a suitable dirty-weekend hotel. 'It has to be somewhere seedy,' she had insisted. 'Regency-cum-Fifties renovations and very Graham Greene-ish where correspondents give courses in adultery.'

At first she had irritated him. In his judgement she was

238

stuck up, conceited and ambitious and would make him nervous. He was right. But she was much more besides. She was fun, she was entertaining and, when she chose to be, she was passionate. Competitive by spirit she looked upon sex as another role in which to excel. It was not that she did anything novel or extraordinarily imaginative. It was rather that she enjoyed so much and therefore gave so much enjoyment in return. That night in Brighton, the bed creaking noisily, the photographer had learned something about bright girls: their cleverness does not stop at the bedroom door: their energy is not all consumed by their work.

The following morning as he had dragged himself back to London, his body aching, he had stared across the railway compartment at Clover. As beautiful and poised as ever she had sat silently reading, her eyes betraying no sign of the night's carnality. She was an enigma to him and would remain so, sunny and generous when it suited her, restrained and cool at other times. But never emotional: Clover never showed any emotion.

Now he was strangely uncertain, timid almost, and mistaking this for tiredness Clover undressed him. Once again a bed was a refuge as the sheets rolled over him. He lay still, feeling the warm pulse of her body neatly folded against his. Sensing his distraction Clover kissed him. He was exhausted and pushing his head against the firm flesh beneath her arm, his face into the side of her breast, he blocked out the world, holding on until very slowly a tear welled in his eyes, a tear which came from Africa and an albino boy, a tear which splashed against her skin and ran down her body until blotted by the sheets.

A little while later the photographer made love to Clover Merrifield, while she had sex with him.

'Tell me about Nicola Reynolds,' he said as she dressed.
'I can't really. She's been dead for donkey's years

. . . well, ten at least. They were all friends in the Sixties apparently. They say Hudson never got over it. That's about all I know.' She zipped up her dress and turned to him. 'So, now are you ready to start work?'

Chapter Twenty-Six

(i)

There was hardly enough wind but they flew their kites anyway, the three of them scampering along the grass launching their excitement into the sky on this Sunday morning. These were the days Emily wanted to remember, the important days for the children, so she had allowed them to hurry her out of the house before ten leaving Richard still sleeping.

There had been, as anticipated, a minor industrial dispute at *Sunday Morning* the previous night and Richard had not arrived home until after one, grumbling to himself about the vengeance Hudson was certain to wreak on the saboteurs when he took control of Federated British. Emily, who had been reading in bed since eleven, had smiled ruefully to herself and put out the light. Hudson always enjoyed a good row with the printers. One of the first things he had done with his initial success had been to buy out J.W. Purley and Sons of Cricklewood and sack the entire staff, though it had cost him a fortune in redundancy payments. They had taken him for a boy during the early *Witness* days and he had never forgotten. They hadn't known: Hudson always got even.

The kites were Chinese and colourful, flying dragons which reared and turned languidly on the light breeze, their tales twisting around their strings before crashing back to earth. Only Benedict was wholly successful in coaxing his dragon to any great height. He was good with toys. Tom, at five, bit back his tears of frustration.

'Come on, we'll get him up highest of all,' Emily said, as she raced across the park hurling the paper

241

dragon into the air, while Catherine helped her little brother hold the string. In the end it did fly, not very well, but enough to blink away the tears.

Who wants to be writing silly interviews for a newspaper when I can be flying kites with the children? Emily asked herself, as the three dragons hovered tentatively above their heads. A warm April morning in Holland Park and she was as happy and fulfilled as life could make her.

They played for over an hour before, with the wind dying completely, the dragons were refolded and their tails and strings rewound for another day. They had to get home and changed for a lunch party at Willie Simmonds', but under pressure she stopped at the gate into Abbotsbury Road. An ice-cream van had parked and after much debate the children each chose a cornet with a chocolate flaky bar tucked inside. On a bench by a flowerbed a girl and boy of student age were enjoying the sunshine, sitting together reading the Sunday papers.

'Look,' whispered Catherine, excited. 'They're reading *Sunday Morning.*'

Emily nodded as the children giggled. Even from a little distance the photograph on the centre spread was arresting. *Mupangare: what happened* ran the headline. Richard had always favoured the direct approach.

'Come on, hurry up,' she called as the children dawdled, 'we'll be late for the party.'

(*ii*)

It was like watching an elaborate courtship ritual: gracious, elegant answers following formal questions, but the real conversation lay in their body language. The subject under discussion was newspapers, the building of a publishing empire. The subtext was sex.

That, at least, was how Charles Latymer saw it, cosseted alone in the green felted visitors' viewing suite watching his wife Dominique on the monitor toying

242

answers out of Hudson as they transmitted *Around The World* live from the studio below.

As a duel of wits it was a non-starter. Hudson was far too well briefed for Dominique, even had she been looking to catch him out, which she clearly was not. A kind man might say it was an expository interview: others might see it as a mismatch or a fifty-minute publicity pitch for Hudson International. To Charlie Latymer it was a beautiful woman making an overt pitch for an attractive man.

He drank his Perrier and contemplated the screen. They looked so good together, his wife and his new employer.

'It is sometimes feared that the concentration of newspapers and magazines in the hands of a small number of proprietors is very dangerous in a democratic system.' Dominique lobbed him an easy one in her deep Gallic drawl, a question, Latymer knew, Hudson would have mentally rehearsed many times.

Hudson nodded emphatically. 'I would agree entirely with that. In fact, that's one of the reasons that we feel it's important that Hudson International succeeds in the take-over of Federated British, in that we'll be offering a new and independent voice. When we started out with *Witness* fifteen years ago it wasn't because we wanted to be the same as everybody else but because we had something new to say.'

'But isn't it possible . . . ?'

Smiling all the time Hudson, the professional interviewee, kept talking. 'Now *Sunday Morning* is different, providing a new voice in Britain, and whatever we do with Federated British will be different, too. And, of course, we're offering guarantees of non-editorial interference as part of the take-over package.'

'All the same there has been concern that someone who owns 20 per cent of the British magazine market should now be moving so rapidly . . .' she smiled to herself '. . . some people would say mushrooming into newspapers, television and radio.' She pronounced mushrooming as though it were some kind of lightly whipped soufflé.

Hudson smiled wider, dropped his voice, leaned forward in his chair and began to speak almost intimately. Latymer recognized the trick. Hudson knew from experience that the director's response would almost certainly be to go in for a close-up.

'You know, Dominique, when I hear arguments like that I think to myself, well, maybe the Luddites didn't all die out after all. Because that's what these people are who come along wanting the brake put on us. They're Luddites. They want to stop progress. But the fact is, one way or the other, information is going to become the currency of the last quarter of the twentieth century. The technology is already there. And more information means more choice for everyone. More democracy if you like. If you don't like the newspapers and magazines published by Hudson International, fair enough, you can buy those of our rivals. And, believe me, we will have rivals, more and more. And I welcome them. Right now there are, as we all know, some problems with some of the trade unions, and I can understand the point of view of unions worried about the welfare of their members. But there's nothing we can do to uninvent the technology we already have. And sooner or later, and I hope it's sooner for everyone's sake, the problems will be resolved and there will be an explosion of newspapers, magazines, TV and radio stations. All we at Hudson International want to do is to be a part of that explosion. We want to help bring honest information, truth, in whatever form, to the people. Is that such a very bad ambition?'

Whatever Dominique might have planned to say in conclusion was denied her. As though he had been watching the clock Hudson had finished the interview dead on time. Fixing him with a look of earnest admiration Dominique simply had time to say: 'Thank you, James Hudson.'

'Thank you,' said Hudson.

Latymer freshened his Perrier, and, studying his reflection in the window between the visitors' viewing suite and the studio, adjusted his hair. He liked what he had heard. He had joined the right team. If Dominique could manage to make her infatuation a little less obvious there was no limit to where Hudson could take him. She was wasting her time, anyway. Anyone could see that.

He finished his drink. He would go downstairs now to the hospitality room and congratulate them both on stunning performances. He was, after all, Hudson's chosen right-hand man, the image-making supremo for Hudson International. He knew about these things.

(*iii*)

Unlike most of Willie Simmonds' friends Penelope Chilston had actually seen *Toffee Ration*, though, in truth, she hadn't thought much of it. Wordy, smutty, altogether too light on dramatic effect and too heavy on *double entendres* would have been her assessment: but the audience had laughed because they knew that was expected and the critics had been kinder than the piece deserved. The critics had always liked Willie, and now he was behaving as though he had another success on his hands, a new *Two-Backed Beast* or sequel to *In Flagrante Delicto*, when actually Willie was whistling past the cemetery of his talent. No wonder he was so grateful to Hudson, she thought, grateful enough to host this Sunday lunchtime party for him. Without Hudson's investment *Toffee Ration* might well have languished for ever on Willie's agent's bottom shelf where it properly belonged. Perhaps, she allowed herself the tiniest criticism, perhaps Hudson's generosity wasn't always properly directed. But Willie was an old friend. Hudson wouldn't have been able to help himself.

Naturally Penny had not admitted to thoughts such as these when she had accepted Willie's invitation to his lunch party. 'Terrific . . . wonderful,' had been her lies and because Willie was now such a success, his faculties for scepticism no longer oiled by journalism, he had believed her. And he was a success. Absolutely. Success and Willie Simmonds had become so established in the public mind as to be indivisible. To have suggested that perhaps *Toffee Ration* was not quite the new work of genius for which the world had been waiting, would not only have been an act of great personal disloyalty, it would have questioned the tenets upon which much success is built and enjoyed: that something stated loudly enough and frequently enough must, surely enough, be true.

With thoughts such as these in mind Penny wandered crabbily around the Simmonds' Pelham Crescent garden, a drink too large for lunch in her hand, a worry in her mind. She shouldn't really have been at this party at all. Richard had given her permission to go to Karachi to interview ex-President Bhutto who was under sentence of death. But now technical and legal problems were being strewn in her path at the Pakistani end. And she didn't trust this new fellow, President Zia, not one little bit.

She glanced at her watch. It was not quite one. She had arrived early, leaving home as Dominique Fayence's interview with Hudson for *Around The World* had come to an end. He had been so impressive, while Dominique had looked as though she could not decide whether she wanted to interview him or seduce him. 'Mushrooming,' she had said, or was it 'meursh-rreumming'? What the hell was 'meursh-rreumming', anyway?

Penny was feeling better now. Perhaps she needn't have had that drink at home. She was intrepid, after all. Why should she need Dutch courage for a lunch party with old friends and colleagues? It didn't make sense.

The garden was quickly filling with guests and their children. There were lots of children, the Gimmelmanns' two pretty little girls, here without their mother today, she noticed, the Tarlo kids in their American clothes, and then the two boys Willie had inherited when he married Ginny. They went with the house, it was said.

She took off her cardigan and, spreading it on a large upturned plant pot, sat upon it while a smiling waiter served her chilled salmon and refilled her glass. It was a lovely day. Trust Willie to throw a lunch party on the only day in April when it would be warm enough to hold it in the garden. He had to be the luckiest man in London. And such a smart garden, too, paved in York stone, furnished in wrought iron, clematis and wisteria clad walls, and even a raunchy looking nude statue, a shameless Venus emerging from the hydrangeas. 'She h..elps the mu..ses fl..ow,' Willie would explain.

Emily was waving at her from the steps, leading a little boy of about five by the hand, shy in this big, new garden. She waved back, and then watched as the boy was taken away by an elder brother to examine a tortoise in the flowerbed. How quickly the guests were multiplying. Willie had so many friends these days, and Hudson so many admirers. Everyone wanted to meet Hudson. There was scarcely room to move, so she stayed where she was, finished her drink and had another. Chat, chat, chat. *Sunday Morning* this, *Sunday Morning* that.

She looked again at her watch. He would be here soon. It couldn't take that long to get from the television studios. Now where was that wine waiter?

(*iv*)

'I was told you'd been to Wildwood.'

The photographer was standing alone by the statue nervously holding a glass of champagne in his hand, staring at the well-stocked flowerbeds, an escape from awkwardness for a moment. He had not noticed her approach and turned quickly when she spoke to him. 'Yes.'

Emily smiled. 'I know the house. A friend of mine lived there. I stayed there once.'

'That would be Nicola Reynolds, wouldn't it?'

Emily nodded. 'Nicola and I were at college together,' she said.

'Ah!'

He was younger than she had imagined, taller, gawky almost, with spiky fair hair and a short stumpy nose which was badly scratched, and his outdoor, almost rugged, look was slightly out of place in South Kensington. In normal circumstances she thought it unlikely that such a young photographer would have been invited to such a party, but with his Mupangare pictures Rob Barnes was definitely this week's hot photographer, and that sort of thing mattered to Ginny Simmonds. Emily smiled. 'I'm Emily Blake, by the way,' she said.

'Oh yes . . .'

She noticed her name registering in his eyes. 'Richard was telling me that you took shelter in Wildwood for a couple of days after . . .' She didn't finish. She knew that everyone else had asked him about the events in Mupangare. *Sunday Morning* was full of it. She went on: 'Nicola always loved the house. I was afraid it might have been damaged by the war.'

'No. Not at all.'

He visited her grave, thought Emily, something that she had never done. How strange that this young Australian, this stranger, should recently have been so close to her.

It was a stilted conversation, the photographer being obviously ill at ease in such smart circumstances. And it *was* smart. Willie Simmonds had always had the most sordid and dank of West Hampstead flats in the old days. Now he lived in one of the best crescents in London. Suddenly stout Ginny, Willie's newish wife, her bosom steaming through the guests like a vast pink prow floating on a sea of lemon meringue, appeared at Emily's shoulder.

'Do you mind, Emily, two of my dearest friends are absolutely desperate to meet the man of the moment. Might I just steal him away for two minutes?' And with the most insincere of smiles she led the unfortunate photographer back through the crowds towards two cooing, fortyish, glamour pusses.

'If that was a rescue bid she led him the wrong way,' Penny Chilston commented from behind her glass. Her voice was slurred.

Emily was not at all upset. No one had ever accused Willie of having taste when it came to women.

It was a typical Willie gathering, dressed with lots of beautiful, clever people, but until Hudson got there it would be only half a party, all eyes shifting towards the house whenever newcomers arrived. In the car on the way Richard had been talking quickly and excitedly about the Mupangare pictures and Clover Merrifield's article. 'Did you read it? Wasn't it perfect?' he had said. 'So straightforward and uncluttered. It's a pity we didn't have more like her in the old *Witness* days.' That was a rare compliment, and Emily had noticed, too, his delight when he saw that Clover had been invited to the lunch. Girls like Clover, she thought, started at the top, but inevitably managed to climb higher.

By two the garden had taken on the animation of a salon as friends and neighbours formed little groups of mutual admiration: a novelist and his wife who were crippled with envy at the style Willie had now acquired; an Irish lady poet of forty, snow-white-haired and beautiful; a young theatrical impresario, his wealth inherited, who arrived with delicious identical twin models; a CBS documentary producer over from New York whom Willie was hoping to interest in a programme about the old Hollywood screenwriters; and a heavily built Lebanese estate agent who was renting the Simmonds a small Tuscan *palazzo* for the summer. Then there was the choreographer, a tiny silver crucifix around his neck which, on closer observation, Emily discovered not to be a symbol of Christianity at all but an intertwining of tiny metallic figures engrossed in congress devious, and a well-known television sports commentator, looking around for someone who would listen to him, and generally making too free with the champagne. And finally dandy Willie himself, his blond hair thinning now, his smile welcoming, his fingers wandering, his suit of pale blue and white pinstripes, his speech an occasional hammer drill of frustration. He was very happy today, he said. *Toffee Ration* was booking until Christmas, which was not strictly true but which went unquestioned.

Hudson arrived just before three apologizing for his lateness, smiling around like royalty and towing Charlie Latymer and Dominique Fayence in his wake.

'He looks well, doesn't he? I mean *really* well,' said Penny. Emily smiled. Penny's devotion had never wavered, but on this occasion she was right. It was a long time since Hudson had looked so happy.

After a little while he saw Emily watching and scooping Tom up into his arms, over his head and down the other side, he strolled across to her.

'I was thinking of you this morning,' he said, joining her on the steps of the summer-house as Penny disappeared in search of the wine waiter.

'That's nice. Or isn't it?'

'Nice memories. I was driving along Charing Cross Road on my way to the studio and I suddenly remembered you dragging me into that cinema there to see some very long Italian movie because you thought I was cinematically illiterate.'

'You were. And I was a terrible snob. What was it? Antonioni or Pasolini?'

'Neither. Visconti. *Rocco and His Brothers*, and you were wearing your green duffel coat over a grey V-necked sweater . . .'

'Selfridges.'

'. . . and you had to dig me in the ribs when I fell asleep.'

Emily was pleased but the past was always dangerous for them. She changed the subject. 'The papers keep saying you're trying to take over the world,' she said.

His eyes lit up. 'I hope so. And with all the old team to help me.'

'Why?' she asked.

'Why?' He looked puzzled.

'Why so many people from *Witness*?'

He shook his head in genuine surprise. 'Because they made everything possible, Emily. You know that. They're like . . .'

'Family?' she said.

(v)

He examined his fading scars in the bathroom mirror, allowing the cold water to run off his soaking head into the basin. It was after four and he had drunk too much, too quickly. He felt over-praised, over-patronized and out of gear in these surroundings. He wondered where Clover was, with whom she was talking. She was so pretty, so accomplished. Every man at the party had been taken by her: even Dominique Fayence had felt the draught of competition; even the mighty Hudson had noticed. Hudson. This was the first time he had seen him. He was younger than he had expected, no more than forty, surely, and so tall: Hollywood film star tall. Someone so famous and so powerful ought to be older, and not so good looking. He pushed his head under the water once more, wetting his shirt collar and cuffs, ignoring the knocking on the bathroom door.

It should have been the most wonderful day of his career. He had been up at eight to buy *Sunday Morning* off a news-stand, to see his pictures. They had worked out better than he had dared hope, and now there was talk of them being entered for some pictures of the year competition. Not bad for a first assignment. Yet he was disappointed. Everything Clover had written had been accurate but there had been something missing. The double-page spread bore his by-line, photographs and story by Rob Barnes, and was factually accurate. But it could never be anything more than fragments of the day, a selection of moments which barely scratched the surface.

Perhaps he had expected too much. For reasons he did not understand he had made no mention of Michael, the albino boy, and, although Richard Blake had wanted to know about his night at Wildwood, he had said only that he found it by accident and left when someone turned up to lead him to Umtali. No explanations. It was as though talking about it would betray Michael's trust. The tormented pale eyes followed him everywhere: 'My father. I know where he is buried. I know how he died. He was executed. They said he was a murderer and they hanged him in the prison. He is an unhappy ghost with Miss Nicola Reynolds now.' There would have been no space for that in *Sunday Morning*.

That morning he had helped tell the background to a not uncommon event. Villagers and soldiers had been killed in an attack. Because he had been there the world knew about it. He had done his job. He had passed on the word. But it wasn't enough. News was a commodity. It was mined or harvested, processed, packaged, marketed and sold. It was the best that could be done, but it somehow wasn't real.

Drying his hands and face on a towel he unlocked the door. Clover was waiting on the half-landing outside the guests' bathroom. 'Are you all right? You've been an absolute age.' She sounded more irritated than concerned.

'Is it time to go yet?' he asked.

She pulled a face. 'P'raps you should go if you want to. I'll stay on here. I'll see you tomorrow.'

'I meant we should both go. You and me. Together.'

A tiny cross vertical line appeared between her brows. 'I'm not ready. Besides . . .'

'Besides what?'

'Well, if we left together it would look as though we were together . . . I mean, living together or something, a pair. And we're not, are we? Don't worry about me. I'll get a taxi.'

He did not answer. She moved to one side to enter the bathroom, kissing him fleetingly on the cheek as she passed. Then she went inside, closing and locking the door.

For some moments he did not move. Pride demanded he should leave immediately. But he did not.

In the garden he found the wine waiter and despite his headache took another glass. He would wait for Clover until the party was over. She was probably overwrought from the pressure of work. Things would be different when they were alone. Dignity is the first casualty of love.

'Have you met Rob Barnes, Hudson?' The editor, Richard Blake, suddenly had a hand on his shoulder.

Hudson was already smiling: 'Well done, well done. My, did you do well for us! Terrific! Are you all right? No damage, no problems . . . ?' His face was kind and generous.

'Absolutely none at all. I'm fine, thank you,' the photographer was almost embarrassed by his boss's enthusiasm.

Hudson grinned. 'Of course you are,' he joked. Then gently he lowered his tone. 'And Wildwood? Richard told me you were there. Is everything all right at Wildwood?'

The photographer nodded.

Hudson became momentarily reflective. 'Good, good. I've often thought . . .' He didn't finish his sentence, but turned to Richard. 'You never went there, did you? It's a most wonderful place. Well, of course, you know that . . .'

There was a silence.

'Rob will be joining us full time on the staff,' Richard said after a moment.

Hudson brightened. 'Oh really. That's fabulous. Terrific news.'

The photographer was flattered. Hudson was so enthusiastic.

'And take my advice,' Hudson joked, 'don't let them beat you down. Stand out for what you think you're worth. I'll back you. OK?'

'I'll do that. Thank you.'

Clover had now reappeared at his side. She was smiling, pleased to be with him.

'Thank *you*, Rob,' Hudson insisted. 'It's great to have you with us.' He turned to Clover. 'And you, too. Both of you. You're the people who are going to make *Sunday Morning* a success.'

With that Hudson turned away as Dominique Fayence and Charles Latymer made their way down the garden accompanied by Emily and Tim Gimmelmann. Immediately Dominique moved to Hudson's side. Latymer was smiling happily.

'It was so nice to meet you,' Emily came across to the photographer, simultaneously putting out a hand to catch her youngest son as he was running, tripping past, then colliding safely into her skirt. She ruffled the child's hair. Her voice dropped. 'We still miss her, you see. All of us. We all loved Nicola.'

With that she was gone. The garden was suddenly almost empty. At the end where a tortoise had been entertaining the children a very big, plain woman was half-snoozing in a deck-chair, her mouth falling open, her eyes closing, an empty glass at her feet. The photographer watched as Willie Simmonds went across and, pulling a deck-chair alongside, refilled her glass.

'Well, P..enny, looks like it's just you and me, old g..irl. You know, you didn't tell me . . . what did you really th..ink of *Toffee Ration*? Honestly!'

The woman opened bleary eyes. '*Toffee Ration*? Honest opinion?'

'Honest op..inion,' insisted Willie.

'Absolutely bloody brilliant.'

'Liar,' said Willie. And kissed her.

The photographer still didn't know half the members of the *Sunday Morning* staff but he realized now who this woman must be. It was a pity about the drink. They said that she was a terrific journalist when she was off the booze.

254

Suddenly he realized that she was staring at him. Embarrassed, he tried to turn away.

'Well, what do you say, pretty boy? Did you get your toffee ration today yet?' She laughed. 'Did you? I bet you did. With eyes like that, no problem. If you didn't, the number's in the book. OK?'

'Oh dear, Penny,' Willie murmured.

But the photographer wasn't embarrassed. For the first time all day he found himself grinning. He liked this big, plain woman. 'I was thinking perhaps we could do some stories together sometime,' he said.

'Ah,' said Penny. 'Promises, promises,' and blowing him a kiss put the glass to her lips.

Chapter Twenty-Seven

The face was bruised, with welts under swollen eyes, the bottom lip cut, as though sliced in two by some sharp instrument. The cheeks and jaw were unshaven. The expression was frightened, uncomprehending, timid, bulging eyes looking up into a light, a scattering of pimples betraying the man's youth. He would, thought the photographer, have been considered a handsome young man in other circumstances, his tight, curly black hair cut neatly, a thin wispy moustache running along his top lip. But the face, frozen at that moment, told only fear and confusion. *Marco de Sampaio, the man accused of the murder of Nicola Reynolds.*

The photographer had begun the day in the library leased to *Sunday Morning* by Federated British, but as publishers of the tabloid *Reporter* the cuttings there had been bigger on headlines than detail. The British Museum's Newspaper Library offered better coverage, the day-by-day, on-the-spot reporting of local Rhodesian newspapers. It was important to him to find out what had happened.

The murder had been the lead for three days running in the *Rhodesia Herald*, and the trial, front-page stuff for a full week later in the year. In Rhodesia Nicola Reynolds had been an important person. On the first day there had been a photograph showing a pretty young woman. *Newly wed heiress murdered in Vumba mansion*; on the second a picture of a very boyish Hudson, tears on his cheeks, as the police had searched the hills and the Mozambique border for *three missing assailants*. And on the third day had come the picture of the accused, a black man, a thief, caught hiding out in the hills, a

256

vagrant Shona from over the border in Mozambique.

Vainly the photographer looked for something of Michael in the young man's picture. Almost embarrassed with himself he realized he had been half-expecting to see the face of another albino. This young man would never have had to suffer the taunts of others because of his looks. Marco de Sampaio would have been a favourite with the girls all right.

Very carefully he shifted the microfilm in the frame and, adjusting the focus slightly, read the caption. *Marco de Sampaio, twenty-three, arrested on the Mozambique border and charged with the Wildwood killing.*

There was another photograph of the dead girl, a Sixties wedding-day picture, Hudson at her side, friends around her. Emily Blake's voice stole quietly into his consciousness. 'We still miss her, you see. All of us. Wildwood . . . I know the house. I stayed there once . . . We all loved Nicola.'

PART FOUR
1964

Chapter Twenty-Eight

They arrived in the morning, a sharp, clear winter's day in August when the earth was brown and dry. All the way down from Nairobi Nicola had been excited, insisting that Emily sit by the window and see Africa at dawn. But, though the Britannia cabin had flooded with pink, new light, the banks of mist below had hidden the earth until, with a bump and a slight bounce, the aeroplane had touched down at Salisbury.

Emily's surprise was immediate. The airport was so small, so local.

A night flight to the residue of the Empire and the plane had been stuffed with lightly tanned faces, fair hair, and many-pocketed cotton jackets: chaps for mopping-up operations in Northern Rhodesia, soon to be Zambia, for post-natal assistance in Malawi, until recently Nyasaland, and for shoring-up tactics in Southern Rhodesia.

Stepping down from the plane – Nicola defiant in a skirt too short and Emily sensible in trousers – they made their way to the small airport terminal where families and friends, floral-dressed wives, blond children and fair girls in the longer, flowing skirts and fitted bodices of a couple of years earlier, waved their menfolk greetings. A customs official, with long shorts, high socks and brown, scuffed knees, pointed the way into the arrivals' hall, casting a sly look at Nicola's exposed legs. 'A massive English county that got misplaced in Southern Africa . . .' A phrase of Nicola's was caught in a groove in Emily's mind.

Africa started at the airport doors where a middle-aged black man with grey hair, and wearing a thin jacket and trousers, a royal-blue pullover and a white shirt, was waiting to greet them. He beamed when he saw Nicola.

'Joseph, how are you?' she was already laughing.

'Oh, very good, Miss Nicola. Very good. The car is just here.' He turned to the two porters who had hurried to take the girls' bags and indicated a cream Citroën DS Safari Estate.

'Joseph, this is a friend of mine from London. Emily Robinson. She's going to be staying with us for a few weeks.'

Emily put out her hand. 'How are you?'

Very politely Joseph greeted her. 'I saw the aeroplane coming. Very big and very noisy.'

'And very far,' said Nicola. 'We're exhausted.'

'Oh yes, very far. Too far,' Joseph said and held open a rear door of the Citroën.

Smoothly the estate car pulled away from the airport. And as Emily listened to Nicola chatting, solicitously asking Joseph about his family, the car, the recent weather and his orchids, she began to understand what she had meant when she warned that she might behave differently in Africa. She was talking like a little princess.

'And what about Mashona, Joseph? I hope you haven't been spoiling him too much.'

'Oh no. He is very well.'

'Not fat?'

'Not too fat.'

Nicola laughed. 'Fibber. I bet he's as plump as an old pig.'

'I think he is looking forward to you coming home.'

'Home, yes,' mused Nicola. 'Home where the eagles fly.' She sagged back in her seat and followed Emily's gaze out of the car window. 'I'm afraid it's a long drive to Umtali, Emmy. But there's quite a lot to see. And Joseph promises to do a Stirling Moss for us, isn't that right, Joseph?'

Emily thought it doubtful that Joseph would have known much about an English racing-car driver called Stirling Moss, but he understood the request and accelerated the big car away from the smart villas and English

gardens of suburban Salisbury. At her side Nicola pointed
out landmarks as they went: a wooden cottage offering
traditional English cream teas, a giant lunar landscape
of balancing rocks, and a pole and dagga early settlers'
house built in the thatched style of the native African huts.
'Bring her back safely,' Richard had fretted at the airport,
as Nicola, hyperactive with excitement, had disappeared
back into the bookshop to find an additional gift for
the housegirl, Fortunate. 'Of course I will,' Emily had
promised. Hudson had slipped a lucky token into her
hand. It was a tiny silver drummer boy. Hudson liked
to give presents.

The previous day they had all been down to Wimbledon for the afternoon, Richard's parents and sister being
away, picnicking on the lawn, playing on the swing.

For eight months the spirit of the foursome had
governed their lives, hardly a day passing when they had
not spoken, scarcely a weekend when they had not been
together. Days out driving in the Cotswolds, a day at
the Cheltenham Races on Nicola's twenty-first birthday
when she had won fifty pounds and then spent all of it
and more on the most lavish dinner any of them had
ever seen, another on the river with Hudson as a mean
punter, visits to the cinema, four in a row, a trip to see
the Rolling Stones at High Wycombe; swimming in the
sea in Sussex, Hudson the best by far, and a night together
in a haunted room at a friend's tumbledown stately home,
when they had laughed until dawn. None of them had
ever had so much fun before. Just before Easter Nicola
had become convinced that she was pregnant and had -
had six desperate days. It had been a false alarm but
she had not taken any more chances. An appointment had
been made with Dr Withy in Wool Road and a diaphragm
had been fitted. A few days later Emily had paid him a
visit, too.

Only during finals had there been an enforced separation, as Nicola had panicked and forbidden Richard
even to call. 'The trouble with men is they're such a

distraction,' she had reflected ruefully on the first morning of judgement. 'If you hadn't met Hudson you'd have walked an upper second . . .'

'And you'd still have been up all night reading what you should have read two years ago,' Emily had replied.

'I wasn't reading, I was praying.'

'For a miracle?'

Nicola nodded. 'But it won't do any good. "The words fly up, the thoughts remain below. Girls without knickers, never to heaven go."' She walked on. 'It's all Richard's fault.'

Even had the flat in Chepstow Villas been large enough Emily and Nicola would not have moved in. They were starting their careers and wanted their own place, although it had already been agreed they would both work for *Witness*. So a two-bedroomed flat over a florist's shop behind Sloane Square had by July replaced South Park Road.

It had been Nicola who had insisted Emily go with her to Africa. 'Don't tell me you can't afford it because I'm treating you and I won't take no for an answer this year, especially as it was my fault about your degree. Besides my uncle's going to be away in South Africa for most of the time so it's an opportunity not to be missed. See Africa with the sun shining.'

'He can't be that bad.'

'No, but he can be grumpy enough to curdle a crocodile's milk when he's in the mood. Anyway, no arguing, you're coming, and it's on me.'

In the end Emily's parents had insisted upon helping, slightly disappointed though they were with her lower second. For Nicola the same degree had been a tiny miracle of flair over application.

What exactly they thought of Hudson had never been easy to tell. He was Emily's first serious boy-friend, and, though he made every attempt to be respectful towards her father and complimentary to her mother, Emily felt that judgement was being reserved. 'He's very handsome,

Emily . . .' her mother would say, in a tone which suggested that he was perhaps too handsome for her daughter, while her father would suck on his pipe, smile his secret thoughts through family dinner parties where Hudson would shine, and wait to see what happened. 'Love is a long-distance race, Emily,' he had told her one night. 'It has ups and downs and detours around the houses, and it's usually best when it's a slow start. But never forget your friends.'

And now the friends were in Africa, driving swiftly across the farming plateau of Eastern Rhodesia. 'What d'you think, Emmy? The Garden of Eden on five dollars a day?' Nicola grinned, yawning her jet lag and snuggling her face against Emily's shoulder.

Emily stared out at five black children in descending height who were walking in single file along the side of the road. 'It certainly beats the hell out of Middle English with F. W. Barrington,' she said.

It was night when they reached Wildwood, the Citroën's hydraulic suspension easing gently over the bumps of the dirt road. Emily had wanted to stay awake, to see everything, but long before they had reached the Eastern Highlands she had been asleep. Now Nicola suddenly shifted alongside her and wound down the car window, breathing in the air in great gulps. 'I can smell it, Joseph,' she said. 'I can smell home. Isn't it wonderful?'

'It is always good to come home,' said Joseph.

Pulling herself up Emily stared ahead at the track, yellow in the car headlights, as they wound their way up the mountain. In front of them a large bird, the size of an owl, flew directly towards the windscreen, before darting away at the last moment. A cold, pine breeze blew from Nicola's open window. Emily gazed into the darkness. It was more remote than anywhere she had ever been.

After some minutes the car pulled clear of the bushes and the house came into view, large and white on the hill above them.

Nicola squeezed her arm. 'Welcome to Wildwood.'

It was not what Emily had expected, although, in truth, she had not known what to expect in this little piece of Africa which reminded her of Scotland. Scarcely before the car had drawn to a halt Nicola had been through her door and into the arms of a small, stout black lady in blue serge, whose thick hair fitted her head like a helmet of grey wool, and whose round wire spectacles were balanced across a wide nose. At her feet two dogs barked excitedly. 'Alice, how are you? It's so wonderful to see you. Let me look at you. Fantastic! You get younger every year. How's the hip? God, it's good to be home.'

The woman laughed and took Nicola's kisses with evident delight although she did not kiss her back. 'I think you are not eating enough in England, Miss Nicola,' she chirruped at last when given the chance to speak.

Nicola giggled. 'Well, you know the English, Alice, all dandruff and thin blood. I brought the best of the bunch back for you.' And she turned to introduce Emily.

That was how Nicola was that whole first evening as, ignoring Alice's disapproval at the length of her skirt, she led Emily around the house, to the guest bedroom where a pine log fire was already burning, to her own room with her stacks of records and books, to the flag-stoned kitchen, rich with the smell of a roast in the oven ('fatted impala time, eh?'), and to the large, panelled drawing room with its heavyweight furniture, rugs and brocade curtains. Everywhere she went light broke into the gloom.

Apart from Joseph and Alice there was only one other full-time servant, Fortunate, the timid housegirl who hovered in the kitchen, afraid to join the welcome. 'I'll talk to her later,' Nicola said, as Fortunate fled from Emily's outstretched hand. 'She takes a little time. My fascist uncle has probably half-terrorized her to death.'

Before dinner and because they were in Africa, they

266

both had a large gin and tonic and Nicola gave potted histories of the characters in the silver-framed photographs in the drawing room. 'My entire family,' she said, 'and except for Uncle Alec, all dead.' Apart from the half-dozen pictures of Nicola herself there was a great-uncle, Ernest Reynolds ('famous for his bush wives, bad breath and the burst appendix which carried him off'); her father, a jaunty young officer in RAF uniform; Uncle Alec as a boy big-game hunter, rifle in hand, his foot on the head of a dead leopard, her parents on their wedding-day in London; her mother a striking young woman in a plain square-shouldered suit with a posy of flowers in her hands; and lastly a faded photograph of Nicola's mother and two brothers in sailor suits as children in Poland.

'Do you ever feel lonely?' Emily asked later as, to her surprise, they had dinner alone at one end of the carved oak dining-room table. 'I mean, you've hardly got anyone left any more.'

Nicola mused for a moment over the roast lamb. 'Well, yes, I suppose I did. Until I met you, anyway. Not now. I've got all I need now. You and Richard and Hudson. You're more than enough for me.'

Emily awoke in fear, choking, a terrifying dream she couldn't remember, not knowing where she was or what was happening as an explosion of noise struck the house. Afraid to move, catching at her breath, she huddled in the blackness beneath the sheets: somewhere above something large scuttled on the roof or in the rafters. The room lit up and lightning leapt in at her through a gap in the curtains. Another roar of thunder bore her down. From the ceiling came more urgent noises. Outside the dogs barked and whined.

Pulling herself up Emily reached across to where she remembered there had been a bedside light. It did not work. Again the tympany struck, the lightning illuminating a picture of an English church on one wall, an old-fashioned dresser, her underclothes left on the back of a chair. Then blackness again. Somewhere close by there was a crashing of glass and a roaring, as the wind raced like a vandal into the house, sending doors crashing. Again the scuttling, louder and directly above her. Outside her window a shutter, having broken free, was creaking and whining.

Pulling back the covers, shrinking as she put her feet on to the carpet, she felt her way to the window and gazed out on the mountain as sheet lightning momentarily made day of night. Rain lashed horizontally against the glass. Feeling her way across the room she stepped out on to the landing. A door at the far end of the house was swinging on its hinges. Moving down the passage, her fingers against the wall for security, she reached for the door handle. Without warning a sudden draught of air wrenched it from her hand before slamming it shut in her face.

It was then that she saw her, caught in the flash of lightning, standing in her bedroom doorway at the far end of the landing, her fair hair shining white, her face pale, a beautiful ghost, the old shirt of Richard's she wore for sleeping luminous almost. Then she was gone, back into the blackness and thunder.

'Emmy . . . Emmy, are you all right?' Nicola was padding down the landing.

Emily could not answer.

'Emmy . . . what's the matter?' Suddenly she was there, the comforting arms, the breath warm and close.

'I thought I saw . . .' Emily was shaking.

Nicola held her closer, a hand stroking her hair. 'Nothing to worry about. It does this sometimes up here, though not usually at this time of year.' Another flash and roll of thunder. 'Gosh, they're playing every kettledrum in heaven tonight all right, aren't they?'

Emily shivered. 'I thought there was something in my room . . . or the ceiling . . . something moving . . .'

'It was probably just a squirrel or a monkey on the roof ... something like that. They don't like the thunder any more than you do.' She held her close. 'Crumbs, Emmy, you're shaking.'

'I'm sorry ... I ...' The image of Nicola frozen in her doorway at the moment the lightning had struck would not leave her.

There was the sound of a door being opened downstairs and some hurrying feet. Then the beam of a torch appeared, finding them on the landing. 'Nicola? What's going on? What's happening up there?' The anxious voice of Alice echoed up the wide staircase.

'It's nothing, Alice, just a window blown open, I think. We'll get Joseph to fix it in the morning. Nothing to worry about.'

Emily could see her now, the squat black lady in a long, patterned flannelette nightdress and nightcap.

'No one is hurt? You are not hurt, Nicola?'

'No. We're fine. We're going back to bed now, Alice. See you in the morning. Good night,' said Nicola, and led Emily back along the landing. By Emily's door she stopped. 'I tell you what, Emmy. Come in with me for tonight. There's plenty of room. No monkeys in there, I promise.'

The sheets were warm and scented already of Nicola, and once in bed she immediately cuddled up unselfconsciously, her arms around Emily, holding her close, protecting her from the storm.

'I'm sorry ... I feel so stupid.' Emily was embarrassed now.

'Don't think about it. I've been doing my best to get you into bed for years,' Nicola mocked and, giving her a final hug, kissed her on the nape of her neck. 'Good night. God bless.'

The storm raged for half the night after that but Nicola did not move again. At first Emily listened to the thunder and waited for the lightning. But there was no more scratching from the roof. Alongside her, Nicola's body was warm, the rhythm of her breath comforting.

In the morning there was no sign of her. It was nearly ten when Emily awoke and with the sun playing through the window she was ashamed of her fears of the night. Moving her head across the pillow she found the indentation where Nicola had slept and, turning her face into it, she closed her eyes. Suddenly from downstairs came the havoc of very loud laughter. Pulling on Nicola's dressing gown she opened the door, and, creeping along the landing, peered down to the hall. Nicola was standing with Joseph, Alice and Fortunate, all four of them wearing Beatle wigs brought from London, while Nicola did an extraordinary imitation of John Lennon singing *A Hard Day's Night*, a tennis-racquet for a guitar. It was a comical, Marx Brothers sight, Alice and Joseph laughing so much that tears fell from their cheeks, while behind them the house-girl Fortunate tapped timidly on a large tureen with a wooden ladle. '*When I'm home, everything seems to be right, When I'm home feeling you holding me tight, tight . . . oh . . .*' sang Nicola through half-clenched teeth, her eyes peering short-sightedly at an imaginary audience down the hall, her Beatle wig lop-sided on top of her hair. It was Pith-Helmet and the Dandelions in improvised performance, thought Emily. On the mahogany dresser alongside were the presents Nicola had brought home, the Old Spice aftershave lotion and new shirt for Joseph, a polka-dotted skirt and blouse from Marks & Spencer for Alice, and a pretty necklace of imitation pink ochre and paperback copy of *The Wind In The Willows* for Fortunate.

'*Dum, dee-dum-dum dee-dum, diddle-liddle-liddle-liddle-liddle-liddle-liddle-liddle-lum . . .*' Suddenly the laughter went into gales as Nicola began to sing her approximation of a guitar solo, simultaneously hopping, one knee bent, across the hall, her racquet thrust out in front in an approximation of what Chuck Berry called his duck walk. Emily smiled. No wonder they loved her so much.

After breakfast Nicola took her around the grounds, past the outhouses beyond the kitchen where the staff had their small, private, whitewashed rooms, and on to the lawn and pool, the two dogs, a sheepdog and a collie, padding along behind them, quiet today. It was grander than Emily could have expected in a place so remote, a small estate of ornamental gardens, bamboo copses, paddocks, rock gardens, sweeping lawns, a summer-house and a lake filled by a mountain stream where glints of gold and silver flitted beneath the surface. At the end of the lawn was a large msasa tree, with rough-hewn steps up to a tree house. Nicola led the way up.

'This was my windy house,' she said, as they stood on the little sheltered platform and gazed across the gardens to the house.

'You mean Wendy house?' Emily corrected.

'That's what it should have been called but when my uncle had it built the carpenter who made it always called it a windy house, and that's what I called it. I imagine I thought it was called that because it was windy up here in the tree. It wasn't until I read *Peter Pan* at school in England that I realized I'd got it all wrong. But it was too late by then. Even the servants call it the windy house.'

In the vegetable garden two Africans were working ('the deal is that they grow it, we take what we need for the house, and whatever is left over they keep for themselves or sell'), while Joseph was with his orchids in one of the greenhouses. 'Didn't I tell you, Emmy, Joseph grows the best orchids in the world?'

Emily looked around at the dozens of different specimens in their pots. Although few were in bloom the fragrance was heady, and around a corner of her mind she saw again Nicola dragging her into the orchid house in the Botanic Garden in Oxford 'for a quick drag of home'.

At midday they went riding, Nicola beating the path on her black pony, Mashona, taking the forest track to the side of the house, up past the jacaranda tree, and on to the smooth open hillside. Emily followed more cautiously on a docile grey, especially hired for her by Joseph from a riding school near Umtali.

Nicola was a confident rider, knowing the open meadows where her pony, as plump as she had feared and shaggy now with a winter coat, would break into an automatic canter; Emily trotted behind. The previous day as they had driven towards the mountains it had seemed to Emily that the silver-trunked eucalyptus trees and commercial pine plantations dressed the region in alien, unAfrican colours. But colonization had never reached these rounded heights where the ancient red mahogany forest gave way to sparse grassland and outbreaks of smooth, grey, granite kop.

At the highest point Nicola reined in her pony and waited for Emily to join her. 'This is my idea of heaven, Emmy,' she said, looking down across the mist of the valley into Mozambique. 'When I was a little girl I would beg my mother to bring me up here. We'd sit and pretend we were on top of the world and could command the clouds and tell them which way to blow.'

Emily stood in her stirrups and gazed around. 'How far is Mozambique?' she asked.

'A mile maybe, perhaps two,' said Nicola. 'The border runs all along here. Children come over the border to go to school. Men wander by looking for work. They're Shona first and Rhodesian or Mozambique second. Alice always sends them on their way when they come knocking on the door asking for jobs. I'm afraid she likes to think of herself as a good old Brit, loyal to the Queen and everything. They stand a better chance with Joseph.'

A few miles away to the south and west a single, thin plume of smoke was rising into the air. 'What's that?' Emily asked.

'Probably someone cooking *sadza* in Mupangare,' Nicola ventured. 'That's the village where the servants

272

come from. Technically our nearest neighbours, I suppose.'

'Can we see?'

A slight hesitation, then: 'Well, yes, of course, why not? Follow me,' Nicola said, and, digging her heels into her pony, she led the way back down the mountain.

Mupangare was pretty, a small settlement of huts set in a sheltered curve of wooded hills and surrounded by maize gardens. All the way from Salisbury the African villages had fascinated Emily. For some reason it had never occurred to her that Africans would still live in thatched huts.

'They'll be wondering what on earth we're doing here,' Nicola said, as women working in the small fields, babies on their backs, stopped and stared. 'White people don't often call at Mupangare unless they have a specific purpose, usually a complaint, I suppose.'

'Not even you?'

Nicola shook her head. 'That sort of thing isn't encouraged among Rhodesian girls. I still feel a bit odd, to be honest.'

Emily could not be certain but as they approached the village she fancied she sensed Nicola's spine straighten and her chin go up.

They didn't dismount. Stopping at the beginning of the open space where the village began Emily smiled at the children while Nicola called greetings to three or four women who came out of the huts to see them. 'We were just passing,' she said awkwardly. 'We just thought we'd say "hello", if that's all right.' She sounded very stilted.

The women looked at the girls, perplexed and amused. One of the younger ones giggled. No one knew what to say. Emily would have liked to look inside one of the huts but she thought it impolite to ask.

'Just wait until Alice hears we've been here,' Nicola said quietly. 'She's such a snob. She'll have a fit. Anyway, we'd better get on.' And turning her pony around she waved politely. 'Thank you very much,' she called, and began to walk Mashona out of the village.

Emily followed. It had been an odd moment.

Turning to look back Nicola caught Emily's eye. 'I know,' she said. 'But you didn't grow up here . . .'

All afternoon Nicola led the way from one viewpoint to the next, proud of her home, pleased to have someone with whom she could share it. There was so much to see: the winter sun turning the hills orange; the large family of baboons, strong and aggressive, which chattered and called in the bush and made the ponies nervous; the single eland grazing on the heath far below: the vastness.

'It just seems so endless. Is it all national forest or park or something?' said Emily as, their ponies grazing below, they sat on a smooth granite headland and ate the apples and sandwiches they had brought as a picnic.

'Well, yes, some of it is, I suppose. But this particular bit, here and up there to the north, and behind us as far as the border, in fact most of what we've seen today, that's ours.'

'Ours?'

'I mean, the Reynolds family. Wildwood. We own it. Quite a lot of it, anyway.'

'But it's huge?'

'Well, quite huge, I suppose. By English standards it is, yes. Fortunately it isn't much use for farming so it's been pretty well left alone, apart from the pine plantations. The Tribal Trust areas like Mupangare are separate, of course. They're owned by the Government for the villagers.'

Emily was astonished. 'I'd no idea . . .'

Nicola looked awkward. 'You have to remember that the Government was virtually giving land away only a few years ago. I know it wasn't exactly theirs to give, but that's what they were doing. To be absolutely honest, Emmy, Wildwood is just the Reynolds' holiday house. It's home to me because I was here as a child but my uncle has one or two other places he would far rather live in. I think he only keeps this place on because I like it, and . . . well, it's in my name, anyway, his for use in his life and then mine. That's what the trust fund says. He doesn't spend much time up here. He can't make any money on the top of a mountain.'

'I knew he had another house in Salisbury . . .'

'The business is based in Salisbury, so there's a house there, yes, and offices. Then there are some pretty big farms down towards Bulawayo and more land out to the north-east towards Lomagundi. You can grow anything there, they say. I don't know a lot about it, to be honest, but there's property and land all over the place and mining here and up in Northern Rhodesia – though God knows if we'll be able to hang on to that now. Quite a packet altogether, I suppose.'

'I never realized . . . I mean, I knew you were pretty rich . . .'

'You never asked. You didn't want to know. And as you can see we don't exactly live the champagne and jet-set life. The Reynolds got rich by turning out the lights at night and sharing the hot water for a bath.'

'All the same . . .'

'All the same, nothing. Yes, I'm a rich girl, and will get richer, but that doesn't mean anything. It isn't as though I'll inherit Wiltshire or Gloucestershire or anything. It's all relative . . .' With that she fell silent and lay back on the grass, the subject closed. After a few moments she caught sight of an eagle soaring on the wind, seeking out its prey, and pointed. 'Now there's a life,' she said. And they watched together, their heads back on the mountain, the wind in their ears.

At four they were caught by surprise as it suddenly turned cold, rain clouds sweeping in from the east, hiding the hilltops. 'Everywhere else gets a winter drought and what do we get . . . Manchester,' said Nicola as, remounting, they turned for home, trotting through the dripping, misty woods, their shirts and jodhpurs sticking to them.

By the time they reached the house the evening was closing in.

'You have been very long, Miss Nicola. Too long. It is not good. You can get lost or hurt.' Alice was standing fretting, rocking on her heels, muscular, blue-black arms akimbo as she waited on the kitchen steps.

Nicola slipped from the saddle and held Emily's pony's head for her to dismount as Joseph hurried forward to lead the horses away. 'I'm sorry, Alice, we sort of lost track of time. You aren't upset, are you?' Seeing Alice's worried expression Nicola looked suddenly shamefaced. 'I really am sorry, Alice. Honestly.'

Chapter Twenty-Nine

(i)

Charles Latymer was late and Hudson was already there, waiting patiently on the pavement outside the bank. He was, Latymer noted, wearing a navy-blue suit, blue shirt and what probably passed in America as an old school tie, a striped affair of various hues of blue and mauve. Latymer was pleased. Banks could be fussy about the appearance of those with whom they did business, even second- to third-division banks like Fiske-Forrester. 'A lot will depend on whether or not we like the look of him,' Neil Fiske had vaguely warned. 'It's all very speculative, you know, even though you say he isn't looking for very much.'

Not much to a bank, perhaps, but a fortune in *Witness* terms.

The conversation with Hudson had been accidental. Hudson had always been polite to him, always friendly, but Latymer knew he did not consider him part of the inner circle. And he wanted to be. More than anything Latymer wanted to be important.

They had bumped into each other in the Portobello one lunchtime, where, over a slice of steak and kidney pie and a half of bitter, *Witness* staff would gossip in pairs or read their copies of *Private Eye*. On this occasion only he and Hudson had been present and quite quickly the conversation had got around to the future of *Witness*. To expand *Witness* needed money, they agreed, and at that moment Latymer had seen his opening.

'Look, I don't know whether this is of any use, or whether they'll even be interested,' he had said, 'but a couple of pals of mine are doing quite well in banking. I could mention *Witness* to them, if you'd like me to.'

Hudson had smiled. 'By all means, do that, Charlie. Thank you very much. We've already got a few feelers out, but you never know.'

Latymer had seen in Hudson's expression that his offer had not been taken seriously: for his part Latymer had rarely been more serious. Immediately he had set to work on his networks. Neil Fiske, cutting his teeth in the family firm of Fiske-Forrester, had been the one to make a tentative bite.

'I thought for a minute you might not be coming,' Hudson said as they opened the heavy doors into the bank.

'I'm sorry,' Latymer said, but offered no reason. The truth was his Underground train had been stuck in a tunnel for fifteen minutes, but if Hudson had become even marginally anxious that was perhaps no bad thing. It made Latymer more important. It suited him to be the go-between who could help find the financing. It celebrated his view of his own importance and it secured his position at *Witness*. The tiny percentage finder's fee that Fiske-Forrester were offering, should they go for *Witness*, was incidental . . . in as much as any fee was ever incidental.

Neil Fiske had been an acquaintance, almost a friend, at Cambridge. Friends were important to Latymer, the right friends, the right ladders. Today was the first rung, nothing formal, just a preliminary meeting to see if Fiske took to Hudson. His office was on the fourth floor at the back of the building, a small room, almost devoid of any personal items. An office boy showed them the way.

If outside in the street Latymer had fancied Hudson might be displaying some slight diffidence, once in Fiske's office that notion was dispelled. He dazzled. Latymer had never seen a performance like it as Hudson laid out his plans. Everything was perfect: the confidence, the charm, the smile, oh yes, the smile. Even Fiske, with his long top lip, ferret teeth and cardigan under his suit, looked impressed.

'And how much would you be looking for . . . ?'

'A hundred thousand pounds.'

'To do all this?' Fiske had in front of him a sheet of paper on which Hudson had outlined the proposed expansion: *Witness* was to go weekly with a national readership; there would be special *Witness* projects including a *Witness Students' Cook Book*, *Witness Movie* and *Rock Music Guides*, a *Witness Cheap Travel Book*, a *Witness Cartoon Book* and perhaps even a compilation of *Witness* interviews, all part of the *Witness* way to living in the Sixties.

'To build the foundations for an expanding organization,' replied Hudson evenly.

'And the present shareholders and structure of the business . . . ?'

Hudson handed Fiske another sheet of paper meticulously prepared by Adam Smith bearing the names of himself and Richard. Then, over tea and biscuits, and in response to more questions, he produced further sheets containing details of advertising and circulation revenue, salaries, rents and expenses.

At about this point Latymer caught sight of his own reflection in the window and was momentarily distracted. His hand went to his hair. It was thick and already quite grey. He ruffled it very carefully as Hudson continued to talk in that open, friendly American way which was so beguiling. Fiske listened. Latymer congratulated himself. It was going well. Hudson would be very grateful to him if this came off. Perhaps he could persuade him to lean upon Richard to put a photograph alongside the Latymer by-line in future editions. Readers felt more secure when they could see what the writer looked like. He smoothed his hair down. He didn't want to leave Fiske-Forrester looking dishevelled.

Neil Fiske was smiling at him. 'Well then, Charles, I think I've got a pretty fair idea. Let's say we speak again in a week or so, when the partners have had a chance to take a look. I must say I think it's . . .' He became cautious. 'Well, certainly it's an interesting proposal. But we'll have to see what older and wiser heads think.' Standing, his hand went out: 'Thank you very much for coming in. May I keep these . . . ?' He indicated the papers. 'Jolly good.'

Fiske would be grateful to him, too, Latymer reflected happily as he stepped back into the lift. The trick, the big trick in a successful life, was to be able to use one's contacts.

'I was wondering, Hudson . . .' he began as the lift began its descent. 'I mean *Witness* doesn't have a deputy editor . . .'

'No, that's true. D'you think we need one?'

'Well, it had crossed my mind. Someone to help Richard.'

Hudson smiled to himself. 'It's an idea,' he said. 'I'll give it some thought, see what Richard thinks.'

(*ii*)

For everyone else August crawled by. The office was as sleepy as *Witness* had ever been, and without Nicola to distract him, Richard, like all editors at slow times, could not help but make a nuisance of himself. Willie Simmonds was always good to talk to. Virtually licking his lips he was labouring over a piece predicting that before the Sixties were through not only would full nudity be commonplace in cinema it was only a matter of time before full sexual intercourse became a standard part of every romantic film.

'You mean we're going to have film stars having it off on the screen?' Richard said. This sounded a lot like Willie's wishful thinking.

Grinning happily Willie stammered his convictions: 'It is in..evitable. As n..ight follows d..ay, as doffed kn..icker follows unclasped bra..ssière, as de..tumescence foll..ows or..gasm, as regret follows all. Art mirrors life. The new liberal real..ism of cin..ema will demand it.'

'I thought the thing about film was that it was all about pretence. I mean no one actually dies in a cowboy film, so why should they actually have to have sex. They can pretend that too, can't they?'

Willie shook his head. 'It isn't the same. Sex is f..un. Every..one likes it. We can all st..op being re..pressed now. God bl..ess the P..ill, and may the d..evil take the hind quar..ters. For too long the only real s..ex has been on the b..ack row of the st..alls. N..ow we are going to see it up there on the sil..ver screen, in close-up and Tech..nicolor at the Emp..ire Leices..ter Square.' Willie paused and then added wickedly, 'Did you know I was con..ceived on the b..ack row of the Guild..ford Gau..mont during *Jezebel* with Hen..ry Fon..da and Bette Da..vis?'

Richard said he had not known that, but was not surprised. As usual Willie's article overstated his case, but, in the dog-days of summer, magazines needed a little controversy to hold on to sales. 'Out of the back row and on to the screen: sex in the cinema, Sixties-style,' he mused. 'What d'you think? Something like that for the cover?'

Willie smiled. 'And maybe "Coming Soon" as a teaser.' When he had a joke to deliver Willie's speech could be as fluent as anyone's.

For once Peter Berridge was neither on the telephone nor baiting Latymer. Latymer had, Berridge insisted, gone grouse shooting with the ugliest daughter of an ugly duke, although everyone knew this to be untrue. He was, in fact, having a wisdom tooth extracted.

'Which means he'll be even more stupid now,' said Berridge.

'Why don't you like him?' Richard asked, leaning over Berridge's desk.

'He's two-faced,' said Berridge blankly.

Richard moved on. He had no wish to get into a

debate with Berridge about Charlie Latymer. Hudson liked Berridge but so far as Richard was concerned the sooner Fleet Street came poaching him the better. It wouldn't be long. No one who was any good would stay at *Witness* once they had been noticed. And in his way Berridge was good, and never two-faced.

Richard had lunch with Penny Chilston. She was pleased. Since Nicola and Emily had come to work at *Witness* Penny had been withdrawn. Now she only wanted to talk about Hudson.

'I can see it's obvious to everyone but what can I do?' she said. 'I know I'll never have an earthly with him but I've always known that. And honestly I'm not unhappy. I like Emily, I really do. I can understand. If I were Hudson I wouldn't look twice at me, either.'

'He's very fond of you,' said Richard, and then wished he hadn't.

Penny smiled. 'Of course he is. But he's not exactly likely to suddenly look at me and think how blind he's been all these months, and to suddenly drop Emily and whisk me off my feet. I mean, he's not even likely to come around drunk one night knocking on the door demanding I succumb to some instant rogering, no questions asked, no strings attached. And I would succumb, believe me, Richard, I'd succumb on the spot and roger till I split, much as I like Emily.'

'I don't think it ever enters Hudson's mind to . . . I mean, he's in love with Emily.' Again he sounded wet.

Penny was thoughtful for a moment. Then she said: 'Yes, Emily. And who can blame him? She's lovely. They're both lovely.'

'Both?' Richard didn't follow.

'Well, Nicola, too. I mean, you and Hudson, you've both done terribly well. Congratulations. And honestly I'm not miserable. I would be if I left *Witness*. I've thought about it. A girl has some pride, though not much, I grant you. At least so long as I'm here I'm doing what I want to do, and I do get to see Hudson every day. Quite honestly, if it's a choice between the pain of not seeing him and the pain of seeing him always with someone else, I'll settle for the latter, pathetic though I may be.'

'I don't think there's anything pathetic about being in love,' Richard mused.

'You don't? You should see my lodger.'

'Vasco? The one who says he's in love with you?'

'He's now telling the same story to a Korean cellist who works on the umbrella stand in Whiteley's. She's called the police twice and had him thrown out. He set fire to himself the last time so they turned a fire extinguisher on him.'

'He's crazy.'

'No. But like me, he is pathetic,' she said, and ordered another bottle. A drunken, gossipy lunch with Penny which went on until four in the afternoon, everyone away and nothing particularly exciting to do: that was the other, not altogether disagreeable, side to being the editor of *Witness*.

Chapter Thirty

(i)

The portrait painter came to Wildwood in the second week, a sallow, long-jawed woman in her late forties who drove an old grey Austin Cambridge and wore a pleated brown skirt, brown cardigan and see-through, cream, nylon blouse which showed her straps beneath. Her name was Diana Pugh and she lived in Umtali, where her husband was deputy finance manager at a logging company, and where she had achieved minor celebrity status for her portraits.

'Why?' was Emily's only question as Nicola hunted irritably through her clothes for something suitable to wear. Pugh the Portrait, as Nicola called her, was already downstairs setting up her easel by the window in the drawing room.

'Don't ask, Emmy. Yes ask. I'll tell you. I promised my uncle. Every year he mentioned it, and every year I put him off. God knows why he wants it. That's the way they are out here. *Nouveaux riches*. He's been saving a place on the wall for it. Personally I think he'd be better with a stuffed warthog's head, but no, it's me he wants in a nice dress and some tat around my neck. So don't just stand there, choose something.'

Between them they selected a blue ball gown (there were only two to choose from, blue or pink – hated left-overs from adolescent parties), and some white beads, and Emily tied the cream hair loosely back off Nicola's face. With the minimum of effort and no make-up the effect was stunning.

In the drawing room Pugh the Portrait was ready

o begin, drinking tea which was being served by Fortunate, and pointing with a cigarette holder as Alice and
Joseph moved a wicker chair nearer to the window. 'I
hear you're becoming a journalist in England, Nicola.
It'll be nice to read the truth about things out here for
once, instead of all those lies they tell in the English
papers.'

Nicola was not to be drawn. 'What d'you think? Is
this all right?' She sat in the wicker chair and looked at
the artist, who gazed long and hard at her before getting
up to edge the chair more into the light.

'If that's how you're comfortable . . . yes . . . pretty
dress. Perhaps if you could bring your hands together
. . . that's better . . . and your head, if you could just
raise your chin a fraction . . . ?'

From the back of the room Emily watched with Alice
and Joseph as the artist prepared her subject. Both servants were beaming. They certainly liked the idea of a
portrait of Nicola hanging on the wall after she had left.
Although Joseph had been friendly from the start Alice
had not spoken very much to Emily. In Alice's mind Emily
was, she knew, associated with all the things which would
tempt Nicola away again.

'Alice was always there,' Nicola would say. 'Even
before my mother died it was Alice I'd follow around the
house, Alice who taught me to bake, who played in the
garden with me, showed me how to make mud pies, fed
me, bathed me, made me *sadza*, put me to bed, told me
a story. Alice was home. She still is. She never changed.
I can't imagine her anywhere but here. She's always been
here. I've never even seen her go to Umtali. She's getting
on a bit now which is why Fortunate has been hired to
help out.'

Emily looked towards Fortunate. Now that the initial
sketching had begun the girl had lost interest and was
standing at the side of the room by a window, staring at
a glass dish containing an assortment of pastel-coloured
and speckled polished stone eggs. Very carefully she

285

picked one up and admired the seams of quartz which ran through it.

'They're pretty, aren't they?' Emily said softly, as she moved towards the girl.

Fortunate started, looked embarrassed and quickly replaced the egg. Then in embarrassment she hurried out of the room.

Oh dear, thought Emily.

Across the room Pugh the Portrait was going about her work, sliding in new details of a massacre by members of a religious sect in Northern Rhodesia as she sketched. 'These people aren't ready for elections, Nicola. They're barbarous. Don't fidget, dear.'

Emily wandered into the garden. Although winter in Rhodesia, it would have been considered a fine, summer's day in England, and with her tube of Ambre Solaire she sat in a deck-chair by the pool and began a letter to Hudson, wondering what he would be doing at that moment. Some distance away, at the end of the lawn, two monkeys played, chasing each other up and down the msasa tree, in and out of the tree house, only to be then chased themselves by the dogs, which barked excitedly before Joseph came out of the house to summon them away.

She stared at the notepaper. She would like to have written an affectionate, effusive letter, but that was not her way. Instead she wrote details, information and observations of how Nicola lived, of the beauty of the mountains and of how so much seemed 'familiar, but once removed, if you know what I mean, like a cousin with a distinct family resemblance but who thinks and acts altogether differently'. Then, feeling a complete pseud, she tore it all up and, raising her skirt a little higher, closed her eyes and enjoyed the sun. Hudson: there would be so much to tell him, and she toyed with the little silver drummer boy he had given her, which was now attached to her bracelet.

At twelve o'clock Fortunate brought her a jug of

home-made lemonade on a wooden tray, approaching, head down, across the grass. Emily had rarely met any-one so shy before, which was surprising because she was not an unattractive girl. She had a round, even face, her hair cut short to her head, and her figure, beneath her pretty, green patterned dress was, Emily realized, slightly voluptuous.

'Thank you,' Emily said. 'That's very kind of you. I'm sorry if I startled you in the house. Those eggs are very pretty, aren't they?' She smiled, hoping to reassure, and tasted the lemonade. 'Oh, heaven! You should have brought two glasses then you could have had some with me.'

Fortunate did not answer, but simply backed away, before turning and hurrying off across the lawn and into the house.

Emily sipped her drink. Not even Hudson would be able to charm a smile out of poor old Fortunate, she thought.

So the holiday passed, Pugh the Portrait governing Nicola's mornings with her easel and paints and hor-ror stories, while Emily read or roamed the grounds, or watched Joseph working in his greenhouse with the orchids. In the afternoons the two girls would go riding or take the car and tour the Highlands, north up to Inyanga, with its waterfalls and ruins, south down to Chimanimani. Everyone was pleased to see them and sometimes, a drink in hand on a veranda, talk of golf or tennis in the air, Emily would forget for a few moments that she was in Africa. Then the insecurities would emerge, the name of Ian Smith would be invoked, and Nicola would change the subject.

On a couple of occasions they stopped off in Umtali, a white-painted, old colonial town of wide, low streets situated in a saucer-shaped mountain pass where the railway ran over the border into Mozambique and on to the Indian Ocean at Beira. There they would buy a newspaper and sit in a tea-shop reading of events in the outside world. Violence was everywhere that August: in Vietnam after the Tonkin incident, in Cyprus and the Congo where there were civil wars, in Harlem where there were riots and in Mississippi where the bodies of three missing civil rights workers had been found.

'As Richard would say, "It's a hell of a time for news",' said Nicola one afternoon as they exchanged parts of the newspaper.

'To which Hudson would probably reply, "Pity we don't own the paper" . . .' Suddenly Emily smiled mischievously. 'Or do we?'

Nicola grinned. 'Not that I've heard. But it's an idea, isn't it? Mmm. Now that would be something.'

(ii)

Alec Reynolds arrived home from Johannesburg at the weekend, tearing up the dirt road in front of the house in a cloud of red dust. The servants heard him from afar, as he dropped his Mercedes down through the gears better to negotiate the climb, and immediately hurried to make him welcome. Nicola, who was teaching Emily the rudiments of croquet on the lawn when they heard the car, grimaced slightly. 'Don't worry,' she said, 'he likes young women. He doesn't see them as competition.' And dropping her mallet she went ahead to greet him.

By the time Emily reached the house Reynolds was out of the car and holding Nicola in his arms, a tall, once-handsome man of over seventy with thinning white hair, who, she noticed as he turned to approach her, walked with one leg permanently straight, the result, Nicola would explain, of a bad mining accident.

With his arrival the atmosphere in the house became uncertain. 'He's slightly intimidated by the English and he'll want to put on a good show,' Nicola confided. 'So be a darling, dress up and make him feel good, will you?'

She was right. Dinner was a formal affair and Reynolds, in a white dinner jacket, tried hard at first to make

Emily like him. He was charm itself. He enquired of the journey, the success of the holiday and the comfort of his home. Anything she wanted was hers for the asking. When Alice came in to serve dinner he was friendly and complimentary towards her and he expressed great satisfaction when she told him of the success Joseph had had with his orchids in the Umtali Flower Show. He was, it occurred to Emily, nothing less than a Victorian millowner, an apparently benign despot, whom everyone went out of their way to make happy. The servants had their reasons, of course. Working at Wildwood was a good job with accommodation. Lose that and it would be back to a hut and subsistence farming in the Tribal Trust Lands.

'I've been very interested in this magazine you've both been working for . . . *Witness*, you call it, don't you?' Dinner was nearly over and Reynolds was playing to Emily as the audience.

Nicola nodded.

'Yes, I read your piece about the Rhodesian Front. I thought it was very well written.'

Nicola caught Emily's eye, as though to say, 'Wait for it'.

'Very well written, but perhaps just a little bit disloyal.'

'Disloyal?' Nicola repeated the word quite evenly, as though savouring it. 'Disloyal.'

'Well, after all, Southern Rhodesia did give us everything we have . . . everything you have.' He looked at Emily to make sure that she had understood this last point.

Nicola ate in silence, her message clear. If he was looking for an argument he would have to argue with himself.

Feeling awkward Emily tried to enter the conversation. '*Witness* is a great success. Circulation's soaring.'

'I'm very pleased to hear it. Pay you well, does it?'

'Well, not much yet, but . . .'

Nicola interrupted. 'Now that isn't fair. It's a new

289

magazine and we're all starting out. No one's earning anything out of it yet other than a living wage. But give it time . . .'

Reynolds snorted. 'Time! You mean these guys who own it are taking you both for a ride?'

Emily was surprised. *Ride*. He had said the word quite deliberately so that a *double entendre* hung in the air for a moment.

Nicola was ready for him. 'Or vice versa,' she came back, quiet, steely, before adding playfully, 'sometimes vice, sometimes versa . . . sometimes naughty, sometimes worser . . . if we play our cards right.'

For a moment Emily thought an explosion was at hand. Nicola and her uncle were staring at each other as though testing the other's nerve, sensing out who would break first. Then suddenly Nicola smiled and leaned across the table.

'Crumbs, if you could just see your face. No one's going to take advantage of two clever clogs like Emily and me. Just let them try. Just watch us when we get back to London. We're going to set the world on fire.'

Reynolds grunted sardonically to himself. 'And you watch out you don't get burned, that's all,' he said.

After that the conversation drifted to talk of neighbours, business, the drought in Matabeleland, the price of copper and a new exaggeration about how the first of the Reynolds had lived two years in the bush before the wife realized it wasn't Australia. It obviously wasn't true, but in the serious mood of the evening it was funny.

After dinner Fortunate served coffee in the drawing room, her head lower than ever. Any progress Nicola had made in drawing her out of her shyness disappeared with the appearance of Reynolds. He began talking about her before she had even left the room. 'Not exactly one for long conversations on the relative merits of Marxism over capitalism in the newly independent countries of Africa,' he laughed to himself, 'but Alice tells me she's a demon with the ironing.'

Nicola held a tin of sweeteners disdainfully over his cup. 'I can't remember, Uncle, was that one saccharine or two?'

At ten-thirty the telephone rang in the hall and Reynolds hurried off to answer it. His face appeared around the door a moment later. 'Someone called Hudson wants to speak to Emily Robinson long distance and person to person,' he said, with almost a wink. 'What d'you think, Nicola, should we let him?'

They were both there at the other end of the telephone in Chepstow Villas, Hudson and Richard sounding young and silly, Hudson excited saying they were planning a sixty-four-page edition, and Richard telling Nicola she'd better come home quickly and start writing if they were to have any chance of filling it. Between the four of them they talked for half an hour and Emily despaired of the phone bill. But at twenty-one there's no denying that it's good for girls to have boy-friends who will telephone from one hemisphere to the other just to say 'hello'.

'You never say, you know, what Hudson's really like.'

They had been discussing the phone call, thrilled and flattered by the extravagance of it all, lying by the pool in bikinis in the few midday hours when it was warm enough to sunbathe. The month's holiday had passed the three-quarter mark and they were impatient to be back in London and getting on with their lives.

'How do you mean?' asked Emily.

'Well, I mean Richard is so straightforward, so determined and honest and you know, everything like that. But Hudson, well, I'm never sure what he's really thinking, what he's up to. So what's he really like?'

Emily considered this. What was Hudson like? Who could tell? After all these months she knew so little about him. He was a person who talked of the future, rarely of the past, hardly ever of his family. There had, she was certain, been some falling out there. What was he like? He was generous, certainly, clever, yes, energetic, enthusiastic, loving, secretive, positive, enigmatic, tenacious, loyal, ambitious. These were just colours in a paintbox. There was something else about Hudson, something almost childlike, naïve, perhaps, yet he was more self-assured than anyone she knew.

Nicola was watching her, waiting for an answer.

'I don't know,' she said at last. 'Most of the time, no, all the time he's just absolutely wonderful. But I sometimes think that somewhere deep down inside, when he's quiet and thoughtful . . . well, it sometimes seems he's humming a different tune from the rest of us.'

There was a long, long pause before Nicola suddenly groaned. 'Crumbs, Emmy,' she said, 'no wonder you only got a II.2.'

Chapter Thirty-One

(i)

Hudson drew the red Alvis to a halt under the plane trees in Soho Square and rechecked his watch. For half an hour they had been driving around central London, loud music on the radio: two young men in a huge and classic, red open sports car on this hot, late summer evening. Only a couple of thousand Alvis TB 14s had ever been made and that had been fourteen years earlier for the rich and leisured. Now in this slightly bulbous, low-waisted, grand tourer of the early Fifties the publisher and editor of *Witness* were collecting envying stares.

Hudson smiled as he listened to the idling of the retuned engine. That day the Alvis had come back from the workshop, serviced, resprayed and with much of its chromework refitted. 'Not bad, eh?' he said.

'Runs like a rabbit,' said Richard. He knew nothing about cars. Noticing that it was almost nine he leaned forward to retune the radio for the news.

Hudson's hand caught his arm. 'Don't touch that.'

'What?' The radio was playing the Animals' *House of the Rising Sun* for the fifth time that night. Radio Caroline, the pirate station which had begun broadcasting that Easter, had only a small reservoir of records. 'You like this one?' Richard was surprised. He had always taken Hudson for a blues purist.

Hudson turned up the volume. The record was ending. 'Listen!' he said. 'Now . . .'

Richard listened as out of the fading organ arpeggios of the Animals something more than familiar emerged, crisp, sharp and American. '*Witness the time, the place, the feeling. Witness the moment. Witness the sights. Wit-ness the sounds. Witness London as it really is. Witness the movies, the theatre, the clubs. Witness the records. Witness the events.* Witness: *the magazine of the Sixties. Out now. Can you get a* Witness? *You bet. Every good newsagent has one just for you,* Witness. *Sixty-four pages, two shillings and sixpence. Can you afford to be without a* Witness?'

Hudson with their own radio commercial. For a moment Richard did not speak.

'Hey, close your mouth, you'll catch flies. What do you think? Be kind. I mean, lie if you have to. It's my first shot. I'm sensitive.'

'What do I think? It's terrific. On the radio? Are you kidding? We should have taped it, got people to listen . . .'

'No need. There'll be more. Twenty spots a week.'

'But why, I mean . . . you should have told me.'

Hudson turned off the radio. 'I wanted to surprise you. A birthday surprise.'

'You've amazed me.'

'Good. Happy twenty-second birthday. Now, come on, your pasta will be getting cold.'

Hudson explained over dinner, sitting in a basement arch in an Italian restaurant on Romilly Street. 'To be honest it was all Willie Simmonds' idea.'

'I didn't know he ever had any clean ideas.'

'So this is a collector's item. Some guy at *Queen* he knows said that Radio Caroline were offering these ridiculously low rates and it seemed to me they were getting right into the homes of our potential readers every day. So I did a deal.'

'*Witness* can't afford radio commercials?'

'We got a special rate. Radio Caroline take space with us, we get space with them. That brought the price down. And by doing it myself we didn't have to hire an actor. That was Willie's idea, too. He thought the American accent might help. We borrowed a studio one lunchtime last week off some people he knows. Got it for free. I made him promise not to tell you in case something went wrong.'

'Jesus! All the same . . .'

Hudson was grinning. He loved surprises. 'There's more.' Feeling in his jacket pocket he pulled out a letter. It was from Fiske-Forrester, a summary of an offer, 'subject to references, full accounts and contract', for an investment of one hundred thousand pounds.

Richard's eyes skimmed the figures.

'It arrived today. Quick work for a bank. Very quick. Basically what they're talking about is twenty thousand to buy them 10 per cent of the company, and eighty thousand as a convertible loan at 2 per cent over bank rate over three years. So, what do you say we have some champagne?'

Richard was too stunned to think. He knew about the Fiske-Forrester talks, but Hudson was meeting and talking to people every day. He had never taken them particularly seriously. 'You don't like champagne,' he said at last.

'Oh, come on, Richard, give me a break, will you? This is your night. It's your birthday. *Witness* was just on the radio. We're the hottest thing in London.'

The champagne was ordered and the celebrations began. Champagne and tagliatelle. Almost before he was into his second glass the volume of Hudson's voice had begun to rise and other diners were turning around to see the young American doing all the talking. He really couldn't take drink.

Between forkfuls of tagliatelle he outlined his strategy. 'Tonight is the start of *Witness* Stage Two. No more the cottage industry. We're going weekly just as soon as you can organize it, and national as soon as I find a distributor. There's no point in doing this thing by half.'

'Absolutely not.' Richard smiled. This was some birthday present. 'A hundred thousand pounds . . .' He found it difficult to believe. 'A fortune.'

'For what I have planned we'll need every penny. And you did it. It was the quality of the magazine that decided them. All you have to do now is do the same again only much bigger and twice as often. And, oh yes, get used to formal board meetings once a month. They're putting Latymer's friend Neil Fiske on to the board to keep an eye on us.'

'Latymer will be very pleased.'

Hudson hesitated. 'He wants to be deputy editor.'

'He's not right,' Richard said flatly.

'That's what I think. We'll give him a rise to keep him happy.' He held his hand out for the letter. Richard passed it back to him. 'You know, we should think about radio. It's good fun. *Radio Witness*. Can you imagine, Richard? *Radio Witness?*'

Richard tried not to laugh. He was twenty-two, a baby, *Witness* was barely nine months old and Hudson was building an empire out of tagliatelle, day-dreams and champagne. 'I'm beginning to,' he said.

'You bet you are,' Hudson poured more champagne. 'Come on, drink up, fella, we're creating our own legend here. So, trust me. OK? Happy birthday.'

Hudson raised his glass and together they finished the champagne.

The suggestion that they visit Tim Gimmelmann was Richard's. Earlier he had slipped an envelope of prints into the car boot, intending to drop it off at the late-night post office in Trafalgar Square. As they returned to the car he realized he'd missed the post.

'D'you mind if we run up to Primrose Hill. I promised him definitely he'd get these prints by tomorrow morning. We can just pop them through the letter-box.'

'Sure, why not? Maybe one day we'll do a *Witness* courier service, too? D'you have the address?'

It was still warm as they drove through Regent's Park, and, with the wind on his face, Hudson was quickly sobering up. While Richard thought about Nicola (only two more days until she came home), Hudson sang: *'There is a house in New Orleans they call the Rising Sun, And it's been the ruin of many a poor boy . . .'* He had a good voice which changed effortlessly with the song he was singing. Tonight it was his blues voice. 'You know, Richard,' he said as they passed the zoo, 'when Emily and Nicola get home we should all go away some place for a weekend before the good weather goes. Maybe Devon or Cornwall. One of those places. Somewhere by the sea. Would Nicola like that, do you think?'

'Great idea. I'm sure she'd love it.'

Hudson smiled again. 'Good man,' he said, and went back to his song. *'Oh mother, tell your children, not to do what I have done . . .'*

Primrose Hill was a mixed area of either pastel-smart or peeling-shabby Victorian villas: Gimmelmann's place was almost the last house on Chalcot Crescent. It was the first time either Richard or Hudson had been there. Hudson sat in the car, double parked, while Richard ran up the steps to post the envelope. Seeing that it would not fit into the post-box he knelt down and tried to push it under the door. A draught excluder blocked the way.

Frustrated he stood up. 'The Tim Gimmelmann Company,' he read to himself as he looked at the brass name-plate by the bells. Trust Gimmelmann.

'OK?' Hudson called from the road.

'Just a minute.' Reluctantly Richard pressed a button. Somewhere inside the building he heard the echo of bell upon linoleum. It was twelve-thirty.

The light in the hall came on almost instantly. Cautiously the door opened six inches and Gimmelmann peered out.

'Sorry to bother you so late, Tim, but . . . I brought the prints . . .'

'Oh . . . thanks . . . yes . . .' The door opened further and Gimmelmann took the prints, nonchalantly insincere as ever.

'That's OK, Hudson and I were passing . . .'

'Hudson? Is he here?' Gimmelmann peered down into the street, his face lighting up. 'Look, come in. Both of you. Have some coffee. We heard him on the radio.'

'Thanks anyway, but we don't want to disturb you. I'm sorry it's so late.'

'You're not disturbing us. Not at all. Look, you get Hudson, I'll put the coffee on and tell Holly.'

'Oh no, really . . .'

But before Richard could argue further Gimmelmann had disappeared back inside the house. He trudged down the steps to the car and explained. 'We'd better go in. One quick coffee. He'll be upset if we don't.'

Richard waited as Hudson found a space a little way along the street and parked the Alvis. 'Pity we couldn't bring the hard top,' Hudson worried as they walked back to Gimmelmann's. The Alvis was the first car he had owned.

'We heard you on the radio,' Gimmelmann fawned as he met Hudson on the steps.

'You did? That's good,' Hudson smiled. 'Are you sure we aren't too late?'

'You were very good. Holly said. We both said,' Gimmelmann repeated as he led the way into the living room.

It was a large, square surprise of a room. On the white painted floorboards were four very large black cushions and a black table which had had the legs sawn off so that it stood just ten inches high. Above the table was one large, low-hanging, cylindrical, white, paper lantern. The walls were white, but in the centre of each was a very large, silver-framed, black-and-white photograph of Holly. There were no curtains, just a white venetian blind pulled down. Gimmelmann wore a black shirt buttoned to the neck and black trousers and shoes.

'Hey, this is just terrific, Tim. Isn't it terrific, Richard?' Hudson's voice was still a fraction loud from the drink.

Richard was not sure if it was terrific or not, but, with not one item of colour in the room, it was unusual.

Gimmelmann looked simultaneously proud and embarrassed. 'Look, er, sit down, the kettle's boiling,' he said, indicating the cushions. From an adjacent room came the brusque march of the Supremes singing *Where Did Our Love Go?*. Gimmelmann hurried off into the kitchen.

They chose a cushion each and sat down. On the table a Gauloise cigarette smouldered in a British Railways ashtray alongside several books. Gimmelmann, who had switched to Gauloise when he became successful, had obviously been working when interrupted. Casually Richard looked at the books. The first two were part of a correspondence course in business. That's ambitious, he thought. Another was called *Shakespeare's Stories*. He replaced the last book as soon as he saw what it was, a primer on the correct use of English grammar. Alongside, a notebook with an incomplete grammar exercise lay open on the table. He immediately wished he had not seen either.

'I'll just get Holly,' Gimmelmann said, coming back into the room and sweeping up his books in one deft movement as he headed out of the other door. 'Holly . . . Holly . . .'

Hudson looked at Richard. 'Don't worry about it,' he said quietly. 'We'll go just as soon . . .'

He didn't get any further. At that moment Gimmelmann returned, followed a second later by Holly. Now Richard understood about the black and white. Holly was the colour, and the colour was red: crimson, pouting, sensuous lips, blood-red nail varnish on her fingers and on her toes, and a deep red shirt, two buttons undone at the collar, two more at the bottom, where it hung open slightly, revealing the tops of her thighs.

'Hello,' she said and slipped into the room. Her voice was hoarse from too many cigarettes. She gazed at Hudson. 'You were ever so good on the radio. Ever so good. It was such a surprise.' She slid on to the cushion nearest Hudson and sat looking at him, crossing her legs under her body.

The bounce left Hudson at once: the easy fun of the evening had gone. For almost the first time since Richard had known him he looked unsure of himself.

'I've always wanted to be on the radio . . . or the television.' Holly was speaking very slowly, giving every word equal weight.

'I'm sure you will. Very soon,' said Hudson. He looked towards Richard.

Helpfully Richard nodded. 'No doubt about it. You'll probably end up a famous film star.'

Holly ignored Richard's contribution. Her eyes were set on Hudson. 'We'd been wondering when you were going to visit us,' she said. As she talked she very slowly turned a ring on her finger, an expensive cluster of stones in the shape of a cartwheel.

Awkward, Hudson looked away and complimented her on the photographs on the wall.

Her eyes did not move. 'I just stand there,' she said. 'Timmy does all the real work.'

'It's a partnership, right Holly?' Gimmelmann said, bringing in the coffee.

'If you say so.'

She had come a long way from the caravan, Richard thought. A year ago she had been an adolescent with a knowing look: now her look was everywhere.

They didn't stay long. The coffee was not very hot (Gimmelmann was embarrassed and wanted to make some more, but Richard and Hudson said they preferred it that way), and after they had been shown around the basement studio, which was hardly more than a bare room, they were back on the steps, saying good night.

'Any time you're around here, call in.' Gimmelmann was grinning at Hudson. Holly rested one hand on the pillar of the porch and said nothing.

'We'll do that, and, ah, thanks a lot . . .' Hudson said as he led Richard away back up the street.

With a quiet click the door closed behind them.

300

'They probably deserve each other,' Richard said as they reached the car.

Hudson shook his head. 'I don't think so,' he said. Then he stopped, his expression crumpling.

Richard followed Hudson's gaze to the Alvis. Where the neat new radio had been there was now just an ugly hole ripped into the dashboard, from which some loose wires now projected. 'Oh no.'

Silently Hudson leaned over the car and examined the extent of the damage, holding the wires in his hands, running his fingers over the jagged tear in the dashboard.

'The lousy creeps,' Richard sympathized.

Hudson said nothing. His face was dull with disappointment. He looked up and surveyed the street. Suddenly there was a scuffling sound. Two youths had appeared from behind another car and begun to run towards Primrose Hill, one of them dropping something metal on to the pavement as they went. In the light from the street lamp Richard saw the radio shatter.

The boys should have been warned. Hudson was built for sprinting. Even before they had reached the end of the street he was closing on the slower, stouter of the two. As they turned the corner, out of Richard's sight, Hudson was no more than ten yards behind.

The second might have got away had he not come back to help his accomplice. By the time Richard reached them Hudson had one boy by the neck. The other was cowering on the floor. There was blood on both their faces as Hudson kicked and lashed at them.

'Hudson, Hudson, OK . . . OK.'

Hudson did not stop. It was a violence that Richard had never seen before, street fighting by someone who knew about fighting. He grabbed hold of Hudson's arm. 'Hey, come on, that's enough. That's enough.'

With one last dismissive wrench Hudson hurled the fat boy against a garden wall, and stood panting, as though willing either thief to attack him. They did not. There was a moment of fear as both boys, expecting another attack, covered their heads with their arms. Then, realizing that it was over, they pulled themselves to their feet and scurried away down the street.

Richard and Hudson walked back towards the car in silence. Hudson's jacket was smeared with blood, the breast pocket was torn off his shirt. The smashed radio lay on the pavement. Richard picked it up.

They drove away from Chalcot Crescent without speaking further.

(*ii*)

Gimmelmann went back to work after his guests had left. Holly went to bed. She needed her beauty sleep, she told him, straight faced. It was a warning he did not need: he did not intend to disturb her. Fetching his grammar books he laid them out neatly on the table again and lit another Gauloise. He looked around. It was a nice place he had now. Hudson had been impressed, he was sure. He liked that. Distracted, he pulled out an advance page proof of the cover for the new fashion magazine, *Moment*. It was a photograph of Holly. The picture credit would read, *Holly by Gimmelmann*. He liked that, too.

Holly and Gimmelmann. They had emerged together and they were learning quickly: fashion photography could be learned quickly. Holly had the face of the moment and Gimmelmann had the camera. *Queen* had followed *Witness*, then had come *Town*, *Honey* and the *Daily Express*. Everyone wanted Holly. For Gimmelmann it was becoming money-to-burn time. He had taken an assistant called Kevin, whom he bullied, and a part-time secretary called Shelly. Shelly did the bookings and sent the invoices and hauled Holly out of bed at four in the afternoon on the days when she wasn't working. And sometimes when Holly went for fittings with the fashion editors Shelly would be especially nice to Gimmelmann in his studio, the door locked, the lights out and the music deafening. Gimmelmann liked having girls in the studio,

302

his studio. It was one way of getting back at Holly. If he had had the nerve he would have told Hudson.

One evening in July Holly's father, Jack Carter, had appeared at the door wanting to 'talk to my Dolly'. Gimmelmann had told him that Dolly was out and suggested a meeting outside a pub at closing time. Then he had telephoned a couple of pals from Finsbury Park, lads he could trust who were impressed by his new-found status, and had given them careful instructions. Days later when he had casually mentioned the visit Holly had smiled and said, 'I hope they bloody well killed him.' They didn't. But Carter knew they could have done and never bothered his Dolly again. Just part of the North London old-boy-network service, Gimmelmann had joked. If he'd known what Hudson was up to at the end of his street he would have found that very funny.

How much Holly enjoyed a joke, a real, funny joke, Gimmelmann had never been able to tell. She never joked herself. She said she didn't see the point in it. She wanted money, an easy life and fame. He had spotted her, photographed her and promised her all those things. And because very quickly he had given her the first instalments on fame and money she trusted him to run her career in tandem with his own. He made her beautiful: he advised her on clothes, make-up, hair, and he photographed her brilliantly. But best of all he gave her money, 50 per cent of everything the photographs earned going straight into her own building society account, her own paying-in book kept in her bag at all times. That was where Gimmelmann knew he was smart. He had realized how to play the money card from almost their first meeting. Others had taken everything Holly earned: Gimmelmann made her a partner.

Pouring himself another cup of cold coffee he imagined her in the next room, her face innocent in sleep. He smiled bitterly to himself. What she thought of him he could not tell. She never said. Did her derision for the world extend to him? He thought it likely. He did not love her. He did not think he even liked her. She was already spiritually crippled by her background; nothing would change her. There was nothing to like. And yet he was obsessed with her, trapped, not only in their shared route to success, but ensnared in eroticism. There were other girls: Shelly, the secretary, though her pink face was covered in light down, and silly, easy models who saw him as the creator of a star and thought that if they favoured him the camera would somehow like them more. But they did not know the things Holly knew.

If Holly was aware of what happened when she was not there she did not complain. Perhaps it amused her. Perhaps it excited her, as he would become excited when she told him details of her former childhood profession. At first he had refused to listen: but she knew how to make him listen. With her the past and the present became intertwined. While speaking of one, reflecting on past details of men and places, she offered him the joy of the present. She would not separate the two. And he knew that sometimes when a fitting or shopping trip finished early she would tie back her hair, paint her eyes, and wait for the cars to stop. Just for the hell of it, and so that she would have something to tell him when she got home.

The Gauloise had burned down to his fingers. Viciously he stubbed it out in the British Railways ashtray. 'Bitch,' he murmured. 'Disgusting, bloody bitch.'

Then, very conscientiously, he went back to his English grammar lesson. It might be the Sixties style to be a Cockney working-class photographer, but it was also a badge of ignorance. Gimmelmann knew he could never get rid of his accent, but at least he could get the grammar right.

Chapter Thirty-Two

(i)

It was Hallowe'en before they could get away for the weekend they had promised themselves, not to Cornwall as Hudson had first suggested, but to a cottage in Dorset which Emily found advertised in a copy of *The Lady* someone had left on the seat of a bus. They drove down in their two cars on the Friday, Hudson and Emily going ahead in the Alvis in the late afternoon, Nicola waiting behind until Richard had seen the following week's edition off to the printers.

It had been a busy time since the girls had returned from Africa. Hudson had chosen the perfect time for *Witness* to go weekly. October was a month of events: there was a general election in Britain, observed in wicked fly-on-the-wall commentaries by Nicola; the Chinese detonated their first atomic bomb; Khrushchev was toppled; and Martin Luther King was awarded the Nobel Peace Prize. On top of that there were the Olympic Games in Tokyo, while Penelope Chilston anticipated the abolition of the death penalty in an extraordinary interview with hangman Albert Pierrepoint: '"Hello Tish," said the murderer. "Hello Tosh," said the hangman. Then he hanged him,' she had written.

Most exciting of all, though, had been Emily's interview with John Lennon. Nicola had gone, too. 'I'll hold your pen, in case you get tired taking notes, or chaperone you, in case he pounces, or translate Liverpudlian, in case you can't understand, or do anything on earth you want, Emmy, but please, please take me with you.'

In the event Lennon had not pounced, but they were

happy just the same. He had made them laugh. He liked journalists. 'I used to think I might be a reporter,' he told them. 'I mean, I wanted to be a writer and the only kind of people who wrote for a living that I knew about were reporters on the *Liverpool Echo*.'

'You could write for *Witness*,' Nicola had blurted out, although she had promised not to say a word.

He didn't, of course. But, with his picture on the cover and Emily's piece inside, the first issue of the new weekly *Witness* sold out again. Hudson was very pleased. He'd always been a Lennon man, he reminded everyone.

Every day the tempo in the *Witness* office grew more giddy. Willie Simmonds got his fingers caught in the knickers of a marchioness and was cited in a divorce case, Peter Berridge was threatened with a libel suit (the first of many), Ben Tarlo and Jessica were married without telling anyone, had a party and then went off to live in New York, and Hudson had another row with the sons of J.W. Purley of Cricklewood for shoddy printing.

In the meantime Hudson found a national distributor, Farrow and Fox, publishers of a series called *Fun and Profit* hobby magazines, who were looking for outside titles to reduce overheads. And, though an unlikely marriage, a distribution deal was pushed through just in time to handle the *Witness Election Special*.

Emily and Nicola now lived their lives in a three-cornered race between their flat, the office and Chepstow Villas. Somehow there was never enough time. Deadlines for articles were more pressing than those for essays had ever been.

It rained all the way down to Dorset, with Hudson either talking or singing as he drove. Looking at him in profile Emily was reminded again of just how good looking he was. In the ten months she had known him his hair had very gradually become longer until it now covered his ears, his only nod in the direction of fashion. But if he was vain he never let it show in what he wore, the conservative American slacks and jackets hardly changing with the seasons.

They arrived at the cottage just before dark, the Alvis making a careful way through the puddles of the cart track as Emily read out the directions. In the summer it was probably a pretty place with good views and roses, but in the mud of October, high on a hill which looked down towards a grey sea, the wind having taken most of the leaves from the surrounding stunted oaks, the stone cottage looked, thought Emily, like some sullen animal, its head down against the elements. They parked against a copse of gorse and, carrying their bags and the boxes of provisions Emily had bought, hurried to the door.

Inside it was low-ceilinged and cream-walled, thinly carpeted and rudimentarily furnished, one all-purpose living room with a kitchen behind. The wide, deep, blackened fireplace commanded the room. To one side was a dresser, to the other an upright, ancient piano. The stairs were narrow and open, ascending from the living room to two tiny bedrooms set in the eaves which smelled of damp and moth balls.

The first thing they did was to light the fire, a basket of logs and kindling wood having been provided. Then, while they waited for the cottage to warm, and after Hudson had opened the piano and judged it playable, they went upstairs and made love between cold, stiff sheets. They did not speak very much. They were happy. There was not a lot to be said.

It was after ten when the others arrived, Nicola bustling through the door giggling and shivering, hanging on to Emily in the kitchen, tasting the soup, standing over the oven breathing in the smell of over-roasted chicken, kissing Hudson, putting more wood on the fire, dizzy with energy. Behind her Richard watched and smiled, proud of her vitality.

'I have a present for us all,' she said enigmatically after dinner, as they huddled in sweaters around the fire. 'But you must promise you won't be shocked, Emmy.'

307

'Nothing can shock Emily,' Hudson said, cuddling Emily's thighs affectionately. He was sitting on the floor in front of her as she sat in a large armchair. 'Interviewers can never be shocked.'

Richard, sitting on the sofa with one arm around Nicola, was very tired and a little drunk. 'If it's one of those dirty postcards Willie Simmonds was showing around the office this week . . .'

'No, much better than that. I think so anyway,' said Nicola getting up. 'Right. Everyone close your eyes. Come on, you too, Hudson.'

Obediently eyes were closed, Richard saying he could hardly keep his open, anyway. Emily had no idea what the present might be. She felt Hudson's hand stroke her leg, and was warmed because of him. A log on the fire spat.

'No cheating,' warned Nicola. 'If the house burns down I'll tell you.'

She was over by the door, rummaging about in her coat pocket.

'Right . . . almost ready.'

Now Emily could sense her returning to the fireplace. She heard the sharp strike of a match.

'All right. You can open your eyes.'

Nicola was standing by the fire, a cigarette in hand.

'Well?' said Richard. Then he saw Hudson smiling.

Nicola took a drag on the cigarette. It was fat and the tobacco was spilling out.

'Wow . . .' said Emily, as she realized.

The sweet smell of Acapulco Gold filled the room. Nicola took one more draw and passed the joint to Hudson whose hand was already out waiting. 'I only managed to get enough for one, so nobody be too greedy,' she said.

Richard was now wide awake. 'Pot!' he mouthed.

'Hash, actually,' corrected Nicola, knowledgeably.

Hudson passed the joint to Emily. She had hardly smoked even a cigarette in her life. Timidly she drew on the joint and passed it quickly to Richard, who took his glasses off before he tried. He took it all very seriously.

This is so naughty, Emily thought. She was actually a little nervous, and wondered how long it would take before she felt the effects. Then she wondered if she would know what it was when she felt it.

The joint had reached Nicola again. Apart from Hudson everyone was very intent, Emily fancying she saw Richard's eyes flick to the window, as though wanting to reassure himself that they were not being observed in this illicit activity. When her turn came again she drew too deeply, and then had to fight very hard to prevent herself from coughing. She was not at all certain that she wanted to smoke any more, but it would somehow have seemed impolite to refuse.

So it went on: around and around.

'Where did you get this?' Richard wanted to know.

'Oh, I couldn't possibly tell you that. Let's just say I have friends in low places.' Nicola was smiling, talking in a rather loud voice.

'Lower places than ours?' asked Emily. 'Impossible.' And she began to giggle.

That started Nicola giggling. Hudson smiled at her. Richard watched and wondered what they were laughing at.

And the more he puzzled the more they laughed.

In the night Emily heard the bed in the adjacent room creaking, the soft mew of relief from Nicola and the wind which capered in the chimney. Hudson slept. He had been quiet all evening, watching them as the older child would mind the little ones, tolerant and amused, but saying little. Before they had made love Emily had asked him what he had been thinking about. But he had kissed her and told a lie. 'I can't remember,' he had said.

She kissed his shoulder but he did not stir.

Emily was cutting triangular slits for eyes in a large pumpkin when Richard went down the following morning. Nicola was still asleep.

'Hudson's gone to look for a shop that sells newspapers,' she said, scouring the flesh and seeds from inside the pumpkin. 'What d'you think? Are these eyes big enough?'

Richard looked at the pumpkin. On one side Emily had drawn a face with a felt-tipped pen: everything carefully planned. 'Yes, I think so. Don't you?' He put the kettle on the gas stove and spooned some coffee into a mug. 'I forgot to tell you last night. You did a terrific piece on Peter Brook.'

'You did tell me. Twice.'

'Really? I'm sorry.'

'You were very tired,' Emily said and smiled.

'Oh yes.' He thought about the joint they had all smoked and of how he had pretended to be high and wondered if the others had realized that whatever it did to them it did nothing at all for him. The idea of drugs made him uneasy, although he knew that made him appear very old-fashioned.

Emily was now cutting the nose out of the pumpkin. He watched her in silence. Despite all the hours they had spent as part of a foursome or working in the office they had not often been alone together.

'Why don't you write for *Witness* any more?' Emily asked.

'Me? Oh, I'm too busy doing everything else. No time for writing.'

'Is that the only reason?'

'Oh yes. When I get more time I'll start writing again.'

'Ah . . .'

There was another silence. The kettle had boiled. 'Actually, that's not true,' Richard suddenly said after a moment. 'The reason I don't write is because I don't think I'm very good at it. Not good enough, anyway. I only realized that after *Witness* had started. I suppose that's why I never managed to sell anything, though I didn't realize it then. My ideas are all right, I think they're good, but I'm better at editing, getting other people to write. Penny Chilston, you, Nicola . . . even Charlie Latymer can write far better than I can. But I can spot a good piece.'

'And is that as good?'

'Oh yes. When the piece is right, and the magazine is right . . . when it all comes together, there's nothing like it.'

They walked down to the sea in the afternoon, four in a line, through a shady patch of evergreen and out on to a wide beach of drying pebbles. The previous day's rain had cleared and the sky was blue and white and hurried from west to east. Beneath their feet the pebbles crunched and shifted. Swaddled in sweaters and overcoats they wandered while the wind caught and stole their voices, inflamed their cheeks and made their noses run. Like a scout troupe on a reconnaissance they spread across the beach, enjoying the freedom of space.

At the water's edge Richard watched as Nicola played ducks and drakes on the swell behind the receding tide. Though hidden under her red woollen hat and enveloped by an old Royal Air Force greatcoat she had bought from a stall in Portobello Road she still dazzled. After a few minutes Hudson joined her and sent a series of flat, smooth pebbles bouncing across the sea. Above the sound of the waves and wind he heard Nicola shrieking with laughter, insisting that Hudson was a cheat. A little further down the beach Emily wandered alone staring into rock pools.

At five-thirty they squeezed into the Alvis and found a pub in a village. It was a working men's place without charm or comfort where three weather-stained local youths, mute and expressionless, drank their beer and observed the girls, until Nicola complained quietly that they made her feel uncomfortable. 'They think we're tarts, Emmy,' she said as they retreated back into the car.

Richard doubted this. To him the blank, watchful eyes had suggested curiosity, guarded admiration and envy. The foursome had everything that anyone might want. Most of all they had each other. And he was embarrassed to think how pleased with themselves they must look.

(iii)

There were four cooks in the tiny kitchen that evening. While Hudson grilled the steaks and Emily and Nicola prepared the vegetables, Richard made the soup and dessert. That was how they wanted it, locked away, cosy and complete in each other's company.

Just before eight Richard turned out the light while Hudson lit the candle in the pumpkin.

'Well now . . .' Hudson stood back, one arm around Emily. A thin vapour of black smoke rose through the chimney where the stalk had been cut out.

'Well done,' said Richard, and pressed a glass of mulled wine into her hand. It was very hot and tasted slightly bitter.

Nicola stared at the pumpkin: 'It isn't exactly malevolent-looking is it, Emmy? I mean, hardly frightening. Almost cherubic.' She smiled. 'In fact, you know, it looks a bit like you.'

'Really?' Emily said rather doubtfully.

'Mmm. It's a self-portrait. See the oval face, the wide eyes, the little *retroussé* Russian nose.'

'Russian?'

'As in Anna Karenina.'

'Oh, nice. Thank you. But my mouth isn't jagged like that.'

'Post-impressionist's licence. It's you, all right, all lit up on a Friday night when you've just got your copy in, smiling like a salamander and making chains with paper clips.'

'I see what you mean . . .' Richard began to tease.

Emily laughed. 'Wow, you too! How clever of you. Of me. D'you think this might become known as my pumpkin period?'

'Absolutely,' said Nicola. 'To be closely followed by your turnip period, and then your carrot period. What d'you say, Richard, should *Witness* have a vegetable arts section? Are we missing something?'

'Good idea. We could put it in between Living Alone and Cooking on Empty. And we'll get Emily to interview herself.'

'She'd never agree,' said Nicola. 'I'd never let any friend of mine be interviewed by Emily Robinson.'

It was all silly. Emily glanced at Hudson. He was amused, but not attempting to join in. 'What do you think?' she asked.

Hudson grinned. 'To be honest, she looks kind of tasty to me. If it is a she.'

'Tasty? Is that good or bad?' demanded Nicola.

'I suppose that depends upon how much you like pumpkin pie.'

'And do you?'

'I like this pumpkin pie,' he said.

Richard looked at Nicola. 'Is he talking dirty?' he asked. Everyone knew that Hudson never talked dirty.

Over dinner, with the benign pumpkin guarded at either end of the table by lighted candles on sentry duty, they persuaded Hudson to tell them about Hallowe'en in California, of painted faces and masks, and trick or treating at neighbours' homes.

'Who was your best friend there?' Nicola asked. 'I mean, who did you hang around with?'

Hudson thought for a moment. 'Well, let's see, they changed a little as I got older, you know the way you

313

grow out of friends, but I guess closest . . . that would be
. . . Bobby Yates. He ended up at UCLA medical school.
Or maybe Spider Menoza.'

'Spider Menoza,' repeated Richard. 'Great name.'

Hudson nodded. 'He was an amazingly thin kid
whose dad worked in the filling station. When I last saw
him he was headed, no doubt about it, for a career as a
cat thief. He could climb into anywhere. You would see
him going up and down drainpipes, arm over arm, very
slowly and certainly, just like . . . well, just like a spider.
He was really crazy. One Hallowe'en he sent off for some
magic dye to put on his hair. He had really thick, black,
wavy hair. Very nice. He was very proud of it especially
after Elvis Presley hit and all the girls started to like long
hair. We were meeting at Bobby's place and Spider turns
up with . . . well, marigold hair, I mean bright orange. He
looked terrible. So we went out and knocked on doors
and everything. He wore a sort of home-made skull
mask, too. Really freaky. But the trouble was the dye
wouldn't wash out. Spider being Spider had apparently
decided it didn't look outrageous enough so he'd added
some of his mother's peroxide to the magic dye. It took
months to grow out. In the end his dad made him have
the shortest crew cut ever seen outside Devil's Island.'

'El Fuerte, California, sounds a more fun place to
grow up than Wimbledon Common,' said Richard.

Hudson disagreed. 'Not really. Just a typical small
town. Like anywhere else really.'

'And what about Spider, and the other boy? You
don't keep in touch, right?' Nicola said.

'Bobby, well, no . . . none of us is much for letter
writing . . .'

'Nobody you know is,' said Richard.

'Well . . .'

'No one writes to you at Chepstow Villas.'

'I guess that's my fault.'

'That's sad,' said Nicola.

'I think so.' Hudson smiled at her.

Emily said nothing. She no longer asked Hudson about his family.

They played Nicola's Game after supper. That was how Richard had christened it because it had been Nicola who had dreamed it up in the car on the way down to Dorset. 'And I must warn you,' he said, 'it's impossible. Nobody will ever be able to do it apart from Nicola.'

Nicola frowned. 'Nonsense. It's easy. What we do is separate into two teams, say Emmy and me against you two. Girls against boys. The team who start first think of a line of a song and sing it, then the opposing team have to take the last word of that line as the first word of another line from a different song and sing that and . . .'

'Hey, wait a minute. Give us an example,' said Hudson. He was sitting alongside Nicola on the sofa. Emily and Richard were in the easy chairs which flanked it.

'Right, well let's say I begin with, *What do you wanna make those eyes at me for? . . .*' Nicola started to sing in a pleasant alto. 'You have to start with a line in another song which includes *for*. You can start in the middle of a line if you want to.'

'You're right, Richard. It is impossible,' said Emily. 'Let's play Scrabble.'

'Oh, come on, Emmy. It isn't impossible. You just have to think. There are thousands of songs with the word *for* in them. Virtually every song ever written, I imagine.'

'Name one.'

'What about . . . *for me and my gal?*' Hudson suddenly sang.

'What's that?' asked Richard.

'Something about bells ringing.'

Nicola nodded. She was exultant. 'That's it! Wonderful! See how easy it is. Our turn now, Emmy. What was it? *Gal!* Is *girl* all right? Right. *Girl . . .*'

Richard looked doubtful. 'I think Emily's right. Scrabble's the best bet. I can't sing, anyway. Or what about Monopoly? We've got that. I found it in the dresser.'

'Just give me a second . . . Come on, Emmy. Think. *Girl!*' Nicola's face was screwed in concentration. 'I know . . . *the girl from Ipanema* . . . Follow that, Bossa Nova,' she smiled at Hudson, pleased with herself.

He laughed. 'OK. Your round. Do we start now?' He was enjoying himself.

'No, we do. Go on, Emmy.'

'Oh God, I don't know.'

'Of course you do. Any line will do.' Nicola was insistent.

'Well then . . . what about *When the saints go marching in* . . . ?' Emily sang in a meek, small voice.

Now Hudson assumed a high doo-wap tenor: '*In the still of the night* . . .'

Richard frowned.

'*The Five Satins*,' Hudson explained. 'You must know that one.'

Richard shrugged. Emily shook her head. This had to be the worst game ever devised. Nicola was practically jumping up and down on the sofa. She had never seen her so bossy.

'Very good, Hudson,' Nicola said. 'Come on, Emmy. Us again. *Night* . . . the word's *night*. I know. *Night and day* . . .' she sang in the style of Ella Fitzgerald.

'Ah, yes,' Hudson congratulated. 'Well, Richard, a song with *day* in it.'

Richard looked miserable. 'Right! *Day*. Erm . . .'

'*I waked, she fled, and day brought back my night*,' said Emily to herself. This was worse than boring.

Nicola frowned at her. '*Day*, Richard,' she insisted, the team captain now.

'Oh yes, *days of wine and roses* . . .' Richard had not been lying about his voice. It was scarcely more than a croak.

'I'm not sure we can allow *days*, can we, Emmy?' said Nicola. 'It's a plural. Oh well, p'raps just this once. *Roses!* I know. That Bobby Vinton song . . . *Roses are red* . . .'

'*Red roses for a blue lady*,' Hudson crooned immediately.

Emily yawned.

'*Lady! Lady?*' Nicola rubbed her fingers impatiently. 'Wow . . . *Lady.*'

'Do we have to play this game?' Richard complained.

Nicola ignored him. 'I know, *The lady is a tramp*! Follow that!'

'Terrific!' Richard stared at the fire.

Hudson had now turned to Nicola. Slowly he grinned. '*Tramp, tramp, tramp, the boys are marching . . .*' he began to sing.

'*Marching! Oh dear! We've already done When the saints . . . Marching*! Crumbs, I dunno . . .'

For one happy moment Emily thought Nicola might be stumped and the game aborted. 'Well then . . .' she began.

But, with a shout of glee, Nicola cut her off. '*When Johnny comes marching home again, hurrah, hurrah, when Johnny comes marching home again, hurrah, hurrah . . .*'

It was pathetic of them, but moment by moment Emily and Richard allowed themselves to disappear, two invisibles sitting on the sidelines, at first unwilling and now unable to take part in the game, excluded by their own anger.

Now the game moved to the piano, Nicola jumping up, opening the lid and then pulling out and sitting on the piano stool. She was no pianist, but, one-handed, she could find a tune. Soon Hudson joined her.

With stops and starts the game continued for over an hour: Hudson and Nicola close alongside each other on the piano stool, a singles' match of an undetermined number of sets, full of flowing lyrical rallies, speculative unrhyming lobs, and sharp, volleying, ungrammatical and disharmonic exchanges. Though he frequently sang old blues numbers to himself Emily had had no idea that Hudson knew so many songs. Nicola was no surprise:

317

how often had she come upon her in the Kemp reading the *New Musical Express* hidden inside a copy of the *Guardian*? Together they made a pretty pair, Hudson playing everything that Nicola threw at him. Emily hadn't known he could play so well, either.

After a while Emily got up and made some coffee in the kitchen. Richard did not speak again and began to look through the latest *Private Eye*. Irrationally Emily was irritated by his sullenness.

Finally the game bored even Nicola. 'I'm sorry, you should have said if we were being selfish,' she fretted, getting up from Hudson and the piano as though suddenly awakening to the chill around them.

Emily tried a wan smile, for which she immediately hated herself. Richard pretended he had not heard.

'Sorry, Emmy,' Hudson threw another log on the fire and sat down at Emily's feet. It was the first time he had called her Emmy. Only Nicola ever called her Emmy.

It was too late. Though they finished the evening with a game of Scrabble, the carelessness of the weekend had been replaced by a studied politeness.

They went to bed early, Hudson and Emily, and made love efficiently and silently.

On the Sunday morning Hudson went again for the newspapers which were read over coffee and toast. What conversation there was concerned the news: the anticipated landslides in Tuesday's American election and Friday's referendum in Southern Rhodesia. And, as always, Vietnam. The previous evening was not mentioned, but it was there. And when in mid-afternoon they took to the cars to return early to London, *Witness* and work nobody was sorry. It was already November.

Chapter Thirty-Three

(i)

Holly Carter made the cover of *The Sunday Times Magazine* just before Christmas. *The face of 1965*, predicted the headline, and Gimmelmann bought fifty copies. He had posed her, in the briefest, torn-off tunic of Chairman Mao workers' cotton, inside a factory which produced jets for aeroplanes, a brazenly suggestive black-and-white picture of dimpled flesh against gleaming, polished engine outer-casings, puppy-dog insolence alongside white-hot technology, as the saying then went. Inside the magazine there were three and a half more pages: Holly in matelot shirt and peaked cap alongside a new Mondrial container depot; Holly in white, calf-high boots and white skirt and sweater on a Derbyshire slag heap, surrounded by grit-blasted local miners, a white, miner's helmet pulled down over unsmiling eyes; and Holly on a moor in walking boots, shorts and sweater, looking down on a Northern industrial town of blackened mills, smoke and chimneys. This was what social commentators called Sixties innovative fashion journalism, and, though Holly was the face the public saw, it was Tim Gimmelmann's name the professionals noticed.

Gimmelmann and Holly had been busy all year but now the rhythm had changed. Fashion-conscious London was a village society, a boy's gang consisting of pushy, young working-class men with cameras and guitars and scissors and creative accounting, of actors and shopkeepers, of traders in tat who worked on their image, of copywriters and copy cats and catalogues of women; smooth-legged women, fringed, pretty, made-up, up-market pony-club girls, more girls than anyone had ever seen before, who looked better than anyone had looked before. Or so they thought. It was a small gang whose members worked alone, but who ate in the same few restaurants, sold their products to the same advertisers and magazines, and who all found themselves earning more money than they had ever known existed before. And it was in this crowd that Gimmelmann and Holly now found themselves welcome.

Holly the foundling from the waste land was a celebrity and Gimmelmann was given credit for having created her.

Now that she was a success she was, of course, rarely free to work for *Witness*, but she was free for the New Year's Eve party at Mama Vecchi's. They both were, turning up late, dressed super-cool, Gimmelmann in a black velvet suit and black silk shirt without a tie, Holly in a black-and-white harlequin outfit. Gimmelmann liked it when Holly dazzled. He was confident with other photographers and boastful in the art and fashion departments, but he was still timid around writers. With Holly to show off he felt good.

New Year's Eve, 1964. *Witness* a year old. A party five times as big as the previous year but again Hudson had provided presents for everyone, Hudson at the door welcoming, or on the floor, smooching with Emily, jiving with Nicola, the only two who remembered how to do it properly, while Richard talked news and newspapers. Gimmelmann didn't say much. 'A fish wouldn't get caught if he kept his mouth shut,' he had once been told, sound advice for someone who had a long voyage to make. But he missed nothing, the increasing self-importance of Charlie Latymer hanging out with some bloke from a bank now; the new woman with Willie Simmonds, a forty-year-old ash-blonde who looked rich and randy; and Nicola sizzling with person-ality as if she wanted to dance with every man at the party, but particularly with Hudson.

Hudson. Most of all Gimmelmann's eyes were on Hudson, and the barrier which Hudson erected whenever Holly approached, the long arms folded protectively across his chest, the rocking back on his heels. Every other man he knew wanted to get close to Holly, Willie Simmonds trying for a cuddle, stealing a kiss and having a quiet feel under the disguise of *bonhomie*; Latymer, despite his contempt, preening before her; and Berridge, sweating and biting his lips. Even Richard could hardly take his eyes off her, though he was embarrassed when she stood too close, as she would purposely do, toe to toe, thigh to thigh, as she talked. Only Hudson stayed away.

'Well, Tim, not dancing?' Emily had caught sight of him watching Hudson and Nicola on the dance floor. The music was now quiet and they were slow dancing in the style of the time, not touching, simply smiling and talking to each other through the song.

He shook his head. He never danced. He couldn't dance. And he watched as Emily's eyes strayed back to the floor.

(*ii*)

'Should auld acquaintance be forgot and never brought to mind, should auld acquaintance be forgot for the sake of auld lang syne . . .' Shoulder to shoulder, arms crossed and linked, they sang. Midnight had surprised them and Big Ben had been chiming before they had turned on the television. Kisses and good wishes and then the song, people forming the chain where they stood, Emily alongside Richard and Latymer, Nicola over at the far side of the room with Hudson and Penny and Willie Simmonds, who was holding on to Holly. 'For auld lang syne, my dear, for auld lang syne . . .' Arms pumping up and down they surged forward to the centre, drunk, happy and excited. It was the beginning but it was also an ending. Emily felt her eyes wet, her throat tighten. Across the room Nicola

321

was smiling at her, laughing as Hudson kissed her 'Happy New Year', his lips grazing her cheek. Emily fought back the tears. *'We'll take a cup of kindness yet for the sake of auld lang syne.'*

June 1965

Chapter Thirty-Four

(i)

'Could we have the editor of *Witness*, please? The editor of *Witness* . . .' Richard's jaw sagged open in astonishment. It was the first prize he had ever won. Around the table people he had only met that day were pumping his hand in congratulations, urging him to his feet. 'Richard Blake . . . the editor of *Witness*, please . . .'

He rose and, smiling around at the applause, made his way through the tables, up on to the dais and to the outstretched, freckled hand of the chairman of McDonald-Crawford, self-appointed media judge. Hudson should be here for this, he thought, as he accepted the inscribed plastic prize. And then he wished that Nicola had been able to fly up to Edinburgh, too.

'Edinburgh?' she had said. 'I've never been there. Drat! I'd love to come, I really would. But I've got to finish this piece.'

For just a moment the lover in him had wrestled a losing battle with the editor. But that morning he had flown alone to the magazine editors' convention, had spoken briefly, as requested, on the problems facing the independent magazine, and now at the grand dinner had won a prize which a few days earlier he had not known existed.

Thanking the chairman he returned to his table. He would telephone Nicola as soon as dinner was over and tell her the good news. Hudson, too. And he smiled inwardly at the thought of Hudson lounging back in his office, feet on the table, laughing. 'Of course we won,

Richard,' he would say. 'How could we do anything but win?'

They had moved into 1965 with Nicola's hair and skirts shorter, and her white Courrèges boots the first pair seen in Notting Hill Gate. Sometimes they would go clubbing, Willie Simmonds getting them into The Bag O'Nails and Scotch of St James, fashionable places of the time, or the cinema, or even, though rarely, the theatre. But later on, when Richard would look back, this would be the time he remembered least well. *Witness* dictated everything. There was no time for reflection, no time for the good times.

For the foursome things had changed after Dorset. They did not go around as a gang any more. On one occasion after Richard had noticed Nicola talking with Hudson he had asked her whether she thought Hudson was still in love with Emily. Nicola's reply had been oblique: 'I'm sure he is. And if he isn't, I am.' Emily, for her part, had seemed slightly distracted, and outside the office he had seen little of her. Recently her father had been unwell and she had been spending more time at her parents' home.

There was no answer when Richard called Nicola after the dinner broke up at eleven, and, because his hosts were anxious to drag him away to an all-night bar in the Cowgate, he did not have time to telephone Hudson. At two o'clock when he emerged from Jimmy's Place it was too late. A plump, pretty girl called Jennifer, an assistant fashion editor on a magazine for teenage girls, appeared to have attached herself to him, but he thought little of it, not even when she dawdled in the corridor outside his room in the Caledonia Hotel. He wondered whether Nicola had finished her piece.

The following day's timetable for the convention had been that after a jolly morning at the McDonald-Crawford distillery, where it was believed lavish gifts were prepared and packed, the journalists would return to their magazines. But at 6 a.m. Richard quickly packed his bag and checked out of the hotel. He didn't drink whisky, anyway.

On the plane he had only coffee and examined his prize again, mentally debating whether it should hang in the living room in Chepstow Villas or be given to Hudson as a present for his office. He decided on the latter. A couple of times during the flight he wondered whether the assistant fashion editor had expected anything more the previous night, and whether she would feel offended that he had left without saying goodbye, but mainly he planned his day. There was so much to do. Flying made him feel dynamic.

From Heathrow Airport he took the bus to Cromwell Road's West London Air Terminal and then a taxi to Chepstow Villas. It was a bright June morning, and the wind which had caused turbulence to the plane was now whipping white clouds across the sky. It was just before nine-thirty when he opened the front door of the house. Pretty good timing that, he thought.

At first he thought the flat was empty. He crossed the hall and went towards the bathroom in search of some Alka Seltzer. It was only as he realized there was none that he heard the sounds, quiet and rhythmical. They were coming from Hudson's room. 'Oh dear,' he smiled, and, thinking it better not to disturb, he quietly closed the cracked old medicine cabinet and tiptoed with his bag into his own room.

He didn't want to but he could hear the sounds more clearly now through the thin partition wall. The sighing of bedsprings, the murmurs of passion. He was embarrassed and surprised. Emily frequently stayed overnight, but it was unlike her not to be in the office by nine-thirty. It wasn't like Hudson either. He tried not to listen and took out the prize.

Beginning to feel like an eavesdropper, he hurried to leave, to get away from the sounds. He was frightened. Something was wrong. He went down the hall. He had to get out. But at the door, a soft, muffled, familiar cry arrested him. He turned and looked towards Hudson's door. And then he saw what had been there all the time. Lying on a chair under Hudson's coat was Nicola's new jacket, the smoky-blue short one she had bought from Mary Quant to go with her Courrèges boots.

'Oh, yes . . .' A gasp from Hudson's room. Nicola. There was absolutely no doubt about it.

The wind had caught the front door and slammed it noisily behind him. But he had hardly been aware of it. He had to be somewhere else. Alone. He had hurried away down the street, aware that he was crying, that people were looking. At one moment he had run and dropped his glasses. At another he had stopped and leant against a wall and wept into the ivy.

At midday he found himself on a bench in Holland Park: at two o'clock on another. He did not know what to do. It grew cold and began to rain, but he did not seek shelter. He remembered his prize and the applause, 'Could we have the editor of *Witness*, please? Richard Blake, the editor of *Witness*', and he realized he had left it in the hall at Chepstow Villas. He thought about how he had first seen her in the cinema, that bright, beautiful face in the light from the Exit sign, as the tidal wave of hysteria had swelled towards her, of the lift to Oxford and of their first night together. And because everything had been spoiled he did not try to hide his feelings. 'Are you all right?' a woman with a spaniel asked in mid-afternoon. He had not known that she was watching him. He nodded and, thanking her, hurried away.

He bought a bar of chocolate, roasted almond, and looked for a café. His hair and coat were wet. He walked towards Hammersmith, though he did not know why. He thought about her body, her scent, her taste. He thought about her skin, the honey tan of her arms, the gentle, warm dampness of her mouth. And he thought about how she had taken him into her and hidden him, of her kisses, of her breasts, of her butterfly touches and smooth body. Then he thought about Hudson.

'I owe you one,' Hudson had said as they put down the trunk. The easy, gracious American who had done so much for him. Then he imagined them together, their clothes scattered on the floor, their skin warm against each other, their secrets and their shared delirium, and tears welled up. He wondered about Emily. And then forgot her. Pain is selfish. It demands concentration. Pain has no time for other sympathies.

(*ii*)

Emily listened in silence. They were in the street, Hudson stammering, his eyes averted, unable to look at her. A bus roared past half-drowning what he was saying. 'I'm sorry, Emily. Neither of us . . . we didn't want ever to hurt you . . . either of you. Don't hate Nicola.'

She had been at the office by nine, going there straight from her parents' house where she had stayed the previous night. When Nicola had not turned up for work she had assumed she was working from the flat. The morning had been too busy to wonder why. At nearly half-past eleven Hudson had telephoned and asked if she had seen Richard, if he had come to the office. She told him he had not. 'Look, Emily, can we meet somewhere . . . ?' he had said.

'Can't you come here? I'm in the middle . . .'

'I'm sorry . . .' He broke off.

'Hudson?'

'Not in the office. Can we meet now, please? We have to talk . . .' He had not been able to finish. She had known then.

She asked no questions, wanted no details. Hudson was anxious about Richard. He said they had heard the front door slam, had found his bag and his prize in the hall.

'Prize?' she asked, confused, not listening to his answer.

Hudson nodded. 'He must have . . . he dropped it . . . when . . .'

329

She stared at him. Even distraught like this he was the most beautiful young man she had ever seen. 'I must go now,' she said, and turning from him walked quickly away.

She was just finishing packing her immediate belongings when Nicola arrived home. She heard the Morris Minor draw up, the car door slam, and then the feet, soft and slow on the stairs. A numb sense of practicality governed her. 'I can get the other things later,' she told herself, closing the suitcase.

Nicola stood in the doorway, her creamy hair falling across her eyes. Her nose was running and her mascara was smeared, staining her cheeks. Slowly she came into the room and, sitting down on the bed, buried her face in her hands.

Emily looked at her. Then, standing, she lifted the case and left the room.

(iii)

Penny was not surprised to hear the front doorbell, not surprised to see Richard, though it was after twelve. After a day of tension and rumour in the office Hudson had taken her to one side, explained that 'there may be a problem' and asked her if she wouldn't mind acting as editor until Richard turned up. 'Where is he?' she had enquired. Hudson had just shaken his head.

Richard looked wrecked. Somehow he had broken his glasses, explaining that they had fallen off when he was running. He did not say what he had been running from.

'You can have my room,' she said. 'I'll sleep in Vasco's bed. He doesn't come home much any more.'

He thanked her, gave her his coat to dry on the boiler and, taking a cup of cocoa, went into her room and closed the door.

Penny sat alone at the tiny kitchen table and finished her wine. Surely he couldn't be surprised? It had all been

330

so inevitable. She had seen it coming for months. Everyone had.

She poured some milk into a saucer for the stray tabby cat she had adopted and, filling a hot water-bottle, went through into Vasco's room. It smelled sweet. She hoped he was not going to be disappointed by his Korean cellist who sold umbrellas, but she thought it likely. He would come back then and tell her how much he preferred her. She wouldn't believe him, but she would be pleased to see him.

She thought then about an article she had recently written which had been headlined *Plain Girls Have Twenty-Twenty* in which she had put the proposition that the plainer the girl the clearer she saw things. She had been writing about the Sixties, the dolly girls and the mini-skirts, the obsession with youth and form and sex. Penny could never wear a mini-skirt: she would never look sexy, and she would never be pursued. But she watched from behind her typewriter those who were, noted the mating displays, the smiles and accidental meetings on the stairs and by the filing cabinets, the little, nervous, early looks, the long glances across the office, the flatteries, the invitations and assignations. And inevitably the betrayals.

Then she imagined Hudson and Nicola together and wondered why it had taken so long.

Chapter Thirty-Five

(i)

They were the golden couple. Everybody loved them. *Born for each other,* that was the phrase most popularly used, and not with sarcasm because they did not provoke envy. They were so handsome, so accomplished and so bright that people felt good just to know them. They were glamorous, a winning team, Hudson so charming, the smile more devastating than ever, Nicola vivacious, unpredictable. In the minor constellation in which they shone they were stars.

The opening of Willie Simmonds' first play, a two-week run in a room over a pub in Richmond, marked their first public appearance as a pair. Almost everyone from the *Witness* hierarchy was there, with the exception of Emily and Richard. Emily was known to have gone back to live in her parents' house and had declined the invitation, sending a good-luck card, while Richard had suddenly disappeared. He had stayed at Penny's place for several days at first, moping about the flat, lying in bed long hours, and walking alone on Hampstead Heath. In the beginning he had hardly spoken, and never about Hudson or Nicola. Hudson had tried to call him several times, but Richard had not picked up the telephone, and when Nicola had visited the flat he had not answered the doorbell. Then on the Saturday, hearing that Hudson and Nicola had gone to the Cotswolds for the weekend, he had returned to Chepstow Villas, packed his belongings and moved into a small apartment in Old Church Street, Chelsea, leaving a cheque behind for his share of the outstanding rent. He was always meticulous about money. Afterwards he had taken Penny to lunch.

'I don't know what to do,' he had said. 'And I don't know how I feel about anything. I know everyone will say that I'll get over it eventually, but I don't want to. I don't want ever to get over Nicola. I don't want to stop hurting. There's a comfort in pain. Does that make sense? I suppose I ought to hate them, both of them, Hudson perhaps most of all. But I can't even do that. I still love her. I'd start again tomorrow, pick up the pieces and forget it ever happened. But I know she doesn't want that. She wants Hudson. And I can't stop thinking about him as my best friend.'

'And partner . . .' Penny had said quietly. There had been some talk in the office that *Witness* could not survive the break-up of the friendship.

Richard had nodded. 'Until this week, until this happened, I thought he was the greatest guy in the world.'

'He is,' Penny had said, and wished she hadn't.

Richard had looked away.

'For what it's worth, my advice is to do nothing. Take some time off. You must be owed some. Even editors get time off. Go somewhere.'

'Where?'

'Anywhere. Don't think about *Witness*. We'll keep it ticking over for you.'

That was how they had left it, and by the time Nicola and Hudson returned from their weekend Richard had gone.

Willie's play opened at the end of the month. Richard had known about it, but, until the publicity began and the cards arrived, few others at *Witness* had realized they had a playwright amongst them.

'Please come, dress outrageously, stay until the end and impress the critics by pretending that you like it, even if you don't,' read the invitation, and, by and large, the *Witness* staff did Willie well. There was no one from sport, but fashion, reviews and advertising, where there were apparently still some girls Willie had not yet tried to seduce, all sent delegations, and all the heads of departments were there. Latymer, who could not drive, was passenger to a horsy girl in a Land-Rover, Berridge was accompanied by a coarse, white-faced, purple-eyed Cockney reporter in a lime-green mini-skirt, orange blouse and red bow called Celia McCabe, instantly and unforgettably nicknamed the Mascara by someone ('she looks like a badly disguised traffic-light,' Charlie Latymer had sniffed), and Adam Smith, the accountant, went down by Underground. Even Neil Fiske, now on the board of directors, turned out.

Penny Chilston had been pleased to be invited along in the Alvis with Hudson and Nicola. It was the first time she had been alone with them. With Emily Hudson had been a friend as much as a lover: but with Nicola he was more subdued, as though overawed by her presence. Penny had noticed it in the office months earlier when he had occasionally become tongue-tied in Nicola's presence, but she had not expected to find it now. He was, she realized, totally, and slightly madly, besotted.

Willie was waiting and welcoming in a small courtyard at the side of the pub, holding a tray of champagne and dressed like an eighteenth-century dandy, a burgundy velvet suit of large lapels over a white ruffed shirt. 'This is the great..est n..ight of my l..ife,' he said repeatedly as his guests climbed out of their cars, his blond flop of hair newly washed and electric and curling over his ears and down the back of his neck. He looked, said Nicola, like a Kink.

Gimmelmann, to whom Willie had always been friendly, and Holly were already there, but on this occasion all *Witness* eyes and smiles fell on Hudson and Nicola as they stood bashfully together fencing back small talk. At seven-thirty Willie ushered his guests and the few paying customers up to the tiny theatre, glasses replenished on the way.

'If they're drunk perhaps they'll laugh louder,' Willie

whispered to Penny as he pushed a typed programme at her. 'We've got a couple of cr..itics in, so we must st..art pr..omptly or they'll m..iss their dead..lines.' With that he hurried off to seat some late-comers. Penny looked at the programme. '"*The Two-Backed Beast* is an adult comedy of bad manners",' she read aloud. Hudson and Nicola alongside did not hear. They were talking quietly together. 'Emmy would have enjoyed this,' she heard Nicola say.

The performance began. There were no curtains and the stage was just a triangular corner of the room with doors at either side. The only props were two upright chairs, a sofa and a bucket. In the front row Penny felt as if she were actually on the stage, taking part in the performance, which after just one minute was proving to be, at the very least, surprising.

Two young men stood facing the audience wearing nothing other than Y-front underpants. One held a mop in his hand, the other a map. Surreptitiously they looked towards each other, then on meeting each other's eyes, turned quickly back to the audience. Somewhere off-stage a lone trumpet played the Last Post. The lights dimmed. Very gradually the two men put down the map and the mop, slipped to their knees and, approaching each other like two inquisitive dogs, sniffed the air. Shuffling forward on their knees, they next sniffed each other's noses and ears and then, beginning to move around each other, heads to hind quarters, as it were, began to sniff at each other's Y-fronts. At the back of the stage two girls wearing only bras and pants necked furiously together on the sofa. The audience was shrivelled with embarrassment. At Penny's side Hudson shifted slightly, his legs so long they protruded out on to the stage area. She glanced up at him. His features were expressionless. Someone coughed. Someone else tried not to giggle. The familiar smell of smouldering marijuana drifted around the darkness. On stage the sniffing of underpants continued. Only Willie Simmonds could have written this, thought Penny, and

335

settled down for an evening of provocative smut.

But it turned out not to be quite like that. Certainly Willie's play was rude, and absolutely intended to shock, but it was also funny. At the interval no one knew quite what to say, but no one left. Willie had used a pellet-loaded shotgun to attack every example of establishment sexual repression he could find, and if some of the shot missed its target by miles, the rest, judging by the nervous laughter, scored bull's eye, backside hits.

The show was over just before ten when the entire audience and cast went downstairs into the pub to celebrate. 'B..b..etter enjoy our..selves n..ow, b..efore the re..views come out and ruin ev..ery..thing,' Willie said, punting around for compliments, a hand furtively kneading the bottom of one of the actresses. Nobody really knew whether they had actually enjoyed the evening, nor had they the slightest idea what the reviews might say. In fact Penny was astonished that Willie had been able to tempt serious critics from *The Times* and the *Daily Telegraph* down to Richmond at all.

It was a noisy pub with a juke box, largely given over to records by local heroes the Rolling Stones, and alongside which Holly set up court, obviously enjoying being stared at. It would have been difficult for anyone not to stare. She was wearing the shortest skirt Penny had ever seen, a pink ribbon of cotton perhaps nine inches long, which matched exactly her lipstick. Her shirt and tights were black. As always she looked slightly dirty, and for the first time Penny noticed that when she smiled, which tonight, on display, she did frequently, her right cheek dimpled.

'Isn't she just the biggest trollop you've seen in your entire life, Penny?' Nicola was gazing across the pub. Hudson, returning from the bar carrying drinks, had become involved in a scrum, his passage blocked by Holly and Gimmelmann. As they watched Holly was leaning up to whisper something into his ear, her breasts deliberately pressed firmly against his chest. He seemed to be straining backwards, but, locked in, and with three drinks in his hands, there was little room for manoeuvre.

'My mother would call her a tripehound,' said Penny. 'And she ought to know.' She was surprised at the ice in Nicola's tone. Surely she couldn't fear the competition.

'What did the black widow want then?' Nicola asked as Hudson prised himself free and delivered the drinks.

Hudson shook his head. 'Oh, nothing really,' he muttered, and then before he could be pressed further, added, 'I suggest we go when we've had this one.'

The reviews surprised everyone, not least Willie. *The Two-Backed Beast* was 'daring', 'innovative', 'inventive', 'electrifying theatre', according to the *Daily Telegraph*. *The Times* thought that 'William Simmonds, while still immature and wanting in theatrical device', had 'an original, barricade-braving mind'. 'Impudently good', was the opinion of that weekend's *Sunday Times*, while the *Observer*'s critic led with 'this sexual broadside, this stunning and pertinent savaging of a society struggling to cast off its metaphorical chastity belt'. Beckett, of course, was mentioned, as were Ionesco and Pirandello. And that didn't hurt. And when, just one week later and by miraculous good fortune, a small theatre became suddenly available in Charing Cross Road, Penny knew that Willie Simmonds' real career was just beginning. *Witness* had another star.

(*ii*)

Richard went to New York. A helpful contact at the American Embassy hurried his visa through and Icelandic Airways provided the cheapest way across the Atlantic. The ten-hour refuelling delay in Reykjavik did not matter. He had nothing to hurry for. He was, he knew, only partially aware of what was happening around him. For most of the time he sought companionship in his memory.

337

He arrived at Kennedy Airport at eight in the morning. It was very hot, already in the high seventies, and stunningly bright. The smell of aeroplane fuel made him gasp as he stepped from the plane.

Early morning Kennedy and everyone was hurrying, all with somewhere to go. He had no real plan and had a cup of coffee and a doughnut while he plucked up courage.

At ten-thirty he called Ben and Jessica Tarlo's number. An hour later Jessica met him off the bus at the Port Authority Bus Terminal in mid-town Manhattan.

'You should have told us you were coming, Richard. Ben would have met you at the airport. Of course you can stay. There's room. We'll make room. We've got a nice place. They pay real money here, you know.' She was suddenly more American than she had ever seemed in London, generous in a tough and practical way. She was also heavily pregnant, her eyes smiling with happiness, and she was wearing a pair of paint-spattered, sawn-off dungarees, swollen huge at the front. 'You look terrific,' he said honestly.

'You don't,' she laughed.

The Tarlos had an apartment on Ninety-Third and Park and they took a cab there. On the way he told Jessica what had happened. She nodded but showed no surprise. 'If you're running away there's nowhere better to run to than New York. I'm glad you came.'

Through the cab window he watched Manhattan, a shock now as it would always be, taller and deeper, the avenues wider than he had ever imagined: heat, glare and noise, the rutted surface of the roads, the combustion of people competing for their space on the sidewalks, a wash of shimmering street-level yellow, then rusts and greys turning into blue above.

It was a small two-room apartment on the third floor of a brownstone house. Jessica said it was a palace for the rent they were paying in this part of Manhattan. They used the north-facing room which overlooked the street as both bedroom and Jessica's studio. A picture sat on an easel. To Richard it looked like a lot of wavy lines, but he said he liked it, anyway. She laughed and said he didn't have to lie. She was hurrying to finish in time for her first exhibition. The back room was for living and because he was tired she pulled out a camp bed and left him to sleep.

When he awoke it was evening and Ben was home. He was doing well, working as a copywriter on Madison Avenue. The successful professional couple: and he envied them their happiness.

They had dinner at a Chinese place on Lexington Avenue where he passed on all the news from London. They made no comment about Hudson and Nicola. Ben had always liked Hudson.

Richard stayed with the Tarlos for three days, during which Jessica gave up her painting in the mornings to show him the sights, though she was too pregnant to walk very far. He did not need company and in the afternoons would patrol the pavements of the city, watching and listening, his pain distracted by New York's vitality.

He was embarrassed to have taken their living room, but on the fourth day a solution appeared when Jessica suddenly asked him if he'd like to apartment-sit for a friend. The owner was a girl from a few blocks away, who, when they arrived at her house, was already shoving a large bag into her Volkswagen. She was a rounded New Yorker in shorts, T-shirt and tennis shoes. Her only advice as she gave him the keys and hurried away was 'treat it like home'. Her name was Lois.

It was nothing like home. She was rich: the floors were polished, the rugs were thick and discreetly patterned and the furniture was of old, dark woods. On the wall hung paintings which, since they made Jessica sigh, he gathered to be either good or valuable, and possibly both. Only one room was bare: a small guest room. He felt more comfortable there; it was a place to seek out his melancholy. Nicola lay with him during the nights, the creamy hair falling across her face as it had in the café in Oxford, listening as he talked, on and on, an endless one-sided discussion in which every fibre of their relationship was dissected. Sometimes she spoke, repeating lines she had said months ago. But she had nothing new to say. Sometimes he imagined he spoke with Hudson, like the conversations they had shared back in the Lamborne when they first became friends. But mostly he just lay and sweated.

He had some phone numbers, people he knew, a girl from Trinity College, Dublin, who was now at NYU, and a cineast who had written a few pieces for *Witness*. He called them and others, and they met him for a drink, took him into their networks and passed him on.

Sixties New York was different from London which was a silly, gimmicky place. In New York there was a preoccupation with the war, with civil rights issues. There was a worry on the streets that was new to him. He watched and noted, and read everything on the news-stands.

He talked to people, too. At a Sunday afternoon anti-war demonstration in Washington Square he fell in with a former army chaplain who had seen service in the Pacific and then Korea, a square, grey, crew-cut man in a black shirt buttoned to the neck. For some reason he told him about Nicola. They were sitting in a bar on Thompson Street, their faces green and red from the light of a neon beer sign, and they had drunk more than Richard was used to.

'The thing is, I'm frightened to go back. I don't know if I can face it. I didn't know I could feel this way about anything . . . About anyone.'

The ex-priest was silent for a long moment and then smiled. 'It seems to me you're a lucky guy.'

'Lucky?'

'Well, yes. To have feelings the way you describe, to

have such powerful emotions. Sure, it's painful, a kind of tyranny, but think of all the people who never have an experience like that, people who never love anybody and are never loved in return. Think of all the people you know who've never had anything to remember. Think what they've missed.'

'That doesn't make it any easier.'

'No, maybe not, but would you rather be without it? Would your life have been as rich? Yes, it is cruel that the girl you loved now loves someone else. I can see that. Your best friend, you said. I guess it happens all the time. But wouldn't it have been worse if you'd never met this girl, if the car hadn't stopped to pick you up? You're young. You've experienced something special. You should treasure it. One day when you're older maybe you won't be so lucky.'

'I don't understand,' said Richard.

'Of course you don't. You're only a boy. Single-minded. Not corrupted by life. Perhaps you never will be corrupted by life. I hope not. Perhaps that was why I always liked the young fellas best. Their needs and problems were so simple, physical yes, but their hearts were usually in the right place. In the passage of a lifetime we change, in many ways we become weaker. Little corruptions eat at us along the way, vanities, greed, varieties of experience, all these things. You say you had a perfect love. I say you're a lucky man.'

Just talking made it easier, talking and time. The healing process had begun. But Richard knew that in every moment he did not hurt the first love of his life suffered a little death. He knew also that he would soon go home.

A few days later, on his last night in New York, Jessica had her opening. It was along with two other artists in a two-room gallery down in the East Village and Richard spent the day helping transport her pictures and supervising the hang while she kept her appointment at the ante-natal clinic. She was the youngest and newest of the artists and had been given the darkest corners and narrowest corridors for her paintings. That worried him but she didn't complain. 'I'm in an *exhibition*! In *New York*! Just around the corner from *Greenwich Village*! And I should *complain*?' she said.

It wasn't a very big exhibition, and the private view didn't attract anyone famous or rich. But it was exciting for Jessica whose parents came from Philadelphia and for Ben who brought some friends along in their cotton summer suits from Madison Avenue, one of whom actually bought the painting of wavy lines. It was Jessica's first professional sale and she was both thrilled and embarrassed. Richard, for the most part, hung around in the background, drinking the wine and changing the Rolling Stones and Motown records, which the gallery owner, a bearded, bald, Mephistophelean-looking character with a whisper, insisted be played very loud.

'D'you have *Fingertips, Part 2*?' It was after ten, the gallery was about to close and a very tanned girl was looking down at him as he sifted the records.

'What?' He probably knew less about rock music than any man in New York.

'Little Stevie Wonder. You don't recognize me, do you? You've been living in my apartment for two weeks and you don't recognize me. My God!' She grinned. 'I'm sorry, I should have warned you that I was coming home.'

When the gallery closed a gang of them went for dinner in the Village. Lois didn't know anyone either apart from Jessica and Ben and so she and Richard sat together. He must have been distracted when he had first seen her climbing into her Volkswagen because he had not noticed that she was attractive. Now she was very brown, and casually chic in a jacket and trousers. She had, she said, been sailing for two weeks out at Montauk on Long Island where her parents had a summer home. Richard knew less about sailing than he did about rock music, so instead they talked about the war and Lyndon

Johnson and demonstrations and *Witness*. She was, she said, a professional 'part-timer'. 'Part of the time I'm doing courses in art history, part of the time I help out in a friend's workshop restoring antiques, part of the time I take photographs and part of the time I write about movies, the ones that nobody else wants to go and see, for the *Village Voice*.'

The taxi back up town dropped Richard and Lois first. Now that she was home he had offered to go back and stay with Jessica and Ben but she would not hear of it.

They got on well. In the apartment she put on some music, Bach, and lit up a joint which they shared. In Dorset he had been anxious, almost scared when Nicola had produced some hash: in New York it was the only thing to do. Still he didn't get much out of it. She put on the television with the sound turned off and showed him some of her photographs, portraits of people who looked like other rich New Yorkers to him. But they were good.

At about four in the morning she said, 'You don't have to sleep in the guest room, you know. You can come in with me if you'd like to. I mean, I'd like it if you did.'

It was so long since he had thought about sex with anybody other than Nicola, so long since he had slept with anyone else. When it was over he lay back and wondered why something that had been so enjoyable should have left him so disappointed. It was already light and Lois was watching him. 'It takes time to get over these things,' she said kindly. 'There's no short cut.'

The telephone at the side of the bed woke him in mid-morning. It was Jessica. Lois had gone off to college. 'I just got a call from Ben in the office,' she said. 'He bought an airmail copy of yesterday's *Daily Telegraph* on his way to work. Apparently Willie Simmonds is a big hit in London with a play he's written. Did you know about this and why didn't you tell us?'

He read about Willie's success on the flight home.

West End theatre in sex-play storm, read a story in the *Daily Express* he had found at a bookstall at Kennedy Airport. It had all happened so quickly, he felt as though he had been away for months. Then he noticed that Willie's surname had been spelled wrongly and was reassured. Some things never changed.

He didn't notice Hudson waiting in the crowd at Heathrow and was heading for the buses when a hand reached out to his shoulder.

'Hey, fella, what's the hurry?'

He stopped in surprise, and looked around, thinking for a moment that Nicola might be there, too.

Hudson read his face. 'It's OK. Just me.'

'Ah . . . right.' Richard searched his mind for something casual to say.

'Ben called to say what flight you were on. Is that all right?'

'Yes. Of course.' He knew that Ben and Hudson had spoken earlier, shortly after he arrived in New York. 'You must have had a hell of a wait. I'm sorry.' The plane had been due in at two-thirty but it was now nearly seven. Icelandic Airways were late again.

'That's OK. I managed to get a little reading done.' Nervously Hudson tried a joke. 'Most of Tolstoy.'

Richard smiled.

Hudson became hesitant. 'How . . . er . . . how are you? We've been worried.'

Richard tried to shrug. 'Oh, you know . . . fine. Fine.'

They stood looking at each other for several seconds. Then quite unexpectedly Hudson threw his arms around him. 'Jesus, it's good to see you again,' he said.

Richard did not respond. He felt faintly foolish standing in the middle of Heathrow Airport being embraced by a man. Hudson would have called it English reserve. Prising himself free he gently mimicked Hudson's accent: 'So, what do you say we go to work? OK?'

They drove back to town in the Alvis and had dinner together in one of their regular Notting Hill Gate haunts where they talked about *Witness*. The distributors, Farrow and Fox, were doing better all the time and both display and classified advertising were up.

'Looks like you can manage without me pretty well,' said Richard, looking at the magazines published while he had been away. 'Penny's done a great job.'

Hudson nodded. 'She followed your formula. It's your magazine, Richard. How did you like New York?'

'It was, you know, interesting. I analysed every magazine in the city. I may have learned a new trick or two.'

'I thought you were on vacation.'

Richard could see that Hudson regretted that as soon as he'd said it. 'No, that wasn't what it was,' he said quietly.

Nicola joined them for coffee, slipping into the banquette next to Richard, leaning up to kiss him, her scent catching him by surprise with its memories. It was a cold evening and she was wearing her old duffel coat. She put her arm through his below the table and sat close and for an hour they all tried desperately to be grown up, faking smiles and jokes. Miserably Richard remembered Lois and began to understand the disappointment he had experienced with her. It was as though he had been unfaithful, not to Nicola, but to their memory.

At one o'clock they dropped him off outside his Chelsea flat. Nicola let him out of the car on her side. 'I'm glad you're back,' she said softly, then leaning up kissed him again, holding on for just a moment. 'See you tomorrow.' Then, turning, she climbed back into the Alvis.

And Richard went in alone.

(*iii*)

'She brands people, you know.' Peter Berridge was

sitting on the edge of Penny's desk, playing with some loose change in his pocket. Gaunt as a grave, his cadaverous cheeks were stretched into a thin, mysterious smile.

'What?' Penny had been expecting something. Berridge had purposely waited until the office was quite empty before he had approached her. It was eight-thirty at night, Richard was back, and now, just when she thought *Witness* was returning to normal, Berridge was being gnomic.

'Holly Carter. She brands all the men she screws. And she screws lots of men, believe me.'

'What kind of brand?' Nothing that Holly did would have surprised Penny. On the cover of a magazine Holly came across as cheeky and cute: the reality was grubby.

'Some kind of scratch,' they say. 'A kind of cross, I believe.'

'Who says?' Penny asked.

Berridge smiled. 'My sources.'

Penny was unimpressed. 'Yes?' she said blankly.

'All right. A hairdresser in Mount Street. He says she's done it to stacks of fellows. You know, the sudden flick of her hand at the moment of ecstasy, as they say, and the chap's got a brand on his shoulder, or wherever.' He was smiling rather unpleasantly now.

'Why would she want to do that?'

Berridge shrugged. 'Why does the praying mantis always kill her mate? Who knows? But she does it, and so does Holly.'

'So, who cares? She's only a . . .' What had Nicola called her? 'She's only a trollop, anyway. The world is full of freaky people nowadays. It's called Sixties dissolute.'

'You mean you don't think it's . . . interesting?'

'As gossip?'

'Well, yes, and maybe . . .'

'You mean you think it's a story. "Randy model brands lovers." That sort of thing? What about Tim? I

346

thought you and he were quite friendly. Have you asked him what he thinks about her screwing around?'

'I'm sure he knows. I think he turns a blind eye.'

'Which is exactly what you should do.'

Berridge was beginning to look awkward. 'I wasn't suggesting running it in *Witness*, you know.' He sounded almost petulant.

'You're bloody right you weren't.'

'I just thought that one of the Sundays . . .'

Penny put her hand up. 'Well, don't think,' she said. 'For better or worse Holly Carter is *Witness*'s discovery. Our first cover girl. If you want to keep your nose in here keep it out of Holly Carter's knicker drawer. All right?'

Berridge looked almost hurt. 'It was only an idea, Penny. No need to come on like a winged avenger.'

Penny pushed her typewriter away and got up to leave. 'I know,' she said. 'No reason at all.' Then friendly, she said: 'Come on, I'll buy you a drink.'

For a moment Berridge hesitated. 'Ah . . . well, oh dear, sorry, old girl. I can't make it tonight. Gosh, is it really so late? I must dash. See you tomorrow,' he said, and grabbing his raincoat he scuttled out of the office.

Penny, lumpen-shaped, plain and intrepid, watched him go. She thought about Holly. Men were never too busy to have a drink with her. In the end she went for the drink alone.

(*iv*)

To Charles Latymer in his St John's Wood flatlet, pristine, neat and tidy and well hung with wall mirrors, it was all incomprehensible. Everyone knew that Penny Chilston had the next best thing to a drink problem and would juggle with her bubbies in the middle of Trafalgar Square if Hudson asked her to. Yet who was it who got promotion when the lovelorn editor went walkabout? Latymer complained to everyone: he told his sometime girl-friend with the Land-Rover, good at three-day eventing and well connected for weekends in the country, and he told Willie Simmonds: he even told Gimmelmann, though he was less in evidence these days, and he made jolly sure all the secretaries, the druggy art department and the fashion girls knew how he felt. He even hinted to Neil Fiske in his cardigan that he was just a tiny bit less than satisfied. But *Witness* was doing well and Fiske did not seem to hear him. Then one day he looked in the mirror and saw what had literally been staring him in the face all along. It was so obvious he could not imagine how he had missed it. He was in the wrong job, anyway. He was simply made for television.

Chapter Thirty-Six

Emily's father died in October, slipping away quietly during the night after a summer of pain. She found him in the morning. He looked older than fifty-five, his thin body worn out by the effort of breathing.

In the past two months he had taken to sleeping in a bed in his study as though fretful that every moment was precious, that every second should be invested in his novel.

To Emily it was a shock, but not a surprise. He had been ill for so long, that she had had time subconsciously to rehearse the moment. She was glad now that she had come to live at home.

Her mother took it badly: she had not been there. She put on a grey fitted dress and pearls and drew the curtains. Then she sat and wept silently as the doctor came and wrote out the death certificate. Emphysema. When he had gone she gazed for a long time at the body of her husband, until Emily insisted she leave the room.

At eleven Emily telephoned her brother's lodgings in Bristol where he was technically at university and left a message. He had not been home for a couple of nights, they said, but that was not unusual. Musicians were gypsies. Then in the afternoon, after the undertakers had been, she called all those who would need to be told and listened to the sudden silences, regrets and offers of help. At tea-time, when her mother's elder sister had come up from Wiltshire and everything had been done, she called Nicola at *Witness*.

They met outside a pub in Kensington Church Street, and for the first time all day she could not hold back the tears. Her father had always loved Nicola. 'What about it, Emily?' he would say during those last months. 'What about Some Floozy Named Flo? I'm sure she's longing to hear from you.' But Emily had just shaken her head. Although he had never offered much of a comment on Hudson she knew he had been hurt for her. 'It's a long-distance race,' was the only thing he said. He often said that.

It was a mild, almost sticky late afternoon and she and Nicola walked in Kensington Gardens. By the Round Pond they watched two schoolchildren sailing a model yacht while their father waited. 'It doesn't seem five minutes ago,' said Emily.

Emily talked and Nicola listened, of holidays she remembered, of her father's terrible jokes and his quiet amusement at her mother's smart friends. 'He was never very successful, you know. I mean when I was younger I used to think he was because he had books in the library and nobody else's father did. But he never sold very well and when the critics bothered to review him they were usually terribly patronizing. But he never stopped hoping. I think he wanted to show Mummy that she'd married the right chap after all, though I'm sure she never doubted it for a minute. It was always a struggle for him.'

'A happy struggle,' said Nicola. 'A happy family. He made it happy.'

They walked on. Since leaving *Witness* Emily had written some interviews on a freelance basis for the *Evening Standard* and Nicola complimented her on them. By the Serpentine they watched young people splashing about in boats, as they had once watched the punts. Finally Emily said it. 'How's Hudson? Is he all right?'

Nicola nodded, and then shrugged. 'I think so. Mainly . . . I mean, he was . . . shattered . . . when . . .'

Emily put a hand on her arm. She did not want to hear this. She pointed at an arrow of ducks skimming over the surface of the water and they watched in silence as the birds bombed to a stop, feet first. 'Hudson always loved you. I suppose in a sense I realized. I think I knew it before he did. After Dorset there was no hiding it. We were all just waiting for what happened, perhaps not consciously, but I can see now there was an inevitability.'

'I'm sorry, Emmy. You know that, don't you?'

'Yes. I know.'

Nicola was thoughtful for a while. At last she said: 'I can understand what you meant now . . . about Hudson humming a different tune from the rest of us. I don't think I know what he's really like, either.'

'We should ask Richard some time.'

Nicola shook her head. 'He used to ask me to ask you,' she said.

He had made arrangements, a burial not a burning, and a small service was held in St Mary Abbot's Church, though he had never been there since Emily and her brother had been christened. And, because Emily asked, Nicola knelt with her in the front pew with the family. Her father would have wanted that.

She had not expected it but Hudson and Richard were also there, standing together at the back of the church, their eyes cast down.

A few days later Richard telephoned and asked her if she would like to write for *Witness* again. There was no reason why she needed to. She was doing quite well as a freelance. But of course she said yes.

Chapter Thirty-Seven

(i)

Without Nicola there was a void in Richard's life and he filled it almost entirely with *Witness* as week chased week chased month, through 1965 into 1966. With no distractions his addiction to news became stronger as American astronauts walked in space, race riots erupted in Los Angeles and the Beatles were awarded MBEs. Then there was a war in Kashmir, the illegal declaration of independence in Rhodesia (Nicola wrote long and angrily about that), a Christmas truce in Vietnam, the Aberfan pit disaster, Burton and Taylor and *Who's Afraid of Virginia Woolf?*, a wonder horse called Arkle at Cheltenham, bombs on Hanoi, anti-Vietnam war protests everywhere, the Moors murders, the World Cup, marijuana, Eleanor Rigby, Chairman Mao's Cultural Revolution and *Time* magazine's late discovery of Swinging London: thousands of stories and pictures on an endless roller of changing news.

Of course, there were girls, though not many. Jennifer, the fashion assistant, who had attached herself in Edinburgh got in touch, and was reattached for a couple of nights, and an actress friend of Willie Simmonds came on like a vacuum cleaner. But they weren't Nicola, or anything like. So most evenings he worked at the office until after ten, occasionally calling in at Emily's home on Campden Hill on his way home, so that they might talk about *Witness* or the news, but, most of all, so that they could discuss their old friends. Neither was bitter about what had happened. But, though the infatuations were fading, the bruising still showed.

Hudson and Nicola for their part were becoming increasingly famous, taken up by the gossip columns and trend makers in the same way that Gimmelmann and Holly had been. Nicola would squirm to see items about herself in the newspapers ('Crumbs, Emmy, they write about me as though I'm Princess Margaret, for God's sake'), but it would amuse Hudson, who understood the value of free publicity for *Witness*. Certainly they made a beautiful couple in a London dedicated increasingly to the young and beautiful, and, when gossip was thin, *Rhodesian heiress and American millionaire* stories were easy fillers. 'At least they're half-right,' Hudson would mock, without ever attempting to correct the half that was wrong.

'He likes it when people think he's richer than he is,' Emily said one evening as she showed Richard a copy of *Queen*. On a double spread were Gimmelmann portraits of both Hudson and Nicola in a feature about those most likely to succeed.

Richard agreed. He remembered the times when Hudson would go without food all day so that he could pretend to be casual when doling out the *Witness* petty cash. 'I know his folks are well off and got him started, but they never helped out along the road. Every penny he's ever made has gone back into the business.'

Emily was silent for a moment and then said: 'I never knew anyone talk less about his parents.'

Richard nodded. 'If you ask me there was some almighty bust-up sometime before he came to London. Maybe they didn't want him to come.'

'I suppose he's just one of those people who never really talks about himself,' said Emily, 'unlike Nicola who will tell you anything you ask her, no details spared.'

'Oh dear,' said Richard.

In a perverse way Hudson's dedication to Nicola amused them both. He had always been generous with everyone, but with Nicola everything had to be perfect. He courted her with style: gifts of jewellery, first editions, a surprise weekend in Siena, another in Brittany. Never particularly interested in food himself he became a restaurant expert, taking her to only the best places, where he would buy expensive wines which he hardly drank. Early on in their affair he was so proud of her he accepted invitations to social occasions, premières and charity balls, events he would once have shunned, where he would sit and stare at her across the table. These ended when she began to tease him about being a social climber. The attentions didn't. Instead they went to the races, where she betted extravagantly, won and lost again, and hatless outshone all the other ladies; to the Henley Regatta, where she drank too much champagne but was still the prettiest sight on water that year; to the Wigmore Hall to hear John Ogdon play the piano and to the Royal Albert Hall to see Bob Dylan on the night he went electric; while every Saturday morning he took her shopping, insisting upon paying for everything, though she could well afford things herself. She was already beautiful but it pleased him to help dress her in the styles of the day that would make her glamorous. And when he took her to parties, and there were so many parties, he would flush with pride as heads turned to look at her.

His devotion sometimes puzzled Emily. 'It's as though she is quite simply the most wonderful thing that ever happened to him, the culmination of his life's hopes, and he wants to celebrate her in every way possible. It's more than touching. It's lovely. But it's also slightly sad.'

It also puzzled her that Hudson and Nicola did not live together. Richard knew better. 'His pride won't allow him. In a lot of ways he's incredibly old-fashioned. He won't want to live with her until he can build her a home he thinks is good enough for her, a palace, I suppose.' So while Hudson stayed in Chepstow Villas Nicola invested some of her inheritance in a small two up, two down and two further down, a fashionable, dinky cottage just around the corner from

354

him in Notting Hill Gate, where she and Emily would meet and talk together, as close again as ever.

There was much to talk about. It was an exciting time, perhaps the most exciting time. Things were happening everywhere, to almost everyone they knew.

(ii)

Fame was changing Willie Simmonds' life more than he could have imagined in his wettest dreams. An instant celebrity, often to be seen on cultural television talk programmes, invariably outrageous and quotable, hardly stammering at all in his performing personality, he had given up journalism for ever when he realized that his first month's royalties from the West End production of *The Two-Backed Beast* amounted to more than a year's pay from *Witness*. Suddenly he was famous for being himself, and now that he was also, by his standards, rich, he was discovering that 'the p..pastures of c..c..c..crumpet, golden acres of h..h..honeyed thigh, butt..ock, breast and limb' were virtually limitless. He was, he told Richard, the luckiest man in London, as every week willing and breathtaking young actresses, and some not so young, not so breathtaking, often married but even more willing, sought dramatic inspiration between his sheets.

'Fame is a terrible aphro..disiac,' he would say, 'but I think God will for..give me if I take back the empties.'

No one knew whether Peter Berridge had any personal interest in sex, but he enjoyed writing about other people's interest in it, not for *Witness*, where he was limited to political and media intrigue and gossip, but, under all kinds of pseudonyms, for the Sunday smuts. He was a natural librarian, keeping and constantly updating files on anyone and everyone who might conceivably be of interest. No item of gossip was too trivial, no name too small to escape his careful collecting and collating. 'I bet the beggar even has files on us, like some kind of KGB sex policeman,' Richard would joke. Berridge was

355

devoted to his work. To see him and his girl-friend, the Mascara, in action at parties, buttering up and knifing down, 'the most ruthless double act since the Thane of Cawdor and his lady', as Richard described them, was to see a new kind of professionalism in dirty journalism. What they did was appalling, but they were very good at it. Hudson was always amused. 'Having him around is like having a hungry jackal chained up in your backyard in case anybody tries to break in. Isn't it refreshing to meet a guy you can rely on to always write the worst thing he knows about anybody. He doesn't know it, but he's a walking gold mine. His day will come.'

For Charles Latymer it was a case of keep trying. Every morning his mirrors told him that his future lay on the screen and though the BBC had turned up its several and diverse noses in his direction he remained determined. It was only a matter of time before his true talents were spotted. Wherever one looked in television Latymer was cultivating, stretching his web of contacts, a lunch here, a drink there, and lots of flattery everywhere. He was convinced: with his looks, his intelligence, his education and his contacts it was only a matter of time.

(*iii*)

Penny Chilston said goodbye to Vasco at her front door on the day after the World Cup Final. She had wanted to go with him to Heathrow and see him off, but he had dissuaded her. Flights to India were always being delayed, he said. She might find herself waiting for days to wave him goodbye. She had no idea whether that was the true reason but she accepted it. They had really said goodbye the night before, anyway, when they had cracked open some champagne and 'rogered like champions'. She was sorry that he had failed his examinations. She blamed the Korean cellist. She was sure he would have made a very good gynaecologist.

When he had gone she went and lay down on his

bed. It smelled of roses as it had always done. Closing her eyes she pictured him sitting in the taxi going down to Victoria to catch the airport bus, his long eyelashes curling, his skin dark and velvetine. She would miss his beauty and his declarations, insincere though they were. It was a warm July day and outside in the street she could hear boys kicking a football about, shouting out the names of recent glory, Charlton, Moore, Ball.

She dozed, there hadn't been much time for sleep the night before, and she day-dreamed, one ear tuned to the cries and celebrations from the street, and, as always, she shared her day-dreams with Hudson. He was smiling at her, beautiful in a cream, summer, linen suit and powder-blue shirt, his skin browner and eyes bluer than she had ever seen. Behind him Nicola was sitting by a stream. 'Isn't she beautiful, Penny?' he said. 'Isn't she wonderful?' Then very slowly he walked back to Nicola, and, taking her hand, led her away.

In the hot afternoon Penny heaved her weight from one side to the other, and, with her mouth open, snored gently into the pillow.

(*iv*)

For Holly and Gimmelmann life was rich as they trawled the fashionable world in search of ever more lucrative assignments. Paris was never likely to be interested in anyone as scruffy as Holly, but there was always work in Rome, or Amsterdam, or Hamburg. And after a slow start the New York fashion editors were beginning to commission. Holly now had her own agent, but Gimmelmann still made sure he got most of the work. Holly liked New York, not the work particularly, nor the pace, but the nights. In the night, in New York, a girl like Holly Carter could have real fun. And she loved the money.

In fact she liked New York too much. It wasn't good for her. The main job in being a model was taking care of oneself and Holly was never any good at that.

So Gimmelmann took her to Los Angeles, which for most people is a sleepy, go-to-bed-early kind of town. At first she said it was boring, but the work was good: Holly in Hollywood, a major spread for *Italian Vogue*, the street urchin gone glamorous. They stayed in a bungalow in the garden at the Chateau Marmont on Sunset Boulevard and Gimmelmann shot her in every glitzy location in LA. Then one night in the Whisky she met some new friends and all of a sudden Los Angeles wasn't so boring after all. She stayed awake for two days and two nights after that, but her pupils were so small he couldn't shoot her. The excuse went out to the crew that she had a cold. No one believed it.

She was more self-destructive than anybody Gimmelmann had ever known. She said she worried about her weight, the propensity to fat around the chin. But she would then sit in bed all afternoon, watching TV with the sound off, her records so loud the Chateau management complained, spooning pecan nut ice-cream by the tub into her mouth.

'Beats a bag of chips in a clapped-out old caravan down the back of the Scrubs, doesn't it?' he told her on the third day of enforced idleness as she lolled back on her pillows, the venetian blinds down, magazines and comics all over the bed. She didn't even bother to answer.

He went out into the garden and sat on a bench under a tree and wondered what Hudson would have done in such a situation. Hudson was pleased with the way he'd come on as a photographer, he could tell that by the way he spoke to him. They'd had quite a few chats, him and Hudson. He wasn't afraid of Hudson any more, not embarrassed the way he had been. The success had helped, naturally. And the courses. He'd got a diploma in English language, though he'd never had the nerve to show anyone, least of all Hudson. Still, no one could look down on him now. He'd done as well as any of them, more or less, and could hold his own without getting his grammar screwed up. Certainly he was making more money than any of them, except perhaps for Willie Simmonds and his *Two-Backed Beast*. He was a dirty little bugger, that Willie. No wonder he couldn't talk properly. It seemed amazing that a bloke who couldn't get his words out without twisting his face up and spitting all over the place should be able to write a play which was nothing but people talking, quick and fluent and witty and rude. What was even more amazing, when you considered it, was the success Willie had with women. They flocked to him: couldn't get them down quickly enough. Every time you saw him he was giving it to someone new, not just scrubby little models with their press-stud tits and crabs like the crowd he hung about with, but heiresses and film stars and the wives of dukes. He'd caught him at it once at a party. He'd gone into the bedroom to get his coat to go home and there was Willie and some blonde bint on the floor banging like an entry gate in a gale. Willie had been very cool about it. 'S..orry, old b..oy,' he'd said. 'I don't th..ink you've b..een intro..duced, have you? Tim Gimm..el..mann, Candida Parkinson-Routledge.' He'd got that bit out all right. Candida Parkinson-Routledge. Very nice, she was, too. Late thirties and married. He liked them married, did Willie.

Gimmelmann lit the last of his cigarettes and worried. He still hadn't decided what to do about Holly. He could go inside and give her a good hiding. That was what he felt like doing. But it wouldn't do any good now. She was blowing up like a soufflé. Perhaps they'd be able to get a doctor's certificate and claim the lost days on the insurance. It would take a week to get her back to work now. Reflectively he wiped a piece of loose tobacco from his lips. Holly! There was something wrong with that girl. It wasn't only that she was lazy. There was something else. Something missing. Perhaps her father had beaten whatever it is that makes people want to get on out of her. She'd been all right, in her way, at first. But the minute she'd made a few bob she got bored. He'd tried to get her to read, not to study, necessarily, but to try to improve herself just a little bit. But reading came slowly to her and she never showed much interest. She'd had even less education than he had and didn't regret her loss. 'The only thing I needed to learn was how to read the instructions on a Durex packet,' she had laughed. It was around that point that he had realized she had actually quite enjoyed being on the game. She liked putting out and she liked being paid for it. In a way that's what she was doing to the camera, putting out and being paid for it. Certainly that was how she saw sex, not romantically, like the silly bitches who wanted you to say you loved them, more like some kind of negotiation. What she liked about sex were the fringe benefits.

Getting up off the bench he wandered out of the shade of the Chateau Marmont gardens on to Sunset Boulevard. The thought of going back inside the bungalow to a pilled-out Holly and her ice-cream tubs was too depressing. It was a hot, hazy afternoon and the sun shone pink through a filter of fine smog. He liked the idea of Los Angeles more than Los Angeles itself. Being there made him feel small and grey-skinned. He wandered on westwards along the pale pavements, looking into the single-storey florists, funeral parlours, banks and restaurants. Catching sight of his reflection in an insurance broker's window he realized how out of place his black jeans and black shirt looked in the land of pastel. Then he wondered from which part of California Hudson had come.

Just past Tower Records he found a bar and wandered inside for a beer. The chill of the air-conditioning and the gloom disoriented him for a moment as he climbed on to a bar stool. Ordering a Coors from one of those twitchy, nervously smiling Los Angeles bar girls, he gazed around the place.

At first he thought he was the only customer, but then

a shadow moved in a booth at the back of the bar and he saw a young man sitting reading a paperback book. Quite deliberately the young man was looking at him, scrutinizing him. He turned his eyes back to the girl who was sliding the beer and the tab across on a cardboard mat. Obviously not having caught his English accent in the two words he had spoken, 'Coors, please', she had already decided he was a nobody and her smile had gone out. From the juke box came the muffled sound of Trini Lopez.

He sipped his beer and tried to imagine Hudson in a place like this. He knew Hudson had worked in bars as a student, even played in piano bars, but that must have been a different Hudson from the sophisticated chap he knew.

A movement in the mirror behind the bar caught his eye. The young man was now sitting more directly facing him in the booth. He was small, fair-haired and fringed, and quite muscular, with a good tan, and wearing blue jeans and one of those pale blue Western shirts with flaps and buttons on the two breast pockets. One button was undone and sticking out of the pocket was a pack of Winston cigarettes. The young man caught his eye, and he found himself holding the gaze for a moment, before turning back to his beer. He liked the idea of being watched.

He was out of cigarettes so slipping from his stool he crossed to the cigarette machine, and, finding his quarters, bought a packet of Winston. It was difficult to impossible to get Gauloises in California. Tearing off the top corner of the packet he put a cigarette to his lips, lit it, tucked the pack into his breast pocket, and carried on down the bar to the neon outline of a man in a large Mexican hat.

The toilet was bright, the strip lighting making his skin look blotched and ugly in the mirror above the basin as he washed his hands. He took his time, there was no hurry, his cigarette hanging from his lips, as he washed,

361

his eyes screwed up against the smoke. He began to dry his hands on the roller towel.

'Hi.' The young man from the bar was suddenly behind him. He did not do anything, did not move towards the stalls or the urinals, but simply stood looking at him, blocking the door, a half-smile on his face. Close up Gimmelmann could see that he was hardly more than a boy, with a small tattoo on the back of his left hand.

Suddenly Gimmelmann felt nervous. He did not answer. This guy was making a mistake, he told himself.

'Well . . . ?' The young man's expression seemed to expect something.

'Sorry, mate. You've got it wrong. A mistake,' Gimmelmann said at last, his voice catching in his throat.

The young man smiled. 'I don't think so,' he replied softly and a hand went out towards Gimmelmann's shoulder.

Gimmelmann reacted as though bitten. Snapping his cigarette from his lips his arm went up to ward off the overture.

The young man stopped, confused, and then with a smirk to himself turned back towards the door. 'Your mistake, I think,' he said, and with that went out of the bathroom.

When Gimmelmann emerged back into the bar the young man had left. By the cash register the bar girl sat oblivious to him reading a newspaper. He didn't finish his drink. He was ashamed to be in this place.

Leaving some change on the tab he hurried out of the gloom into the warm Los Angeles afternoon and turned back towards the Chateau Marmont and Holly.

He was, he realized, still shaking.

PART FIVE
February 1979

Chapter Thirty-Eight

(i)

The connection was poor and the line hummed. The voice of the telephonist was distant: 'Just putting you through.' In this time of sanctions there was little money available to improve telecommunications.

The photographer cupped his hands around the telephone to smother the extraneous sounds of the *Sunday Morning* office. He had been trying for some time to be connected with a Mr Ronald Harris, manager of Barclays Bank in Umtali. 'Hello, hello . . .' The line spat static.

'Yes . . . manager speaking. How can I help you? And can you speak up, please, you're very faint?'

The photographer raised his voice still higher. 'My name is Barnes, Mr Harris. As I explained to your assistant I want to enquire about an account for a friend of mine.'

He had already been through his request twice now, to ascertain that Michael Mavangwe had opened an account with the money and letter he had given him some months ago. Both times he had been told that it was not bank policy to give details of customer accounts and both times he had requested to speak to someone senior.

'In normal circumstances, Mr Barnes . . .' the jargon was repeated. 'But, as you say this was rather exceptional because of the . . . er, the age of the customer involved, and I can confirm that the boy did, according to our files, come to the bank some months ago with a letter of introduction and some currency, and was helped to open a deposit account with the bank acting as guardian, *vis-à-vis* the account.'

The photographer smiled. 'That's terrific. Thank you very much. Now, if it's OK with you, I'd like to make a further deposit on his behalf,' he shouted down the phone. 'Could you give me his deposit number, do you think?'

He could not hear it but he was certain this new request would have caused a sharp intake of breath at the Rhodesian end of the line.

'Well, I'm afraid that's going to be rather difficult, Mr Barnes . . .' Very carefully the manager explained that not only was that against banking regulations, it would also be contrary to the United Nations sanctions which forbade cheques to Rhodesia being honoured by British banks.

The photographer had anticipated this. Some Swiss banks were known to be regularly ignoring sanctions. He would, he explained, send the money through Switzerland. 'It's just that I know Michael doesn't have anybody looking out for him, and I'm sure that growing up an albino has to be some kind of handicap, so I thought another five hundred pounds might make things easier.'

'Well . . .' For just a moment the bank manager hesitated, then his agreement crackled down the wires. 'Well, yes, I think in this case that would be in order. Now let me see . . .' And very slowly he spelled out the boy's account number. 'I only hope he'll be grateful to you, Mr Barnes. He's a very lucky boy indeed. Five hundred pounds will be a considerable fortune to him.'

'Lucky is one thing he isn't, Mr Harris, but *I'm* very grateful to *you*.' Then explaining how he would be sending the draft with an accompanying letter of confirmation he put down the telephone. He smiled. That morning he had received a surprise five hundred pounds royalty cheque for the US syndication rights to his Mupangare pictures. He felt good. It was the first time in his life he had ever had five hundred pounds to spare and he was enjoying giving it away. Turning to a typewriter he began, slowly and two-fingered, to type his letter to Barclays Bank in Umtali.

Around him in the open-plan office the energy of *Sunday Morning* crackled. There was a rumour that Hudson had been seen in the building earlier that morning: the presence of Hudson always got everyone's adrenalin running.

During his nine months with the paper he had not got to know Hudson any better than at their first meeting. Hudson had always been friendly, and had helped him secure a good contract, but it was clear he felt awkward in the photographer's presence. It was as though an old wound had been reopened. He felt sorry for the man. Everything he had read or been told about Nicola Reynolds described a terrific girl whose life had been stolen. He felt sorry for Michael Mavangwe, too, a ten-year-old unwanted albino, who wanted to believe his father had not been a murderer. His mother had told him that and he had believed her. Michael Mavangwe. It had been suggested in the court reports that Marco de Sampaio had been attracted to Wildwood because of a friendship with a housegirl there called Fortunate Mavangwe. But Fortunate had made no appearance at the trial and the court had had no doubt about de Sampaio's guilt. He had hardly even put up a defence.

Since returning from Rhodesia the photographer had built a reputation for war coverage, being sent to photograph demonstrations against the Shah in Teheran, to Nicaragua, where he lived in the forest with the Sandinistas, and to Cambodia, as a guest of the Vietnamese Army; while with Penny Chilston, he had done stories in Northern Ireland, Brazil and West Germany. He had not been back to Rhodesia. As Richard had put it: 'We've had our slice of Rhodesia. Now go and do as well for us somewhere else in the world.'

And there had been much to photograph in this first year of *Sunday Morning*'s publication, a year made easier when the previous November *The Sunday Times*, under attack from the print unions for years, had closed down until agreement could be reached. Hudson had been lucky there. In the end he would have eleven months to establish *Sunday Morning* before *The Sunday Times* was back on the streets.

There was no luck involved in his take-over of Federated British, however. That was pure business guile. First the seduction and agreement to let *Sunday Morning* print on *Reporter* presses, and then, links having been forged, a grab for the whole organization. By June it had become his, with teams of shining new accountants and designers flooding into the old Federated British building within an hour of the papers being signed.

'Jeez, talk about the invasion of the body snatchers . . .' the photographer had exclaimed as he and Clover Merrifield had stood and watched the new regime of style and youth move in to replace the middle-aged and grey. Hudson moved so quickly. While others were talking he was buying, dismantling and rebuilding. Within weeks the *Reporter* had been replaced by a new tabloid daily newspaper, *Night And Day*. Peter Berridge was editor.

'They say his brief is to do whatever it takes to be successful,' Clover had said as she and a group of *Sunday Morning* journalists had examined their new sister newspaper.

The photographer had shaken his head at the infection of nipples, the prying, intrusive sex investigations, the yobbish soccer coverage. 'Just so long as they don't want to reprint any of my pictures . . .'

Hudson never made that mistake. The two newspapers were kept completely separate in the readers' minds. Richard Blake had apparently insisted upon that.

'Ah, that's better. About time you learned to do something useful.' Clover was swishing past him on her way out of the office. The photographer looked up from his typing. Her comment might have been read as office banter by anyone else, but he recognized the put-down. Her brisk pace gave no opportunity for response. He was being used, he knew, for companionship and for sex until something better happened along. He knew also that sometimes she was unfaithful to him as the whim of the moment took her. Everyone knew. It hurt but there was nothing he could do about it. He lived for her, wanting with every photograph to please her, to show her how fine a photographer he was. She dominated his thoughts. When they were together, when she was in a good mood, his life was exultant: when he was alone, wondering where she might be, with whom she might be sleeping, his days and nights were wrecked.

To hide from the misery of uncertainty he absorbed himself in his photographs. No one took better war pictures than Rob Barnes. No one got nearer to the action. No one took greater risks. She had, she said, been impressed by his work in Rhodesia: his pictures from Teheran, Nicaragua, Cambodia and Belfast surprised her, too. He began to live for danger, not because he enjoyed it, he was always frightened, but because it was his way of impressing Clover. 'If Clover could see me now,' he would think to himself, curled up in a ditch in South Armagh, a guest of the Provisional IRA as, masked, they mined a road, or knee-capped their former comrades. Before the year was out his cameras could smell their way to war, and the events of Mupangare had become just the first in a diary of death. He should have become hardened by the blood and tears and excrement of his profession. Perhaps he had. But, like a first love, the memory of Michael Mavangwe had traced his every step. 'Perhaps when the war is over I will buy a passport and come to England,' he would hear in his sleep. He prayed, he actually prayed, that God, if He existed, would keep a careful eye out for Michael's welfare. That was why he was sending the five hundred pounds: to give God a hand. He finished typing. He would not tell Clover about the money. He had not told her very much about Michael. She would not have understood.

He looked at the clock which hung on the wall

over the back bench. It was already after twelve. He would have to leave shortly if he were to be down in East Sussex in time for tea.

Clover Merrifield almost collided into Hudson on her way out of the office. He was distracted, discussing something as he climbed the stairs between Ben Tarlo and Peter Berridge, when, hurrying around the corner, late for an appointment at the House of Commons, she nearly flattened the three of them.

'Hey, wow, what is this . . . ? "Hackette mows down senior staff in management coup,"' Ben Tarlo joked, putting an arm out to stop her from falling.

'I'm sorry,' Clover said, steadying herself on the brass banister. She didn't like the way Peter Berridge was looking at her. She was certain he had a file on her somewhere, tucked away, ready to be produced should she ever leave Hudson Communications.

'No, *we're* sorry,' said Berridge, his skeleton's head bobbing from side to side like one of those toys which hung in the back windows of salesmen's cars.

Hudson said absolutely nothing. He rarely did. A couple of times she had attempted to be friendly with him as he put in an appearance at office functions, but the reserved politeness had never broken. Now he simply smiled at her, waited while his colleagues fussed, and then carried on up the stairs.

Rather more carefully Clover continued her descent. Hudson was a funny chap. She really didn't know what to make of him. Glorious to look at, he was aloof to her. A few months earlier she had been asked by *The New York Times Magazine* if she was interested in writing a short profile (under a pseudonym, if she wished) about Hudson, 'the American who was shaking up Fleet Street'. At first she had tried the open approach, calling Charlie Latymer and asking if it was possible to arrange an interview. But Latymer had been doubtful to the point of useless. Hudson never did personal interviews, he explained. 'If you're very lucky he might talk to you about his plans for the future of Hudson Communications, but absolutely nothing personal. Besides I can probably tell you everything you need to know.'

Of course he couldn't tell her anything she really wanted to know. Hudson's official biography, as issued by Latymer, was almost as spare as his six-line entry in *Who's Who*, which gave his place and date of birth simply as Los Angeles, California, 1939. No parents were mentioned and for education it simply listed Berkeley and Columbia, without dates. The cuttings files at *Sunday Morning*, and also at the *Daily Telegraph*, were hardly more use. There were snippets on the start of *Witness*, and then increasingly large pieces on its progress, rather more on the death of Nicola Reynolds (which she read with interest), and business reports on the move into mass-market magazine publishing: but there was nothing on Hudson's background. This was not particularly unusual among businessmen, especially those not born in Britain. Clover had then made a few tentative enquiries: Richard had been hardly more forthcoming, mentioning a town called El Fuerte and quite wealthy parents, now, he believed, both dead; Penny Chilston had been suspicious of her motives and Willie Simmonds had been sweet but unhelpful. 'To be ab..sol..utely honest, I think Hudson's one of th..ose people who was hatched fully gr..own. I mean even at the beg..inning he always seemed s..o much more gr..own up th..an the re..st of us, if you know what I mean. He kn..ows a lot of bl..ues songs, if th..at's any use.'

It hadn't been. For a group of journalists they all seemed very uninquisitive, until she thought about her own friends and realized she knew virtually nothing about half of them. Had it been important enough she could have called El Fuerte, Berkeley and Columbia, discovered dates, and perhaps eventually found old classmates, friends and relations. But it wasn't. In the end she had cried off, telling New York of the problems she was encountering, but by then they had lost interest in the story, anyway.

There were so many things more important to pursue. Hundreds of things. Like today, she thought as she waved down a taxi by a mountain of uncollected rubbish on Farringdon Road, and set off for her appointment with the Leader of the Opposition. Today should be a good one. 'Tell me, Mrs Thatcher,' she rehearsed in her mind as, sitting in the cab, she checked the batteries in her tape recorder, 'if Jesus Christ came back on earth and wanted to be a politician how could you possibly sell him the Conservative Party?' Something like that should get her going, all right.

(iii)

If he looked carefully Charlie Latymer could just about make out the reflection of his face in the polished surface of his desk. This was made possible because the desk was bare. The desk was bare because he had nothing to do. This puzzled him. He had the most highly paid job of his life, he had the status of sitting on the board of the newly named Hudson Communications, he had an expensive and attractive, if bored, secretary, a chauffeur-driven company car, a small but healthy shareholding in the company, large expenses, long lunches, long holidays, short hours and a more than generous pension plan. But for most of the week he would sit twiddling his thumbs wondering just what Hudson had intended when he had rescued him. Or, to be more precise, why Hudson had rescued him. Admittedly, occasionally he would be wheeled out to address a second-rate news conference, to appear on television, when no one was watching, and put Hudson's point of view. He was sure he did it very well. He was good at being his master's voice. But there were lots of chaps in the organization who could do that, perhaps not quite so professionally, but efficiently enough. So what was Hudson playing at?

Dominique had arrived home at two o'clock the previous night. He had been still awake, sitting up in bed attempting to read a novel, trying to pretend he didn't know where she had been. She had lied, of course, and had told him that she had gone back to her producer's flat for some pasta after a late filming session. She hadn't known that her producer had telephoned just before eleven with some trivial message. He hadn't told her. He didn't much go for confrontation. Instead he had watched her as she undressed, first the earrings, then the bracelets, then the necklace, then the little combs from her hair, everything measured, every movement graceful. He had noticed that her hair had been slightly wet around her shoulders, though it had been a fine evening, and that her lipstick had been recently re-applied. She was very tired, she had said, as she had climbed into bed and, switching off her bedside light, had immediately turned away from him and closed her eyes. Had she had a nice evening? he had asked. 'Yes, not bad, darling. Good night,' she had murmured into her pillow.

Turning away from his reflection he played with a model Bugatti he had on his desk, running it from one end to the other. Hudson had given it to him. When it ran off the side of the desk into the waste-paper bin he let it lie there.

If the only thing Hudson had wanted had been a quick affair with Dominique why had he gone to so much effort and expense. She was hardly difficult, Latymer had known that when he married her, and she'd made her infatuation with Hudson so obvious it would almost have been difficult for him not to have taken her to bed.

So why had he given him the job, the status, the chauffeur, the shares, the salary – all to do virtually nothing? And why did he carry on in public with her so blatantly? Wives often had affairs, and why not?

Let's face it, he'd even had the occasional wife himself, the discreet well-heeled tumble in the afternoons in a pleasingly appointed *pied-à-terre* wasn't altogether disagreeable. And for a famous television face like himself sometimes it was easier to dally than desist. Where was the harm in that? Dominique had never known, nor, so far as he was aware, had the husbands. That Dominique should occasionally do something similar wasn't totally unexpected, nor actually even that upsetting. What was disturbing was that Hudson was making very sure that everyone knew. Hudson, who had always been so discreet. It didn't make any kind of sense.

He considered his options. He could confront Dominique. Lay the law down. Tell her this behaviour had to stop. Or he could have it out with Hudson, resign and tell him where to stuff his money. He liked the idea of that. Decisiveness. Let him know it didn't matter how rich and powerful he was he couldn't screw Charlie Latymer's wife and get away with it. He smiled to himself. It would give Dominique a shock, too.

There was a tap on the office door. Pulling a sheaf of papers in front of him he glanced busily up just as Samantha, his secretary, looked in. 'Just to say that your car's waiting and I'll go to lunch now if that's all right, Mr Latymer.'

He looked at his watch. 'Goodness, how time flies,' he said crisply. 'Yes. Very good.' He tried a businesslike smile.

The girl closed the door behind her. He relaxed again. He was having lunch at the Garrick Club with Harry Chatterton, an old friend from Cambridge who had gone into publishing and become very poor.

At least he wasn't poor: and the Garrick was the best place in London to be seen.

Getting up he went into his private bathroom which ran off his office and began to wash his hands.

In the mirror his reflection studied him. Perhaps it would be better to sleep on things: see how it all worked out. Infatuations rarely lasted. What if a few silly tongues did wag? He had a broad back. It would be a pity to give up so much in a fit of pique.

Carefully he dried his hands. They were well manicured. He would give it time, and then when it all cooled down, as it inevitably must, he would take Dominique away. New York perhaps. She liked New York. They would do well together there on the circuit. They made such a handsome couple. She was such an asset.

Once more he checked his look in the mirror. He liked what he saw. Old Harry Chatterton would be sick with envy if he discovered he had his own driver. His reflection was smiling at him now. He'd make sure Harry knew by offering him a lift back to his appalling publisher's office after lunch. 'Yes, Harry,' he would say, 'it certainly beats bicycle clips . . .'

Then chuckling to himself he went off to find his driver and car for the short drive to the Garrick Club.

(iv)

'If they want to dry me out they should peg me out on a washing-line and leave me blowing in the wind like a pair of old lady's knickers,' Penny Chilston said bleakly. 'Whatever they did couldn't be worse than being stuck in here with all these boring old drunks.'

The photographer grinned as they strolled on across the field.

'I mean, for God's sake, one drunk is a bore, twenty is on the scale of a natural disaster. You should hear them, getting up there every night whining on. No, not *whining* on, not unless it's a non-alcoholic wine anyway, *whingeing* on about their "problem". Jesus, it isn't the drink that's the problem. They're the bloody problem, being so bloody boring. I promise you, Rob, you spend two nights in this place and you'd kill for a drink.'

'So you're enjoying it here, are you then?'

Penny laughed. 'I am now that you've come. I bet

they're all at their windows watching us, wondering where I found you. Drunks do a lot of wondering, you know . . . usually wondering who they are, where they are, what time the pubs open and how the hell they're going to get home. Thanks for the card, by the way. I put it on the sideboard in my cell next to . . .' She stopped, unsure of herself.

He looked at her.

She shrugged, great heavy shoulders. Why shouldn't she say it? 'All right, next to the flowers Hudson sent.'

'Hudson sent you flowers? That was thoughtful of him.'

'He's a very thoughtful man. I suppose Richard must have told him I was coming in here. Pity, really. He didn't need to know. Ah, what the hell!'

They walked on in silence. She was trying not to show it, coming on the bluff and the tough, but the arrival of Rob Barnes was more than a treat. He was so fresh-faced and eager, terrifying to be with on a story if you valued your survival, but a complete softy when the all-clear had sounded. Amazingly for a war photographer he hardly drank: even more amazingly he put up with her, and took care of her, when she did.

It was the drink that had finally brought her to this place. She had gone on a bender two weeks earlier, one of those disgusting marathons which had begun one lunchtime and continued for two days until her body had been so dehydrated she felt as though she were being consumed by some internal fire. She didn't really know what had started her, or what had made her carry on. That was just the way it happened sometimes when the chemicals took over. Drinking into oblivion. At first it was grand, everything seemed so much sharper, simpler, rosier. And then not so sharp, until in the end it didn't matter, anyway.

It had been Rob who had come looking for her when she hadn't answered her telephone. 'I know you're in there, Penny Chilston, so open the bloody door,' he

376

had called through the letter-box when, trembling with fear and nausea, she had ignored the ringing of her front doorbell. She'd eventually let him in, ashamed that he should see her in this state. He'd stayed that day and that night, sleeping in the room Vasco used to have, while she had sweated and shivered herself sober.

The following day he'd put it to her quite simply. He was brutal and he was kind. 'It seems to me you've got two choices, Penny. Either you can carry on drinking and delude yourself, like all the other drunks in the world, that you're as good an operator drunk as you are sober. And now and again you will be, but less and less until you're an embarrassment to everyone who knows you and they only keep you on at *Sunday Morning* because Richard and Hudson haven't the heart to fire you. Or you can accept what everybody else knows but won't tell you, that when you're drinking you're about one-third as effective and that, in effect, the paper carries you. And, if you can accept that, the next thing is for us to do something about it.'

If she hadn't felt so wretched she might just have clouted him for his impudence. What did he know? He was so young. But she had just sat there taking the pummelling. Later she would be moved by his blunt honesty. This daredevil Australian boy, who took his life in his hands every time he went out on a job, really cared. It was because of him she had committed herself to this rhododendron, croquet and lemon tea concentration camp hidden so deep in the middle of the East Sussex countryside it would take a compass and a degree in orienteering to find anything remotely resembling a pub.

Two weeks, they'd said, was the minimum stay, and halfway through her second week she was enduring, though with some difficulty. Part of the time her body screamed for a drink. But most of it was passed with her head inside a book, or out, as she was now, walking the grounds, avoiding the company of the other inmates.

'What about the gossip?' she asked as they opened a gate and began to wander through a copse of young oaks. 'What's going on in the office that I'm missing in this green and smiling backside of hell?'

'Gossip . . . well, I dunno, really. The purge on expenses didn't last long, thank God, Andrew Northey's setting up a full-time office in Washington, Henry Walker's in Teheran covering the return of the Ayatollah, the editor's been getting very stroppy about the recycling of PR handouts . . .'

Penny held up her hand. 'Please, spare me. I said *gossip*. Gossip. Like, who's having who. That's gossip, dear boy.'

The photographer went quiet.

Was there a slight blush? Penny wondered. She'd hardly been tactful. Everyone in the office knew about Clover Merrifield's lapses. Men always talked.

'Well, there's Hudson and Dominique Fayence,' he replied at last, carefully.

'Yes?'

'People say he's in love with her.'

Penny snorted. 'Fiddlesticks.'

'They're making it very public. He obviously doesn't care what people think. Doesn't give a bugger how Charlie Latymer feels.'

'I wouldn't be too sure about that, if I were you.'

'I don't understand.'

'Well, no, you wouldn't. But you don't know Hudson like I do.'

'Does anyone know Hudson?'

'What?' The boy was now beginning to irritate her. She knew exactly what the Dominique Fayence affair was about, and it was certainly not about love.

They had now come to the end of the woods and were looking out over the sharp side of an escarpment. It was nearly five and the February light was fading, forming mist patches below them on the downs.

The photographer pushed his hands into his coat

pocket to keep warm. 'Well,' he said, 'he is a bit of a mystery, isn't he?'

Penny shook her head. 'Mystery? Not to me, he isn't,' she lied. 'But now, if you've seen enough perhaps you'll escort your great aunt back to the asylum where, if you're very lucky, she will reward you with a large slice of fruit cake and a refreshing pot of tea.'

Slowly they began to retrace their steps.

He was right. Hudson had always been a mystery, the solitary man, untied to anyone or anything other than his friends, the shy dictator who revealed so little about himself and his feelings, and who never felt it necessary to explain.

Chapter Thirty-Nine

(i)

News of the death of Alec Reynolds at a hospital in Johannesburg came just before Easter. Barney, the chief sub-editor, had spotted it in an item of copy from *Reuters* and, marking it 'Editor to see', had sent it across to Richard's office. Richard immediately telephoned Hudson. He had already heard.

'I had a call from the hospital this morning. It's very sad,' he said. 'He was a very lonely old man.'

'And he never went back to Wildwood?'

'No. I spoke to him a couple of times recently but he was really too frail to travel. I'll be going out there for the funeral, of course. I imagine it will be in Salisbury. His office is looking after everything.' There was a moment as they both remembered the old man. Richard had only met him once and disliked him intensely, but Emily had urged him to be more understanding.

'And what about Wildwood, what will happen to Wildwood now?' he asked after a moment.

'Wildwood . . .' Hudson's voice trailed away. 'I don't know, Richard. I've always put off, you know, going back there. I was never sure he would have wanted it. Now I'll have to sort things out . . . decide what to do . . .'

Suddenly Richard realized. 'Of course. It's your house now.' Wildwood had been in Nicola's name, but for the use of her uncle during his lifetime.

Hudson's reply sounded distant, as though only now was he, too, realizing what had happened. 'Well yes, that's right, I own Wildwood now.'

After he had put the telephone down Richard considered calling Emily, but decided against it. She would probably be still at school. Wildwood. It had seemed such a magical, exotic place to him. He stood up and, going to the window, let in some fresh air. Looking down on the street below he could see the distribution vans lining up outside the circulation bay, already repainted with the new Hudson Communications logo. 'Communications' was becoming the buzz word of the age, 'communications' and 'media', and Hudson's communications network never stopped spreading; not just in Britain, where one by one he was taking over local giveaway papers and printers and buying into radio and television consortia, but in Europe where there were French, German, Spanish and Italian versions of the most successful *Fun and Profit* magazines, and in the US where he had recently bought a large printing works in Michigan.

Lying discarded on the window-sill was a copy of that morning's *Night And Day*, delivered by order of the chairman to all executives, but rarely read by this one. Picking it up Richard glanced at the front page. The lead was another non-story about a Cabinet minister caught in adultery. At any given time it was generally reckoned that 30 per cent of the Cabinet were adulterous, a peccadillo generally overlooked unless the girl was a talkative tart, a spy, the wife of a Cabinet colleague or all three. That Hudson should allow Berridge and his *Night And Day* morality stormtroopers to pillory an otherwise perfectly harmless member of the Cabinet while he was blithely sleeping with the wife of one of his senior employees was more than puzzling. He dropped the newspaper into his waste-bin.

It was the speed of Hudson's expansion which most astonished him. The newest newspaper proprietor in Britain, and arriving at a time when the old regime were looking around to give up and get out, it was as though Hudson was involved in a race to develop his plot before others noticed the potential. 'We have to build now . . .' he would say, a talking clock of opportunism, '. . . stake our claim to the orchard. If we wait five years the other guys will have got there first and stripped it bare.' No matter how much advice to stay out, he had no doubt that he could make it work. To Hudson everything remained possible: any problem could be solved if approached from the right angle. Hudson Magazines was providing a hugely profitable basis, and now fast, cheap, new print technology was coming to newspapers no matter how the unions tried to prevent it.

The emergence of *Night And Day* had been sudden and astonishing. It was, in its way, brilliant, a neat, cheeky, daily package of sex, innuendo, witty headlines, smear, sneer, astonishing photographs, crudely funny cartoons and total amorality. Social historians would one day peer in vain for Hudson's political or .philosophical slant as perceived through *Night And Day*. There wasn't one. It existed solely to make money, even if that meant taking exactly opposing lines on an issue two days in a row. This was one publication of which Richard was definitely not editor in chief.

'What do you think, fella?' Hudson had asked him one night after three months of publication. 'Come on, give it to me with both barrels. Tell me the truth. I can take it.'

'I think it's appalling.'

Hudson had guffawed at that. He had been sitting in his Knightsbridge office, his legs stretched across his desk, his shirt sleeves rolled up to his elbows, outrageous advertising campaign mock-ups littering the carpet. 'You're damn right it is. And it's perfect, too. The perfect throwaway product. Right? Remember? The transport café in Kilburn High Street all those years ago?'

'It's actually worse than I expected. I didn't think even Berridge could crawl so low.'

'Berridge will go as low as it takes and lower. That's what I like about him. And the lower he goes the more he makes possible for everybody else in the organization. I promise you, Richard, *Sunday Morning* will never have to struggle the way *Witness* did. *Night And Day* will make it possible for you to have everything you want, make it possible to turn *Sunday Morning* into the best newspaper in the world. Isn't it worth bending the rules a little bit to achieve that?'

Richard closed the window and went out on to the main editorial floor. At her desk Clover Merrifield sat rigidly erect, speaking on the telephone. She had such good posture, he noted, not for the first time. She had once told him that as a child she had hoped to become a dancer. As he passed she saw him looking and caught his eye. Always the eager smile. They had had lunch or drinks together several times during this first year of *Sunday Morning*. Though busy to the point of distraction he had always had time for Clover. On a couple of occasions, when driving himself, he had given her a lift to her home in Chelsea. But, though she had invited him, he had never gone inside. The moment had never been right.

Thoughtfully he walked to the back bench and sat down. His presence there would inevitably start the conveyor belt again, the endless loop of choices to be balanced and decisions to be made. He looked again at Clover. She had begun to type, leaning into her typewriter, peering at the words as they fell on to the paper.

'I was right in assuming that Alec Reynolds was Nicola's uncle, wasn't I?' the chief sub-editor asked, breaking into Richard's day-dreams.

'Oh, yes . . . yes, thank you, Barney. He was an old man. I think it was expected. I'll get features to arrange a short obit.'

The chief sub nodded and went back to his work.

Alec Reynolds: 'wiser than God and twice as old . . . just a cantankerous old Nazi'.

'You don't like him?' he had asked as they had sat in the Greek restaurant off Queensway.

'Oh yes. I love him,' Nicola had said, wincing at the Retsina. 'He's sweet. But I can imagine he takes some getting used to . . .'

(ii)

Willie Simmonds was the only one to miss her, at least the only one to mention it. 'Wh..at, no pictures of Holly C..arter, Tim . . . ?' he said, as he gazed around the reception area.

Gimmelmann did not answer. He winced and drew on his Gauloise. Willie was right, there was no Holly Carter, no space for her on the sparkling, white, thirty-foot walls where two levels of the old carpet wholesalers had been knocked into one. Her presence, her image, would have been a stain on his achievement. He didn't want to hear her name

The opening of Hudson-Gimmelmann, the six-storey headquarters of the film facilities house in Great Marlborough Street, hadn't been planned as a large reception, just a few selected friends and some good champagne. Hudson-Gimmelmann wasn't for everybody, it was to be at the select end of the market, offering the best-equipped studios and cutting-rooms for quality TV commercials makers. Hudson-Gimmelmann was class. Gimmelmann liked that. There were other film and television facilities houses which Hudson owned and in which Gimmelmann had a small share and advisory capacity, factory-run places for everyday work, but this was the jewel in the collection, slap in the middle of the West End, a stone's throw from most of the biggest advertising agencies.

He had designed it himself, from the yucca tree growing out of the marble-chipped patio in the lobby, to the computer-lit studios, the changing rooms, each complete with silver-framed examples of Gimmelmann's photographs, and on to the deluxe, twenty-seat viewing theatre, a temple to the wealth to be generated from commercials. It hadn't come cheaply, in fact his original plan

384

for a personal holding of 20 per cent had been halved by the time the building was complete. But other than lining up the banks and helping out with the investment Hudson had not interfered. Now Hudson was striding around, Dominique Fayence, svelte and intelligent, at his side, her lobes, wrists and neck murmuring discreetly of gold on expensive perfume.

Apart from Willie Simmonds, Gimmelmann had not invited any of the old *Witness* crowd. They would probably have stuck up their noses and been quietly scornful. Journalists and advertising people never mixed well, the journalists pretending that the advertisers were thick and greedy, the advertisers knowing that the journalists were drunk and poor. Willie was his one exception. Though he was often drunk, he had not been poor for a long time. And he was famous. Earlier in the evening Willie had been complaining of writer's block, which Gimmelmann rather equated with some malfunction of the shutter on a camera. But now Holly Carter was on Willie's mind.

'What happ..ened to her any..way?' Willie stammered amiably. 'She was won..der..ful at seventeen.'

Gimmelmann tried a shrug. 'Same old story. Went off, didn't she? Haven't seen her for years.' He looked around for some distraction. Two of the prettiest models of the moment were sitting together at the foot of the wide spiral staircase which led from the lobby up to the main studios. 'Have you met Trish and Eva? They were telling me they're having a girls' night out tonight because their boy-friends are both abroad.'

Willie followed Gimmelmann's eyeline. 'Really. G..inny's away, too,' he smiled. 'Now there's a co..incidence.'

'And Jenny had to go to the school for some parent-teachers meeting,' Gimmelmann smiled. 'Tell you what, why don't I see if they're free for dinner later on. The four of us, what do you say? It might be a giggle.'

'You know I'm a happ..ily married man ag..ain, don't you, Tim?' Willie smiled.

'Me, too, but our wives aren't here, are they? So
. . . all right?'

Willie looked at the girls and sighed. 'You know, I
sw..ear to G..od that if ev..er I come back on earth again
it will be in the f..orm of a fash..ion phot..ographer or a
comm..ercials direc..tor.'

Gimmelmann grinned: 'Well, let's not count our chickens too soon, all right?'

At two o'clock in the morning Gimmelmann climbed
from between tangled sheets in the bamboo and silk
bedroom of a Fulham cul-de-sac. A languidly beautiful
girl lay in the darkness watching him. She was, she said,
sorry that he had to go so soon. 'Perhaps there could be
another time . . .'

He nodded. He hoped so, he said.

He didn't understand it. When he could so easily have
women like this, beautiful, eager, fresh young girls, why,
just a few days ago, had Holly been able to drag him
back? He felt dirty at the memory. Five hundred pounds
left on a Formica fold-down table-top in a filthy caravan
next to an empty milk bottle which had not been rinsed:
the price of an hour's degradation.

The girl in the bed wanted to talk, to make a plan.
Her boy-friend was away for another two weeks, she said.
Gimmelmann did not answer. In his mind he saw Hudson
strolling around the studio, so pleased with everything
he saw, and slightly amused by something Dominique
Fayence had said. He liked it when Hudson smiled. He
had such a terrific smile.

Chapter Forty

All birthdays were special but an eleventh birthday was particularly important: ten had come and gone with no change in the pattern, but eleven meant being almost an adult. That was certainly how Catherine Blake viewed it.

Emily had expected she would ask for a party, possibly even a visit to the cinema for half her class. But when one Sunday morning that was suggested Catherine was almost disdainful.

'I'd like,' she said, drawing herself up in a way which suggested she had given the matter considerable thought, 'a dinner party.'

'Dear God,' Richard gulped from behind his *Observer*.

The boys giggled and imitated her. '"I'd like . . .",' Benedict mocked, '". . . a dinner party",' Tom finished.

Emily kept a straight face. 'That's a . . . good idea. Who are you going to invite?'

'Hudson,' came the reply.

'Hudson?'

'I think he's very nice . . .'

'A bit old for you, isn't he?' Richard said, putting his newspaper down.

'. . . and he plays the piano very well.'

'That's true,' Emily agreed. 'But you know he's terribly busy. Flying off to America and Paris and all over the place all the time.'

'I'll send him an invitation.'

The boys giggled again. '"I'll send him an invitation",' Benedict chimed as Tom choked on his Shreddies.

Over the top of his newspaper Richard smiled. 'It still works, you see,' he said quietly to Emily. 'He still knows how to charm them.' Then very softly: 'And this one isn't married.'

Emily pretended to frown. Details of Hudson's women were not for the children's ears. 'Right then,' she said, 'that's Hudson invited, who else?'

Catherine shook her head. 'No one. Just you and Daddy and us and Hudson.'

'But supposing Hudson can't come, it won't be much of a birthday party, will it? Hadn't you better ask some other people?'

'He'll come,' Catherine said. 'He loves coming here. Anyone can see that.'

Of course, Hudson did come to the dinner party. Catherine wrote the invitation herself on an embossed white card, and Hudson had his secretary telephone to say that he would be delighted to accept. Emily watched her daughter take the call in the kitchen, standing on the stripped pine settle, repeating the time and place. 'And thank you very much for telephoning,' she finished, very seriously, as Emily bit her lip trying not to laugh.

The birthday fell on the last day of the Easter holidays, when Catherine dragooned her brothers into preparing menus, English on one side, a sort of French on the other. Tom had suggested they have fish fingers (*doigts de poisson* according to their French, Emily presumed), but Catherine had become very high-handed. 'You can't have fish fingers at a dinner party,' she bullied. 'Fish fingers aren't sophisticated.' Instead she instructed her mother to cook chicken with pineapple slices, which she had had once on a memorable occasion at a Berni Inn.

Hudson arrived right on seven, Josh, his driver, dropping him off. He had flown back from New York overnight, and spent a day in the Knightsbridge office before coming to the party. Although she had had a day to prepare Catherine was not ready when her guest arrived, so Richard took Hudson downstairs to the kitchen to talk to Emily, pouring them glasses of wine each as the boys ran riot around the house in self-induced over-excitement.

Hudson looked tired, thought Emily, but excited about something: almost before he had finished kissing and greeting her he was telling her about it.

'Actually, I'm glad we have a couple of minutes,' he said, 'because I was wanting to ask you both a kind of favour . . . particularly you, Emily.'

Lifting a hot plate with the hem of her pinafore Emily moved the chicken from the grill to the oven. 'Granted,' she said.

Hudson was almost bashful. 'Well, I hope so. It's about the Foundation . . . the er, the Hudson Foundation . . .' He took a glass of wine from Richard before he continued. 'The idea is that we set up a charitable trust so that we can spread around to others what I probably have too much of these days, and I wanted to ask you both if you'd mind serving as trustees. Actually, Emily, I wanted to ask you if you'd like to be the chairman or chairperson, sort of thing.' Suddenly he fixed her with such a smile, a smile she hadn't seen in years.

'The Hudson Foundation . . . ?' Richard was surprised.

'Yes, well, it's been in the back of my mind for quite a while. I mean, I like creating things, building up businesses, expanding, buying new ones, getting rich, if you like. I've had ten fantastic years when, in a business sense, it's all gone right for me. And the next years will be even better, maybe ten times better. So I'm not going to stop. I'm going to build and build, and we're going to make Hudson Communications into one of the great media empires.'

Richard began to smile at Hudson's certainty.

'The thing is I already have everything in life, every-thing material, that I'm ever going to want for myself. When we were starting out all we wanted was enough money to pay the printer's bills and put some gas in the van, but we did it because it was fun. And it's still fun. But I don't want to buy castles or have great art collec-tions or any of that stuff. Think how much more fun it would be if we were divvying the profits around a little bit.'

'Divvying it around to whom?' asked Emily.

'I don't know. Some kind of educational programmes, I thought. That's what I'd like to sit down and talk with you both about. Maybe when the children have gone to bed we can work something out.'

Richard was ever-cautious. 'You're expanding like mad at the moment. Shouldn't you wait a couple of years and see how it turns out?'

'I don't think so. We can start now, maybe in quite a modest way and then build as we go. What do you say, Emily? Will you help me? Will you, please?'

Emily felt herself blushing with pleasure. Hudson was such a rogue. Who could say 'no' to him? 'Well, I don't know if I'll be any good at it, but I'd love to help,' she said. 'Whatever it is . . .'

Once more Hudson smiled, and putting his hands to her waist was kissing her again when Catherine made her entrance, followed by her two brothers. 'Oh wow, you look just terrific . . . happy birthday,' Hudson said and lifted her up in his arms to kiss her.

She did look pretty, thought Emily, in her new, navy-blue velvet dress trimmed at the hem and neck with lace, and bought especially for this day: so proud of herself and so grown up. And, unless Emily was imagining things, wasn't that just the slightest trace of lipstick?

Together the family moved into the dining room. Under Richard's supervision the children had set the table, each place with a named menu, so that Catherine could be sure that Hudson sat next to her.

'*Soupe de tomate, poulet et ananas, et glace vanille,*' read Benedict carefully, then looking considerately at Hudson he said, 'That's tomato soup, chicken with pineapple and vanilla ice-cream, in case you can't read French.'

'Oh, thank you,' said Hudson.

Catherine's face was a picture of mortification. She

looked at Emily in despair. How could her brother embarrass her so much? Of course Hudson could read French. Hudson could do anything.

The boys went to bed at ten o'clock, Tom worrying that he wouldn't be able to wake up for the first day back at school, and Catherine at ten-thirty, carrying her presents (Hudson had brought her an address book from New York with his name and personal numbers already written in), thanking and kissing everyone good night, especially Hudson.

'Little flirt!' Richard pretended to grumble jealously, and then cuddled her himself.

It had been such a pleasant evening, and had ended up with the children sitting around Hudson as he played the piano and they sang songs.

Emily had expected that when the children finally went to bed Hudson would stop playing and join Richard and herself to finish off the wine and discuss his plans for the Hudson Foundation. But he didn't. He carried right on, playing and singing to himself, all his old favourites, his blues songs and his barrelhouse, sitting alone at the piano at the far, narrow end of their large L-shaped sitting room, lost in his own lonely world.

PART SIX
1967

PART SIX

Chapter Forty-One

(i)

'I was thinking of asking him to marry me, if that's all right with you. Is that enough milk?'

For just a moment Emily couldn't answer.

'Well? Is it?'

'The marriage or the milk? Yes. Of course. Both, I mean.'

'That's good. You should have it black, Emmy, it's far more invigorating. Do you think he'll have me?'

'He's obsessed with you.'

'As a girl-friend, a lover, a bit of fluff on his arm, an accessory for the Alvis, yes. But what about as a wife?'

'You mean it, don't you? You really are going to ask him.'

'It's called proposing.'

'Yes. Why?'

'Why? Well, a girl isn't getting any younger.' Nicola pulled a comical face.

'Do you love him?'

'Oh, Emmy, of course I love him. Second best in the entire world, but you're disqualified.'

'And . . . ?'

'Well, I suppose I think . . . and this might sound terribly conceited, though it isn't meant that way, I think I'd be good for him. I mean, I think a wife would be good for him. Perhaps any wife almost. He's such a lonely person. He tries to hide it all the time, but I've never met anyone so alone. Sometimes I look at him when he doesn't know I'm looking and his face is completely . . . well, it's more than empty, it's as though it has been washed of any emotion. Then he sees me watching and smiles that smile and the world melts. You know what I mean, don't you?'

Emily knew.

'You don't think I'm completely mad then?'

Emily shook her head. They were sitting in Nicola's tiny conservatory, the french windows of which were open on to the small, square, whitewash-walled garden. It was a sunny Sunday morning in April and the piccolo trumpet of *Penny Lane* could be heard from an open window somewhere nearby. 'Has he ever mentioned marriage?'

Nicola frowned. 'You don't think the blackguard will turn me down, do you?'

'No chance.'

'Good, because there are two conditions attached to this wedding. One is that I keep my maiden name. I like being Nicola Reynolds. So that won't change.'

'And?'

'You agree to be bridesmaid. And don't say no, because I'm not listening. So that's decided. Good.'

'So all you have to do now is pop the question.'

'I'll get him drunk. You know he can't take drink. I'll make an honest man of him before he knows what's hit him.' She laughed, and then began to sing quietly along with the music coming across the gardens, a famous flip-side now. 'That's how it'll be, Emmy, *Nothing to get drunk about, strawberries and cream, for ever*,' and stretching her legs, she put her feet up on the wicker sofa, tucking them under her bottom. She was wearing a tiny fragment of a Paisley cotton dress, so short that modesty was marginal to impossible. For three years hemlines had been going up: now there was nowhere left to go. 'If Alice and Joseph could see you now,' said Emily.

Nicola frowned slightly. 'Oh don't. I feel so guilty about them. I got a letter from Alice last week advising me not to go out without my cardigan because she had heard on the wireless that it was very cold in England over Easter. Can you believe it?'

'She'll be upset if you get married without her blessing.'

'Yes, but she'd be a lot more upset having to leave Wildwood to come here and give Hudson the once-over. I'm sure she'll love him. Can you imagine how he'd charm her. She'd be jogging around him like a seventeen year old. Perhaps we could go home for our honeymoon.' She smiled. 'Now there's a thought. First we'll go to Wildwood and then on to California.'

'Doesn't Hudson have any say?'

'Emmy, he has all the say. I'll do whatever he wants. But it never hurts to have a plan, does it?' She looked mischievous. 'Like you, for instance.'

Emily shook her head.

'It would be perfect, you know. The four of us again. They were the best times.'

Emily did not reply.

(*ii*)

Hudson told Richard the next morning when he arrived at the office. He even had a date: Thursday 1 June. All he needed was a best man.

Without hesitation Richard accepted. 'Congratulations. I'm very pleased for you both. I mean that,' he said.

Hudson grinned. 'I know you do. Seems like I owe you another one now.'

'And does this mean that we finally get to meet the Hudson seniors?'

Hudson laughed. 'That's exactly what Nicola wanted to know. I don't know. It's a long way from California. I'll call them tonight, and see how they feel about coming over. They'll probably be all crabby and cross because I never write or anything, but I guess it's a family failing.'

'Perhaps you should go and see them sometime.'

'Yeah, maybe I should. They're both over eighty now. Quite an age.'

'All the more reason . . .'

Hudson cut him off. 'You're absolutely right.'

'Hudson, can I have a word?' Adam Smith was walking across the editorial floor towards them, a sheaf of invoices in his hand.

'Oh no, here comes trouble,' Hudson laughed, and getting up put an arm around the financial director's shoulders. 'How are you today, Adam? Still worrying? Didn't I tell you to leave the worrying to me?' And with a 'see you later' thrown in Richard's direction he led Adam out of the office.

Richard returned to his work, careful editing of an article about LSD. 1967 looked like being a very druggy year. He thought about Hudson marrying Nicola and for the first time in months he felt empty inside.

(iii)

The *Evening Standard* carried the news first as a diary item, picked up the next day by the *Daily Express* William Hickey column. *Rhodesian heiress to marry*, ran the modest-sized headline with a copy of Gimmelmann's portrait of Nicola. It was the photograph which drew Gimmelmann's attention.

'What is it?' Holly was sitting on a stool in the Primrose Hill studio, her hair in curlers. A make-up artist in granny glasses was waiting to begin work on her. There was a lot to do. Another model, Jenny Quinn, fair, with even, doll-like features, was watching nervously. Holly was the star, Jenny the debutante.

Gimmelmann handed Holly the newspaper.

She read slowly to herself, then began to laugh quietly.

'Hudson getting married,' she said. 'What about that then? What about that then, Timmy?'

Gimmelmann turned to the other girl. 'Sorry about the delay,' he said. 'We shouldn't be very long.'

Behind him he could hear Holly continuing to laugh. That was when he probably hated her most of all.

(iv)

Penny Chilston couldn't quite remember why she had decided to get drunk. Something she didn't want to think about kept hovering about at the back of her mind, waiting its moment, preparing to swoop and torment her if ever she became sober enough to let it. She refilled her glass.

She was alone in her flat and two-thirds of the way through a new bottle of gin. Her mother had always drunk gin when she had entertained her friends. Gin and orange, gin and tonic, gin and It. Penny had known then that It was short for Italian Vermouth, but her mother had managed to endow it with some quite different interpretation. 'What'll it be, darling, gin and It?' Then the silly, flirty giggle.

She wondered how Vasco was getting along. He had never written. She hadn't expected him to. He had probably shacked up with some dolly girl on the ship going home.

She wasn't enjoying the taste of gin any more. This drinking couldn't go on.

Hudson and Nicola strolled languidly across her mind, hand in hand. She raised her glass in celebration, but as she put it to her lips a salty tear ran down her nose and rolled into the gin.

Hudson. She imagined she heard him singing an old blues song.

'You have a lovely voice, you know.' A Friday night and they had been the last two to leave the office, Hudson going around tidying up, emptying overflowing bins into a plastic bag, publisher turned janitor, singing to himself all the time.

399

'Oh, thank you, Penny . . . that's really nice. I think most people wish I would just shut up most of the time.'

'I don't think so, and you know an awful lot of songs.'

'Yes, well, quite a few. I like songs. I've worked in a lot of bars, you know, and you get to hear the same songs every night.'

'Bars in California?'

'Oh, all over. New York, Los Angeles, Chicago. That was where I learned the blues, Chicago.' He moved on and began to sing again.

They had gone for a drink together after that. He was so warm and encouraging, so easy to get along with that she had forgotten that men were not supposed to fancy her. She had wanted to make a pass at him, just to see what would happen. But, of course, she hadn't.

She finished the bottle.

Chapter Forty-Two

Latymer's audition had gone perfectly. He was tanned from a few days in Perpignan, so the sunny smile which had greeted him in the make-up room mirror had been wonderful encouragement, and his mind was sparklingly clear. He had learned from previous failures and now he spoke more slowly and more intimately into the camera. Even his little jokes had come off. He had planned them carefully and rehearsed them so that they fell out as casually as off-the-cuff asides.

It had been the third and final audition, the one where he had had to host a political forum, with four Members of Parliament as participants. If he had been allowed to choose the MPs himself he could hardly have found more suitable subjects. They had been as predictable as the seasons. The money invested buying drinks for the researchers had been well spent.

The summons to Harvey's office sealed it. Harvey, with his horn-rimmed glasses and blue and white striped shirts, was the executive producer and it was his job to find an anchor man for the show, 'someone young, but responsible, in touch with the times, but with an overview of history, someone the viewers could trust . . . but most of all someone who can communicate . . .' Someone, Latymer was certain, exactly like himself.

'Well, Charles . . .' Harvey was pouring the drinks, 'I'd say that wasn't bad, wasn't bad at all. What I'd like to do is offer you a contract for seven programmes, at the end of which we can both review our positions. What do you say?'

Latymer lifted his glass to his lips: 'Cheers.'

The Sixties had found another star. Charlie Latymer had made up his mind about that.

He bumped into Neil Fiske of Fiske-Forrester not entirely accidentally that evening and told him the good news. He was going into television. *Witness* was behind him, and 'Just in time, I'd say, wouldn't you?' he added casually.

'I'm sorry?' Neil Fiske looked puzzled.

'Oh dear,' said Latymer. And very slowly shook his head.

'We should talk,' said Neil Fiske, and led the latest star of television away to dinner.

Chapter Forty-Three

(i)

Whether Alec Reynolds' trip to London so soon after Nicola and Hudson had announced their engagement was entirely coincidental Emily never knew. Probably Reynolds had business interests in London anyway, but there had never been anything important enough to bring him hurrying over before.

He arrived early in May and booked in at the Mayfair Hotel, Nicola having failed to persuade him to stay at her house. She was still driving her Morris Minor but, because she knew he would expect something better, she met him off his flight from Johannesburg in a hired Rover.

'Already throwing your money around, I see,' had been his first comment upon seeing the car.

He was, Nicola would tell Emily, even more querulous than usual. 'You can't win with him. The thing is he's distrustful of everyone's motives,' she explained. 'And that can be very difficult to take.'

The dinner party was Nicola's idea, something to break the ice. Emily was unsure, particularly when Nicola insisted that she bring her mother. 'Come on, Emmy, I've been coming to your house for years. It's time your poor mother met my only surviving relative. She'll be fascinated. People like him are practically extinct outside safari parks. Besides if she's there perhaps it'll put the old bull on his best behaviour.'

The old bull arrived by taxi, half an hour earlier than expected, complaining about how wet it was. Nicola, who had been preparing dinner since four o'clock, was still in the shower, so Emily got him a drink and apologized for the weather, a warm summer evening of fine rain. He seemed to expect her to apologize. He had come, it seemed to Emily, determined to be difficult.

'She calls this a house?' he gasped, looking in perverse astonishment at the cottage rooms and narrow hall, mirrored to look larger. 'What did she say she paid for it?'

Emily ignored the question. 'It's terribly handy for everything,' she said. 'She was very lucky to get it.'

'Oh, luck! Is that what you call it here in England?'

He looked out on to the small, paved garden and shook his head. Emily waited. Virtually every person she knew was envious of Nicola owning such a pretty town house at this stage in her career. Nicola had chosen well, and she was sure he knew it.

'And what about this Hudson then? I thought it was you he was sweet on.'

The bluntness surprised her. 'That was a long time ago. We've all changed a lot since then.' Then stepping into the momentary silence as he seemed to wonder how best to reply, she said: 'I still think of that holiday at Wildwood, you know. I had such a wonderful time. How are they all, Alice, Fortunate, Joseph?'

He sniffed. 'Not being helped by the sanctions Harold Wilson and your British government have imposed on us, I can tell you that. It hurts them more than us, you know. He should try living there before he tells us how to rule our blacks . . .'

Her mother arrived next, and the old man's charm temporarily returned. With her soft voice and extreme politeness she seemed to demand good manners.

Wisely Nicola chose to wear the longest skirt she possessed, almost knee-length, and there were no sarcastic comments, and when the boys came Emily was relieved that Richard was wearing a jacket. Reynolds liked to dress for dinner, she remembered. Hudson, as expected, was wearing his light linen suit, and with a half-hearted stab at fashion, a floral, kipper tie which Nicola must have bought. He looked every bit the successful young American businessman.

At first the evening passed amicably, Nicola successfully steering the conversation away from anything vaguely controversial. Hudson started quietly, but, as the company relaxed over pudding, his confidence increased and he began to chat far more than was usual for him, amusing everyone with stories of the vacation he worked as a door-to-door magazine salesman in St Louis, Missouri.

'No kidding, they'd have us out there from nine in the morning until nine at night, with maybe a half-hour break for a hamburger and another for coffee. At the end of the day if we hadn't sold we'd have a two-hour indoctrination and self-criticism session in the motel where we were staying. The North Koreans had nothing on those guys. We'd all have to stand in a circle, never allowed to sit even though we'd been on our feet all day, and be harangued by the man and woman running the team. "Why didn't you make a sale? Whose fault was it? It was your fault? Right? Right! Why? Because you didn't want to make a sale, right? Right!" Hour after hour. Then the next day they'd put us out to work the same streets, starting all over again until we did sell. In the end we'd be virtually begging the people to order the damn magazines.'

'And did you sell?' asked Nicola.

'I guess I made my quota most days,' Hudson said.

'I bet you did,' said Richard. 'Can you think of anything more frightening than a Hudson who daren't go home without a sale?'

Emily was fascinated. Hudson had never mentioned this before. It was sometimes as though he saved up his lifetime's experiences for when they might be most useful. Tonight he had evidently decided that Nicola's uncle would want stories of his pioneer work in the spirit of capitalism.

'And was that when you decided to go into magazine publishing?' Reynolds asked.

Hudson shook his head. 'I don't think so. That was because of Richard. He sold me on the idea of journalism and publishing. He was so dedicated. He still is. And he's right. He showed me the way.'

'So you repaid him by taking his girl.'

There was a terrible silence. Hudson flushed. He had been lulled into a false sense of security, had thought he was doing well. He didn't often make misjudgements like this.

Nicola recovered first. 'That's unforgivable,' she said icily.

Reynolds deliberately misunderstood. 'I think so, too,' he snapped back.

Emily stole a look at Hudson. He was ragged with anger.

Reynolds looked around the table, gleeful and challenging at the same time. Everyone avoided his gaze.

Richard finally found the way through. 'No one stole anybody,' he said quietly. 'The fact was that as time went on it became clear to us all that Nicola had more in common with Hudson than with me. That's part of growing up. People grow up, you know.' He said it so deliberately, it was a rebuke which invited no debate.

Suddenly, inexplicably, Reynolds looked tired. The fight went out of him. He sighed and fell silent. It had been an extraordinary moment: the gesture of a man, like his country, bitter with the way the world had gone. He didn't know Hudson, didn't know whether he approved of him or not, and had no idea what his motives might be. But he distrusted his youth and his style and his winning of Nicola.

They had coffee in the sitting room, where Emily's mother valiantly guided the conversation to the relatively neutral ground of wildlife preservation, a subject Reynolds, almost surprisingly, was keen on. 'When I was a boy the whole country was alive with game, with buck, sable, elephant, warthogs, lion . . . everything you could imagine. We've civilized the place, stumped it out and

406

ploughed it and built it into a nation. But for what? For whom? What kind of people will inherit it? I don't know if we shouldn't have left it a wilderness, the way it was.' And he looked across the room to where Nicola was speaking softly to Hudson.

(ii)

The rain had stopped so they walked for a while to sober up and for Hudson to calm down. Up on to Campden Hill they went and around the Square, staring up at the tall Georgian mansions as they walked, all dark now in the early hours: a part of London where the rich people lived.

'You know what he was saying, don't you, Richard? That I'm marrying Nicola for her money. Like some gigolo or one of those guys.'

'He's an old man. It doesn't matter what he thinks.'

'It matters to me. As far as he's concerned I'm just some jumped-up kid out of nowhere, some guy on the make who figures the way to an easy life is by marrying his niece.'

'Hardly jumped up. You're only publishing the best magazine in the country.'

He shook his head. 'To him *Witness* is the kind of thing people do for a hobby.' He went silent, and then said quietly: 'Maybe that's what it is to me, too. It certainly isn't a money winner.'

'What? Come on! We're doing wonderfully. You know we are.'

Hudson pursed his lips but said nothing more. They walked on. It was the first time Hudson had ever questioned *Witness*'s success and it was so unfair. Month after month at the regular board meetings Hudson and Adam Smith produced figures showing steady growth. The distributors, Farrow and Fox, with their stable of *Fun and Profit* magazines, were doing a tremendous job.

Richard tried to ease the gloom. 'Reynolds will be all

right when he meets your folks. You know how some of these people are: background is everything to them. It'll be fine on the day.'

'I don't know, maybe I should call the whole thing off.'

'What?' Hudson was serious. This was no gesture. He never made gestures. 'You're mad.'

'No. It'll be years before I can keep her in the style she expects.'

'You *are* mad. Apart from owning a house she lives just like the rest of us. She doesn't expect anything.'

'You know what I mean. Look at these places. This is the sort of house Nicola belongs in.' They were walking past the large Italianate white mansions of Holland Park. 'Nice, right?'

'Yes, sure.' Richard hardly looked at them.

'One of these days . . .'

Richard didn't doubt it. Hudson always got what he wanted. It had been a strange conversation. For the first time Hudson was showing signs of vulnerability.

(*iii*)

Emily's telephone rang at one o'clock. She had been expecting the call and had not gone to bed. After the dinner party she and her mother had walked home not quite knowing what to say to each other. 'He certainly seems a very opinionated man,' was about as much a judgement as her mother was prepared to make. Neither of her parents had ever been much critical of others.

'Sorry about that,' Nicola said down the phone. 'You were right. It was a bad idea. I'm afraid he's just a regular, old, hairy-backed one. He was the same when my father married my mother, apparently. He was convinced she was just a dedicated little gold digger.'

'And was she?'

'Probably. I certainly would have been in her circumstances.'

'Where is he now?'

'Oh long gone, probably to take it out on some poor tart in Shepherd's Market, I imagine. No, that isn't very fair. I didn't mean it. He's too old, anyway. I suppose it'll all be fine in the end, though he won't be there on the first.'

'Is that definite?'

'Yes. He has to get back, he says. "Things are tricky with these Harold Wilson sanctions",' she mimicked. 'Hudson's going to have a tough job getting around that one. It'll take more than a bag of sugared almonds and a bunch of flowers.'

'He'll do it.'

'Mmm.' Nicola went quiet. Then she said: 'You know, Emmy, I didn't tell you, but when I mentioned marriage, when I proposed . . . well, Hudson didn't exactly leap for joy. He was pleased, but almost the first thing he said was, "I'm not good enough for you yet". Can you believe it? *Yet?* What has yet got to do with anything? And what does it take to be good enough for me?'

Chapter Forty-Four

(*i*)

Gimmelmann put on his pale beige summer jacket: it looked good with his patterned Indian shirt and maroon flares and the neat little moccasin shoes he'd bought in Marrakesh. He was glad he'd had that job in Morocco because he'd come back with a tan, which was an envious thing to have in London so early in the summer.

He smelled Holly before she reached him. She was wearing oil of patchouli which was strong and spicy, penetrating even the burning joss sticks. It made him think of cool nights in southern India, though he had never been to any part of India. For a while she stood watching as he admired himself in the mirror. It was a warm evening. She was wearing only an old shirt. She looked mischievous. Behind her in the living room the music played as always. '*We skipped the light fandango, turned cartwheels across the floor.*' The song that was everywhere that summer.

'Very nice,' she said at last as he finished preening himself.

It was so rarely that she had an opinion on anything he was surprised. 'The shirt?'

'The lot. Very nice. A nice little package. If I didn't know better I might think you were going out to see that Jenny Quinn.'

'But you do know better, don't you?'

She gazed at him. 'I know you better than she ever will.'

'*. . . as the miller told his tale, that her face at first just ghostly . . .*'

410

'I never imagined Hudson having a stag-night,' she said after a moment.

'It was Willie's idea. I think he just wanted an excuse for a party. Willie loves parties.' She was watching him so closely it made him nervous.

'Shame the way some people always need an excuse, isn't it?'

He didn't know what she was talking about, but he nodded anyway. He wasn't used to having Holly make idle chatter. He picked up his car keys off the table. 'You staying in, are you?'

Holly shrugged. 'I might be,' she said.

He didn't know why he had asked. He no longer cared whether Holly came or went, hadn't cared for years. She was lazy and she was trouble, and, as her agent was tired of pointing out to her, she was too heavy these days. The dimpled urchin child of sixteen was now twenty: the cuteness had matured into a sullen indifference. 'Well, OK then, I'll perhaps see you later,' he said and went to the door.

'You won't forget, will you, give Hudson a kiss from me,' she called after him. She was standing in the centre of the black room with the evening sun shining directly through the windows, silhouetting the outline of her body beneath the shirt. Despite the tendency to plumpness, she was still pretty, still the sexiest woman he had ever known.

'That her face at first just ghostly, turned a whiter shade of pale . . .'

He went out and closed the door.

(*ii*)

At eight Richard took a taxi to Chepstow Villas. The plan was that he and Willie would escort the bridegroom on his last bachelor night. He found Hudson in thoughtful mood, listening to Billie Holiday, lounging on the old leather sofa they had inherited when they had first moved in together, his legs dangling off the end. Scattered around him were bundles of invoices, sheets of figures. Always working. Other than that the place looked much as it had when Richard lived there. How strange that Hudson had never bothered to find a better home. He could certainly have afforded to. He would be moving into Nicola's house when they got back from honeymoon.

'Nicola made me promise to look after you tonight,' Richard said. 'And to make sure you don't drink too much.'

'Don't worry. I'm a big boy now, you know. If you want a beer there's one in the fridge. Willie's bound to be late.'

Richard helped himself. When he returned to the sitting room he found Hudson lying back with his eyes closed. 'Are you OK?' he asked.

Hudson smiled. 'Sure. How's our baby looking for next week?'

'A special edition on the hippy generation, written by genuine pot-heads, cranks, acid-freaks and assorted self-abusers. At last *Witness* tunes in, turns on, drops out and floats downstream, even if the editor doesn't like the idea very much. We've got the word "love" all over the cover, surrounded by flowers. It seemed appropriate this week.'

'Sounds good to me.' Hudson closed his eyes again. 'It's been good, hasn't it, Richard. The past four years. We've done OK.'

'What do you mean, "We've done OK"? You're only getting married, you know. We'll still be here when you get back from Rhodesia.'

'Of course you will. I guess I'm just tired.'

'It might be an idea to think about delegating a little bit more. Nicola will probably insist anyway. Adam and you have been working yourselves to death.'

'He's a good man, Adam. Weren't we right about him now.'

'I think we were probably right about everyone.'

Hudson considered, and then said: 'Yes, we probably were.'

Richard slumped in an easy chair. 'I take it your parents aren't going to be with us on Friday.'

Hudson shook his head. He didn't offer any excuse and this time Richard did not ask for one. He was never going to meet Hudson's parents, he knew that. It didn't matter. 'But yours will be there, won't they?' Hudson had insisted that Richard's parents and sister and Emily's mother were invited.

'Just try and keep them away.'

On the stereo player Billie Holiday began to sing *Strange Fruit*. Hudson listened as though hearing the words for the first time. Richard watched him, his long body and legs folded in three places across the sofa.

'One thing I always meant to ask you,' said Richard, wiping beer from his lips. 'The little scar on your chin. How did you do that?'

Without opening his eyes Hudson put his hand to his face. 'That!' He traced the white line with his thumb. 'That, I seem to remember, was the result of some kind of accident in the school gymnasium. I was always too tall to do gymnastics, better at basketball, but they would never listen. They never do. It bled like a gusher and Spider Menoza became so worried he tore off his T-shirt, rushed to a tap and then held it tight against the wound to stem the flow of blood. It worked, too. He was a good guy, Spider.'

'Maybe you should have invited him to the wedding.'

'Maybe I should.'

The doorbell rang. It was Willie, dressed for the night in a kaftan and a pair of white cotton trousers. Around his neck was a single string of blue beads, while across his lip and down the sides of his mouth were the beginnings of a soft, blond Zapata moustache.

'You do realize you look ridiculous, don't you, Willie?' Richard said, smiling.

Willie laughed. 'B..ut of course. Isn't that the f..un of it all? To look ri..diculous and not to c..are.'

'You look terrific, Willie,' said Hudson, pulling himself up and beaming. 'So what do you say, you guys? Shall we go and enjoy ourselves?'

(iii)

'*Terry meets Julie, Waterloo Station, every Friday night . . .*' It was some time since she had seen Nicola so happy, singing, chattering, hopping distractedly from subject to subject, an item of gossip here, now a joke, now a line of a song. 'Come on, Emmy, you sing, too. *As long as I gaze on Waterloo Sunset I am in paradise.*'

They had spent the evening together, first a drink in the Hyde Park Hotel, then an early dinner in a French restaurant in Knightsbridge. Very smart for a special occasion. And now a dawdle through the park on a balmy, scented evening, a little drunk on Sancerre, Nicola linking her arm through Emily's as she always liked to do. 'If I were an African I'd hold your hand, Emmy. Even if we were boys.' Just the two of them. They had never had close girl-friends outside each other. There had never been the space for anyone else.

'The fact is, Emmy, I can't help wishing Alice could be here. And Joseph. Their presents came, you know. They made me cry. Alice sent a smooth stone carving of a man and woman joined together so that they have only one body, a bit like Siamese twins, I suppose, which had been done by her nephew in Salisbury. It's terribly good. Joseph sent a white shawl, the sort you wrap babies in, so I suppose he's presuming I'm pregnant. I can just imagine poor Joseph not knowing what to send and Alice bullying him to go down to Umtali and buy something. With all those children he can hardly afford to throw money away on me.'

'What about Fortunate?'

Nicola smiled. 'Poor Fortunate. She's got some boy-friend who Alice seems to have decided is quite unsuit-able. Apparently he's from Mozambique and can't speak English, which, to Alice's way of thinking, is not at all the sort of young man for Fortunate. I bet she's giving her a really hard time. I'll have to see what's what when I get there. He's probably a perfectly likeable chap.'

'And your uncle?'

'Oh no, I don't think he's very likeable. Not really. Do you?' She laughed. 'He's sulking, of course, which is what he always does when he can't have his way. He says he's leaving Wildwood free for us for our honeymoon, which is no great sacrifice because he'd far rather be in Salisbury, but I suppose he means well. He's probably embarrassed now and doesn't know how to get out of the situation. Bless him. I'll get around him, you wait and see. He'll think of Hudson as his long-lost son and heir by the time I'm finished.'

They were walking now on the grass and Nicola had slipped out of her shoes. 'D'you know I hardly wore shoes until I came to school in England? Alice would always try to get me into my sandals but as soon as she went back into the house off they'd come. I hated her for making me, but when I was sent here I wept for weeks promising God I'd wear my sandals all the time if I could only go home to Wildwood again.'

At the children's playground in Kensington Gardens they stopped and dawdled on the swings for a while, each busy with her own thoughts. They both knew things would inevitably be different when Nicola was married. After a long moment Nicola began to sing quietly to herself again. '*As long as I gaze on Waterloo Sunset . . .*'

(iv)

It was Willy's acting voice: totally fluent. 'There was this pair of newly weds and, armed with a carton of

French letters, they went to stay on a farm for their honeymoon.' Groans heaved around the room. Willie, quite drunk, his new kaftan disfigured with a red wine stain, was not at all put out. 'As soon as they got there they hurried up to the bedroom, jumped into bed and, to cut a short story even shorter, got at it, hammer and tongue.'

'Be specific. How much hammer and how much tongue?' shouted Trevor, the *Witness* rugby correspondent, to ribald laughter.

'History doesn't record, but I suspect a considerable amount of both,' came back Willie. 'Anyway, the first morning there the farmer's wife knocked on their door: "Breakfast," she called. "No thank you," called the groom, "we're not hungry today. We're living on the fruits of love." The same happened at lunchtime and at dinnertime. And for four days in a row. No food. Just the fruits of love. Then on the fifth day it was the farmer who banged on the door in the morning. "No breakfast today, thank you," called the groom. "We're living on the fruits of love." "The fruits of love, is it?" said the farmer. "In that case would you mind not throwing the cores out of the window because they're choking my chickens."'

It was an old joke which they had all heard before but they laughed just the same. At the top of the table Hudson, with Richard and Willie at his sides, smiled broadly as his friends thumped the table. One of the Mama Vecchi's waiters was moving around the long refectory table putting out yet more bottles of wine, the waitresses having been advised to keep away from drunken stag-nights. Earlier there had been dinner, speeches and toasts, Richard leading the ceremonies, and throughout which Hudson had grinned, drinking as lightly as his friends would allow. Now was the time for traditional smut.

The room was packed and rowdy. They were all there: Gimmelmann, looking very pretty and successful tonight; Peter Berridge, hunched in a corner at the end of the table, a malevolent, grinning harvester of spite, no doubt taking notes for his files; loyal Adam Smith, smart in his new light-weight suit; Ben Tarlo, who, with Jessica and their babies, had flown over from New York especially for the wedding; the boys from advertising and distribution; all the various *Witness* male writers and sub-editors; and those who had been and gone, who had worked for *Witness* on their way to bigger things. Only Charlie Latymer was missing. Typical, thought Richard. Since Latymer had landed his job in television he'd been even more arrogant.

As it had been Willie who had organized the party the nature of the 'spe..cial sur..prise' was not unexpected. Just before midnight, with only wine bottles, glasses and candles left on the table, the door was opened and two fair-haired girls, dressed in white, ankle-length robes and with flowers in their hair, entered and climbed on to the long table.

Willie rose to his feet again. 'Will some..one turn out the l..ights, pl..ease?' Momentarily, as he had ceased to perform, the stammer had returned. The electric lights were turned off leaving only the glow and flickering shadows of the burning candles. 'Gentlemen, as the cabaret for tonight's occasion we're very fortunate indeed in having with us two lovely free spirits of the universe, the karma whom you will all become better acquainted with very shortly. They are like ying and yang, the two sides to every coin, the opposites in personality, the ultimate celestial balance, Sister Golden Hair Delight and Sister Sunshine, who have been transported back specially from a standing room only engagement . . .'

Someone guffawed at that: 'Standing room only. Not half!'

'Ying, yang, paddiwack, give a dog a bone, this old man came rolling home,' sang a drunken sub-editor.

'. . . a standing room only engagement in the Temple of Heavenly Promise and Spiritual Freedom in Kathmandu.'

'Get 'em off,' shouted rugby-playing Trevor untranscendentally.

Willie grinned at him.

Hudson was shaking his head in amusement. 'Only Willie,' he murmured.

Everyone looked towards the girls who waited calmly until there was a silence in the room. Reaching down Willie pressed a tape recorder by his foot. At first faintly, and then more loudly, came what sounded like the chanting of Oriental monks. The two girls knelt down, face to face, then in a slow balletic movement leaned forward and kissed. Richard wanted to giggle.

Very gradually the girls began to undress each other, first the buttons, one by one in carefully rehearsed routine, then the sashes which held their robes closed, until with a flourish the music changed to Ravi Shankar and the girls fell to the floor to rise immediately without their gowns.

'Like b..utter..flies climbing out of their dis..carded pupae,' whispered Willie, overloud, with what sounded suspiciously like pride.

In the darkness someone sniggered.

Suddenly the girls had been transformed into flower children in white shifts, daisy chains around their necks, buttercups at their wrists. At this Willie began to applaud, and it occurred to Richard that, amazingly, he was taking it almost seriously. But then he was drunk. Richard looked at the girls, one with long hair, almost to her waist, Sister Golden Hair Delight, the other, Sister Sunshine, with her hair in a bob, and wondered if either of them was particularly special to Willie. Of all the people he knew Willie was the most dedicated Sixties man.

The two girls were now helping each other out of their white dresses, first one, unpeeling to reveal a white, lace-trimmed slip, then the other unveiling to a tiny, white bikini bottom.

Alongside him Hudson took a sip of his wine and shone a smile at Ben Tarlo who was gazing in concentration at the two girls on the table in front of him. Who would have believed? Ben Tarlo, the happily married father of two, mouth open in wonder at a strip show?

Suddenly, so suddenly it was quite unexpected, one of the girls, Sister Sunshine, was naked. With the revelation came a belated chorus of cheers from some of the revellers. Willie applauded politely.

'We've come a long way, Richard?'

'Sorry?'

Hudson raised his voice. 'A long way since Health and Efficiency down at the Café des Artistes.'

That first night out together. They had been together almost every day since then but still Hudson kept his mysteries. Women still threw themselves at him but he was always careful not to encourage. Was he ever tempted? What had happened to the red-headed lawyer, to Britt-Marie and all the other girls? When they had been a part of Hudson's life he had hardly talked about them. After they had left they had never been mentioned. And Richard wondered whether Hudson ever thought about Emily, really thought about her, as he still thought about Nicola.

On the table Sister Golden Hair Delight carefully snuffed out all but one candle. The music now was quiet. Slowly Sister Sunshine began to undress her companion. One naked, one clothed, yet somehow it was the girl still clothed who was the object of all eyes. They were pretty girls: nimble, flat-chested androgynes, acting as though they were alone, making their audience feel like secret onlookers to some private act. Gradually, sinking down, they stretched out between glasses and bottles, and, very slowly, began to make love to each other.

Around the table the stag-night was hushed. In Willie's hand a column of burnt ash from a fat joint, minutes without being smoked, collapsed. Tim Gimmelmann, his elbows supporting his chin, tugged distractedly at his almost shoulder-length hair, and Ben Tarlo, having taken off his glasses, had his wide, dark head virtually on the back of his chair, his body slumped nearly to table level. Next to him Adam Smith rested his forehead on his hands, his eyes watching everything through the bars of his fingers, and further on Berridge looked up through hollow eyes over sunken cheeks, his rapidly balding, sweating skull shining in the candlelight.

Things hadn't changed that much, thought Richard whimsically. Sex in the permissive society was just as fascinating as it had been in the repressive society. The only difference was that there was more of it.

The party broke up at one with most people well and truly drunk, spilling out noisily on to the Westbourne Grove pavement, Willie with kaftaned arms around the celestial sisters, who had now transfigured into a rather dazzling West German ballet student and a trainee shoe-shop manager from Balham. Willie's smile to Richard seemed to say it all: 'I know I look ridiculous, but look what I'm taking home tonight.'

There was probably not a man there who did not envy him. The rituals of stag-nights are about sex and the company had been aroused. In another generation they might have all ended up in a whorehouse. Some of the design team and younger sub-editors did indeed want to go on to a club they knew called the Speak-easy, where all manner of loose girls were said to parade, and, after noisy debate, climbed into cars and drove dangerously away towards Oxford Street. But the backbone of the old network was ready to call it a night.

'By the way, I forgot to tell you, Holly sends her best for you both,' Gimmelmann told Hudson.

It sounded so unlikely that Richard wanted to laugh.

'That's very . . . ah . . . very encouraging,' Hudson said politely.

'Well then . . .' It seemed that Gimmelmann did not want the evening to end. He stood there gazing at Hudson.

Along the pavement other guests were shaking Hudson's hand and wishing him well, before wandering unsteadily away.

Adam Smith appeared at Hudson's side, quite drunk. 'Just to say, don't you worry. You can leave all the worrying to me this time. Isn't that right?' His speech was slurred.

Hudson patted him fondly on the shoulder. 'Are you OK, fella? Are you going to be able to make it all right?'

'I'm fine,' said Adam, although he clearly wasn't.

'Let's grab this cab for you,' Hudson said, and, holding Adam steady, put his fingers to his teeth and whistled expertly.

The second cab he tried pulled to a halt.

'You've got precious cargo here,' Hudson smiled at the driver, and passed him a ten-pound note. 'Take care of him, will you? He's going to Hammersmith.'

The driver, who had looked a bit fed up when he saw the condition of Adam, brightened at the tip.

'Can I give you a lift back then, Hudson?' Gimmelmann said as the cab pulled away. It was beginning to drizzle.

Hudson shook his head. 'I'll walk if you don't mind. The rain should help clear my head.' Then glancing at Richard he added: 'Richard could do with a ride home, though. You can go by Chelsea, can't you?'

Gimmelmann viewed the prospect of giving Richard a lift with little excitement. 'Oh . . . well. OK then . . . you'd better come if you're coming,' he said, ungraciously, and led the way towards his Mini Cooper.

The street had suddenly cleared and Richard and Hudson were standing alone on the pavement. The lights over the door at Mama Vecchi's went out.

'If you're sure . . .' Richard began.

'I'm sure,' said Hudson, turning up his jacket collar. 'See you tomorrow, and thanks for everything.'

A couple of minutes later when they drove back past Mama Vecchi's Hudson was still standing there, his hands deep in his pockets, his tall shoulders hunched, as he gazed unseeing at the pavement.

(v)

There was no sign of Holly when Gimmelmann arrived home. The bed hadn't been slept in. The bitch was obviously out on the razzle again.

Chapter Forty-Five

(i)

Nicola started the giggling. They were standing in a row in front of the registrar, a small, precise man with a ginger, V-shaped beard, when Emily felt the unmistakable tremors of building hysteria. She bit her lip. It was without doubt a very rude-looking beard. Even ruder than John Donne's or Shakespeare's. The pre-nuptial drinks hadn't helped. It was the first wedding for all of them and they were silly with nerves.

It had been at Nicola's insistence that Emily was alongside her. The registrar had prissily tried to insist that Willie Simmonds, who, in the absence of her uncle, was giving Nicola away, should stand closer, but Nicola had held firmly on to Emily. 'I want Emily next to me. Willie can give me away very nicely from the end of the row, can't you, Willie?'

Willie, in a white suit and flowery shirt, all cuffs and collar, had just grinned. He was completely stoned.

There had not been quite so many giggling fits recently, not like the solemn Oxford moments when both girls would be doubled up, tears flooding their cheeks, chests and lungs aching from straining to keep control. Glancing along the line Emily could see that both Hudson and Richard were staring ahead, determined not to look at each other.

At her side Nicola was looking beautiful. They had shopped for her dress together, Nicola, never having the patience to have anything made, finally settling on a cream, mid-calf-length dress, with blue forget-me-nots embroidered delicately up the bodice. On her feet she wore open sandals, and in her hair, darker now, almost golden, reflecting her years in England, a simple, cheap butterfly clip that Emily had given her the first Christmas they had known each other.

The registrar was hurrying through the ceremony. It was all so fast. 'Do you take this woman, Nicola, to be your lawful wedded wife . . . ?' Hudson assented, with just the slightest smile. He was shining today, it seemed to Emily. So tall, not so worried looking as he had been recently, wearing a pale blue shirt under a light summer suit. He looked very American. 'Do you take this man . . . ?' She looked at Nicola. She was smiling. She said 'I do' before the registrar had finished asking her, she was so eager. Along the row Richard, fidgeting uncomfortably in a new, navy-blue suit, fumbled as he passed the ring.

The kisses, the handshakes, the book to be signed, and suddenly out they went into the showers of confetti, where photographer friends snapped everything, Gimmelmann wanted to pose everyone and the Mascara pulled out a Brownie she must have had since school. Ben Tarlo asked Adam Smith if he was feeling better and Willie Simmonds stood at the back of the crowd applauding as though watching a show, which in some ways it was. Such clothes and such colours: flared lime or burgundy cotton suits, wide-brimmed turquoise, peach and avocado hats, Sioux head bands, flowing Indian dresses, scanty snatches of floral shifts, dandy shirts, Bengali beads, Italian earrings; banker Neil Fiske getting it wrong and dressing in tails; the new girl Heather, from the art department, having hardly bothered to dress at all, two inches of linen pelmet, knickers minimal and much admired, and more flowers in hair than buttonholes. A fancy-dress party spilling over the pavement into the road outside the Kensington Register Office: Berridge, in a striped suit he must have stolen from his grandfather's grave, congratulating Hudson, a dry, hard kiss on the cheek for the laughing bride; Willie grinning inanely, Sister Sunshine and Sister Golden Hair

Delight in saffron robes at his side; and Penny Chilston, tears shining in her eyes as she showered everyone in champagne.

And then suddenly from nowhere there was Holly, her skin chalk white against the blood red of her dress, moving through the crowd, easing her way past Nicola, approaching Hudson to kiss him deliberately, lasciviously, on the lips in front of everyone, while Gimmelmann turned away and pretended he hadn't seen. Hudson's face fell and he pulled back. It was too late. Too late for Nicola to turn away and ignore it, and her face crumpled as this moment was spoiled for her.

Emily watched unable to help. Poor Nicola.

'You're looking lovely.'

'I'm sorry?' She turned around.

It was Richard. 'I've been watching you, watching everybody else. You do a lot of that.'

'Yes.'

'Your dress . . . it's very pretty. You look . . .' He didn't know the words.

It was a simple pale blue dress Nicola had noticed in a window in Beauchamp Place and insisted Emily went to see. She had seemed more interested in what Emily wore than her own bridal dress. 'Thank you. Nicola bullied me into buying it,' Emily said.

'She was right to.'

(ii)

They sat together at the reception, Richard with Emily. It seemed the most natural thing in the world. They were such good friends.

Nicola had chosen the Arethusa in the King's Road, probably at Willie's suggestion, which was the smartest place of the moment. She had also chosen the music: *Sergeant Pepper's Lonely Hearts Club Band*, released that very day. Although she did not often write about music any more she had made an exception to do a colour piece on the making of the album, an event she had not wanted to miss. *'I get by with a little help from my friends,'* she had sung around the office all week, *'I get high with a little help from my friends.'* That was true.

After lunch the speeches, and after that the dancing. Everyone watched Hudson and Nicola: they made such a stunning couple. Richard held Emily and felt so very comfortable. There was no sign of Holly. The rumour was that Gimmelmann had beaten her up around the back of the register office, but, although no one quite believed it, no one wanted her back. At a large corner table Emily's mother and brother sat with Richard's family. All were agreed the bride and groom made a lovely couple, although Richard's mother thought Hudson looked a little tired. He still dazzled her.

Nicola was more than the bride, she was the spirit of the day, moving from table to table, thanking and gossiping, laughing and teasing. Everyone wanted to kiss the bride, boys and girls alike. Even Penny Chilston. She was the breath of life. If she had any regrets that her uncle had refused to attend, or that Hudson's parents had not made the journey, she did not show them.

The afternoon passed too quickly. At six the limousine came to take the newly weds to a hotel in the country. The following day would be the flight to Johannesburg and on to Rhodesia and Wildwood.

The guests followed them out into the King's Road to wave goodbye, mobbing the car, spirits over-high, voices over-noisy, Penny Chilston drunk and wet-eyed now, earning a quick kiss from Hudson.

Richard and Emily stood together as the squall of excitement raged around them. They had both said their goodbyes privately, Emily when she had helped Nicola into her going-away suit. In a private room at the back of the restaurant Hudson had given Richard a final bear hug: 'We'll call you from Wildwood,' he had said.

'Goodbye . . . good luck . . . bye . . .' the chorus cried, and the car began to pull away.

Suddenly the car stopped and a window opened alongside Emily. Nicola leaned out. 'Write soon, Emmy, promise,' she demanded.

'Promise.'

And with a final kiss the honeymooners were on their way.

Chapter Forty-Six

(i)

The best man and bridesmaid went to Paris for the weekend: a spur of the moment champagne suggestion by Richard. To have gone back to their separate homes after so much excitement would have seemed so flat.

The last flight of the day was at nine. They collected their passports but there was no time to change or pick up much else. Because the banks were already closed Willie lent them some money. Since his success he always carried a thick wad of ten-pound notes in his inside pocket in case of sudden extravagant whims. He would have insisted upon driving them to the airport had he not had to look to the needs of Sister Golden Hair Delight and Sister Sunshine.

'With the compliments of the cabin crew,' the stewardess smiled as the plane sailed over the Sussex coast. 'And congratulations.' And she placed a small bottle of champagne together with two glasses in front of Richard in the aisle seat.

'I'm sorry?' Richard looked up, surprised, flushed and a little drunk from the day. Two other stewardesses were standing by the curtain to the cockpit looking at them and smiling.

Emily giggled. She was still wearing her bridesmaid's dress. In the button-hole of Richard's suit was a white carnation. 'Thank you very much,' she smiled, and taking one glass raised it to Richard. 'They think we're honeymooners,' she whispered.

The plane landed at Le Bourget at eleven, Paris time, and with no idea where they were going to stay they took taxi to the Boulevard St Germain. They found the Hotel de l'Université down a side-street near the Sorbonne, and, though the assistant manager viewed them with some degree of suspicion, requesting that they pay in advance, they were given a room.

'I hope you have a very nice time here,' the young porter, sixteen and already trying to grow a moustache, smirked as Richard tipped him.

They had never even kissed before, though they had been friends for so long. And now as they lay back on the small double bed together, reflecting on the events of the day, Emily kicking off her shoes, and, without shyness, snuggling close to him, a stillness came over them. They were at peace with each other, relaxed, unembarrassed and unhurried. There was so much to think about.

For so long they had been joined together because of relationships with other people: with Nicola and Hudson. Now they were together because of each other. It was a new beginning.

Without awkwardness, in the dim light of the bedside lamp, they undressed, and squeezed between sheets tucked so firmly under the mattress that once in bed they felt strait-jacketed. Their bodies were warm alongside each other and though they were both exhausted their desire was insistent, keeping sleep at bay. When they made love it seemed to Richard the most natural thing in the world and he wondered why they had never thought of it before.

(*ii*)

They felt foolish at breakfast in their wedding outfits and as soon as the shops were open hurried out to buy jeans, shirts, underclothes and sandals for the weekend. It was the only haste they made all day. Although Emily had been to Paris with her parents and brother and once to interview Roger Vadim, Richard had only ever passed through on school trips. Certainly neither could say they

429

knew Paris, and, as it was their beginning, they wanted to discover it together. Because there was no hurry, and it was sunny, they walked everywhere, enjoying each other.

They missed lunch, settling for a beer at a pavement café near Notre Dame, spent the afternoon on a cruise along the Seine, and went back to the hotel to make love before venturing out for dinner and a movie.

They chose *Jules et Jim*, although they had both seen it before. This time, without the subtitles to read and not enough French to follow the dialogue properly, the story seemed slighter, the changes of affection more capricious. At the end Emily had tears in her eyes, just like the first two times. Jeanne Moreau seemed so impossibly, wonderfully, wilfully female; almost familiar.

On the walk back to the hotel they stopped for a drink in a late-night bar. As they talked Emily tried to remember something her father had once written. 'Sex is all very exciting, and romance can be exquisite and dramatic, but the real bricks and mortar of a relationship are laid down in all those hours together when nothing much happens, when the chief purpose for being together is companionship. Good companions invariably make the happiest couples.'

(*iii*)

Gimmelmann had called on Jenny Quinn after the reception. He liked the way her flat was spick and span and modern. She was so uncomplicated, someone like himself really, a North Londoner, getting ahead in life by using her native talent. He knew she fancied him rotten. She hadn't been able to disguise it. She had asked if he was hungry and had made him some scrambled eggs. Then they had gone to bed. Everything about Jenny Quinn was clean. She had a good face, too, delicate as porcelain, her agent liked to say. He could do things with that face. But the best thing of all was that she wasn't Holly. Lying between the clean sheets at Jenny Quinn's he could hide

430

from the venom of Holly, imagine she had never told him all those things, make believe she had been lying to him. He didn't believe her, anyway. Not really. She just said those things.

Holly wasn't there when he arrived home at lunchtime the following day. Pinned to the outside door was a message from the Metropolitan Police suggesting he call at the police station. Wondering, though not quite worrying, if it was something to do with the good hiding he had given Holly after the wedding, he opened the flat door and looked inside. Hardly anything had been left in one piece. Holly had gone, leaving only smashed glass, ripped prints, torn clothes and singes in the cushions and carpets where she had tried to start a fire. Nothing had escaped the systematic destruction. The sheets on the bed were torn, the cushions ripped open and their contents scattered, and the stained-glass window showing Bambi eating magic mushrooms, for which he had paid so much, had been smashed when a glass Buddha (picked up cheap on a shoot in Thailand) had been hurled through it. In the studio she had taken a kitchen knife to the roller blind, and smashed the lamps and his four cameras. His Rolleiflex, the camera he had first used to photograph her, a collector's item really, lay in fragments.

He should have been angry, but after the initial shock his only emotion was one of relief.

At the police station he was asked if he knew of anyone who might have a grudge against him. He said he did not. The police had, he was told, been called by a neighbour who had noticed that the front door had been left open in the middle of the night. When asked if he lived alone he said he shared the flat, but the young lady in question was away working at the moment. He didn't know when she would be back.

'She's gonna be very upset when she sees what's been done, isn't she?' the sergeant on the desk mused.

'Maybe,' Gimmelmann said. 'But she'll get over it. She's a resilient girl.'

The policeman wearily closed his book. Why should he care if this poncy little photographer didn't?

When the refuse collectors called at Chalcot Crescent on Monday morning they found two dustbins filled to overflowing. Had they looked carefully as they emptied the bins they would have discovered hundreds of ripped prints and several boxes stuffed with negatives, all of Holly Carter. Even the negative for the original *Witness* cover was there, the picture of a young, cheeky gypsy girl on scrubland behind Shepherd's Bush.

Tim Gimmelmann had broken the cardinal rule of photography. He had thrown away his negatives.

Later that day, as he lay between Jenny Quinn's peppermint striped sheets again, it pleased Gimmelmann to think of reclaimed land out on the Essex marshes growing out of the images that had made the career of Holly Carter. He had buried her. He had no doubts that her career was finished. That pleased him, too. Perhaps he could now forget about her, put her and her taunting out of his mind for ever and get on with his life.

(*iv*)

They stretched the weekend to Wednesday afternoon, going to a bank on the Monday morning and arranging a transfer of further funds from London so that they might carry on with the good time.

On the Sunday they had taken a bus out to Versailles, and Monday was given to the Louvre. Emily was interested in art history, and that made Richard interested. And like all his interests he took to it with the enthusiasm of the convert.

Most of the time, however, was spent getting up late, strolling through the streets, lolling together in the Bois de Boulogne and making love in the hotel in the early evenings, the 'DO NOT DISTURB' sign on the door. Even the outbreak of the Six Day War did not break into their holiday.

On Wednesday, all their money and excuses gone, they bought a cheap suitcase and caught a late afternoon bus to Orly where Emily posted a letter to Nicola in Rhodesia. 'She'll be so pleased with us,' she said. 'It's what she's wanted for ages.' They had hoped to be back in London in time for Richard to call Penny, who was acting editor, but the flight was delayed for two hours and it was after ten when they landed at Heathrow.

There was never any question of Emily going home. It wasn't even mentioned. They simply went back to Richard's flat in Chelsea, and, because they were exhausted, fell quickly asleep in his tiny narrow bed.

It was after nine when the ringing of the telephone in the next room woke him.

Pulling himself from his bed, where Emily was now stirring, Richard took his dressing gown off the hook on the bedroom door and stumbled through into the living room.

'Hello,' he said, picking up the receiver, expecting to hear Penny or someone else from the office.

There was a distant clicking noise, but nothing more.

'Hello,' he repeated.

'Is that Flaxman 2329?' a distant operator asked.

'Yes.'

'Just one moment, I have a call from Rhodesia for you . . .'

Richard came alive. 'Oh yes, good . . .'

'Hello . . . Richard?' Hudson's voice was thin and distant.

'Yes, hello. How are you? Are you at Wildwood?'

'Richard . . . it's Hudson.'

Emily came into the room, a blanket around her. She was smiling. 'How are they? Are they all right?'

Richard put a hand up. For some reason Hudson seemed to be having difficulty speaking.

'Richard, something terrible has happened . . .' The voice faded.

There was a silence. 'Hello . . . Hudson?'

From the other end of the phone he thought he heard what sounded like a sob.

'Hudson! Hello . . . are you there?'

Emily stepped forward.

'Richard, I've got terrible news.' The line crackled, and suddenly Hudson's voice was clear. 'It's Nicola, Richard. She's dead.'

Richard could not speak. He looked towards Emily, standing by the door. Her smile had vanished.

Chapter Forty-Seven

Emily was muddled and distracted, her memory slowly unwinding as Nicola became part of her. They had shared everything, and now that did not change. The conversations continued. The pain was new: it was like nothing she had ever experienced. She could physically feel it, as though she had lost a part of herself.

Richard, his voice and breath broken, had relayed the first, sparse details: Hudson's dawn ride on the mountain behind Wildwood, Alice in hysterics when he returned, Joseph and the police in the drive. And Nicola . . . a single blow to the head, they were saying, trying to stop a burglary. She had still been wearing her nightdress.

Around midday the *Evening News* found them, then the *Evening Standard*, asking for background on Nicola. 'Sorry to bother you at a time like this, but . . .' Then Penny rang from *Witness*. Richard took all the calls, though he could scarcely speak.

Later Emily would not remember getting through the following days. Strangely her mind went off on a tangent and concentrated on Joseph, the kind man in his orchid greenhouse wearing the royal-blue pullover, and Alice, the stout, energetic black lady with the helmet of steel-wool hair. Alice had always been fearful of intruders. A worrier. She had warned Nicola, waiting, fretting for them to come home that first day. 'You have been very long, Nicola. Too long. You can get lost or hurt. It is not good.'

'I'll come out,' Richard had offered immediately, but Hudson had not wanted that. There was nothing Richard or anyone could do. He would phone again when he could speak, Hudson had promised.

Emily did not offer to go to Africa. There was no one there to see. She tried to sleep that first afternoon: the phone off the hook, the curtains drawn. Perhaps she dozed because suddenly she cried out. Richard was there. 'I couldn't see her face. I was frightened. I thought I'd forgotten what she looked like.'

Information came slowly and unreliably. The one o'clock radio news included the murder as a short item after all the reports from the Six Day War. Wars do that to news: they monopolize. East Jerusalem had fallen after house-to-house fighting, and the Israelis were already praying at the Wailing Wall. Already troops were at the Suez Canal and Sharm el Sheikh on the Red Sea. The murder of Nicola Reynolds was a two-line item at the end of the 'other news'. If she had not been rich, Nicola's murder probably wouldn't have been reported at all.

In the afternoon Penny, grey with shock, called around with some sandwiches. She had been talking to someone at Reuters news agency. The word was that a manhunt was taking place along the Mozambique border. Nicola's handbag had been found by a river. All day she had been trying to telephone Hudson at Wildwood but had been unable to get through.

The early evening news, twice its normal length for the war coverage, had more sparse details and showed the Tim Gimmelmann photograph of Nicola. *London journalist murdered on honeymoon*, was the general line. Police were out with tracker dogs, they said. American magazine publisher, James Hudson, had told police he had seen three men making for the nearby border. He was now said to be suffering from shock and under sedation.

Emily went home for a few hours in the evening to comfort her mother. Nicola had been so close to all of them. She was glad that Daniel was still there.

At ten, after collecting some clean clothes, she returned to Chelsea and Richard. Both Willie and Penny were there, Willie's eyes bloodshot with tears. She did not need their companionship. Excusing herself she went through into Richard's tiny bedroom and closed the door.

In the night Richard joined her, his face rough where he had forgotten to shave that day. She could smell duty-free whisky on his breath, but it had not dulled his pain and he was restless and unsleeping. They did not speak.

The arrest of Marco de Sampaio was announced on the eight o'clock news on the Saturday morning, virtually the last item after reports of Israel's acceptance of the United Nations ceasefire. Marco de Sampaio, a Mozambique citizen, the announcer said, had been arrested while hiding close to the Mozambique border and had been taken to Umtali for questioning. 'It is believed,' said the announcer, 'that de Sampaio occasionally worked as an odd-job man at Wildwood, the Reynolds' remote Rhodesian mansion.'

'Marco de Sampaio,' Emily repeated the name to herself. But she felt nothing.

Chapter Forty-Eight

Marco de Sampaio was hanged in Umtali Gaol at seven o'clock one summer morning at the beginning of February, 1968. It was 5 a.m. in London. Emily felt sick. She was eight months pregnant. She had not slept.

'Are you all right?' Richard stood in the doorway to the bathroom wearing his pyjama bottoms. She was sitting on the floor, her dressing gown fastened around her bulge to keep out the cold, her head resting against the wall behind her.

She nodded and looked at her wrist-watch. Would it happen dead on time? she asked herself. Perhaps they would be a little late. She wondered about the legend of the last cigarette, the hearty breakfast, the final walk. Would he die alone or with others? Three in a row, perhaps. She had heard that they did that for convenience in some countries, that hangmen travelled the country and then lined up the recently convicted all together. It was apparently cheaper on the expenses that way. Economy in numbers. Better for the taxpayer. She wondered if it made it easier to face death if one were to share the moment with others. And then she wondered if Marco de Sampaio would be blindfolded or hooded or wide-eyed, seeing everyone. Marco de Sampaio, a Portuguese name for a black, non-English speaking Shona from across the Rhodesian border in Mozambique. He had had an interpreter at his trial. Would he have been given a Catholic priest for this last night, for his last confession, for the last rites? Would he still have denied his guilt? Although a non-Catholic, Emily had been educated in a convent school and knew that according to the teachings of the Church forgiveness was only given to those who were truly sorry for their sins.

They waited, six months married, listening to the squalls of rain scuttling across the flat zinc roof of the bathroom. Pugh the Portrait had written to Emily during the trial describing the demeanour of the accused, sending her a sketch of the courtroom and de Sampaio in the dock, a handsome man, who had looked quite terrified. 'Let's see him try to wriggle out of the noose,' the artist had written, with sickening spitefulness. 'I'll be there outside the gaol on the morning, keeping vigil for poor Nicola, making sure the savage gets what's coming to him.' Sick with revulsion Emily had burned both sketch and letter and never replied. Now she imagined Pugh the Portrait's grey Austin Cambridge parked in a wide, dusty street, under the trees and across the road from the white-walled Umtali Gaol, the long-jawed portrait painter in her cream blouse sitting impassively at the wheel, counting away the seconds of a man's life, the self-appointed guardian of judicial revenge.

Emily did not know whether she believed or not, but she prayed. Please God, make it easy for this poor man. Make him truly sorry. Grant him a state of grace at his time of death. She shivered on the cold bathroom linoleum, frightened. Whatever Marco de Sampaio had done Nicola would not have wanted this.

Hudson had been backwards and forwards several times. Returning to London after the magistrates' hearing he had gone back to Umtali for the committal proceedings, and then again for the trial. The request for an appeal had been turned down on insufficient grounds, although Hudson had been quoted in the newspapers as saying he hoped there would be one.

There had never been much doubt about the outcome of the trial. While being questioned by the police de Sampaio had been unable to give an account of his whereabouts at the time of the killing. His attempts to

439

escape arrest had been pathetic, leaving a panicked trail for the dogs to follow. In his pockets were over two hundred pounds in English currency stolen from Nicola's bag, together with three pastel-coloured, polished stone eggs taken from a collection at Wildwood. Why he should have taken a fancy to them particularly was never explained in court, but Emily had understood. She remembered those eggs. Fortunate must have talked about them. Fortunate was de Sampaio's girl-friend, one of the young men who came over the border looking for work. Usually Alice sent them on their way, but Joseph had needed help in the garden. Later it had become known that he had been dismissed from a farm in Mozambique for drunkenness and petty thieving. Fortunate could not be called as a witness at the trial. She had disappeared into the hills when de Sampaio had been arrested. 'Poor Fortunate's not exactly a great one for conversation, I'm afraid,' Nicola had said. Now she wouldn't have to say anything. At Wildwood the police had found de Sampaio's fingerprints in the drawing room where Alice had found Nicola's body. Explaining the English money he was alleged to have said that Nicola had given it to him when she bought some *mbanje* from him the afternoon before the murder. The *Daily Telegraph* had reported that a ripple of surprise had run around the court at that point. *Mbanje* was the local dope – grass or pot by another name. So de Sampaio was also a drug dealer. It had been a very straightforward case.

Throughout the hearing and trial Alec Reynolds was reported to have sat silently alongside Hudson, joined now in shared grief. Behind them, Pugh the Portrait had written in her letter, 'the servant Joseph sat, tears streaming down his cheeks'. Alice had only attended when called to give evidence. 'They say she blames herself. Nicola's husband has been very attentive to her. Such a lovely young man, a lovely couple. Everyone here thinks so.'

In court Hudson's evidence was the only real hope for

de Sampaio. He had, he said, seen at least three intruders in the vicinity that morning, he watched them while out riding, high on the mountain behind Wildwood. They had been running, he told the court, hurrying in the direction of the border. At the trial he had urged the authorities, through the court, to make every effort to find out who those men had been. But though efforts were made, the men had not been found.

Arriving back for the first time a few days after the initial magistrates' hearing, the tabloid Press had ambushed Hudson at Heathrow Airport wanting to know how he felt. He had not answered and Richard had hurried him through to a waiting taxi, shaken by how gaunt and confused he had looked.

The details of Nicola's and Hudson's last few days had emerged slowly. Wildwood. So beautiful, so remote. Alice excited and giggling, and Fortunate looking from behind her hands at the new bride and her American husband. Somewhere there had been Marco de Sampaio, too, but Hudson had not noticed him at first. Those few days, he told Richard and Emily, had been just wonderful. Everything had been perfect. 'It was like I'd been dealt this incredibly lucky life, that we both had. It was just too perfect to last.'

On the Monday they had gone riding, 'a mosey around the Ponderosa,' as Nicola had put it, although the horse Joseph had arranged for Hudson had been a little on the small side. They had hired a bigger one, complete with an old Western saddle, when they had driven down to Umtali to see Nicola's lawyers the next day. Emily had nodded at that. There had always been lawyers. Nicola had wanted Hudson to get to know them and to sign some papers.

'Joseph drove the horse-box back and we sat in a tea-shop making plans, you know, the way you do. Nicola had decided she wanted to be a publisher, not just as part of *Witness*, but on a much bigger scale. We spent the day planning our future. She was so positive.

We laughed so much. That was the best day. That was . . .' He had paused as he searched for the right word. Then he said simply, '. . . well, I guess that was my life as perfect as it could ever be.'

That was the day they had met Marco de Sampaio, Hudson had said later. He had been with Fortunate as they returned from Umtali, hanging around making her laugh as she pegged out the washing on the line. 'Nicola said she'd never seen Fortunate looking so chirpy before. Like she was really having a good time with the guy. She's very shy . . . right?'

Emily had nodded.

'I guess Alice must have been taking a nap because it seemed to me that she ran the whole house and she'd warned Fortunate to stay away from the guy. That was when Nicola bought the grass. It was no big deal. She just said, "He looks like he knows his way around the town", and went off for a word with him. *Mbanje*, that was what she called it.'

The Wednesday had been their last day together. 'She showed me the tracks through the forest and the mountain-top behind the house where she liked to go. It was so beautiful up there. It seemed like it would be the last place on earth to be tamed, that it had been that way since the beginning of time.

'That night we made dinner ourselves. Alice wanted to do it, but Nicola made a thing about it being our honeymoon, and that even if she didn't necessarily believe in tradition it was the traditional African way that the wife cooked for the husband. We just had a steak and baked potato each and some local wine, maybe too much wine, smoked a little and sat by the log fire.

'The next morning she was still sleeping when I got up. I went up on the mountain again, just after dawn. It was the most incredible sight. Like heaven. The buck at the stream and the birds hovering. It's winter down there and there was a frost. But then the sun got warmer and more and more animals came out to feed. That was when I saw them. They were below me, heading for the border, three of them, running. I didn't think anything of it. I just sat on my pony and watched. I guessed they must have passed right by the house, but there was no reason why they shouldn't, no reason that I knew. I don't know. Maybe they were just passing innocently through, but I saw them up there and I didn't see Marco de Sampaio . . .'

He had ridden on, he said, unsure of his way, and it had been after ten when he had arrived back at Wildwood. He knew something was wrong immediately. He could hear crying as his horse had made its way through the forest. A group of women who worked in the gardens were collected outside the house not knowing what to do. A police car had arrived and Joseph was speaking to two officers. It had been one of the policemen who had broken the news.

The reports in the newspapers had filled in the details. The body had been found in the sitting room by Alice at around nine o'clock. Nicola was wearing the long, white nightdress she had bought for her honeymoon. Death had been instantaneous. The french windows to the garden had been open. If Joseph had been around that side of the house he would have noticed earlier, but he had been busy in his greenhouse. Alice had been in the kitchen with Fortunate.

At first Alice had thought Nicola might have fainted and had attempted to revive her, she and Joseph lifting the body off the carpet on to the sofa.

It had only been at midday when a senior police investigator had arrived from Umtali and asked that all the Wildwood staff should be assembled that Marco de Sampaio was missed. Fortunate could not help. She could scarcely speak, she was so frightened. Two days later, after de Sampaio had been found by sniffer dogs hiding in the forest, Fortunate herself had gone missing.

It had been a milder Alec Reynolds who had returned to Wildwood. He had always prided himself that Wildwood was a safe haven against the world, that if Nicola had

443

stayed she would have a happy fulfilled life, surrounded by people who knew their place. That such violence had reached even Wildwood seemed to him to be the final confirmation that the world he knew had broken down. Despite the brusqueness of his earlier behaviour in London he had, said Hudson, been kind and thoughtful to him. 'He kept saying he wished he had gone to London to see Nicola married. They'd spoken on the phone when we first arrived at Wildwood and she had sounded so happy, he said. He wished he had seen her happy, and been able to be happy with her. He loved her, you know,' Hudson had said sadly. 'Just like the rest of us. In his own way he always meant well for her. He tried to control himself at first, but when he saw Alice he just broke down . . .'

The decision to bury Nicola's body on the mountain had been Hudson's. It was Wildwood land and Alec Reynolds liked the idea of his niece being there rather than in a graveyard. None of them were church-going people, anyway. So, as soon as the court allowed, the body had been reclaimed and taken up on to the mountain. Joseph had dug the grave himself. Many of the local people from Mupangare had come to pay their respects, shocked by what had happened, grateful that the killer had not been from their village. The gravestone had been carved in Umtali. 'Nicola Reynolds, 1943–1967.' She had stayed Nicola Reynolds.

In the small bathroom in Old Church Street, Chelsea, Richard held Emily's hand, her face pressed into his shoulder. She wondered where Hudson was at that moment.

They had married quietly when Emily had discovered she was pregnant. There had been no celebrations, and they had already had their honeymoon in Paris. Daniel and Carol had been the witnesses, the parents the only guests. Hudson would have been there but he had had to be in Rhodesia for the committal proceedings.

According to newspaper reports Marco de Sampaio had not understood when the verdict had been returned. 'Guilty, your honour.' But then as the word and sentence had been translated he had sagged back in the dock as though unable to comprehend what was happening to him.

'Please God, make it easy for him to die,' Emily prayed.

At five-thirty Richard led Emily back to bed. It would have all been over by then.

Chapter Forty-Nine

Witness closed down in the second week of February, 1968. The last issue was devoted to the Tet Offensive and its aftermath. It was a sad day, but there were no tears. The heart had gone out of it over eight months earlier. Ultimately the closure was Hudson's decision, but it came as a surprise to no one. The senior staff had been drifting away to other jobs for months. Even Richard had gone or, to be more accurate, had never properly returned. Although he had remained on the board, and had called into the office several times a week, Penny Chilston had stayed on as acting editor. In the October he had taken a job with the *Guardian*.

Hudson told Penny of his decision one night after everyone else had gone home. He had hardly been seen around for months, calling in to see Adam Smith now and again, but more often having Adam go across to Chepstow Villas for meetings. But arriving late to collect some papers for the following day's board meeting he had found Penny still at her desk.

'I wouldn't bother if I were you,' he said quietly, taking her pen from her hand. 'It isn't your fault. Life has changed for all of us.'

They had dinner together that night, just the two of them. Without Nicola, and with Richard and Emily inseparable as they waited for the baby, Hudson had seemed vaguely at a loss to know what to do. When she had finally plucked up courage and suggested getting a bite to eat he had appeared grateful for her company.

'We could struggle on, but honestly I don't think there's much point,' he told her as they ate. 'Sales have been sluggish and advertising is slow, but I'd be lying to you if I said that was the only reason. To be absolutely honest I really don't have the heart any more.'

'So Charlie Latymer was right?' she said. 'About *Witness* being in difficulties.'

He looked at her. 'No. Not *Witness*. Charlie Latymer told you that?'

She was embarrassed. 'Well, something like that. I think he was just bitter because he didn't think he was being taken seriously enough.'

'You don't remember exactly what he said, do you, Penny?'

'Only something about a cash-flow shortage, and that he was getting out while there was still money to pay the wages. You know what he's like.'

'Yes, I know what he's like,' he said. 'Poor old Charlie.' He shook his head and poured more wine.

She put a hand over her glass. Not too much: she wanted to remember this night.

'It doesn't matter,' he said. 'None of it matters now. The truth is there was a small problem, although it seemed bigger then. Not with *Witness*, but the distributors, and that was making it difficult for us for a while.'

'Farrow and Fox have a problem? I thought they were rolling in it.'

'They had a problem. But I think I've solved it for them.'

'Am I allowed to know how?'

'I've bought them,' he said simply. 'It will be announced at the board meeting tomorrow.'

Penny was puzzled. 'The distribution company or the magazines . . . *Fun and Profit in Greenhouses* and all the rest of them?'

'The whole lot. Everything.' He watched her face. 'You're looking exactly the way Richard did when I told him.'

'But that isn't journalism.'

'Wow, you're such a snob! Just like him. It's the reality of publishing, Penny. Magazines without a mission,

447

the ones ordinary people want to buy. Hobby magazines, do-it-yourself magazines, entertainment magazines, magazines for accountants, race-horse people, stockbrokers. If I can get them right and a lot more like them I'll be able to build a real publishing empire, so that we can do anything we want. Nicola understood that . . .'

The memory of Nicola fell across their conversation again and stilled it for a moment. At last Hudson smiled.

'Look, I don't know if anything we'll be doing after *Witness* will interest you, and somehow I don't see you chomping at the bit to write for *Fun and Profit in Boatbuilding*, but whatever we do you know there'll always be a job if you want one.'

Penny nodded. She knew. And she knew also that Hudson had not found her tonight by accident. He had wanted to let her down lightly. He had always been good at the personal touch.

Chapter Fifty

(i)

The memorial service was Willie's idea. Who else? Hudson had not been enthusiastic but being unable to identify his reasons fully had passed him on to Emily. He would abide by her decision.

'Some of us f..eel that we never s..aid good..bye, if you know what I mean,' he had said, adding that he knew a friendly vicar, who liked the same sort of music as Nicola. That had made Emily frown. 'I don't mean rec..ords, nothing b..rash or vul..gar, but p'raps an organ..ist who's also a B..eatles fan. There are lots of them about, you know. I think it would m..ean quite a b..it to the old gang. And I'm sure Nicola would have loved it.'

Journalists and actors love memorial services. Willie was a bit of both and a good friend. Against her better judgement Emily allowed herself to be persuaded. It would have seemed selfish to say no.

Willie's friendly vicar, a former actor, had his church down an avenue about midway along Ladbroke Grove, a red-brick characterless block of a building, put up in the Thirties, neglected by the Sixties. The chosen day, a chilly April morning which blew sleet among the white apple blossom, would have been Nicola's twenty-fifth birthday. Emily, nine and a half months pregnant and waiting, arrived with Richard by taxi. It was not difficult to spot the church. On the outside wall a local graffiti artist had painted a row of life-size sunflowers in the shape of people, black raisin faces, yellow petals for hair. A new generation of Pith-Helmet and the Dandelions. Nicola would have smiled at that.

Willie was standing on the church steps in a pale green, double-breasted suit, his arms out welcoming, a buxom young Italian film actress at his side. Since the success the previous autumn of his second play, *In Flagrante Delicto*, 'now lash..ing 'em in on Broad..way', he had taken to wearing very expensive, flashy suits. 'It's chea..per and more con..venient than try..ing to have a foll..ow spot acc..ompany one through life.'

'Are you all right?' Richard asked Emily as the taxi drew to a halt.

She looked down at the large, uncomfortable swell of her stomach pushing through the one decent maternity dress she had bought herself. 'I'm fine, but you'd better have hot water and towels ready, I think,' she said, heaving herself up.

They were all waiting, all the *Witness* network, Adam Smith, Berridge with the Mascara, Gimmelmann with Jenny Quinn, his pretty new girl-friend, Charlie Latymer, glowing like the television star he was becoming, and, of course, Penny; then there was the entire staff of Mama Vecchi's, the barman from the Portobello, young journalists just starting out, some actor friends of Willie's Nicola had charmed at various parties, people Nicola had written about, even friends from Oxford, never thought about in years, and a couple of smart young ladies with high ringing voices who introduced themselves as old schoolfriends from Highfield House. Emily's mother was away, staying with her sister, but Daniel came with a new blonde, and Richard's sister, Carol, brought some spring flowers from the garden at Wimbledon.

Hudson arrived almost last, the red Alvis pulling up across the road as Emily and Richard were about to go into the church. Climbing from his car Hudson stared without smiling at the group of friends on the steps. His face was thinner these days. At that moment Emily wished she had stood up to Willie.

Together they filed into the church, Willie putting an arm around Hudson who entered last. It was a small, friendly place inside, shabby certainly, and definitely low church, the only symbolism being a single wooden cross standing on a dais at the front.

Without quite knowing what expression to wear Emily, with Richard at her side, made her way down the short central aisle. She felt enormous and awkward and wished that she might slip into the first row of seats she reached, but the vicar, recognizing the VIPs, beckoned them to the vacant front row. Sliding into the pew she sat back, adjusting her weight carefully. On one side of her was Richard, on the other, Hudson.

What was it, religion, show business or a feast of sentiment? And did it matter, anyway? Willie as organizer had appointed himself both artistic director and priest for the morning, his friendly vicar stepping to one side to turn the pages for the young musician at the Hammond electric organ who, as soon as Emily and Hudson had sat down, had begun to play.

Emily hung her head, trying to imagine what Nicola would have made of it all. Would she have giggled at the theatrical solemnity? Or would she have hummed along? That was more likely. She felt a muscle tightening in her stomach and slipped her hand inside her coat.

The music came to an end and Willie moved to a lectern which stood to one side of the cross. Gravely he smoothed back his hair.

'Nicola Reynolds was not, so far as I am aware, a religious person.' It was his fluent actor's voice. 'I'm not even sure that she believed in God. But what I do know beyond any doubt is that she believed in her friends.'

Around her Emily felt the gentle evangelical murmur of agreement. This was what they had come to hear.

Willie smiled: 'Nicola loved her friends, as I think every one of us here has very good reason to remember.'

Another nodding of heads.

'So may I put this thought to you all, believers and non-believers. If God is Love, then is it not possible that Love is God?'

Well intentioned as it was Emily knew that at this point Nicola would have bitten her lip. The Hippy Gospel according to Saint Willie, she thought. Well, God bless him for trying. At the pit of her stomach the ache pulsed again.

(ii)

In the aisle seat of the fifth row, just about central so that everyone could get a good view of him, Charles Latymer contemplated his skin. Before leaving home that morning he had given himself a quick flash with a sunray lamp and was feeling slightly toasted. He hoped it didn't show too much. The white rings around the eyes where the goggles had been worn were something of a give-away. Better not to make a habit of this: dried-out, wrinkled skin was so unattractive.

It was nice to see that Hudson bore him no grudge. He'd hardly been telling tales out of school, anyway. After all he'd got Fiske-Forrester into *Witness*, the least he could do was keep them informed if Farrow and Fox looked like going under. Neil Fiske, his cardigan showing around the dandruff-dusted collar of his suit, was sitting in front of him. As Nicola's only heir Hudson was now a very valued client to Fiske-Forrester. The old deal had been settled. Now the word was that Fiske-Forrester were to be large investors in the new Hudson Publications which was sprouting out of the rump of *Witness* and the remains of Farrow and Fox's *Fun and Profit* line. Naturally Richard had been given a neat little slice of the new company. Equally naturally no one remembered how he had got Hudson and Fiske-Forrester together in the first place. Latymer frowned bitterly and his burnt skin cracked. He wished he had a mirror handy. He had a feeling his nose might be turning pink. If that little rat-skull Berridge noticed it would be all over the *Daily Sketch* tomorrow. He looked down the aisle at Hudson. Such a tall man, good-looking, too, he supposed, in that even-featured, bland American kind of way. And now, apparently, quite a wealthy man. He had sold Nicola's Notting Hill Gate house without ever moving in. Funny how no one ever got to meet any of his family. They were supposed to be worth a bob or two themselves. Small-town American wealth, though. Hardly the real stuff. The music ended, and, Oh God, Willie was on his feet again.

(iii)

He hadn't expected her to put in an appearance, and it would be hardly likely that she would even know about the memorial service, but, all the same, Tim Gimmelmann was relieved that there was no sign of Holly. It would have been certainly within her warped view of the world to turn up and make some sort of scene. Not like little Jenny Quinn, neat as a pin, in the pew at his side.

He hadn't seen Holly since she had walked out leaving his home a wreck, although he had heard about her from time to time. For a while she had been said to turn up regularly at various London nightclubs where the latest rock musicians would gather after midnight to see what they could pull. The story was that half the names in the current top forty had had Holly, an exaggeration, obviously, but an indication, too. There were other stories. One of the hairdressers had heard that she was selling it again occasionally: she had always liked that, and he remembered the miserable few pounds with which she had returned those afternoons in Kentish Town, a smug expression on her face, as though she had got something for nothing.

At his side he could smell Jenny Quinn's mouthwash as she mouthed the words to the songs. She was so clean. She was never going to catch the moment as Holly had done, but with that bone structure she could work till she was virtually middle-aged. Just so long as she didn't say anything. She could embarrass him then. Holly hadn't embarrassed him. That wouldn't have been the word. Not embarrass. But she'd always puzzled him.

Somebody had told him that she was dabbling with heroin these days. He thought it likely. He had been right about her career. Her agent had dropped her, and no self-respecting photographers were interested. People said she looked so terrible these days she wasn't worth the film.

In the front row Hudson was resting his chin in his hand. Hudson had always been wary of her, never been taken in by the come-on smile into the lens. Holly had said that she frightened him. That was a boast, really. She boasted a lot, and she lied a lot. 'Why don't you ask me about Hudson and me then?' she had baited. 'Don't you want to know? You'd like it if you knew. Come on, I dare you. Can you face it? Or are you too jealous? What is it? D'you want him all for yourself or something? You can't hide it, you know. It don't matter what you do with Jenny Quinn and all the others, locked doors in the studio and everything else. You can't fool me. I know what you really want.'

He forced his mind away. God, what a bitch. She wasn't fit to breathe the same air as Hudson.

Hudson. He was wiping away a tear with the back of his hand. Gimmelmann could see it quite clearly. He'd never expected Hudson to show emotion. He was always so much in control. That was why he knew she'd been lying about him. That was what he liked about him.

He'd been in the studio when he'd heard about Nicola's death, a borrowed studio in Islington, doing pictures for a swimwear advertisement for a Dutch company. He hadn't known how he felt when the assistant had shown him the story in the newspaper. Not exactly sad: that wasn't it. He had never been very close to Nicola, not like Willie and some of the others. She was too posh for him. It was more a matter of astonishment that it should have happened to someone he knew. Of course, he had to feel sorry for Hudson.

Richard had been aware of the hand going to Hudson's eye, but he had not turned to look. He wanted this service, with its piping organ sounds and Willie's wandering oration, to be over soon. He wanted to restart their lives from this moment on, and much as they had all loved Nicola, to draw a line under her and begin again. Nicola would have understood that. She was always the merry realist.

A final tune was playing. He recognized it, the Beatles' *In My Life*. At his side Emily winced. He looked at her. She took his hand.

Relief. The last in, they were the first out, the entire congregation waiting while they promenaded down the aisle. Out on to the steps they went, looking for their waiting taxi. Behind them Hudson shook hands and thanked everyone for coming.

'I think we should go straight to St Mary Abbot's Hospital,' Richard told the driver as he helped Emily into the cab. Her suitcase was already packed and waiting.

The cab driver looked nervously at them both.

'It'll be all right, provided you don't take the scenic route, or go over any large bumps,' Emily smiled, and then whispered to Richard: 'At least I hope so.'

Smoothly, quickly, the cab pulled away from the red-brick church. Looking back through the rear window the last Richard saw of that part of his life was Hudson's arm held high to them as they raced away. Good luck, he seemed to be saying. Good luck.

Being a first baby she took her time, but, after an eighteen-hour labour, Catherine Nicola Blake was born at five thirty-nine the following morning.

PART SEVEN
August 1982

Chapter Fifty-One

(i)

Emily lay on her beach mat and weathered the sharp sting of the sand as it blew against her skin. It had been blowing all afternoon, but being English they put up with it as stoically as they endured the heat on stiller days. Closing her eyes the thunder of the sea filled her senses. Close by she could hear the shouts of Benedict and Tom as they hurled themselves on to their inflatable bedboat, as it bobbed and turned on the incoming tide. Alongside vibrations of rhythm leaked from Catherine's headphones. Earlier in the summer Hudson had returned from a trip to Chicago bringing each of the children an electronic gift: Benedict had been given a computer chess set, Tom, a small music synthesizer and Catherine, the latest craze, Sony Walkman headphones. It was an invention of genius, Richard had announced. At a stroke the decibel level in their home had been halved. Now, bored with the boisterous energy of her brothers, Catherine was blocking out the world.

Emily loved these summer holidays, a couple of weeks washed up on a foreign beach with a pile of books and no distractions outside the family. They had done it for thirteen years in succession, since they had taken Catherine as a one year old to a primitive camp site in Brittany. Now they were better off, well-off even, and the holiday homes they rented were more than comfortable – this year's, an ancient farmhouse in south-west France, had its own tennis court, pool, fields and forest.

As usual Emily had taken the children ahead of Richard, who would never miss more than one week's edition. On Sunday morning they would drive to Bordeaux to meet him off the plane, all talking at once, excited to see him, Richard saying how amazingly tanned they were, the children telling him of the house, the beach and the forest: Emily smiling, quiet as ever, happy to see him.

The beach today was almost deserted and they had chosen the most sheltered spot near a small plantation of pine trees. It wasn't particularly hot, but it was pleasant and private.

Easing herself on to her elbows Emily watched her sons playing together. Benedict was now twelve and Tom was ten. They were engrossed in a game of adventure, sitting together with their legs over the side of the bedboat so that it sank in the middle, paddling with their hands, pretending they were being pursued by crocodiles. 'Look out, Tom, there's one behind you,' Benedict called as they passed a tangle of seaweed, and the younger boy kicked out hard with his foot and hands, making machine-gun noises. 'All right, got it. Watch out for the killer whales.' So it went on as they splashed and kicked, fell off the bedboat and climbed back on again, laughing and shivering in the surf. She wished she could keep them at this age. They were so beautiful and undemanding. So uncomplicated. Catherine, two years older, was at a stage when she could not decide whether she wanted to play with her brothers, hide in a book, moon about after a French boy she had seen (but not spoken to) further down the beach, or disappear into her music. She already had choices, was aware of herself.

Dusting the sand from her thighs Emily considered her body, her shape now rounder, slightly more comfortable than it had been. Thirty-nine was a good age to be. It had all worked out for them, and she was grateful.

Not everyone had been so lucky. She and Richard were at the age when surviving marriages had become the exception. The Tarlos were still together, naturally, and now had five studious children, but, after years of disguising the bruises, Jenny had left Tim Gimmelmann. She had kept the girls and moved into a modern town house in Kew, while Gimmelmann, whose studio complex with Hudson was said to be making him extremely wealthy, was renovating a house in Little Venice. There were rumours about Gimmelmann. Willie Simmonds had been through the divorce courts too, although, in his case, with absolutely no acrimony. With a diminishing theatrical originality he had finally gone to Hollywood where he was now living with a nineteen-year-old dancer in a Malibu house once owned by Truman Capote, driving a Pontiac Trans Am and writing screenplays adapted from current bestsellers (or, more frequently, rewriting other people's screenplays). His was, by all accounts, a life of easy style and occasional depravity. Everyone had always liked Willie, not least his ex-wives and mistresses who were said to meet regularly to exchange, with increasing hilarity, stories of his infidelities and excuses.

For Emily it all seemed very remote. Hers had been a sedate and orderly progression through growing children and schools, from Richard's tiny two rooms in Chelsea, to a garden flat in Fulham and then eventually the house near Holland Park which had become their family home. *Witness* had paid for that, or, more accurately, Richard's small shareholding, which, when *Witness* had closed down, had become an even smaller slice of Hudson Magazines. Hudson had wanted to lend Richard the money for the deposit on the house, advising him to hang on to his shares, but that had never been Richard's way. He didn't like favours, especially not financial ones. So Hudson had bought him out and Richard and Emily had set to work to build their life together.

Compared with some of their friends it was a life which must have seemed dull. Emily could see that. While Hudson Magazines had continued to expand, and the wealth Hudson had inherited from Nicola to multiply, Richard had worked steadily at the *Guardian*, climbing the ladders of responsibility, before moving on

461

to *The Sunday Times* and eventually to *Sunday Morning*. But, to Emily, it was a life as rich as any she could have dreamed.

A lull in the boys' shouts prompted her to sit up. They were quite safe, now busy digging a canal to take the incoming waves. She marvelled at their energy. They played harder than most people worked. She checked her watch. It was nearly four, almost time for the Wednesday afternoon conference when that week's *Sunday Morning* would be shaped. She imagined Richard sitting at his desk surrounded by his army of assistants which, like *Sunday Morning* itself, grew ever larger, doggedly going over some small point, determined to get it right, and the uncomfortable shuffling in their chairs of those who had got it wrong. 'You shouldn't take it so personally,' Hudson would chide when Richard would become irate about sloppiness in some parts of the paper. But he couldn't take it any other way.

At her side the tiny metallic crashing of disco music reverberated from Catherine's headphones. Catherine had been so thrilled with the Walkman, not just for itself but because Hudson had given it to her. Hudson. He had always been there, a part of the family, godfather to all the children, popping in unexpectedly whenever he felt like it, a frequent guest for Sunday lunch, and a regular fixture at Christmas, when he always insisted upon buying and helping dress the Christmas tree. There had, over the years, been many women, a league table of handsome, bright, well-connected ladies, but their presence in his life had always been kept discreet, hidden from the children's eyes, sheltered almost from Emily herself. The exception had been Dominique Fayence. That had been public and unpleasant. Latymer should have realized: one way or another Hudson always got even. When the affair had cooled, so had Latymer's marriage, Dominique eventually going to live with a younger man who interviewed on a late-night BBC 2 news programme. Characteristically, Latymer's reaction had been more one of indignation than hurt. He still had his job, his chauffeur, his salary and his perks. Perhaps in his own view he still had status. No doubt he was useful to Hudson but there was no denying that a peculiar kind of revenge had been exacted, as though all along Hudson had been keeping a register of the loyal and disloyal.

It was the one side of Hudson Emily did not like to contemplate, so seemingly out of character for so generous a man. Emily knew all about Hudson's generosity. As chairman of the Hudson Foundation board of trustees she saw the ever-increasing flow of money which was being funnelled into educational grants for schools and colleges. While the heads of other organizations laboured to create wealth and become rich, Hudson worked so that he would have more to give away. 'Every bad deal I do, Emily, means less goes into the pot for the Foundation, so I'm going to be the meanest son of a bitch there ever was,' he would tell her, grinning widely. He wasn't, but his business ambitions were never satisfied, and, completely absorbed in the making of money, he left it to the Foundation to decide how to spend it.

Catherine was now rubbing Ambre Solaire on to her legs and watching her brothers' excitement as the ocean rushed into their canal, crumbling the sides as it came.

Go on, join them, Emily willed her daughter silently. Be immature. Enjoy a last summer before adolescence consumes you completely. Be a child for just a little while longer. It's such a short time.

Such a short time and Richard was missing so much of it. Fathers did. Again she imagined him, walking around the office now, his eyebrows furrowed behind his glasses, a few pounds heavier than when they had first met, his hair greying, thinning slightly on the crown. She was looking forward to his arrival. That was when the holiday would really begin.

Carefully Catherine took off her headphones and wound the wires around the Sony Walkman. Then getting to her feet she walked across to her brothers and sank down on her knees beside them.

Emily lay back and closed her eyes. Richard would be pleased. He didn't want her to grow up too quickly.

(ii)

Through his telephoto lens the photographer could clearly see the red bandanna of the Palestinian on the roof of the apartment block fifty yards away. He knew the man, he was certain. He had chatted with him only a few days earlier at a PLO check-point, a bright, laughing fellow who spoke reasonable English and had been singing a popular song to himself. He had cadged a cigarette from them, wanting to see what cameras the photographer was carrying, enquiring about the lenses he used: a normal everyday conversation. He wished he could remember his name. Penny Chilston would be able to, but Penny was on the other side of Beirut at the Barbir Hospital which had been hit by shellfire earlier in the day.

That morning, after weeks of siege, the Israelis had begun shelling and bombing Muslim West Beirut, where the Palestinian Liberation Organization had their head-quarters, low-flying F-16 fighter-bombers racing across the city. And though it was useless the PLO were shooting back.

The photographer stared at the apartment block. It was one of the highest on the street, a blitzed wreck, shell-holed and windowless, a crazily exposed place to be used for an anti-aircraft battery, but it offered a good view south over Beirut, particularly the Palestinian camps of Chatila and Sabra.

Stepping back inside the lobby of the office building in which he had been sheltering he looked around for Harry Byam, an American colleague from the Associated Press news agency. Byam was on his knees changing rolls of film. Around him a group of Lebanese waited silently

464

as they listened to the moaning of the earth under the weight of the bombing.

'I want to get up and see it all from the PLO position,' the photographer said, indicating the roof-top.

'What?' Byam looked up from his camera. 'You're out of your mind. Those guys are sitting ducks.'

'They've got a terrific overview of the city. They'll know what's really going on. And you don't get pictures of PLO operating anti-aircraft batteries in Beirut every day.'

Byam snorted. 'Right. And you know why? Because they're not good at it. They can't take on the Israeli Air Force. They've got pea-shooters up there.'

'Are you coming?'

'Do I look like a fool? No, I'm not coming, and don't you go, either. It's too dangerous.'

As if to emphasize the danger a bomb rumbled close by and an old Lebanese lady, who was carefully holding a box containing a set of crockery, uttered what sounded like a prayer.

The photographer shook his head. 'I don't think so. They're aiming at the camps. The pilots probably haven't even noticed that they're being fired at.'

'They know. They'll do something about it. We'd be better off on the sea front or maybe over at the hospital with Penny.'

The photographer didn't want to hear this. From outside came the sound of anti-aircraft fire. He knew where he was going. 'OK, you go to the hospital. I'll meet you both there later,' he said, and without waiting for further discussion slipped out of the lobby.

From the roof-top down the street the boy in the bandanna seemed to be beckoning him.

'For Christ's sake, Rob . . .' was the last he heard from Harry Byam as he ran along the side of the pavement in the shelter of the shell-pocked buildings, his Billingham fishing bag over one shoulder, a Nikon around his neck.

The street was deserted, everyone seeking shelter of

some kind, and he quickly covered the fifty yards to the building. The doorway was unguarded. Inside what had once been the foyer of a modern apartment block had been reduced to broken rubble. He began to make his way up the stairs. This was his second visit to Beirut. He had missed its great days. All he had seen there had been death and confusion, Palestinians, Phalangists, Syrians, Israelis and dozens of splinter groups, all seeking influence, settling scores.

He trotted cautiously up the first flight of steps. Without electricity it was quite dark, apart from on the open landings, and he did not wish to give anyone an unnecessary surprise. There were too many jumpy people in Beirut.

He and Penny Chilston had arrived by taxi from Damascus four days earlier, hungry to capture the city under siege. Before that he had endured six weeks of frustration in the Falklands War, mainly confined aboard the aircraft-carrier HMS *Hermes*. His work had been disappointing. Beirut represented a new chance to prove himself and he was pleased to be working with Penny again. She was a good bloke, frightened of nobody and, now that she had given up the drink, she wrote with a rare compassion, not just for those under attack, but for the attackers, the gunmen and the bombers. 'They have their point of view, too,' she would say. All the same, he was glad that she had decided to go to the hospital that morning. Had she been with him she would probably have talked him out of what he was now doing.

He climbed on. It was a ten-storey building and appeared empty other than for the men on the roof. Presumably the unfortunate people who lived there had taken shelter elsewhere when their home was requisitioned for an anti-aircraft battery. Somewhere across the city he felt and heard the rumble of another bomb and stopped, one hand resting on the wall. He was out of breath and frightened. He was always frightened. His shirt, with its many bulging pockets, was heavy and

466

damp with sweat, smeared in dust. Something Clover had said to him when she had finally ended their relationship played in a corner of his mind. 'The thing about you, Rob, is you get too involved. You're supposed to be a journalist, with a detached view of the world, but you're really just a sponge for every bleeding heart you can find.' And with that she had coolly detached her life from his. It had never been much more than semi-detached, anyway.

He pushed on up the rubble-strewn steps. On the fifth landing he found a girl of about seven standing with her mother, who was carrying a baby. They were staring out from the glassless window across the smoking city. The child was holding a small black-and-white rabbit. They turned and watched him approach, saying nothing. From above he could hear the sound of shouting in Arabic. Putting his Nikon to his eye, he dropped on to one knee, and pressed the shutter, once, twice, three times. The girl gazed unsmiling into the lens.

Suddenly he became stern, and, waving his arms, indicated that the woman must get her children out of the building as quickly as possible, pointing away down the street. 'Not safe here, not safe here,' he insisted. 'You go. Go. Go now. Right.' The woman understood. Wearily she put an arm around the child's shoulders and together they began their descent.

The photographer watched until they reached the next landing. Then, satisfied that they were leaving, he picked his way over a stained, abandoned mattress and continued his climb.

(iii)

Cold watercress soup, poached salmon, mangetout, wild mushrooms, new potatoes, strawberries, grapes, five different cheeses, two chilled bottles of a good Chablis . . . Clover Merrifield prepared for sex as carefully as she wrote. Dinner for two, her living-room table cleared of her books and typewriter, her kitchen warm from bubbling soup. She opened the window to the garden to allow in some fresh air and a passing Underground train caused some wine glasses on a tray to vibrate slightly. In the living room some Chopin played quietly on the record player. '*I'm always chasing rainbows . . .*' she sang along to herself.

London in August. Thin newspapers, muggy weather, too many people away, and not a lot to do. But for Clover it was not a bad time at all.

She stirred the soup thoughtfully, deciding upon what she should wear. She had left the office early in order to prepare dinner, to plan the rhythm of the evening. These things took a little effort if they were to be done properly. She enjoyed making an occasion. There was even champagne in the refrigerator. She frowned. No, not champagne. It might look too celebratory. It was, after all, only an affair.

She would wear blue, she thought: a flimsy, blue, loose, floral summer dress. Very feminine. She liked to dress up: single and well paid she could afford to. She had always been successful, right from university, but now she held more than promise. She was a clever journalist, one of *Sunday Morning*'s established star writers. Four years on and the offers were coming in from other newspapers. There was even interest from television.

She turned off the gas under the soup and going through into the tiny bathroom began to run the water. She would lie and soak and mentally prepare her evening. Let's face it, Clover, she told herself, half the fun in life is anticipation. She smiled. What was that line about adultery being the only game two adults can play that two children can't? But, of course, she wasn't married.

(*iv*)

He had been wrong about the bandanna. It was not worn by the boy he had met at the check-point, but

468

someone quite different, an older man with a bad skin condition. It did not matter. There were four of them on the roof with their AK-19s and their anti-aircraft gun, which they must have carried up the ten flights of stairs piece by piece. He wondered if they had stolen it from the Syrian army.

They had not heard him coming, although he had shouted to warn them several times. But when he had stepped out on to the flat, hot roof their expressions, though surprised, had been not unfriendly. It excited and pleased them to have someone to record their part in the battle for West Beirut. Perhaps they thought he would bring them luck. They knew this was a dangerous place to be. He knew it was an insane place to be.

As if to confirm his fears, almost as he had reached the roof a bomber had streaked overhead shaking the building with its vibrations. The pilot must have had a clear view of them, the photographer thought, as the jet raced away eastwards towards the mountains and the Bekaa Valley. How could they miss us? How could these boys be so brave? Or were they just foolish?

On a clear day the view from the roof would have taken in all of Southern Beirut to the International Airport, near which the Israeli tanks and guns were drawn up, west out to the sea and eastwards up to the hills. But this was a day of guns and bombing, of dust and smoke, fire and noise, and, down there in the camps and in the streets, of blood.

Across the city ambulance sirens and fire engines whined in despair.

The four young men waited for the next bombers, staring skywards, shaking their heads. They were unshaven and dark, with thick, wavy hair: their uniform of jeans and shirts and sweat an outward testament of their machismo. While they waited the photographer took some wide shots of the burning city. A column of smoke rose from the direction of Fakhani where the PLO had their headquarters, and others from the main camp at

Bourj Al Barajineh. In an hour it would be almost dark: then the sky of West Beirut would be glowing pink. He had noticed it before: war is good for sunsets.

'A sponge for every bleeding heart . . .' She'd been standing in her basement living room, her arms folded across her chest, irritated, he knew, that he had turned up unexpectedly. She had been seeing somebody else that evening. They had gone nowhere in four years and he wondered why he had tried so hard. No, that wasn't true. He knew why he had tried so hard. The choice had never been his.

Two of the young men were staring down anxiously towards the PLO camps as though trying to ascertain exactly which areas had been hit. Standing just behind he photographed them as they pointed at the distant, soaring banks of smoke. 'Perhaps his house . . .' the man with the bad skin and bandanna explained in English.

Calmly they waited for the next attack. This was when he could have left, when he could have scrambled back down the flights of stairs to the relative safety of the street. But he stayed.

When they came the two F-16s were almost on them before they could be heard, screaming low across the sea and out of the sun. This was the moment the photographer had wanted. Three of the young men turned to man their gun, the other loosing off his automatic in impotent rage at the heavens. Dropping down on to his chest the photographer framed the group of young men firing up into the sky. As the first plane streaked overhead they swung their heads to watch it go.

The bomb fell from the second plane. They heard it for only a fraction of a moment as it rushed towards them. The photographer was gripping his camera, his finger down, for automatic shot after shot after shot.

It seemed so familiar to him, the flash, the weightlessness, the explosion in his head, the roar, the pictures. 'I am not a thief. I can use this garden. It is permitted.' A young albino boy holding out a camera. 'I do not think it is broken. It will still take cards.'

And then the darkness.

(v)

Penny Chilston saw the bomb. Sitting in the back of a car behind two Agence France correspondents she happened to turn at the moment it dropped out of the sky, perhaps half a mile away. The shock wave of the explosion seemed almost to lift the car. The concrete building crumbled in a vast puff of smoke and dust. 'My God . . .'

(vi)

They saw it on the late news: a picture of the photographer smiling into the camera, taken at Heathrow upon his return to London after the Mupangare massacre, and the bleak announcement. 'Among the dead was prize-winning Australian war photographer, Rob Barnes, who was covering the war for the newspaper *Sunday Morning*. An American colleague from the Associated Press news agency said Barnes had been taking pictures of a PLO anti-aircraft position on the roof of an apartment block when it had suffered a direct hit by an Israeli bomb . . .'

She had switched on the television at his request, pretending to complain that he found the news more alluring than her, and he had kissed her and fondled her thighs as she had flicked through the channels.

They had missed the headlines and joined the report halfway through the lead item on the Israelis' push into West Beirut. The news of the photographer's death came at the end of the main Lebanon battle story.

He felt it, he was sure he felt the raw punch of shock. His heart seemed to crash into his ribs. The air stuck motionlessly in his lungs. Alongside in the bed Clover gasped and made a small cry. They leaned

471

forward to see, to hear better, Clover searching for the remote control, the sheets falling from their bodies. '. . . Barnes, who won prizes for his work in the Rhodesian War and later in Nicaragua and Belfast, was twenty-seven. He was unmarried.'

It had been a forbidden evening, and all the more delightful because of that. There had been others, but this had been the first time she had made dinner for him. The other occasions had been chance opportunities, the first after a retirement party in a Smithfield wine bar for Barney, the chief sub-editor, when everyone had had too much to drink and the act which he had vacantly imagined had come to pass with an ease which had later astonished him. He had not wanted an affair and had not pursued one. That first night had been an aberration, he had told himself. But there had been other aberrations as new occasions had presented themselves, a two-day conference on newspapers in Barcelona, an almost-by-chance meeting in New York, and a handful of times back at her flat, after extended lunches. It had all been infrequent enough for him to convince himself that it was not an affair, hardly even a fling, in fact, perfectly normal behaviour for a man of his age and in his position. And because Emily had never suspected, because no one else had known and because he had become middle-aged and familiar with the thousand compromises of everyday life, conscience had never been given a chance. He had even cheated the photographer without guilt.

The news report moved on to other subjects. He could not speak. Slowly Clover began to cry. He did not look at her, did not even put a hand out to comfort her. He had known that Rob Barnes took unacceptable risks. He had warned him about them. But he had praised the photographs which came from those risks. Did that make him an accessory to his death?

The telephone at Clover's bedside began to ring. She did not answer it. Dressing, Richard went into the kitchen for a glass of water. The remains of the evening

472

were piled in the sink. On the living-room table lay the last of the meal. They had broken off before finishing dinner when desire had got the better of them. The grapes were untouched.

The telephone rang again and again. At last Clover answered it. The caller was the deputy editor, Stephen Symes. He had only just been told himself. He was so sorry that she should have heard in such a way. 'Normally they give us a tip-off to call close relatives,' he told her. 'Something must have gone wrong.'

Clover did not cry for long. Richard watched her as she composed herself. She wanted him to stay, but he needed to leave. He felt dirty. He knew what she had meant to Barnes. Everyone had known. The poor chap had been the joke of the office.

Before he left he kissed her, dutiful lips to her forehead, his hands cradling her face, then, promising to call her first thing in the morning, he let himself out of the flat.

There were almost a dozen messages on his answering machine when he arrived home. Everyone wanted to help; Hudson called asking for details. At three o'clock he managed to get through to Penny Chilston in Beirut. With her went any slim hopes of mistaken identity. She had seen the photographer's body, or what remained of it, lying in the wreckage. She was surprisingly calm.

Just before five he put in a call to the photographer's parents in Sydney; the pictures editor had come up with the number some hours earlier.

They had already heard. There were, the father said, Press and television on the front lawn. They had drawn the curtains. He had been fighting to control his voice. He couldn't help but feel sorry for Rob's girl-friend, he said. They'd been told a lot about her. Then he thanked Richard for telephoning.

At eight Hudson phoned again. 'We'll do everything we can for the parents, Richard, in terms of financial help . . . not that money's much help, I know, but it's the only thing we can offer. And we're arranging for the body . . . it'll be flown home to Australia, if that's what they want. Anything they want, really, we'll do it for them.' The youth club over at Hudson Communications was already efficiently organizing.

Richard was still in his study when Emily phoned from France at just after eight-thirty. She had just heard the news on the BBC World Service. He had not slept. He had been looking out over their small, green London garden, remembering the first time he had had sex, that first night out with Hudson. Solveig, the Norwegian girl who had been so casually unfaithful to her fiancé. Sex and betrayal. He had once been betrayed, and now he had betrayed.

'I'm so sorry, Richard. Really.' Emily's voice was kind and gentle. So trusting. She asked questions, wanting to talk about what had happened, but his answers were dull and confused.

He could sense her suspicions growing as they spoke. He had never been able to hide anything from her. Finally she said, very softly: 'Was he, Rob Barnes . . . was he still seeing Clover Merrifield?'

'Erm . . . well, I . . . I don't know.' He could feel his cheeks burning. 'I mean, why should I . . . ?'

There was a long pause before she said: 'You don't mention her much any more, you see.'

Chapter Fifty-Two

It was a long time since Tim Gimmelmann had seen Hudson in such a mood; perhaps he had never seen him like this. He had been summoned by Hudson's personal assistant, Annabel, to present himself at The Boltons at four o'clock, but when he had arrived, prompt as always, he had been asked to wait a while. Sitting in the ante-room with the two secretarial assistants outside Annabel's office, trying to count the assortment of that week's magazines on display from Hudson Communications, he had become aware of a piano playing in the room above, a soulful, bluesy piano, from which gospel chords echoed down the stairs and around the ice rink that was the hall.

'Is that Hudson?' he asked one of the sentries.

'He sometimes plays to himself,' came the reply as the girl hardly lifted her eyes from her word processor.

'Does he know I'm here?' he asked, slightly irritated.

'Sorry?' The girl looked up coolly from her keyboard. Thinking better of it he shook his head and went back to counting the magazines. He didn't mind waiting a while. Just so long as he was in time to meet Edward after rehearsals. He was so proud of him. Mercutio was such an explosive part. Perfect for Edward. He wondered what Hudson would think of him. He was sure he would like him. Perhaps when they got settled in to Little Venice they could ask Hudson and one of his ladies around for dinner one evening. He might even like to see the play first. That would be nice.

Hudson was still sitting at the small white piano when Annabel led Gimmelmann into the sitting room. It always seemed a bit bare to Gimmelmann's taste, and enormous. He couldn't understand why Hudson had never got around to finishing it off. Annabel put a list of telephone messages and letters for signing on to the piano and then left them. Hudson continued to play, putting out a hand to take Gimmelmann's, indicating a chair.

Gimmelmann waited. On a wide glass table in the centre of the room was a large-scale model of the new mirror-walled Hudson Communications centre which was already under construction on the Thames just beyond Chelsea Creek. It was an extraordinarily precise model, right down to the clutch of satellite dishes on the roof and the dinky Hudson Communications distribution vans lining up outside, waiting to rush *Night And Day, Sunday Morning* and all the other publications off around the country. God knows how Hudson was going to square the new technology with the unions, he thought. But he would. He always found a way.

He looked back towards Hudson, wondering for how long he would want to play. That black-and-white photograph still hung above the piano. He remembered the day he had taken it. Nicola had been in a giddy mood, refusing to take him seriously, and he had become irritated. He preferred photographing models, they did as they were told: Nicola had found the whole thing a great joke. 'Oh, come on, Tim, surely that's enough. There must be one amongst that lot where I don't look too gruesome,' she'd said as he had reloaded his camera.

'It's a serious job taking pictures,' he had chastised sullenly. He hadn't asked to take her picture. He'd only been doing it as a favour to Hudson.

Through the viewfinder he had seen her giddiness dissolve. There had never been any harm in her. 'I'm sorry, Tim. I'm being silly. Of course it's a serious job. I suppose I'm a bit embarrassed,' she had apologized.

She'd been as good as gold after that. But when he'd looked at his contacts after the session he'd realized that it hadn't mattered whether she behaved or not. Her face ad been so full of life. Though she was careless about clothes and forgetful of make-up, she had been one of those girls who are beautiful without trying. In the end the picture Hudson had selected had been the first shot.

Hudson caught him looking at it, and stopped playing. 'What do you think, Tim, does that capture her, the way she was?' He didn't wait for an answer. 'I think it does. I saved them all, you know. Everything you ever took of her. Sometimes at night when I couldn't sleep I'd go through them wondering if I could find one I preferred. But I never did.'

'She was easy to photograph,' Gimmelmann replied. It was only half a lie.

'Peter Berridge was telling me that Richard and Emily ... well, that Richard and Clover Merrifield ...' he didn't finish. Hudson had never found it easy to gossip.

Gimmelmann knew what he was talking about, and that he was being asked to confirm or deny. Apparently everyone at *Sunday Morning* knew about the affair, only Richard believing it to be a secret. 'I don't think it's serious,' he said.

Hudson looked at him for a long time, so long that Gimmelmann had to turn away. At last he said: 'It's always serious.'

A shadow of another life fell between them, Holly gloating up at Gimmelmann from black sheets, her white skin almost glowing in the morning light. He had heard her enter the flat in Chalcot Crescent, she'd slammed the door to make certain he heard, and then she had made an elaborate ritual of undressing in front of the window, sliding her blouse and skirt from her body, one eye in the mirror to make sure he was watching.

Hudson's right hand idled over the piano keys again. 'I loved Emily once,' he said. 'No, that isn't true. I've always loved Emily. Richard, too. I thought they were perfect together.'

'Is anything perfect?' Gimmelmann asked, embarrassed slightly. Hudson stopped playing. 'Yes. I think so. Perfect until we ruin it. We always spoil it for ourselves. Don't ask me why. Perhaps that's what they mean by original sin. It seems to be in us. Some flaw that makes us destroy the best things we have. Greed, desire . . . fear, sometimes, I suppose.' He stood up and, closing the piano, walked to the back of the room and looked down at the garden. 'Did you know the photographer who was killed in Beirut?' he asked.

'I think I may have bumped into him a couple of times. Someone pointed him out, but we didn't speak.'

Hudson was hardly listening to his reply. 'He went to Wildwood, you know.'

'Wildwood?' Gimmelmann had no idea what he was talking about.

'Nicola's old house. In Rhodesia. Wildwood. He stayed the night there. Broke in and slept there three or four years ago when he was hiding out from the guerrillas . . .'

'Ah.'

Again a silence fell between them. Hudson was still such a handsome man, even at moments like this when his day was overcast with sadness. He was still beautiful.

Gimmelmann waited. He remembered wondering if Holly had gone out without her underclothes or if she had lost them along the way? She had been giggling to herself, the way she did when she wanted to attract his attention, when she wanted to bait him.

'The trouble is, Tim, it's all in the balance, all the time, all the way through life. We build and we destroy. Richard and Emily have everything, the perfect family. Then an impulse, a primitive knee-jerk reaction, and it's wrecked, a lifetime's work comes tumbling down. We all do it, and we spend the rest of our lives asking ourselves why . . . if we get the chance.' He sighed and looked towards Gimmelmann. At last he said: 'What the hell was the guy doing standing on the top of a ten-storey building during a bombing raid, anyway?'

Gimmelmann shook his head. Another silence. He had

never known anyone who took such deliberate pleasure in malevolence as Holly. If she had been taking something out on the world because of what had been done to her she must have been terribly wronged.

Hudson was talking again. 'Anyway, what do you reckon?' He had picked up the letters off the piano and was sitting on the sofa facing him. 'Is New York ready for Hudson–Gimmelmann? It'll mean you spending at least half your time there, but if we don't go forward we stand still and that looks dangerously like walking backwards in my book.'

New York. Edward loved New York. And there was so much work for good-looking young actors in New York these days.

Hudson was smiling. 'Look, think about it. Talk it over between the two of you. Let's try and get it right, shall we? I'll be guided by whatever you decide. OK?'

Gimmelmann nodded. He was so happy. Hudson trusted his judgement. That meant a lot.

Chapter Fifty-Three

(i)

It was the loneliness that was hardest to bear. She needed someone to talk to: a girl-friend. Instead, as the weather turned bleak, she took long walks in her raincoat along the beach leaving the children inside squabbling over Monopoly and card games.

She felt selfish that she should allow herself so much pain over an infidelity when a young man had just lost his life. But the scales of pain are not evenly balanced. She had only spoken to Rob Barnes once, at the garden party at Willie Simmonds' house, and, although she had seen him occasionally, and had followed his career with interest, she had never got to know him. She wished now she had been less reticent.

They bought the English newspapers in Bordeaux and during the following days read the obituaries in the *Guardian* and the *Daily Telegraph*. Richard had written a short piece for *The Times*. The tabloid Press all found their individual angles, the *Sun* writing about *Mystery of photographer's suicide mission*, while the *Daily Mail* made him a hero, finding a woman with two children he had shooed out of the building minutes before the bomb fell. Considering that hundreds of other people were dying in Beirut every day that week Rob Barnes did pretty well in terms of space.

Emily thought about Clover Merrifield. *The girl who waited*, ran the *Daily Express* with a picture of Clover looking damp-eyed and exquisite. Sitting on a dry patch of pine needles in the small forest beyond the sandhills Emily watched a rain squall sweep in off the Atlantic as she tried to make sense of her feelings. Occasionally she cried, sobbing out loud, a huddled figure alone among the trees. The children would never have guessed.

(ii)

Clover knew that it was over the moment she had been able to take in the news. Sitting on her bed, the sheets around her face, she had felt Richard's interest in her ebbing away. He had pretended to kiss her good night, but she had known then that there would never be another kiss.

Unable to face the bleating of her colleagues' sympathy she had stayed away from the office for the next few days. When she had finally gone back it had been to resign.

It was the Tuesday after the photographer's death and already the news from Beirut was having to fight for space against other events from other parts of the world. In Paris, in what some would see as a reprisal, six people had just died when a grenade had been hurled into a Jewish restaurant.

Behind his desk Richard looked pale and tired, suddenly older and less attractive. He was, he said, going down to Bordeaux the next day to join Emily and the children. She nodded her head: inside a part of her wanted to say, 'And bully for you.' She did not ask whether Emily knew of their affair . . . well, hardly an affair. She didn't want to know.

Richard did not appear surprised at her decision, nor did he try to persuade her to stay. In fact it occurred to her, slightly annoyingly, that he might be secretly relieved. As an editor he was brilliant and professional, but as an adulterer she could not deny, now that it was over, that the word amateur sprang to mind.

'Do you have any idea where you'd like to go . . . I mean, I'm certain that once word gets around, half London will be beating a path to your door.'

She shook her head. 'I don't know. It might be time for a change, I think. Perhaps another kind of journalism.'

He nodded. 'You mean television?'

'Well, possibly.'

He changed the subject. 'Have you had a chance to be in touch with Rob's parents yet?' he asked.

She was puzzled. 'No. I didn't think . . .' She stopped.

'It was just that when I spoke to his father, he said that he was thinking of you, that Rob had mentioned you to them. Quite a bit, I think.'

'Ah . . .' she said, and flattened her hands down on her thighs. It was, she intended, a gesture of some finality. 'He should have told them that it was finished . . . that it had been nothing serious, anyway.'

'Perhaps it was to him,' he replied, and then immediately apologized. 'I'm sorry, that sounds . . .'

'. . . like guilt,' she said.

He didn't answer.

That was the end. She stood up and put her hand out to shake his. 'Well, anyway . . .'

He came around his desk. 'Good luck, Clover, though I know you won't need it.' He reached to take her hand but she had already withdrawn it. The easy mutual rhythms of just a few days ago had been broken.

'We'll no doubt bump into one another,' she said, backing away, 'and thanks for, you know, everything.' With that she turned and walked out of his office.

(*iii*)

Because she had become close to him Penny Chilston volunteered to clear out the photographer's flat. Death leaves so many loose ends. It had been thought that Clover might wish to be involved; Penny had telephoned, explaining the situation and inviting her along. But Clover had said, very sweetly, but without explanation, that she hoped Penny would understand if she declined the invitation.

482

So Penny went alone, with a shopping bag full of plastic bin-liners, to the apartment in the quiet St John's Wood avenue where a bouncy girl representative from the letting agency was waiting on the pavement with the spare keys.

'You won't mind if I don't come in, will you,' the girl said hurriedly, 'but it's one long dash today. It's the top floor, at the back. The rent is paid until the end of the month. There's usually a three months' notice clause, but . . .' She looked embarrassed. 'We were very sorry to read about Mr Barnes, although I never met him myself. Was he . . . was he a friend of yours?'

Penny nodded and took the keys.

'Ah . . . I must say it sounds absolutely frightful out there in . . . you know . . .' The girl hovered for a moment alongside her black VW Golf. Penny did not speak again, so tossing her long hair back over her shoulders the girl said again that she really had to dash and, climbing into her car, accelerated away down the road.

Penny watched her go, standing on the steps of the large white Victorian villa. It was a hot day and the horse-chestnut trees which dressed the street were heavy and still and sticky with greenfly. Penny was nervous and glad that the girl had gone. She didn't altogether trust her emotions.

It must once have been a grand house, some of the others in the avenue were still smart, but several panes in the large glass porch which stood over the steps were broken and the iron work needed painting. On a panel by the front door was a haphazard collection of bells. Sellotaped to one was the name 'Barnes'.

The house echoed as she opened the front door. The hall was large, cream and in need of redecoration. A strip of threadbare carpet ran from the front of the house to the back. Another wound up the stairs. Lying on a metal storage heater was a heaped collection of unclaimed letters, cards and slips of paper advertising taxi firms, restaurants and local businesses. She looked through the envelopes. Judging by the dates some had been there for several months. This was the London of transient young people, foreign students who came, studied and moved on, leaving behind a paper chase of unclaimed mail.

There were several items for the photographer, sorted and stacked together by one of the other residents. Picking them up Penny began to climb the stairs. Throughout their friendship she had never been to the photographer's home before, though he had frequently visited hers. He did not, he used to say, entertain much.

She found the flat at the back of the house, in the eaves, where the staircase had become narrow. A skylight, half-covered in a green moss, cast a soft yellow light on the top landing. Pausing for a moment after the exertions of climbing six flights of stairs, she put the key into the lock. She was forty and she was panting.

It was a small, musty, functional, two-roomed home, with a tiny kitchen and an even smaller bathroom. The carpets were old, worn and stained and the furniture minimal and cheap. The curtains were drawn in the living room, and, opening them, she was sadly amused to see the untidiness in which the photographer had lived. Opening a window she let in some fresh air. The signs of his sudden departure for Beirut were everywhere. The kitchen bins had been emptied (constant travellers never leave anything to rot when they are away), but the bed was unmade, and clothes lay scattered over the backs of chairs. Half-read copies of several newspapers lay open on the carpet.

What surprised Penny most though were the photographs. Dozens of black-and-white pictures covered every inch of wall in the living room and bedroom. She had seen some before in *Sunday Morning*: the zealous, veiled women of the Ayatollah, the Sandinistas' school for young guerrillas learning arithmetic from a blackboard in the jungle, the famous Mupangare mortar blast picture which had made his name, the neatly stacked pile

484

of white, dry, human bones arranged in front of a temple in Cambodia, and the three street orphans of Rio de Janeiro, snapped in the act of stealing a wallet from a tourist. But there were others which she did not know. A child mother breast-feeding a baby under a concrete South American highway; a photograph of Penny herself, laughing into the camera, taken, she remembered, at Kennedy Airport; and others which looked like family pictures showing a middle-aged couple and two teenage girls standing on a lawn outside a modern single-storey house. From the ridiculous to the mundane, she thought.

And then there was Clover. The beautiful, even face, perfectly arched brows and doe eyes gazing out from between the carnage on every wall. And Clover had not wanted to accompany her.

'Oh Rob, you poor, silly boy,' Penny said out loud, flopping down on a sofa. 'She really wasn't worth it.'

He had never spoken much about Clover. He knew Penny too well for that. 'If I were you I'd look around for someone who deserves you,' she had once told him. 'A boy like you could have his pick of half the pretty girls in London, and then go back for the other half when you're finished with the first lot.'

'But you know it doesn't always work like that, does it, Penny?' had been his quiet reply.

They had had dinner in Christian East Beirut the night before the bombing began, just the two of them, a half-bottle of Fleurie for him, water for her, making plans for when the Israelis came looking for the PLO as they were sure they soon would. He had been in good spirits. He liked Beirut. The adrenalin had been running. 'Just don't let's take too many risks, all right?' she had warned. 'Promise,' he had said. She had known he didn't mean it even then.

'You know, Penny,' he had said, as they had walked the short distance back to their hotel. 'Soon after I first started I seriously thought about giving all this up, pictures of war

485

and everything. It seemed to me I was trading in human misery.'

Penny had been unimpressed. It had sounded like the ramblings of an adolescent. 'But you didn't.'

'No, I didn't.'

She had waited for an explanation, but he had said nothing more.

Somewhere below her in the house Penny could hear music. Someone was playing the same record over and over. A girl was singing. She recognized the tune. He had whistled it endlessly those last few days. *Moonlight Shadow*. A hit of the moment. Something about trees that whispered in the evening. It seemed appropriate now.

Realizing that she was still holding his letters she began to leaf through them; Richard's instructions had been that *Sunday Morning* would clear any outstanding bills. There was the usual junk mail, telephone and electricity demands, with threats to cut off the services, a bank statement showing a whopping overdraft, a postcard from Disneyworld in Florida from the secretary on the *Sunday Morning* pictures desk who was on her honeymoon, and two blue air-mail letters. One was from Australia with the sender's name on the back, Mrs Mavis Barnes. His mother. Penny put it to one side to be returned unopened. The other envelope had been addressed very carefully in block capitals, the postage stamp showing the vast waterfalls of the newly independent African country they now called Zimbabwe. Penny still thought of it as Rhodesia. There was no sender's name on the envelope. She opened it: a page and a half of neat, round handwriting.

Dear Rob,
How is it with you in that blessed country of yours? I hope all is going well and that you are taking lots of good cards for the newspaper. Here I am so eager to do well in my examinations I am really becoming addicted to my studies like billyo.

486

Penny smiled at the misuse of an expression which was now archaic in England.

As you can see I am living now in Musaswa, not too far from Mutare, which is how we now call Umtali since Independence. I am with my uncle. I did not think he would want an albino, because sometimes people who do not have the sense of a chicken or poultry talk about albinos and say that they are witches or devils who will bring bad spirits and 'flu or such like, but he knows that that is just old women's gossip and he is a good man. When I think of how lucky I am to have him as my uncle and you as my friend my eyes fill up with tears until I cannot see to read or write any more.

I have a question to ask you. The people here in Musaswa want to build a school for the children but do not have any money. They do not know that I have a bank account in Mutare because I did not know how to tell them and they would not have believed me anyway. But I have not yet spent any of the money you have given me, waiting always for a rainy day. Now I want to know if I can use the money in the bank to help the people in Musaswa build the school. They are good people and I want to be of assistance to them as you were to me. Then perhaps one day if I work hard I can be a teacher and teach in the school. The Government want all the villages to have schools for the children, but no one knows which trees the money is growing on. I do not think those trees grow in Zimbabwe.

I hope it will not make you angry that I am asking if I can share the money you gave me with these people you do not know. Please write to me and tell me that you are not angry. In Shona there is a phrase, 'Nyadzi dzino kunda rufu', which means 'Shame is more painful than death itself', and that is what I would feel if I went against your wishes.

When I next write to you I will tell you how I have seen my mother again. She is living in Mozambique now and she told me that she can prove that my father was not guilty because she was with him all night in the windy house. But I suppose all that is water under the bridge now. The candle in my hut is almost gone. A woman I know is going to Mutare tomorrow so I will give her this letter to post. I pray for you every night, and my heart is overflowing until we can meet and be friends again.

Please do not stop thinking of me.

The letter was signed, 'Michael Mavangwe'.

Penny vaguely remembered the photographer mentioning an albino he had met once in Africa, but he had rarely given details of his assignments. That he had sent the boy some money was no surprise. Everyone knew he was a soft touch.

An albino? Getting up from the sofa Penny scanned the wall of photographs. She found him almost at once, hiding his eyes behind a hand, a hat on his head, alongside a cheeky little tot who was wearing a Donald Duck T-shirt.

This was going to be a letter she would have preferred not to write. Putting it from her mind she slipped off her jacket and took the bin-liners out of her bag. It was time she set to work, sorting out and throwing away. She had spoken to the photographer's parents, offering to send them everything which had been his, but they had asked for very little. 'He'd never been much of one for possessions,' his father had said. 'The only things he had any affection for were his cameras. It might be nice to have any cameras you find there, them and his pictures. I'd like to see a copy of everything he printed up, see the world through his eyes, so to speak. D'you think that would be all right?'

It was, Richard had said, the least they could do.

One by one Penny began to take down the photographs from the walls.

The sun returned and they bathed every day in the sea, had swimming races in the pool, played family tennis tournaments, went riding through the woods, perused small town markets in pastel shorts, T-shirts and flip-flops, ate candlelit dinners in the restaurants of ancient towns, and wandered the beaches and vineyards, honey-tanned, happy children, and two adults putting on the performances of a lifetime.

It was important to both of them that the children should not know that anything was amiss. Emily could not remember her parents ever falling out and that was how she wanted her family to remember their childhood. 'Nothing we do or say must spoil the children's holiday,' she had said sternly to Richard that first night as they had watched the children playing French cricket on the lawn. He had nodded an agreement. Later he had said, 'Emily, I'm sorry,' but she had simply said, 'Yes,' and turned away.

The energy of the family governed the days, and sometimes it was possible for him to imagine that nothing had happened. But at night after they had kissed the children and gone alone to their room a silence would fall between them. At home in London they had always read in bed, but now they quickly switched out the lights and turned away from each other, Emily always first.

He knew that she would not wish to discuss what had happened: would not want to know the details, that she was retreating inside herself, avoiding him. She was not purposely punishing him. That was not her way.

He remembered how when he was much younger he had wondered why anyone who was happy was ever unfaithful. There had never been any sense of loving Clover Merrifield. She was a bright and pretty girl who had

489

flattered him with her attention. He thought about the sex with Clover, the romantic sensuality of their dinner, the grapes they left uneaten in their haste into bed, the folds of her hair which had fallen down across her face as she had nuzzled his body, the smell and taste of her skin. And then he thought of the television news and the photographer, and shame crippled him.

Though exhausted, he slept badly. There was a balcony off the bedroom, a flat square roof, where sometimes in the very early mornings, a bath robe around him to keep out the dawn chill, he would sit and watch the steel light of the new day as the sun melted the mist on the vineyards. Once when returning to bed at six-thirty he found Emily sitting up, watching him. He asked her if she would like a cup of tea, but she said, 'No thank you,' and, lying down again, closed her eyes and locked him out.

September 1982

Chapter Fifty-Four

The old, dust-covered Chawasarira Bus groaned and dropped down a gear as it wound on towards the gap in the hills, its rear end hanging low and heavy over the back axle. On the roof a couple of free-riding sparrows hopped between the mountain of bags, boxes of farm produce and suitcases piled there, pecking at a sack of ground nuts.

Five rows from the back of the bus Emily watched the woman alongside her discreetly feed her baby inside her blouse. On Emily's knee a little girl of two, her hair in tight knots, dozed. The woman had joined the bus at Marondera, weighed down by bags, the baby on her back, the toddler clinging to her hand, wide-eyed. The woman's eldest, a boy of about four, sat across the aisle. They were well-behaved children, thought Emily, as she held the child in her lap. There had been no tears during the long journey and three-hour wait for a new fan-belt to be fitted to the bus at Rusape. For a while the little girl had been captivated by the chickens in the wicker cage left in the middle of the aisle. Now she was sleepy. 'You don't see African children cry much,' Nicola had once said. 'They don't expect a lot, and there's always someone there to cuddle them.'

Seeking the bus for Mutare at the Harare Bus Station, Emily had attracted astonished looks, as, carrying her suitcase, she had struggled between the hundreds of travellers and the drinks and mealie vendors who served them. White women did not often travel on Chawasarira Buses. The more expensive express bus service, with its air-conditioning and limited stops, was favoured by those who could afford it. Why she had chosen to travel this way Emily was not at all certain. Possibly it had been the whingeing she had encountered from disgruntled whites in Harare. That had disappointed her. She was probably behaving irrationally and emotionally, she thought, as the bus struggled on, but it was an irrational and emotional time of her life.

The bus was full, as had been the flight from London, a wide-bodied jet, a choice of wines with dinner and a movie of astonishing destructiveness which had begun somewhere eight miles above the Sahara. Now sitting, vacant-eyed and dusty, in the heart of Africa, she thought about her children, well into their new term at school, and her mother, happy to be able to step in, aware that something was wrong, but never asking. Richard had seen her off at the airport, a quick brush of his cheek and she had hurried away. Looking back from beyond passport control she had seen him still watching, his shoulders hunched in bewilderment. She had not waved.

He had not wanted her to come to Africa, fretting quietly that she did not know where she was going and that, only two years after the war, it might still be dangerous in remote areas. She had ignored his worries. Since they had been back from France they had hardly spoken, anyway.

Their performances had never slipped, not once during the holiday, or the long drive and stop-overs in Orleans and Arras. On the ferry back to Dover they had sat, silent and alone, while the children had wandered the decks in search of excitement. But as the English coast had drawn closer Emily had realized there were tears in her eyes. While they had been away she had been able to hide from her fear that she did not love her husband any more.

Penny had called around with the letter and photograph their first weekend home. She had found Emily in the basement still feeding the washing machine. 'He seems to be some child Rob befriended and I thought the Hudson Foundation might be interested,' she had

494

said. 'He's an albino, and he writes very well with lots of old-fashioned phrases. I didn't reply because I thought you might like to put it up for consideration . . .' She had stopped speaking while Emily studied the letter.

Michael Mavangwe. The name had been printed at the top of the page along with an address. Emily had not recognized it, but something in her memory had stirred. *Please do not stop thinking of me,* the letter had ended, signed, *Michael Mavangwe.*

'I wasn't sure. Is it one for the Foundation, or do I write and tell him to do whatever he wants with his money? That's what Rob would have told him.'

Emily had been hardly listening, re-reading over and again one sentence. *She can prove that my father was not guilty because she was with him all night in the windy house.* The windy house. Mavangwe.

It seems his father got himself into trouble at some time . . . *but that's all water under the bridge . . .* Penny had smiled at the phrase.

The windy house. 'You mean the Wendy house,' Emily had corrected. Nicola had laughed. 'That's what it should have been called but the carpenter who made it always called it the windy house, and that's what I called it. Even the servants call it the windy house.'

'So what do you think?' Penny had asked. She had never been to Wildwood. The windy house would have meant nothing to her.

Carefully Emily had refolded the letter and returned it to its envelope. 'Yes. Why not? Let's give it a shot, shall we? Thanks, Penny. I'll push it in the right direction. And if you like I'll let him know about Rob.'

'Do you mind?' Penny had been grateful for that. There had, in the end, been so much for her to do, photographs sent to Australia, clothes dry-cleaned and donated to the local Oxfam shop, rubbish burned, bills paid and letters answered. So many letters.

Over the next few days Emily's memory had slowly unwound. Fortunate Mavangwe, the young girl, too shy

495

to speak to her, backing away on the lawn at Wildwood, the startled, guilty look when Emily accidentally caught her admiring the speckled, polished, stone eggs. Fortunate Mavangwe with the pretty face who had been too scared to appear at the trial of Marco de Sampaio: when he had wished to call her as a witness for the defence she had disappeared. She was scared of everyone. The idea that she might have taken up with a murderer must have terrified her. Mavangwe. *She can prove that my father was not guilty because she was with him all night in the windy house . . .*

'There could be ten thousand Mavangwes in that part of Africa,' Richard had said when she told him. 'It's probably a local name. And what if he is some relation, what if he does know Wildwood, what does that tell you?'

'Nothing,' Emily had agreed. 'But if this Mavangwe wants to help build a school . . .'

'You have a field worker go and make a report to the Foundation . . .'

'Yes,' she had said. 'All right. That's what I'll do. I'll be a field worker and make a report.'

'But Emily . . . ?' he had begun. She had silenced him.

'Can't you see, Richard, I want to go? I want to get away.' After that, the silence. They had so rarely argued before.

'Well, if your mind's made up you should give Hudson a call, get him to lay things on for you through the Hudson–Reynolds office in Harare,' Richard had come back eventually. When Alec Reynolds had died Hudson had assumed control of all the Reynolds' family businesses.

She had thought about that for a moment and then shaken her head. 'I'd rather not. You know what Hudson's like, he'll insist they treat me like a princess. I know he'd mean well, but I'd rather make my own way and be anonymous. If I need any help when I'm out there I can always get in touch so that he can wave his magic wand. Don't tell him I'm going, will you? Not yet. There's no point in upsetting him by bringing it all back. And he would be upset.'

After that Richard had given up. They were drifting further and further apart. She had been determined to go and there was nothing he could have done to stop her. It had been more than six weeks since they had made love. With every night that had passed it had become more unlikely. They had never talked about Clover Merrifield: now they couldn't talk about anything.

The child on Emily's knee was now sleeping against her breast. She felt the warm body and regular breath on her neck, and was grateful for the comfort. On the back seat some young men who had drunk too much beer were joking to each other. The woman with the baby shook her head at their rowdiness, and delicately peeled a hard-boiled egg which she had bought through the bus window during the wait at Rusape.

It was a kind of running away, Emily knew that, and Michael Mavangwe's letter had provided the excuse. No one ever does anything for a single reason. That was what Hudson liked to say. The forces drawing her back to Wildwood would, at any usual time in her life, have been resisted. But this was not a usual time. For fifteen years she had lived for and through her husband and children and now suddenly the equation which she thought to be perfect had been broken. It was an everyday story, she knew, but it did not happen to her every day.

Nicola would have known what to do, she told herself, then immediately changed her mind. Nicola would probably have been hysterical. She had been a ferociously possessive girl, possessive even of Emily. No wonder it was now Nicola who was drawing her back to Africa, giving her time to make a reassessment of her life. She would find Michael Mavangwe, whoever he was, and find out what he meant by his reference to the windy house, and perhaps the Hudson Foundation would be able to help him with his school. And she would go back to Wildwood, seek out Alice and Joseph perhaps, and rediscover a time when the future had been brilliant.

The bus struggled over the hill and began its descent towards Mutare. It was not a hot day but the sun on the window pane was warm, and in a half-sleep Emily welcomed Nicola as a travelling companion. She was, of course, talking about Hudson. Why was it always Hudson when there were so many more important things to discuss? Emily dreamed, but Nicola must not have heard. 'The trouble is,' Nicola was saying, 'he puts me on a pedestal, and the truth is I'm not really a pedestal person, as you very well know. Crumbs! Far from it. Did I tell you I'm buying him two presents for marrying me, giving him two rewards? One will be a heavy-duty sledgehammer for the smashing of aforesaid pedestals, and the other is a beautiful white piano I saw in a shop in New Bond Street. Don't tell him, will you, Emmy? I want it to be a surprise. He's always so generous, forever buying everyone presents and never anything for himself. And he plays the piano so well. I want it to be the best present anyone could ever buy him.'

'He already thinks he's getting that by marrying you.'

'Which just shows what a poor sense of direction he has in life. Golly! Girl without pith-helmet marries boy without compass. We don't stand a chance out there in the bush, Emmy. Not a chance.'

Slowly, the old bus ran on through the African hills towards the dusk and into the past.

Chapter Fifty-Five

(i)

In the end it wasn't, as Hudson's celebrations went, very special, no grandees, politicians or even famous faces being invited to brave the roped and planked walkway across the mud to the low wall, the trowel and the mortar. There was a marquee in which green plastic turf had been laid on wooden floorboards, and there was champagne, but otherwise it was a very light lunch for a relatively small gathering. Naturally Charlie Latymer would have preferred something more elaborate, and had originally suggested to Hudson that they might attempt to entice the American Ambassador out, or even a minor member of the Royal Family. But Hudson had just patted him on the back and told him not to worry, that he would take care of that side of things. Since the launching of the Hudson Foundation extravagant parties had been strictly out of style.

So when the day arrived for the laying of the foundation stone of the new seven-storey Hudson Communications centre the occasion was coloured in mystery. Only Hudson knew of the design and the inscription of the foundation stone, and only Hudson knew who would be given the honour of laying it.

The ceremony was set for two o'clock but the cars had begun to arrive almost as soon as the workmen (who had been given a two-hour lunch-break) stopped work at one, wending their way gingerly across the ten acres of mud. First came Rajah Dehwola and other members of Hudson's youth club, their voices loud and smart, all busily ordering and organizing; then the cameramen and photographers, the vans from the caterers, a phalanx of architects; and lastly a small wad of bankers, Neil Fiske among them, now grey and stooped, the cuffs of his cardigan showing at his wrists. Mainly though the guests were executives from the various branches of the Hudson empire, people from newpapers, magazines, radio, and television, everyone full of casual *bonhomie* and pretending not to mind about being dragged out on such a rotten day. Inevitably some of the old *Witness* gang made the journey, although by no means all, Willie Simmonds being in Los Angeles and Penny Chilston back in the dryer. (She hadn't apparently fallen off the wagon, as had been rumoured, but her hold had become pretty tenuous since Beirut and she was taking no chances.) Tim Gimmelmann had arrived though, getting there early to show off Edward, his good-looking actor boy-friend (it seemed so obvious now, why had he taken so long to realize it?), and Richard Blake had turned up with Ben Tarlo who was now group managing director. Latymer was surprised that Emily wasn't there. Hudson would be disappointed.

At ten to two Berridge's car slid across the flats. Latymer nodded towards him. Was Berridge mellowing? he wondered. He had actually been quite courteous when Dominique had finally bolted, almost verging on the sympathetic. Latymer hadn't told him anything, of course. No details, anyway. *Night And Day* wouldn't have printed them, but Berridge was just evil enough to pass them on to a rival who would. Some people had been surprised that Latymer had stayed with Hudson Communications after the way he had been cuckolded, but he had (it wasn't as if the circulation manager had been having his wife: Hudson was the chief executive, after all) and the job had gradually become more fulfilling. And when Dominique had taken up with that working-class oaf from the BBC Hudson had been consideration itself, as though he felt Latymer had suffered enough. He and Hudson would never be close pals, not the way he had once hoped, but the money was unbeatable and with Hudson Communications growing all the time Hudson needed chaps like Charlie Latymer around. Oh yes.

(*ii*)

If I am so successful why do I feel this way? Richard asked himself. He was standing alone on the edge of the mud staring out across the Thames watching a lone sculler in a wet suit making a difficult passage up the river towards Putney. Once he had paddled a stray rowing-boat along the Serpentine, hand after hand . . .

In the car down to Chelsea he and Ben Tarlo had talked about Hudson who was going to Florida the following day to buy another printing company. 'He can't stop buying. It's time he married again, he's becoming eccentric,' Ben had said. Richard was fond of Ben: they had both done so well, Ben the business brains Hudson trusted most of all and rewarded most handsomely, Richard the editorial overlord. Eventually he had managed to impress upon Hudson that no one person could be editor in chief of all the different titles Hudson Communications now published, but, with the exception of *Night And Day,* Hudson had managed to coax him into becoming a director of each company which made up his empire. 'That way I'll at least have someone to blame who isn't afraid of me when things go wrong,' he had joked.

The sculler was struggling. If I'm supposed to be so influential, why do I feel this way? Richard asked himself again. He was influential, inasmuch as a newspaper editor is ever influential. Governments would not be made or destroyed by anything which appeared in *Sunday Morning,* the Prime Minister would hardly quake in her shoes when she read his editorials, but *Sunday Morning* had a voice and an identity and was active in the debates of national life. In his tiny way he was, he could see, just a little bit influential. In the *Sunday Morning* office his

501

staff treated him with deference and fawning respect, even those he encouraged to be friendly. Was it only respect?

The sculler was now disappearing into a heavy shower. The trouble was, he told himself, they saw him as the confident, accomplished, national newspaper editor, while inside he felt like the twenty year old, just starting out, wondering if this was the week they would find him out.

'Well, well, well . . .' he heard, behind him. 'The old Alvis . . .' It was Berridge guiding everyone's eyes across the mud to the entrance of the site.

Along with the other guests Richard watched in surprise as the red Alvis sports car made its way slowly through the puddles towards the marquee. When he had half a dozen cars and a driver at his disposal why, Richard wondered, should Hudson have chosen to drive himself in this car on this day?

'Hi, how're you doing? How are you?' Hudson, in jeans, sweater and Wellington boots, moved easily among his guests. 'Sorry about the mud. If your shoes get ruined put in for new ones on expenses. Hello. Thanks for coming.' It was the easy, friendly performance of the casual multi-millionaire, surrounded by his associates and flunkeys in the formal blue-suited uniforms of their offices.

Already the caterers were beginning to pour out champagne in the marquee, and the site foreman and two assistants from the architect's office were preparing the foundation stone for the ceremony.

Looking around Hudson approached Richard, a question on his face. 'I don't see Emily,' he said.

Richard shook his head. 'She said to apologize. She's away. Sorry.'

It was one of those moments Richard had seen before, when nothing Hudson could do would hide the disappointment. 'Oh no. I really wanted her here . . . I was sure . . . Certain.' He pressed his boot into the mud miserably. Then he said, 'You're a fool, you know that, Richard. She's the best thing you ever had in your life . . .'

Some of the guests were looking. Richard nodded. 'I think so, too.'

Suddenly Hudson put an arm around his shoulder and squeezed it. 'It'll be OK, fella. I know it. You'll make it work. Trust me.'

'Mr Hudson . . .' The site foreman was ready and wanted a word.

The moment had arrived. The guests gathered around the low wall and, as the builders and architects prepared, Hudson sank to his knees, trowel in hand. Then, as the foreman advised, he began to slap mortar on to the low, wide wall, where the foundation stone, a discreet, oblong-shaped piece of marble, was to be laid. Taped over the front of the stone, and hiding the inscription, was a piece of white cloth.

Only now had it become clear that Hudson himself was to lay the foundation stone of his new building. And, like the practical person he was, he was insisting that this stone be properly laid, no simple unveiling ceremony for him. He wanted to lay the foundation stone literally with his own hands.

'OK?' Hudson asked, looking up at the builders as he finished applying a good, even carpet of mortar.

'Perfect,' the foreman said.

Some of the toadies present applauded stupidly.

'Stand clear now everybody,' called the foreman, and as the guests stepped back to take their glasses of champagne, and photographers and cameramen crowded closer, the marble foundation stone of the new Hudson Communications centre was lowered gently and hydraulically into place. A patter of applause broke across the mud flats as Hudson ran the trowel expertly around the edges of the stone, trimming off the mortar which was oozing out.

Finally a waiter passed Hudson a glass of champagne. It was now raining quite heavily, but he did not appear to notice. Holding the champagne in one hand he neatly tore away the covering veil from the foundation stone. There was a rattle of camera shutters. 'Thank you for coming, all of you,' he said, and put the glass to his lips.

Richard leaned forward to read the inscription. He hardly needed to: he had guessed anyway. 'The Nicola Reynolds Building,' ran the top line. 'This stone was laid on Friday, 24 September 1982, by James Hudson in memory of his wife.'

Chapter Fifty-Six

She drove carefully, avoiding the pot-holes and gulleys in the red sand and the branches which reached down from the overhanging trees. The road was narrower than she had remembered, neglected, and the bush at the sides higher, as though the undergrowth was gradually reaching in and reclaiming its own. Because she drove so slowly the mountain seemed steeper, the forest above impenetrable.

She had not needed a map. So little had changed in the past eighteen years. She had stayed the night at the Manika Hotel in Mutare, where they had arranged for her to hire an old South African Ford Laser, and had set off that morning feeling the strangest euphoria, as though about to re-encounter an old friend. She had decided in advance: Saturday was for Wildwood. She would go looking for Michael Mavangwe on the Sunday morning.

She had telephoned home the previous evening. Daddy was still at the office, the children had said, giggling among themselves about something. 'What did you have for your dinner?' Tom had wanted to know. 'Grilled rhinoceros and chips,' she had told him.

The springs and brakes on the car were doubtful, but the engine was solid, and she had quickly passed the timber yards and crossed the railway tracks and begun her ascent into the mountains of the Vumba. It was more beautiful than she had remembered, the hills more rounded, 'female really', as Nicola used to say. In less than an hour she had reached the dirt road which led to Wildwood and Mupangare. Twenty minutes later she had turned the corner of the mountain and caught her first glimpse of the house again.

From the distance of the road it had looked much as Emily had remembered but now, as the car broke out of the forest, she saw with dismay the damage of abandonment.

Shutters hung from hinges, and windows were broken or had been left open so that the vines growing around the front columns had stolen into upstairs rooms, while walls, once sparkling white, were now flaking and washed with green where blocked gutters had overflowed.

Drawing the car to a halt she climbed out and approached the house across the weed-covered gravel of the drive. The front door was ajar. She peered inside into the wide hall. It was quite empty.

She did not enter immediately, perhaps she lacked the courage, but moving around the side of the building she crossed under the heavily overgrown pergola, where what had once been a carefully cultivated vine now rampaged to the roof, and moved on across the overgrown paved rose garden towards the garages and outbuildings which formed the small rear courtyard.

The sense of desertion was everywhere, water in a rain barrel was covered by green algae, window-frames were rotting and birds had nested in the collars which held the drain-pipes. She was baffled. Why would Hudson have let this happen? Wildwood was his house now. She had not known what to expect, but it had never occurred to her that Wildwood might simply have been forgotten.

Stepping through new spring nettles she moved on past the kitchen and the semi-derelict servants' quarters where Alice, Joseph and Fortunate had once made their homes, and the stables where Mashona had grown fat from lack of exercise, until she came around to the french windows which looked out across the lawn. They had played croquet there, she remembered, and for a moment she saw her, Nicola, leaning on her mallet and throwing her head back and laughing as Emily's ball had gone careering away down the hill into the long grass: 'Take that, Gryptight-Thynne.' At the bottom of the garden stood the old msasa tree, and, in its branches, the windy house.

She turned away and looked at the upstairs windows. Her own room had been at the back looking east up the mountain. Nicola's had been on the far corner. She wished now that the house had been locked and shuttered. Every open door was an invitation.

The front door fell back to her touch and she stepped into the empty hall. Because of the creepers growing around the windows it was quite dark inside. She could, however, see that, although the house was open to the world, there was no sign of vandalism. It was as though it had been picked bare of everything that could be taken away and then left to rot.

She climbed the wide staircase, passing memories as she went, Fortunate and the smell of Johnson's furniture polish, Pith-Helmet and the Dandelions and *A Hard Day's Night* that first morning, and Alice in her long, patterned nightdress and nightcap during the electric storm. 'No one is hurt? You are not hurt, Nicola?'

Reaching the landing she gasped as a small lizard, startled by her arrival, suddenly darted along the banister away from her hand, before running up and on to the cream, empty wall where it froze, pulsing nervously.

'Come on, Emmy, pull yourself together, you old cowardy custard,' she heard Nicola mock her. Quickly she walked along the landing, glancing, as she went, into the empty bedrooms. Only the door to Nicola's room was closed. She almost hoped it would be locked. But it swung freely open as she turned the handle.

Her memories of this room had never left her: the doll's house, school pictures, toy theatre, lacrosse stick, books, a record player, an old stuffed panda. Now there was nothing. She was relieved. Walking into the centre of the room she gazed around, remembering where the bed had been, where they had slept together. Then she stood by the open window and looked out across the garden, past the forest, to the top of the smooth mountain.

Turning back to the room she opened the clothes' closet where the two hated ballgowns had been stored. Again nothing: but something written at about chest height on the back of the closet door caught her eye. Opening the door more fully to the daylight she peered at two lines of neat, unjoined writing, the work of a child and now almost faded into the paint.

'*Put another Nicola in, in the Nicola-odeon . . .*'

She went into the sitting room last. She had wondered if she could face it, but the house was so bare, so stripped of its personality, that when she reached the door it held no fear.

This was where they had sat on those cold evenings, huddled around the pine-log fire, talking as always about Hudson and Richard, perfectly happy doing the best part of nothing. She stood by the fireplace and tried to imagine it as it had been. That morning, Nicola sitting in the wicker chair, Pugh the Portrait and her paints, Fortunate touching the speckled eggs. She glanced at the french windows. That was the way Marco de Sampaio must have entered. And this was where Nicola had died.

They were waiting for her by the greenhouse door, five of them, barefoot ragamuffin boys in their shorts and T-shirts and thin little jumpers, the eldest no more than twelve, carrying on his back the youngest, aged about two. They had obviously seen the car because they were not surprised to see her, but they had made no attempt to enter the house and find her. Between them they were holding an old watering-can. Even before she reached the greenhouse Emily had smelled the orchids, 'the quick drag of home'.

The boys looked at her, intensely curious, as if wondering what attitude she would take with them, not prepared to commit their own expressions until they knew.

'Hello.' Emily smiled around at them.

The little ones smiled, and the medium ones looked to the eldest for guidance. 'Hello,' he said. 'Hello,' repeated one of the smaller ones. 'Good morning,' came in a cheeky medium one and giggled. The baby having the piggy-back just gazed in wonder.

'They are very nice orchids,' she said, looking down the greenhouse at the meticulously kept plants.

'Oh, yes, very nice,' replied the eldest boy. 'Very nice,' repeated one of the others.

At least the orchids hadn't changed. Much of the rest of the garden was hopelessly overgrown and turning quickly into an ornamental forest. 'I was looking for the man who used to work here,' said Emily. 'His name was Joseph. Do you know him?'

'Yes, Joseph,' the eldest boy replied. 'He is coming here soon.'

Joseph arrived within the hour, just as the boys were finishing watering the plants, walking slowly, his back straight, across the garden towards her, his expression at first cautious, then thrilled as he remembered. How happy they had all been that time, he told her, when Miss Nicola had come home from the university in England.

One by one he introduced the boys. They were his grandsons. Now seventy, he had, he said, many, many grandchildren, and threw his hands out wide as though distributing seed. They did not live too far away. In Mupangare. Perhaps she remembered.

She asked after Alice. He became serious. Alice had stayed at Wildwood for many years, keeping it comfortable and clean, as it always had been. He did not know why she had stayed. 'Perhaps so that the ghost of Miss Nicola would not be lonely in that big house.' Sometimes Mr Reynolds had visited her. He liked Alice. But he had never stayed. 'She was a very lonely woman after . . .' He left that part unsaid. 'I did not want to be here always so I took a job in a saw-mill in Mutare and would come twice a week to look after the orchids, or to work in the garden. Sometimes we would have *sadza* together, but then she would scold me for dirtying the kitchen with my boots and make me eat outside. She became very old and very forgetful and would talk to herself. She would even forget that Miss Nicola was dead. In the end her sisters came and took her away to their village. I think now she is . . .' He gestured, a graceful finality.

They climbed the mountain together, the boys leading the way, up past the jacaranda tree, now covered in flowers, skirting the edge of the forest on the track which Mashona had known by heart, and out on to the smooth rump of the hill. This is like a pilgrimage, Emily thought. Joseph talked as they climbed. The decision to abandon Wildwood had been taken by Mr Hudson, he told her. 'He is a very good man, Mr Hudson, very kind. After Mr Reynolds died they came and took all of the furniture and curtains in big vans, everything that was inside the house and all of Miss Nicola's belongings. The people of Mupangare were told that they could use the Wildwood land and gardens to grow mealie. They could even use the house, too, if they wished.'

'But the house is completely empty?'

Joseph smiled. 'The people here are still very superstitious,' he said simply. 'They do not like to come too near. The doors and windows are open so that the bad spirits will leave.'

'Do you believe that, Joseph?' she asked.

He didn't answer.

Nicola's grave was at the highest point of the mountain. 'This is my idea of heaven, Emmy,' she had said. She must have told Hudson the same thing. A simple stone cross. 'Nicola Reynolds. 1943–1967.' Poor Nicola. She had missed so much.

Around them the day which had started so brightly was turning misty.

The boys watched her silently. After a few moments Joseph shooed them away, and pretended to busy himself examining a plant so that she might be alone with her thoughts. He was such a gracious man.

She wondered if she should say a prayer, but she couldn't think of anything to say. Nicola would understand. She thought of the last time she had seen her, how pleased Nicola would have been to see her go off to Paris with Richard. She had never seen their happiness. And then Emily thought about Richard.

'What about Fortunate?' she asked as they began their descent. 'Fortunate Mavangwe.'

Joseph shook his head and frowned. 'She went away.'

'Did I hear that she had a son?'

Reluctantly Joseph nodded. 'Oh yes. A son. He is *musope*.'

'*Musope?*'

'Albino.'

'Ah,' Emily said quietly.

'She abandoned him. She was ashamed. He did not deserve a mother like that. He lived in Mupangare with his grandmother. But he is gone now.'

'And did you know his father?'

There was a long pause as Joseph measured his dignified pace down the mountain. 'No,' he said finally. 'No one knew his father.'

They walked on in silence. The path narrowed as they left the smooth grassy hill and entered the forest and they fell into single file, Joseph's grandsons ahead of them, the twelve year old still carrying the little one.

Chapter Fifty-Seven

(i)

He was in the hotel bar, looking somehow smaller
and younger, his jacket too big at the collar. She froze
in astonishment.

After leaving Wildwood she had taken Joseph and his
grandsons back to Mupangare in her car. The boys had
been very excited, crowding into the back, not speaking.

'Sometimes I tell them how I used to drive big cars
all over Zimbabwe for Mr Reynolds and they are very
impressed,' Joseph had joked, 'but now I live in my house
and drive my wheelbarrow.' He seemed very happy with
the arrangement.

His house was a brick-based, circular, thatched African
hut. Mupangare was much as Emily had remembered, the
pretty sheltered village beside the hill. There was nothing
to suggest a massacre had taken place there only four
years earlier.

'You weren't here when the fighting came?' Emily
had asked Joseph.

He had just shaken his head. 'No. I was in Mutare. I
was too old to fight.' He had left it open to her conjecture
as to which side he would have chosen to support.

It had been dark by the time she had arrived back at
the hotel. There was, the clerk on the desk had told her,
someone waiting to see her. She had thought there must
be some mistake.

He had his back to the door, but caught sight of
her in the mirror behind the bar. When he turned, she
realized she had tears in her eyes.

Married love in a hotel room on a winter's evening in Southern Africa. The first night of the second part of their marriage.

He had flown all night and driven all day to be with her, afraid that she would not want him, that she would stand off and politely ask him to leave her alone. He had seen it happen to so many of their friends: the tiny cracks and then the inexorably widening rifts. He had known she would not break up the family, would not leave him. Not physically. But the friendship upon which their lives together had been built had been broken.

He had taken an additional room in the hotel, fearing that she might not want him with her. But it was in her room, in her bed, that they made love. He tried to tell her he was sorry, and would not betray her again. But she stopped him, putting a finger to his lips. 'You don't know whether you will or not. I don't know what I might do. We can only try. But it has to be worth the effort. I learned that today up on the mountain.'

At five to nine, and feeling guilty, they hurried downstairs to the dining room for dinner. An elderly couple at the door to the room opposite watched in astonishment as they left Emily's room together. They had been at the desk the previous day when she had checked in alone. 'They think we've only just met,' she whispered, touching Richard's arm.

'I feel as though we have,' he said.

Over dinner, though his eyes were closing, he told her how he had rushed home and packed and sworn the children to secrecy about his flight to Harare.

'No wonder they were so giggly. What decided you?'

'I think it was Hudson. Something he said. He was worried for us.'

She smiled. 'Worried where he'd go for his Christmas dinner, I imagine.'

She told him about the abandoned Wildwood and Nicola's grave.

'I'll tell you a secret,' he said, pouring the wine. 'In the beginning, when I was with Nicola, I was always jealous of you. She could be so . . . passionate, I suppose, is the word. I'd never known a girl so fond of another girl before. She talked about you all the time. I used to think she was in love with you.'

Emily remembered the letters. 'She had such intense feelings, and was never afraid to show them.' She paused. 'Would you like to see Wildwood? We could go back tomorrow.'

He thought for a moment before answering. 'No. I don't think so. You have memories of the place. But to me it would be just a shell. Besides I came here to help a field worker from the Hudson Foundation spread Hudson's money around a little bit.' He smiled. 'Did I tell you that Hudson laid the foundation stone himself, like Napoleon crowning himself. He did a good job, too, as though he'd been a bricklayer in another life. He'll never forgive you for not being at the ceremony, you know.'

Emily laughed. 'Oh yes he will.'

He was so tired he should have slept easily. At his side Emily lay satin-folded. He touched her face. He had never stopped loving her. Love. It came in so many different guises, one word to express a multitude of differing, perhaps contrary, emotions. Love. A good word for headlines. Short enough for a single column of thirty-six point lower case in Century or Gill or even Bodoni. Powerful enough in June 1967 to fill the entire cover of the old *Witness*. Love. Newspapermen used it all the time. It was a selling word, a verbal chameleon which could change its colour or meaning for whatever the circumstances. He stared unseeing into the darkness. The hotel was silent. It was Saturday night. In London, two hours behind, the first edition of *Sunday Morning* would be going to press.

514

Chapter Fifty-Eight

They found him stacking crates of empty beer bottles outside a bottle store by the side of the road. Everyone in Musaswa knew Michael Mavangwe. He looked older than Emily had expected, a tall and very thin fourteen year old, wearing a wide-brimmed bush hat, a dark blue shirt buttoned up to the neck and long trousers. He even wore socks and a ragged pair of old tennis shoes, and a pair of cracked sun-glasses. The only parts of his skin which were visible were his hands and parts of his face.

Musaswa was not a pretty village. Just off the road it was one of several settlements of thatched huts stretching across a wide hill of over-populated communal land, where almost every bush and tree had had branches torn off for firewood. The bottle store was at a crossroads where men lounged or stood around drinking or watching the day pass by. The albino boy worked alone.

He had not seen them watching from their car and when they approached he was surprised and embarrassed. The men outside the bottle store were glad of the diversion, shifting to get better views of the newcomers. Perhaps he expected bad news because, leaving his work, he led them quietly around the back of the bottle store where they might speak privately.

Carefully Emily explained why they had come to find him. Rob Barnes had been a very good man, she told him, kind and generous, exceptionally brave and a very good photographer. His friends missed him very much.

Michael Mavangwe sat in the shade on a low earth step outside a small storeroom and listened silently. Before long, tears ran down the cracked, pink cheeks from behind the sun-glasses. He was not embarrassed to cry.

'He was my best friend,' he said. 'Nowhere in the world is there another like him. He did these things, sent me money, because he loved me.' He took off his sun-glasses to wipe his face with his sleeve and Emily saw the pale, flickering eyes, the lids red and swollen. 'I thought one day I will go to visit him in England . . .'

'The reason we came,' said Richard, 'is because it may be that the people here can get help to build a school without using the money you were given.'

'He would not like me to give the money for a school?'

Emily smiled. 'I'm sure he wouldn't mind at all. It's your money. You can do whatever you want with it. But the money was intended to help you. Perhaps one day you will want to go to college and learn to be a teacher.'

'If we do not have a proper school here I can never become a teacher.'

'There is sometimes money available to help build schools and buy books,' said Emily.

The boy looked doubtful.

'I think I met your mother, a very long time ago, before you were born,' Emily said at last. 'I came from England to stay when she worked at Wildwood. Your mother is Fortunate, isn't she?'

This surprised him. 'Yes, she is Fortunate. She is living now in Mozambique. Not too far.' He gestured vaguely eastwards. 'Did you know Miss Nicola Reynolds?' he asked after a few moments.

'Yes,' Emily replied.

'My mother said she was very beautiful.'

'Yes.'

He considered this for a few minutes and then said, 'I think the spirit of Miss Nicola Reynolds is not happy.'

They should have left the car at the Mozambique border where customs officials told them that they did not have the correct documents, but Richard had been too long a journalist to be defeated so easily. Showing his credentials

516

and explaining that he was the editor of an English Sunday newspaper and had to drive into Mozambique for a few hours to talk to someone, he then very coolly slipped an American hundred-dollar bill inside his passport. After a few moments the gate opened and the car was allowed through.

'It is not too far,' the boy told them as they drove carefully between the traffic of heavily burdened pedestrians crossing the border, 'we will be there soon.'

'We are doing the right thing, aren't we?' Richard asked suddenly as they waited while the boy talked in Shona to the guards at the Mozambique check-point. 'Delving into the past like this.'

Emily frowned. 'I'm not sure. But it seems important to him. And I want to know. That must be all right, mustn't it?'

It was further than they expected and the roads in Mozambique were more difficult than those in Zimbabwe. In the back seat the boy sat quietly, only speaking when he wished to point the way through the sandy mountain tracks. He had much to think about. Before they had left Musaswa Emily had spoken at some length with his uncle and the head men in the village on behalf of the Hudson Foundation, explaining how she would help them to make an application for funding.

Eventually he guided them down a long, winding path into a deeply wooded gully, where four or five dilapidated huts stood surrounded by small maize gardens. Fortunate could hardly have chosen a more inaccessible place if she wished to hide, Emily reflected. Climbing from the car, they looked around. One by one the inevitable children began to appear.

They found Fortunate at the back of the huts washing clothes in a round tub. Emily would not have known her. The comely, shy young girl with the shapely hips and pretty dresses had aged beyond recognition. She was thin and haggard. She could only have been in her mid-thirties but she looked fifty.

As they approached Michael spoke quickly in Shona to his mother.

'Hello Fortunate . . .' Emily smiled. 'Do you remember me?'

Fortunate stared at Emily but did not return the greeting. Then, looking worried, she began muttering and gesticulating to her son. For some moments an argument ensued. Michael turned back to Emily and Richard. 'My mother is afraid that if she talks to you she will get into trouble.'

Emily turned to Fortunate. 'Nobody will get into any trouble, Fortunate,' she said very clearly. 'You have nothing to be afraid of with us. I promise you that. Michael says that you said you can prove that his father did not kill Nicola. Is this true?'

There was a very long silence, during which Fortunate stared at the ground. She seemed less timid now than sullen. After a while the boy spoke sharply in Shona to his mother. Finally she began to speak, very quietly: 'Marco was with me all the night. We were in the windy house up in the tree, listening to them.'

'In the windy house? Why were you in the windy house at night-time?'

Another silence, then: 'Alice would have heard in my room. The walls were very thin. She would have sent me back to my village. Marco said we could go in the windy house and smoke some *mbanje* and have a good time.' There was another long pause. Again Michael encouraged in Shona. Then she said: 'We were making Michael in the windy house all through the night, listening to the fighting and quarrelling. That is why he is *musope*, because of the bad spirits that night.'

Michael, now without his dark glasses, a hand in front of his face to protect his eyes, stared at his mother and gently, kindly shook his head. He knew better than that.

Emily didn't understand. 'Who was fighting and quarrelling, Fortunate?'

Fortunate sat down on the earth by the tub: her reply was almost inaudible. 'Mr Hudson and Miss Nicola. She was shouting and screaming, very angry and upset. Then she went quiet. I told Marco to go and steal the egg after Mr Hudson had gone out riding because he had left the windows open to the garden. We had smoked too much *mbanje*. I always liked the eggs. They were pretty.'

Emily glanced at Richard. He was crouched down. She was puzzled, disappointed on Michael's behalf. She felt rather foolish to be there at all. She had been over-emotional when she read Michael's letter. Fortunate had got the simplest fact wrong. There had been no row that night. Hudson had said how perfect the evening had been. Come to think of it, she didn't think Nicola and Hudson had ever rowed. She didn't blame Fortunate for making up a story. It was probably what she wanted to believe. She blamed herself for wanting things to be different for Michael, for perhaps hoping that Fortunate had seen the strangers Hudson had talked about.

She tried again. 'Mr Hudson said that when he was out riding he saw three men running towards the border. Did you see those men, Fortunate?'

Bleakly the woman shook her head. Around her six ragged children stood watching silently. Tears of indignation welled now. 'I am telling you the truth,' she insisted, staring always at the red earth. 'Marco was not a bad man. He was a thief, but he was not a murderer. I asked him to steal the egg and because he had had too much *mbanje* he went to do it. Very quick. In and out. Less than a minute. Miss Nicola was sleeping on the floor, I could see. Perhaps she was drunk. I was at the windows with him, keeping watch. He was laughing. I said run quickly and nobody will know. He had had so much *mbanje* he was falling over. I was frightened that Miss Nicola would wake up and be angry. But then Marco saw the handbag and picked that up, too. It had many dollars. I was frightened then. He took the handbag and the money. And then he ran away, like a drunken man, into the forest with all the money. And I went to my room and because of the *mbanje* went to sleep, until Alice came shouting for me, telling me I was a lazy girl . . .' Again she fell silent.

Very quietly Richard now spoke for the first time. 'You said you heard Miss Nicola and Mr Hudson falling out, Fortunate. Did you hear what they were saying?'

'Oh yes. I heard very well. She was shouting about a dolly. Over and over she said it. "Dolly, Dolly", and "Holly" and "Don't come near me, don't touch me. You disgust me". And then, "Disgusting . . . filthy . . ." and "stinking prostitute . . ." Many, many bad words.'

Emily had become a spectator. She could hear Nicola saying the words, yet she could not believe it. She was afraid. She wanted to leave.

'And what did Mr Hudson say?' Richard asked.

'He was quiet, saying, "I'm sorry, Nicola. Nicola, please forgive me." Then he shouted at her. He told her to shut up. And she shouted more and more. She was very angry. He was saying, "Please, Nicola, please, Nicola . . ." For a long time. And then she went quiet. He must have soothed her. Mr Hudson is a very nice man. He was very nice to me.'

Emily had once wondered whether the Hudson charm would work on Fortunate. Now she looked at her, trying to challenge the fantasy in this story, but Fortunate did not meet her eyes, continuing to talk, making up for the years of wretchedness and silence.

'When Alice found that Miss Nicola was dead I was very frightened. The police had dogs and they chased Marco. I thought I would go to gaol with him for stealing the eggs and the money. So I ran away. I thought they would find the guilty men and Marco would come back. But they didn't find them. And then they hanged him. But then I was very pregnant and had to go home. In Mupangare they were glad that Marco was the guilty one because he was not from that village. When Michael was born and they saw him they said it was because I was a bad girl making a baby with a murderer. But he was not. Somebody else was the murderer.'

'Do you know who?' Richard asked.

'No, sir, I don't know that. A bad man who came when no one was watching, perhaps when I was sleeping. Someone from another village.' She finished speaking.

'Why did Marco not tell the police he had been with you all night in the windy tree, that you had been with him when he stole the eggs?' Richard asked finally.

Fortunate shook her head. 'I don't know. He had smoked too much *mbanje*. Very, very much. All day and all night. It made him silly and sleepy and then he would not know what he had been doing. Perhaps he could not remember . . .'

A weekend in Dorset, the four of them around the fire and Nicola producing her present; Willie Simmonds, smiling and smiling in the register office while she and Nicola giggled; and the rain rattling on the zinc roof of the bathroom in Chelsea the night Marco de Sampaio had been hanged.

Emily turned to Michael. He was squatting now on the ground, his hat in his hand, his hair yellow. A thought crossed her mind. At about the time Fortunate and Marco had been making him in the windy house she had been conceiving Catherine in Paris.

And Nicola had been dying.

521

Chapter Fifty-Nine

Murder is different from any other form of death. It calls for investigation. It must be unravelled. It demands certainties. An open verdict is no verdict. It only provokes more questions. Why and how? But mainly, who? Who killed Nicola Reynolds? Who killed Marco de Sampaio?

Richard had sat for some time outside the caravan before plucking up the courage to knock on the door. From time to time he had seen the thin curtains part, and a face peer into the darkness across the common towards his car. Perhaps he was supposed to flash his headlamps, he thought, or make some other kind of signal.

Emily did not know he was there. She would have advised against it. She was frightened. The past was crawling out of its grave and beckoning, with its secrets and lies. He wished they had never found Fortunate, that Penny Chilston had burned Michael Mavangwe's letter along with everything else. Now he had to know. The possibility that a young man had been hanged for a murder he did not commit numbed him.

They had returned from Africa the night after seeing Fortunate, their joy in reconciliation fractured by doubts. Richard had wanted to go immediately to Hudson with Fortunate's story, to hear him explain it. She was obviously exaggerating the row. It had probably been no more than a tiff. But Hudson had still been in Florida negotiating the purchase of the printing company.

Richard had to understand, to colour the new grey areas of doubt. It obsessed him. He remembered Nicola and relived their times together, the happiness and the pain. They had broken apart and their lives had changed, but he had never stopped loving her, not when she had married and not when she had died.

In the cuttings' library he had read again accounts of the Wildwood murder, and stared into the handsome face of Marco de Sampaio. 'I do not know,' the African had said through a translator when asked in court to account for his activities on the night of the murder. 'I cannot remember.' He might just as well have tied the rope himself.

In the end Richard had asked Irene, his secretary, to find out Holly Carter's address. 'Tim Gimmelmann will know,' he had explained. 'Tell him it's personal.'

He climbed from his car and, crossing the sparse grass, tapped lightly on the caravan door. It was raining. Fifty yards away a train thundered through a cutting. Waste paper lay sodden in the mud. An outside light came on. The door opened.

'Well now . . .' Holly Carter leaned against the door-frame, gloating, a cigarette between her fingers. It was almost a replica of the pose she had adopted when he had first seen her, the provocative child beauty on the waste land. Now she was no longer beautiful. She was big, her face and body swollen, her hair stringy and bleached again. She was wearing an old pair of black, tight, satin trousers and a pink blouse with a round neck which hung off pudding-fat shoulders.

'I wondered if I could talk to you?' he asked.

She smirked. 'That's what they all say. I never expected to see you again.'

'Can I come in?'

She stepped back into the light and indicated with her head that he should enter. Now he saw the scar which disfigured her face. It ran from the side of her mouth almost to her right ear. It looked like a razor slash. She noticed him looking. 'A dissatisfied customer,' she said, and closed the door on the rain.

He sat down on the edge of a stained tartan rug which lay across a bunk bed. The interior of the caravan was filthy and cluttered. Underclothes and tights were scattered on the floor and across cushions and furniture. The remains of a Kentucky Fried Chicken meal lay in its carton on the narrow folding table. A cat was eating a sardine from a tin on the floor. A bottle of vodka had recently been opened. An empty one lay on the bunk. The light was dim.

Once Holly Carter had mesmerized. The face of 1965. He had to remind himself.

'Gone off, have I?' she cackled. 'If it's a "where are they now?" number you can stuff it. That's why I'm out here stuck up the backside of beyond, so they won't find me. I don't want to be famous any more. It might put the punters off. And I need the punters, special clients to keep me in the lifestyle I've become accustomed to.'

'Er, no . . . nothing like that,' said Richard, a little too quickly.

She looked at him strangely for a moment, then she said: 'You've done well, haven't you? Timmy told me.' Then she said: 'It's two hundred quid to you, whatever it is.'

'I just want to talk.'

'Two hundred quid for that too. It's all the same to me. Unless you want to do two things at once. Special discount then.' She cackled again, but it was only the scar on her cheek which seemed to smile. Her lips stayed in their sneer.

Without asking if he wanted any she poured two inches of vodka into a plastic cup and passed it to him with a bottle of tonic water. Then she sharpened her own drink.

'I want to ask you something, and I want you to tell me the truth. I don't think it will be important to you, but it is to me.'

Her face was expressionless.

He took a drink. 'I want you to tell me about you and Hudson,' he said.

That almost produced a smile. This was easy money.

524

Hudson? Christ, this is going back a bit, isn't it?'

'But you haven't forgotten?'

'How could I forget? The mighty Hudson. Timmy would never let me forget that.'

'Tell me,' he said, and, taking out his wallet, counted out ten twenty-pound notes and placed them on the bunk between them. He had come supplied.

She picked up the money and, opening an old handbag, stuffed it inside. 'What do you want to know? He fancied me. You all fancied me. I could see it. But he never came on like some of you. He used to look at me as though he knew all about me, as though he knew what it was like and had to stay away. Timmy was wetting his knickers for Hudson. I knew what little Timmy was from the start. He worshipped Hudson. What he wouldn't have done to have changed places with me.'

'You had an affair with Hudson?'

'"Affair!!"' She rasped unpleasantly at the word, but then her smile snapped closed. 'People like me don't have affairs. That's for your sort. Did you never notice that?'

He was embarrassed. 'But you went to bed with him?'

She snorted, clearing her throat. 'If you want to call it that. I gave him a present, didn't I? A nice little wedding present. Showed him what he'd be missing with that stuck-up cow. I thought he might be too drunk. Stag-nights can be a real disaster. But he wasn't. I waited for him, sitting on the steps outside his flat. "You'd better come in," he said, "you're getting wet out here." Always the gentleman, wasn't he? Such a fake.'

'Fake?'

She shrugged. 'Wasn't he?'

He sat in silence for some moments. He wanted to ask her why she hated so much, but he doubted that she would have been able to tell him. 'Did he say anything?' he asked at last.

Now she smiled, showing the tips of her teeth between the bright, full lips. Assuming an American accent she whimpered: 'Don't tell her. Don't tell Nicola. Please don't tell her.'

Chapter Sixty

Hudson arrived back from Florida on a Tuesday but it was not until the following Sunday afternoon that Richard called on him. For days Richard had sought another way, trying, with Emily, to put the matter out of mind. It was impossible. On the Saturday night when he had arrived home from the paper he had found her leafing through an old photograph album, looking at a picture of the four of them taken one day at the races, Nicola in a silly green hat she had made herself, Hudson peering the wrong way down a pair of binoculars.

'He wouldn't like to think we were behaving like this,' Emily had said quietly. 'It's not surprising that if Nicola found out about Holly she was hysterical. She always hated her. Why should he have told us if they fell out? I'm sure they made up again. He was obviously right about the men he saw running towards the border. If they'd listened to him Marco de Sampaio wouldn't have been hanged. The poor man was just too convenient.' She had it all worked out. Still Richard had not slept.

It was already mid-October, and the pavement outside Hudson's home in The Boltons was littered with spiked and squashed husks from the horse-chestnut tree which stood there. Richard parked his car in the road, although there was plenty of space in the drive. Climbing out he paused to pick up a conker and polish it on his trousers. Tom was collecting conkers.

It was at that moment, as he stood up, that he saw Hudson watching, standing in the first-floor drawing room of the large white house. There was no greeting: Hudson simply stared down blankly from his mansion,

527

looking, for once, almost small, framed by the lofty window. It was an expression Richard had seen before, many years ago, very early one morning when he had returned to the Lamborne after his first night with Nicola.

The front door opened electronically as he reached it and he stepped into the white marble of the hall.

Hudson was already waiting at the top of the stairs. In his old tweed jacket and slacks, and with his hair recently cut and his slight Florida tan showing against the blue of his shirt, he looked quite boyish. 'Good to see you, Richard,' he called down. 'Come on up. We've the place to ourselves for once.' His voice echoed around the house.

Slowly Richard climbed the wide steps. He had telephoned before leaving home, asking if it was all right if he popped around for a chat. 'Sure, anytime. Now? You want to come over now? Sure. Why not?'

Hudson led the way into the drawing room. On the rug in front of the sofa lay all the day's newspapers, tabloids to one side, qualities to the other. *Night And Day* and *Sunday Morning* were together. 'I was just comparing the field,' he said. 'We did pretty well for a quiet time, I'd say.'

Richard agreed. He didn't know how to begin. 'I heard Florida went well,' he said at last. Ben Tarlo had been talking. Hudson had even bought a beach house so that he would have somewhere to stay when he was there. He had never much liked hotels.

Hudson smiled to himself. 'Do you want a drink, Richard?' he asked.

This was a surprise. Hudson rarely offered drinks. Because he drank so little himself it never occurred to him. 'No, thank you.'

Hudson made it easy. 'To be honest I've been expecting you since I got back. I'm surprised you took so long.'

Richard must have looked puzzled.

'I heard you went to Africa. I called you at home from New York. Catherine told me. I swore her to

secrecy. She said you'd gone to give Emily a surprise.'
Hudson smiled. 'That was good. I'm glad you came to
your senses.'

He had stolen the initiative. Richard hesitated.

'So, anyway . . . ?' Hudson was waiting.

'I don't know where to begin.' Another pause. 'It's
about Nicola . . .'

Hudson waited.

'This may sound crazy, but I'm afraid they may have
hanged an innocent man.'

For a long moment Hudson gazed at him and then
very quietly turned away and stared out of the window.
The sun was already very low and pink in the sky behind
the trees. 'Yes,' he said. There was no surprise in his voice.

Briefly Richard explained about the letter from the
albino boy, how Emily had gone to find him, perhaps to
try to help through the Hudson Foundation, and of their
meeting with the boy's mother, Fortunate. He paused.
'Fortunate told us that the night Nicola died . . . she
was with Marco de Sampaio. He couldn't have killed
her . . .'

Hudson stared at him. 'Go on.'

'She said she heard you fighting, that Nicola was
hysterical. She saw her lying on the rug. She thought
she was sleeping, and that someone else must have gone
into the house after you went riding, after de Sampaio
had stolen the handbag.'

Hudson's face was washed of expression. 'And what
about you and Emily? What do you think?'

Richard couldn't answer. He shook his head. 'I don't
know. You saw three strangers . . .'

Hudson thought for a moment and then said: 'It
won't bring her back, you know. Nothing we do can
change that.'

'But if an innocent man was hanged the investigation
should be reopened . . .'

Standing up Hudson moved away from him and sat
down at the piano. Again there was a silence, as though

529

Hudson was carrying on a simultaneous conversation inside his head. At last he said: 'Do you remember that first night out we had together, those two Norwegian girls. I knew then we could have a brilliant future together if we could just get it right. I suppose it was the sharing I liked. Doing things together. You and me. Then Nicola and Emily. The four of us. Those were the best times. Do you remember? Everything before had been leading up to that. Everything since has been, I don't know . . . empty.'

He allowed his right hand to trace a few notes high at the top end of the keyboard, but as abruptly as he had begun he stopped playing and closed the piano lid.

'There were no three strangers, Richard. I made them up trying to save Marco de Sampaio's life. I figured I might muddy the waters sufficiently to get him off. I suppose I didn't try hard enough. I guess I didn't want to try hard enough . . .'

He stared down at his hands. Suddenly Richard wanted him to stop now, but it was too late.

'You ask yourself where it all goes wrong. At what moment. Because there is a moment. It's so easily done. A few drinks, a temptation, one last fling, one last woman. Holly. She made it so easy. Nothing very important, you might think. Not even that unusual, not really. It happens all the time. And Nicola need never have known. Except, she wanted to know, and I suppose I must have wanted her to know.'

Now he needed to talk. Richard didn't have to prompt.

'I'd told so many lies, to her, to you, to everyone. I don't know how many of them you believed, all those excuses I dreamed up. I imagine you were too polite to enquire too deeply. But I wanted to tell Nicola everything. To start again. Without any secrets. At first I told her all the problems. We were going bust, you know. *Witness* was about to go under. Charlie Latymer had picked up some gossip about Farrow and Fox going broke and had ratted to the bank that they couldn't pay

530

us. And if they couldn't pay us . . .' He let his hand fall. 'We couldn't repay the bank. I kept it from you. Business was my problem. You were getting your part right, week in, week out. Only Adam knew. We juggled the figures every night to keep it from the board, trying to carry on for a little while longer, all the time hoping for a miracle. They're funny guys, bankers. They'll come and celebrate your wedding, drink your champagne and kiss your bride, knowing all the time they'll be putting you on the street the following morning. Maybe Charlie Latymer should have been a banker.'

He became thoughtful. 'I didn't want anything from her, you know. I wanted to do it all myself. She wanted to get married. I wasn't ready. It was too soon. She was impulsive. She wouldn't even listen to the *Witness* problems until we were married. She said she wasn't having her life spoiled by a few little money troubles.

'I told her on the plane going out to Africa about the bank and *Witness*. You know, she just laughed. She thought I was crazy to worry about it. Crazy? *Witness* was everything I had in the world. I'd borrowed a hundred thousand pounds and couldn't pay it back. To her there was no problem. It was her idea to buy out Farrow and Fox. I'd never properly realized before what ambition she had. "You won't go bust," she said. "I won't let you. We'll get bigger and bigger until we're too big to go bust." She wanted a Sunday newspaper one day, you know. We talked about it at Wildwood. "One day," she said, "we'll have our own paper and call it *Sunday Morning*." That was her idea.'

He almost smiled at the memory.

'Wildwood. I thought it was heaven up there. The hill, the forest, the house. Nobody I'd ever known owned anything like that. Emily had told me how vast it was, but it was still a surprise.' He stopped abruptly and looked at Richard. 'I have everything from there, you know. I sent the vans, had everything packed and stored, Nicola's things separately. They're all here upstairs. But I couldn't go back there. Not after what happened.'

'What did happen?' Richard asked, his voice scarcely above a whisper.

'It was the Wednesday, we'd been down to the town, making plans, talking magazines and publishing. A lot of it silly, honeymoon talk. When we got back Fortunate and her boy-friend, Marco, were hanging around outside. Nicola was friendly towards him. She bought some grass. He was making a name for himself as the local supplier.

'There were just the two of us for dinner. Nicola made it, shooing Alice out of the kitchen. We had a few drinks, some wine. We went to bed for a while, then sat downstairs by the fire, Nicola in her nightdress. Just one of those lazy evenings. We were talking about Fortunate and she asked me if I found her attractive. Just testing, I suppose. It was nothing. Then she asked me about Holly. She had kissed me at the wedding. What did it mean? she wanted to know. I said it was nothing and that I didn't know and tried to change the subject. But I suppose I must have betrayed something because she wouldn't drop it. "Are you sure it didn't mean anything? You can tell me. I won't be angry if at some time . . . I'd rather know. I'll understand." I swore there was nothing, but she wouldn't leave it alone . . . You know how she was?'

In the darkness Richard nodded. Hudson's face was now deep in the gloom of early evening.

'For some reason, I'll never know why, I told her. No secrets. That was what we told each other. We'd never have any secrets again. But it was more than that. I wanted to tell her. Maybe I wanted to have some kind of absolution from her. I didn't want it lying there between us, a guilty secret, ready to be thrown up at us at some time when Holly felt vindictive. And she would have done that. I knew. Holly was destructive.

'It had been this wonderful, wonderful evening, and suddenly I destroyed it. I don't think she believed me at first, you know, because she didn't get upset or mad or anything. She just looked at me in a funny way and asked for the details.'

He stopped. His voice had begun to break. 'I told her about the stag-night and how Holly had been there, waiting . . . that it was a terrible, incomprehensible thing to do and that I was sorry . . . She was so quiet, I thought she understood. But then she began to cry, and when I went to comfort her, she pushed me away, and began to shout, "Don't touch me", "The filthy stinking slut", "You disgust me". She couldn't stop. She became hysterical and began fighting me off. I thought Alice or Joseph would hear. I was trying to calm her down. She was hitting me, beating me, screaming, louder and louder. She said I'd ruined everything, and she was right, I had. But she was out of control and I couldn't stop her. She went on and on . . . I was begging for forgiveness. But then . . .' He stopped. His voice had risen as emotion had charged through. He became quiet again. 'You're right about Marco de Sampaio. He was hanged for a murder he didn't commit. But we don't need a new investigation. We know who killed Nicola. I did.'

For how long had Richard known? A few days: a couple of weeks? But still he did not want to believe it. Not even now when Hudson admitted it. Trust me, Hudson had always said, trust me, from that first day when they had carried his old beige trunk into the Lamborne together, the young American, on his first day in London. 'Trust me.' And Richard had. Everybody had.

Hudson was still talking, this moment mentally rehearsed perhaps for years. 'I killed Nicola, Richard, and indirectly I killed Marco de Sampaio. I could have saved him, but I didn't. When it came to it, the moment when I could have stepped in, I did nothing. I let him die. I murdered him.'

Richard was shaking his head. 'No . . .'

'Nicola was an accident. She finally went too far.

Something she said . . . Something I'd told her . . . a secret, about my mother. She threw it back at me. Said that was the only kind of woman I was fit for . . . She didn't mean it, didn't know what she was saying. But I couldn't take it. I just hit out. Quite hard. Very hard. She fell. Her head hit the edge of the fireplace. I knew immediately. She just lay there on the carpet, as though she'd fallen asleep by the fire. There was no blood. I sat with her for hours. I'd lost everything in one moment. When dawn came I got changed and slipped out of the house. It was so beautiful up there, so fresh. I just wanted to ride and ride. I didn't ever want to go back. When I did I expected to be arrested. I was really giving myself up when I rode back through the forest to Wildwood. But even before I'd dismounted I realized that no one suspected me. Alice and Joseph had found Nicola's body and lifted it on to the sofa. It was just assumed right away that it couldn't possibly have been me. They were apologizing to me that this should happen there. They were ashamed, they said. And I let them be ashamed.'

He stopped to reflect on what he had said. It was dark now, and the contours of his face were lost in the gloom.

'I let them pursue Marco de Sampaio because I thought they would never catch him, that he'd be across the border and gone. The three men I said I'd seen was something to confuse them even more. I'd expected to be arrested. I thought that my life had ended. I'd lost Nicola. I'd lose *Witness*, you and Emily, and everything I'd built up. I'd started with nothing, less than nothing, and I was back with nothing.'

Richard must have shifted in his chair, because Hudson repeated himself. 'Yes, nothing, Richard. No matter what I might have told you. Nothing. There never was a rich family in California. I'm sure you guessed eventually, because you stopped mentioning them. Nicola guessed. I worked for five years, night and day, doing every job I could find to have enough money to come over here and set myself up, to begin again, as the person I thought I wanted to be. It isn't unusual. You know that. Nobody ever checks. You tell a story often enough, get it into a few cuttings, and it becomes the truth.

'The way Nicola died was, I suppose, just another lie, though I never intended it. I never thought someone else would take the blame. That was never the plan. But, I suppose, when I wasn't suspected, I saw a way out for myself. I could make all the things Nicola and I had planned come true. It didn't have to be the end of my life.

'I was certain Marco de Sampaio would get off. The evidence against him seemed so flimsy, circumstantial. I kept telling myself that if things went really badly for him I'd own up and take whatever was coming to me. But as the weeks went by, as the sympathy flooded in – even Nicola's uncle began treating me like a son – I began to somehow believe the part I was playing. When he was found guilty I tried to get an appeal going, but it was turned down. I still didn't believe they would hang him. I couldn't believe it. I kept saying to myself, "Just one more day and I'll own up." But I never did.

'Then on the last night, the night before he was to hang, I picked up the phone and began to make the call. I didn't complete it. The moral courage ran out on me. I was scared. All my problems had been solved, I was rich and the world felt sorry for me. I went and got drunk, stinking drunk, so drunk I couldn't stand up. When I woke up it was too late. He was already dead . . .'

A sodium, yellow street-lamp had come on down the road casting a pale glow around him, an outline now against the white piano. Above the piano hung Gimmelmann's photograph of Nicola. 'Why did you tell me all this?' Richard asked at last.

Hudson sighed. 'You'd found out anyway. Hadn't you? I think you had.' There was a short silence before he said: 'I'm glad.' He breathed out, a short broken gasp. 'I've wanted to talk about it for a long time now . . .' The room was suddenly lit up by the headlamps of a passing car. Hudson must have seen the loss in Richard's face because he said suddenly: 'I'm sorry, really sorry that you had to know. Sorry for everything. But you're my friend, Richard. That's what friends are for. No more secrets.'

Chapter Sixty-One

With a strong recommendation that funds be provided for help in the building and equipping of a secondary school in Musaswe, Zimbabwe, Emily resigned by letter from the Hudson Foundation the following morning. Richard had already been into *Sunday Morning* to clear his desk. Because it was Monday he had not bumped into any of his senior colleagues, had not been asked for any explanation. Emily sent her resignation by messenger. She offered no explanation either.

Richard had arrived home the previous evening in shock, hardly able to speak. Hudson, he had said, had pursued him to his car, telling him how happy he was that everything was now out in the open, beginning, even, to make new plans for them both.

Neither Emily nor Richard had slept. The enormity of Hudson's confession lay across them, an immovable, smothering burden. Nicola's death had been an accident. They could understand that, could see how it had happened, Nicola baiting Hudson, coaxing him to tell her about Holly, and then, in fury and hysterics, turning upon him. 'I'll kill you if you're ever unfaithful to me,' she had once told Richard, while Emily remembered the tantrum by the river at Oxford, the collision with a runner which had erupted into a screaming match. She had been highly strung and insecure: and sometimes frighteningly possessive. Yes, it was possible to imagine the row, the momentary loss of control, immediately and eternally regretted. But there had been nothing momentary or accidental about the execution of Marco de Sampaio.

'It was as though by telling me he felt he was somehow making it all right,' Richard had said suddenly,

537

deep in the night. 'As though he's lived with it for so long he thinks he's paid the penalty. When he'd finished telling me he looked exhausted, but somehow relieved.'

Emily had not replied. She had known and loved Hudson for nearly twenty years. She was in turmoil. It was as though half of their lives had been torn up. They wanted to hide from what they knew.

More than anything they needed time, and when the children came home from school they were greeted with an early half-term holiday. They flew to Venice that night, changing at Milan, where they told them as briefly and evenly as possible that there had been a falling out with Hudson. Their expressions and voices must have betrayed them, because there were surprisingly few questions, not even from Catherine.

For the children the adventure that is Venice was a distraction. For Emily and Richard there was no relief. A street photographer in St Mark's Square mistook them for a happy family and caught them, frozen in a squall of pigeons. Later when Emily looked at the picture in the window of his shop she saw that her eyes were glassy, Richard's smile forced.

They telephoned Emily's mother who said reporters from other newspapers had been trying to find out where they were. She had not asked for an explanation. She never did.

The weather was sharp and cold, and an autumn mist lingered over the canals. They did all the tourist trips and marvelled together, but Emily recognized little, her vision clouded by tears of despair. It was worse than losing Nicola.

After the first two days they did not mention Hudson, not even to each other and, though they tried desperately not to show it, a depression settled over them. They each had a journey to make. The destination was the same, but it was a journey they could only travel separately, as they began to reassess their lives.

After three days Richard bought the English newspapers. There was some Press speculation about a row at Hudson Communications, but as neither Richard nor Emily was exactly a household name, they knew that, unfuelled by further incident, interest in them would quickly die. Hudson, they noticed, was said to be unavailable for comment.

On the fourth night Emily dreamed that Hudson made love to her. They were in the windy house, their bed a mattress of moss and moist leaves on the small, wooden platform. They were both dressed, though she was barefoot, and as she lay back she could feel twigs scratching her bare legs. 'We must be quick or Nicola will find us,' Hudson was whispering, as his hand found the warm cotton of her underclothes. And, though she knew it was wrong, betrayal heightened the excitement as her arms and body opened for him. He was so handsome. How could she resist? 'It's all right,' she heard herself say, 'Nicola's dead, she won't know. We can stay here all day. No one will ever know.' Her skirt around her waist, his hands under her, she pushed her face into his shoulder. Above them the old msasa tree curved and spread. She held him. He was so beautiful. Why should she resist? Now she could smell the msasa leaves, yet somehow they were orchids, could see Richard and Joseph on the lawn holding Mashona for Nicola to mount, knew the fear and excitement of imminent discovery. Through the leaves the house looked bare and abandoned, the windows broken, while across the lawn a black man she knew to be Marco de Sampaio was playing croquet with Fortunate. And then came Nicola, dressed for riding, the young and beautiful girl she had always been, chatting and teasing Michael Mavangwe who, with his pink, albino hands, stroked Mashona's shiny, black neck. Nicola! 'She isn't dead after all,' Emily murmured, her voice breaking, smiling in her dream. 'It was all a mistake.' But urgency was governing her now as she felt her body drawn upwards into Hudson's. 'Don't tell Nicola,' he was gasping, as they clung together, 'don't tell Nicola, don't tell Nicola, don't tell Nicola . . .', over and over as below them Mashona cantered around the lawn, a handsome black pony ridden by a beautiful fair girl, who smiled at them, looking up into the msasa tree and the windy house, laughing and waving. 'Emmy . . . Emmy. I can see you . . . Emmy, Emmy . . . I'm watching . . . Emmy . . .'

The violence of her release awoke her. She was moaning, sobbing into her pillow, panting, her skin wet with sweat as she grasped desperately, futilely at the receding joy of her dream.

'Are you all right?' A dim bedside light clicked on.

Slowly she opened her eyes on the tall, narrow hotel bedroom. Alongside her Richard was watching.

'You were dreaming,' he said.

Then she remembered and was ashamed. 'I'm sorry,' she said. She closed her eyes again, but she was too late. Nicola had gone.

Richard put a hand on her shoulder. She took it and together they lay and waited for another day.

Chapter Sixty-Two

(i)

Penny Chilston watched from the balcony as very gradually the pine tree was tilted and lowered into the hole in the centre of the lawn: a delicate task. The tree had arrived that morning on the back of a forty-foot-long truck, its roots caked in soil and polythene-wrapped, its branches lashed together for transportation, and its growing tip jutting a full ten feet off the end of the tail-board, a hazard sign hanging there. A pick-up truck with a flashing roof light had followed closely all the way from Orlando. All afternoon, with a crane and pulleys, five men had laboured to raise the tree in time for Christmas. Standing by was another truck, two electricians and two hundred feet of rubber-sealed fairy lights. It was Christmas Eve, ten past four in the afternoon, seventy-nine degrees and a Spanish-speaking gardener was spraying water from a hosepipe on to the pine tree's lower branches.

Penny sipped her lemon tea and turned the page of the novel she had been reading. She had promised to write a review during the Christmas break, but the book was heavy going and she was finding it difficult to concentrate. Or could it be that this house, this situation, was not conducive to concentration?

The way Hudson had spoken of the house had made it sound like some no-account shack washed up on the Atlantic coast of Florida, hardly more than a collection of driftwood. In reality it was hardly less than a summer mansion in white-walled Spanish colonial style, a nineteen-thirties folly with nineteen-eighties luxury. 'It even has curtains,' Penny had joked upon first being shown around. Unlike the house in The Boltons this one had been bought already furnished.

Hudson had tried to smile, but he was not good at jokes these days, and, apparently happy that she approved, he had wandered off to greet his other guests. He had promised just a small house party, but now the rooms were filling. Willie Simmonds had arrived from California with his teenage dancer girl-friend, Marsha; someone called Morty, Hudson's New York lawyer, was due at any moment along with his wife, Esther; while a young novelist called Sherman, whom Hudson had met on a plane and decided to help, had moved with his beach-comber wife into the apartment over the pool house. And if British Airways were on time Rajah Dehwola and Hudson's personal assistant Annabel, together with their latest partners, would be there in time for dinner. There might have been more: Tim Gimmelmann and his friend Edward had sent their apologies, having already arranged a week in Thailand, while the Tarlos had dropped out that very morning when one of their children had gone down with chicken-pox.

Penny had not asked Hudson about Richard and Emily. Others had tried during the past few weeks and been met with a grey, empty stare, and a shake of the head. After lying low for all of November Richard had agreed to have lunch with Penny at the beginning of December, but had changed the subject whenever Hudson was mentioned.

It was more than puzzling, more than sad. Hudson, though still smiling, had become distant and restless. And although he had thrown open his home to his friends he seemed less the host than the reluctant guest, more solitary than ever as every day he walked alone on the beach, or stayed in his room, old blues records scratching remorselessly on his record player.

Across the lawn the Christmas tree was finally ver-tical and to everyone's satisfaction. Held upright with ropes from three corners, two labourers shovelled earth around the roots. Standing it looked taller than Penny had expected, as high as the palm trees which mounted guard at either side of the house. When the lights were switched on it would be something to see, she thought.

'What do you think? Will we have the best Christmas tree in Florida this year?' Hudson was at her side. She had not heard him approaching along the balcony. Despite the slight tan he looked, she thought, more tired, more worn than she had ever seen him. Under his eyes were heavy bags. Unusually for him he had not shaved.

'I don't know about that,' she said. 'But it's certainly big. Are you sure such a tall tree can survive being uprooted and moved like that?'

Hudson leaned against the balcony wall and observed the activity. The ropes securing the tree were now being taken away. 'I don't know, to be honest, Penny. They tell me it can. I'm trusting their judgement. They say you can transplant anything if you can take enough of the old soil with you.'

A sea breeze had now sprung up, stirring the palm trees, and together they watched as the electricians began to unwind the fairy lights. From the vicinity of the pool, around the corner of the house, came the low thudding of disco music, as the younger guests began to enjoy their Christmas in the sun. Momentarily Penny thought about the photographer. He had always preferred bars with a juke box, and she remembered sitting with him in a bar that last night in Beirut. She missed him more than she would ever have thought possible.

She looked back at Hudson. The electricians had lost his attention now and he was gazing across the lawn, between a gap in the palm trees and on towards the beach and the sea, his expression alert, concerned, as though he was watching someone in the far distance, someone she could not see.

Suddenly she realized something. All her adult life she had desired Hudson: now, for the first time, she was aware that she did not. Yet she still loved him.

Putting a hand on his she said: 'Penny says, penny for 'em.'

Slowly Hudson shook his head. 'To tell you the truth I really don't think they're worth it,' he said. And turning away he went back down the balcony towards his own private rooms.

Below on the lawn the electricians began to hang the lights on the tree.

(*ii*)

It rained on Christmas Day in London, a grey, heavy day of silent streets and new clothes, and Emily up early to put the turkey into the oven. On the top floor the children opened their pillow cases, tearing apart hours of careful wrapping, and were happy. Richard stood in his bedroom and watched the rain on the road and listened to their excitement. They would make it a good day.

It had been difficult, a strain. A way of life had ended abruptly, awfully. Emily had her part-time teaching, which, during a minor 'flu epidemic, had expanded to fill four mornings a week, but Richard, who had never been a day without a job since he started *Witness*, had found his new idleness bewildering. He had always worked in an office and missed the charge of news and deadlines. Now he had too much time to ruminate. There had been approaches, of course, and invitations to lunch with colleagues throughout newspapers. But, apart from Penny, he had had no appetite to see anyone. In mid-December because Emily had worried at him to get out and do something, he had agreed to write and record a BBC radio series about the role of newspapers in a democracy. It was, he would joke bleakly, the sort of thing out-of-work editors did to keep their hand in.

They had tried not to think about what they knew, about Nicola and Marco de Sampaio. But how could they forget? There was, they were aware, a correct procedure. There had been a terrible miscarriage of justice. They knew what they ought to do, but it had never seriously occurred to them to make a report to the Zimbabwean authorities. Apart from clearing Marco de Sampaio's name it was difficult to see how the re-opening of the case for investigation could possibly do any good.

The family tradition had been that Hudson provided the tree and helped the children dress it a week before Christmas, turning up on Christmas Day to sit between Emily's mother and Catherine. Then Richard's father would tell the jokes he told every year, and his mother would try to catch Hudson's eye. They might just as well have left an empty place at the table, Richard mused later over lunch, as, with studied politeness, everyone went out of their way to avoid mentioning Hudson.

It wasn't the same, but it was Christmas, and the house smelled warm, and was prettily decorated, and the children were thrilled with their presents. A family Christmas, the Queen's Speech and *The Sound of Music* on television again. Nicola, he remembered, had always teased Emily that she was really a *Sound of Music* sort of girl.

As usual Hudson's presents were saved to the last, opened just before tea on Christmas Day when presents from grandparents and other relatives would be exchanged. This year was no different. Josh, Hudson's driver, had delivered them in the Mercedes some days earlier, each one carefully chosen and neatly addressed in Hudson's small handwriting. It had been the first contact with him since October, and, at first, Richard had wondered whether the children should even accept the gifts. Emily had seen things more clearly. Of course they must accept them.

He had not disappointed, each present carefully, affectionately chosen: a pretty necklace for Catherine which made her feel grown up, an illustrated book on American Indians for Benedict's latest craze and a make-your-own space station set for Tom. And, as always, there was a collective present, a family game for playing on Christmas

545

night, this year, *Newscaster*, a new question-and-answer board game from a Hudson Communications subsidiary.

'News is news is news, I agree, but it's also money,' Hudson had once said. He'd got that right, Richard reflected.

They played for hours, the whole family, parents, grandparents, children, Richard's sister Carol, and even Daniel and his new blonde girl-friend, joining in to try and beat the 'newscaster' with questions. 'Who coined the phrase "iron curtain"?', 'Where was the armistice at the end of the First World War signed?', 'In what state was Elvis Presley born?', 'Where is Margaret Thatcher's parliamentary constituency?', 'In what year did Richard Nixon resign the US presidency?'

Around and around they went. News, news and more news, presents, slices of Christmas cake, crumbs amongst the wrapping-paper on the carpet, sprigs of dried holly, cards falling off the mantelpiece in the draught from the fire, the children, eager and competitive, and Emily catching Richard's eye across the room: the kindest of smiles. A family at Christmas.

(*iii*)

They held swimming races in the afternoon, some of the younger ones, Rajah Dehwola imitating a porpoise to show off to his girl-friend: Sherman, the young author, claiming, when he was beaten, that he was too drunk to swim.

Sitting in the shade in her deck-chair, her lumpen shape covered by a sun-dress, Penny watched Willie's topless girl-friend, Marsha, rubbing sun cream on to his back. Californian life suited Willie. His stammer had almost gone, as had his hair, but he looked younger and fitter than she had seen him in years.

It was a strange, unfocused kind of Christmas Day, centred around a large, poolside brunch, where a team of caterers smiled and served and wished everyone a Happy

Christmas, and a barman offered a cocktail known as a Noel special. 'No, thank you,' Penny said politely, and watched while the New York lawyer's wife turned from an elegant, middle-aged woman into a squawking embarrassment, wondering if she had once talked so loudly when she was drunk.

Penny looked around the pool. Hudson would probably be back soon. She had seen him earlier from her bedroom window, swimming alone, length after length. He was a good swimmer. But by the time the first guests had reached the pool he had gone for a walk along the beach.

For almost the first time since Penny had known him there was no beautiful woman in attendance. She had sat next to him at dinner the previous night. For a while he had been more like his usual self, amused by Willie's jokes and stories, bright and attentive to Penny. 'I'm glad you could make it down here, Penny,' he had said. She knew he meant it.

The Christmas tree had been a great success and Hudson had smiled like a boy as the lights had been switched on. But it had been a short-lived delight, and, although Penny and Willie had stayed up late talking with Rajah and the young author, Hudson had left them shortly after dinner. 'Is he well?' Willie had asked. Penny had shrugged.

Getting up from her chair Penny reached for a sun-hat and made her way through the garden to the gate which led out on to the beach. She saw him at once, not far away, standing at the edge of the ocean, watching the waves. At first she thought to join him, to take his hand and coax him back to his friends. But she didn't.

The piano awoke her. It was almost half-past five. She listened for some moments. With such a smooth, bluesy touch she had no need to wonder who might be playing. Hudson was so perverse. After making himself scarce all day, he had turned up for dinner, hardly spoken to anyone apart from her, and disappeared immediately afterwards, despite the Cuban rock group who had taken over the main hall with their Latin soul music.

It had been a good party, too, high spirits, fat balloons, Willie and Marsha doing a Fred and Ginger impersonation, Rajah Dehwola trying to poach the author's wife, and Penny dancing alone happily in a corner.

'I'm sorry if I'm not being a lot of fun,' Hudson had apologized during dinner. 'Maybe dragging you all down here wasn't such a brilliant idea. I guess I'm not really in the mood this year.'

'Don't worry about it,' Penny had told him. 'Everyone's having a terrific time.'

'I suppose I wanted it to be like the old days. D'you remember the old *Witness* parties we used to have?' His sudden smile faded. 'I was happy then.'

She watched from the shadows of the stairs. He was such a tall man, playing alone, slumped over the white grand piano, his eyes closed, his cheeks wet with tears that shone yellow and red in the glow of the fairy lights from the Christmas tree on the lawn. His fingers stroked the keys. He had such a gentle touch.

Chapter Sixty-Three

Ben Tarlo, as managing director of Hudson Communications, was the first to hear. He had been called by the Florida police and telephoned Richard immediately. Emily took the call. She thought it must be a mistake. Then she refused to believe it.

It was late in January, a bright, freezing day, and she had just returned from school. Richard was at the BBC recording his series. She called him and he hurried home immediately.

The mid-evening news brought the confirmation. 'James Hudson, head of Hudson Communications, is feared to have drowned while swimming off the coast of Florida this morning, where he had been staying in his beach-side mansion. He was alone at the time but was seen to enter the sea by a writer and his wife who were living on the millionaire newspaper publisher's estate.'

The head and shoulders of a young couple appeared on the screen. They looked confused. They had not spoken to Hudson for some days, they said, but had noticed him early in the morning sitting on the beach.

The young man spoke for both of them. 'He was a good swimmer, so we thought nothing of it when he went into the water and began to swim out to sea. But then he didn't stop. It was as if he was going somewhere and was in a real bad hurry to get there. He just kept on heading out, further and further. I called Calendar, and she got the binoculars. We still thought he'd turn back. But when we realized he wasn't going to we called the police. We'd lost sight of him way before the Coast Guard could get here . . .'

No body was found. Hudson had simply walked into the sea and disappeared.

PART EIGHT

June 1987

Chapter Sixty-Four

(i)

The racket of war, mortars pummelling, the thudding of heavy bombs; tanks smashing through flimsy barbed-wire barricades, buildings crumbling, dive-bombers strafing the ground; the German invasion of Yugoslavia on black-and-white newsreel with the volume turned far too high.

The voice of Clover Merrifield, mellifluent yet serious, emerged from the tympany: 'James Hudson, publisher and philanthropist, lived and died an enigma. But until today no one ever really knew where he came from: no one still knows for sure why he died.' The war dissolved through to newsreel of Hudson at work in his office. 'But, during nearly two decades, James Hudson built not only a giant international newspaper, magazine and communications network; he also laid the foundations for a worldwide charitable trust for education – the Hudson Foundation. Always a generous man Hudson gave freely in his lifetime, and in his will he directed that his entire personal holding in all his companies should go to his Foundation, thus ensuring that so long as Hudson Communications prospered so would the Hudson Foundation. This week when the new Hudson Communications Centre, the Nicola Reynolds Building, is officially opened by the Queen in London, we take a look at the man who was James Hudson, at where he came from, at what he achieved, and at the mystery of how and why he died . . .' The camera panned along a deserted Florida beach to gaze across an empty ocean: music swelled.

Alongside her Emily felt Richard fidget uncomfortably in his seat. Television, with its postcard images to illustrate the narration, always irritated him, and today he was especially tightly wound. They had arrived late, hoping to slip into the viewing theatre unnoticed, but Clover Merrifield, now in the back row between the director and producer, had delayed the start for them. Emily had seen quite a bit of Clover Merrifield recently. There was her weekly documentary slot on television, now into its third season, and she had been around to the house to interview them both for this programme. Emily had expected to dislike her, but she didn't. Nor did she envy her. The latest darling of television, with, it was said, a steel mill for a soul, was just another part of a past that had died with Hudson. Gently Emily put her hand on Richard's. It would be over in an hour.

Clover was now on the screen standing in a Bayswater square. Behind her Emily recognized the smartly painted terrace of restored Victorian houses which had once been the Lamborne Hotel. Clover looked at the houses: 'It was to this square that in 1963 James Hudson came when he arrived in London, to all intents the son of a well-to-do couple from a small affluent town in California, and a graduate of Berkeley and Columbia Universities. That was what he told his new friends, and, because he was an assured, intelligent and charming young man, his background was never questioned. But the truth was somewhat different. Although James Hudson did attend Berkeley and Columbia it was never as a full-time student, and never for very long. It was true he grew up in California, but his parents were not well off, in fact he never even knew his father, and the "family money" he said was used to launch his first magazine, *Witness*, was not the gift from them he claimed. He had made it himself, scrimping and saving, sometimes doing three jobs a day.'

Clover now looked straight into the camera. 'You see, the enigma that was James Hudson was a self-creation. At some time in the early summer of 1963 a young man called Tomiflav Mirkovic, half-Yugoslav, half-German, but brought up from the age of three in a succession of cheap Los Angeles rooming houses, changed everything about himself, starting with his name. At that moment James Hudson was born . . .'

Emily felt no surprise, only a deep sadness. She had heard the rumours before. Clover and her team had spent time and money discovering a part of the truth, but it would only ever be a part of the truth. Bleakly she watched as Clover told the few details they had been able to uncover: of the German soldier and the Yugoslav peasant girl and the resulting child born in December 1941. Forty-one. He had been even younger than they had believed. Yet always so grown up.

The newsreel of derelict wartime Yugoslavia had given way to black-and-white film of Italy and then Los Angeles. Clover was still talking. 'With the father of her son killed in action, somehow Mirjana Mirkovic got to Italy where, in 1944, she became involved with an American soldier, Bill Cernic. Invalided out of the Army Cernic married her and took her back with him to California. The marriage lasted only four months. By the time Tomiflav Mirkovic was four years old his mother had been abandoned. Hardly educated, with a thin grasp of English and poor health, she scraped a living as best she could.'

An elderly woman with a blue rinse and large glasses was standing in a devastated area of Mexican Los Angeles. 'I was involved in counselling at the time and this poor girl would come in with this little fellow. I don't know how she managed. She was never well. Maybe sometimes she did things she shouldn't. I know she did. I'd tell her, warn her, that she was getting into bad company, but she'd just look at me. She was so young, pretty really. But she didn't have anything. She was a good mother in her own way, I'll say that for her. He was a nice little boy. A very nice-looking little fellow. She did her best, I suppose. After a while she stopped coming.'

There were other interviews. A couple of landlords who thought they remembered, and some junior school teachers. 'He was so quick. He taught himself everything, right from the off. He could read when he came to us.'

But they were short interviews, following Mirjana's footsteps as she had moved through the sprawl of Los Angeles, a young woman and a child going from room to room. No one had known them well. By the age of ten Tomiflav was already helping out by cleaning cars in a used-car lot. There were all kinds of snippets of memories. One teacher remembered an ability for languages: 'In other circumstances he would have been considered a potentially gifted child. He was always wanting to improve himself and would listen to the news in Spanish, because he didn't like the Spanish accent he got off the kids on the block.' Another remembered him for drama. 'He was a good natural mimic, a good actor. He became the part. Even as a ten year old. Then one day he wasn't there.'

The next sighting had been in Anaheim where at eleven he had been part of a team which fastened fairy lights to a pine tree outside a Ford distributor's showroom one Christmas, then at a school in Pasadena where he had won a debating prize. 'He read all the time,' another teacher said. 'What he missed in class he made up for at home, or wherever it was he slept.'

Again Clover was close up on the screen, this time outside a public records office. 'According to records Mirjana Mirkovic died of tuberculosis in December 1953, when Tomiflav was twelve years old. Shortly after her death he is known to have become involved in a fight with a class-mate, José Menoza.' A thin, bald, hard-looking man appeared next. 'We were pals for a little while, Tom and me, although I was a lot older than he was. I guess he always seemed much older than he was because he was so tall and grown up. I think I said something unflattering about his mother and the stories about her, you know, and before I knew it we were rolling over on the floor. He was a hell of a fighter for a young kid. He got a bad cut on the chin when I hit him, but it didn't stop him. Nothing ever stopped him. He was strong all right. And determined, know what I mean?'

There were other accounts: in Sacramento, he had been known as a good pianist, in El Fuerte, he had chopped wood. But there were large gaps, too, when no one knew where he went. By the end of the Fifties he was to be seen hanging out around the campus at Berkeley, studying, working, saving, playing the piano in bars. He had played in lots of bars. There had been no close friends. He had told no one about his past, no one saw where he lived. It was as though Tom Mirkovic was waiting for his new life to begin before he would have time for friendships. In 1962 he had turned up at Columbia University in New York, a part-time student, who slept for a while on the floor of the basement of the Psi Upsilon fraternity house, his few belongings locked in an old trunk, while he worked in a hamburger bar on Broadway.

'He was, by then, a handsome young man, with style and charm, looking older than his years,' said Clover. Then, in 1963, he bought a couple of jackets and a Brooks Brothers overcoat from a student he knew and, with a new name, and seeking a new life, took a Saturday night flight to London.

(*ii*)

There was a cold silence as the credits rolled and the lights went up. For a few moments no one said anything. Then the producer took charge. 'Just to remind you all there are drinks and eats down in the reception room . . .'

Richard stared at his arms, crossed defensively in front of his chest. Next to him Emily was being greeted by Jessica Tarlo. He avoided Ben Tarlo's eyes. He needed a moment to think. Mainly he was relieved.

Did it matter? Did any of it really matter? Hudson

had invented himself and they had believed him. He wondered how much Hudson had come to believe it, too.

They moved down the open staircase into the reception room where sausage rolls and vol-au-vents were being served, the hum of conversation gathering now. He looked around. There must have been sixty guests, mainly journalists or Hudson Communications employees, but there were other, older faces: Willie, deeply tanned, talking to Tim Gimmelmann, Peter Berridge and Charlie Latymer head to head. For a moment Clover Merrifield purposely caught his eye and then, with a look which said, 'See how well I've done', she began addressing the crowd of young reporters surrounding her.

Penny Chilston, tomato juice in hand, touched his arm. 'I often wondered,' she said. 'No, not often, just sometimes. He was so alone in the world. Bless him.'

Richard nodded.

'I thought they might have got you to say why you and he fell out . . .'

'It was nothing, Penny. Of no interest to anyone else except him and me.'

'And still no clue why he walked into the sea.'

The programme had had more witnesses from Florida but no explanations had been offered.

Richard shrugged. 'I suppose he just got tired of living. It happens.' And he thought of a conversation many years ago about a man called Stephen Ward.

Ben Tarlo had joined them, overhearing their conversation. He was now chief executive of Hudson Communications. 'I don't think he ever really got over Nicola,' he said quietly.

'Probably not,' Richard agreed. He looked again at Clover. She was being showered in congratulations. She wasn't that clever. She would never know, but somehow she had missed the story of a lifetime. It happened. It happened all the time.

Penny went to talk to some friends leaving Ben alone

with Richard. 'I think in some ways I'd rather not have known,' Ben said, shaking his head. 'It just makes it sadder.'

'He was always sad. He just hid it very well.'

Emily approached. The post-mortems would go on for days as the programme was shown and reviewed, but they both wanted to get away. He put an arm around her.

'I know there's no point in my asking, but if you ever fancy a career in newspapers . . . either of you . . .' Ben was laughing.

'Maybe one of these days.'

Emily leant forward to kiss him. As she did Willie Simmonds lined up next to him and was given a kiss, too.

'I'm going back next week. Next time you're in Los Angeles, Richard . . . you, too, Ben, or even you, Emily, I can show you nights which would have made Nero blush.' The stammer had gone, but nothing else.

'I'll look forward to it,' said Emily.

Laughing, Richard led Emily out of the theatre on to Piccadilly.

For a while they dawdled among the tourists and discussed the programme, slowly making their way up towards the park. It all seemed so long since they had lived for newspapers. Emily was now happy to be teaching full time, while Richard had a career in radio news, producing, presenting, interviewing. He was becoming quite a celebrity, in a quiet way, famous for his voice. He was a contented man. In radio there was no waiting for the next day's or next week's edition. News never ended. And he could still never get enough of it.

They strolled on. It was almost summer. The boys had examinations soon and Catherine would be coming home from college in a few weeks. It would be nice to be a whole family again.

Life was good for everyone. There had even been a letter from Michael Mavangwe a few days ago with news of the Hudson Secondary School in Musaswa. 'We are now one of the best schools in the country,' he had written. 'I am very proud and grateful to you and to Mr Hudson. One day, when I become a teacher, perhaps I will get a passport and come to visit you in your house in London.'

He would always be welcome.

THE END

CONJURE ME

BY JACK CURTIS

I give a magic show and someone dies . . .

In the seventies they wanted to change the world – a group of young people who talked of blowing up trains, or wrecking the system. Then Lori Cosgrove died and their own world was changed for ever. Now, fifteen years later, someone is summoning them to lay Lori's ghost . . .

First there is Zeno – self-styled magus, illusionist and escapologist, but now he has added another role – murderer. Then there is Sam Pascoe, the lawyer. He used to know Zeno, but which of his old friends has become both conjuror and killer? These two are locked in battle, but beyond that conflict, watching it with cruel detachment, scheming, manipulating, *enjoying*, is Wallace Ellwood, a man whose delight in pain seems limitless.

The stage is set for the deadliest of magic shows.

'Read it, then go to sleep with the light on'
Daily Mail

0 552 13593 3

SECRETS OF STATE
BY PETER DRISCOLL

Eugene Vale — American war hero, multi-millionaire businessman and prospective US Secretary of State — has lived with two terrifying secrets for over forty years.

With the news of his appointment to one of the highest offices in the land, his past threatens to catch up with him, and a series of brutal murders across Western Europe, executed by those seeking to protect him, culminates in a stunning climax in the hills of Northern Greece.

In his electrifying thriller, the author of *The Wilby Conspiracy* and *Spearhead* confirms his place alongside Frederick Forsyth and Gerald Seymour in the top ranks of contemporary spy fiction.

0 552 13217 9

THE DECEIVER
BY FREDERICK FORSYTH

Sam McCready is The Deceiver, one of the Special Intelligence Service's most unorthodox and most valued operatives, a legend in his own time. The end of the cold war has, however, strengthened the hand of the Whitehall mandarins, to whom he seems about as controllable as Genghis Khan, so Sam is to have his fate decided at a special hearing.

As part of the proceedings, four of Sam's key operations are reviewed: a clandestine mission into East Germany in 1985 to contact the top Russian spy General Pankratin; the second involving a KGB colonel who wants to defect – but is he genuine? An audacious Gaddafi-inspired plot to ship arms to the IRA; and the fourth when McCready presided over the aftermath of political murder and mayhem in the Caribbean.

Following the world-wide triumph of his recent novel *The Negotiator*, the master returns with a keenly perceptive view of British Intelligence in the eighties, featuring one of his most memorable characters – The Deceiver, Sam McCready.

0 552 13823 1

HAND IN GLOVE
BY ROBERT GODDARD

Tristram Abberley was an English poet of the 1930s whose reputation was sealed when he died fighting for the Republicans in the Spanish Civil War. Nearly fifty years later his sister Beatrix is murdered during what appears to be a robbery at her home, but robbery – it transpires – is only part of the motive that underlies her death. Beatrix is the victim of a dark conspiracy, one that her loved ones are powerless to defeat.

But nothing is quite as it seems in a Robert Goddard novel. In a narrative that moves between Cheltenham and New York, Paris and rural Wales, Tunbridge Wells and wartime Spain, the conspirators themselves are caught up in a chain of dramatic events that are the consequence of meddling in the dark secrets of the legendary poet.

'A brilliant writer of suspense, Robert Goddard makes no claim other than to engross and entertain the reader'
Maureen Owen, *Daily Mail*

'Combines the steely edge of a thriller with the suspense of a whodunnit, all interlaced with subtle romantic overtones'
Time Out

'Cliff-hanging entertainment'
Guardian

0 552 13839 8

THE LUCY GHOSTS
BY EDDY SHAH

In the dying days of the Second World War many of Germany's rocket scientists traded their expertise for privileged treatment at the hands of both Russian and American invaders. For those scientists, bound together in a secret East–West brotherhood known as *Die Lucie Geister*, the war would never cease until Germany was united once more.

But with Reunification, sinister forces are unleashed. In a rash of assassinations, the scientists' records 'disappear' in the mysterious but systematic destruction of CIA and KGB files, and SAS captain Adam Nicholson is called in. A series of horrific murders leads him and his CIA sidekick, Billie Wood, from New Orleans to a neo-Nazi breeding ground in Germany. But it will be in Berlin, Germany's new capital, that her fragile democracy will be tested as never before, when Adam must gamble his life to unlock the final secrets of the Lucy Ghosts.

Eddy Shah's pulsating thriller transcends the pace and excitement of his first bestseller, *Ring of Red Roses* (also available in Corgi), confirming his emergence as a remarkable new talent on the international scene.

'A breathless, racy thriller'
Sunday Express

0 552 13918 1

A SELECTED LIST OF THRILLERS
AVAILABLE FROM CORGI BOOKS

THE PRICES SHOWN BELOW WERE CORRECT AT THE TIME OF GOIN
TO PRESS. HOWEVER TRANSWORLD PUBLISHERS RESERVE THE RIGH
TO SHOW NEW RETAIL PRICES ON COVERS WHICH MAY DIFFER FRON
THOSE PREVIOUSLY ADVERTISED IN THE TEXT OR ELSEWHERE.

☐	13592 5	SONS OF THE MORNING	*Jack Curtis* £4.9
☐	13593 3	CONJURE ME	*Jack Curtis* £4.9
☐	13217 9	SECRETS OF STATE	*Peter Driscoll* £4.9
☐	12550 4	LIE DOWN WITH LIONS	*Ken Follett* £4.9
☐	12610 1	ON WINGS OF EAGLES	*Ken Follett* £4.9
☐	12569 5	THE FOURTH PROTOCOL	*Frederick Forsyth* £4.9
☐	13275 9	THE NEGOTIATOR	*Frederick Forsyth* £4.9
☐	13823 1	THE DECEIVER	*Frederick Forsyth* £4.95
☐	12140 1	NO COMEBACKS	*Frederick Forsyth* £3.95
☐	09436 6	THE ODESSA FILE	*Frederick Forsyth* £3.95
☐	13561 5	INTO THE BLUE	*Robert Goddard* £4.99
☐	13282 9	PAINTING THE DARKNESS	*Robert Goddard* £4.99
☐	13144 X	PAST CARING	*Robert Goddard* £4.99
☐	13839 8	HAND IN GLOVE	*Robert Goddard* £4.99
☐	13697 2	AIRPORT	*Arthur Hailey* £4.99
☐	13678 6	THE EVENING NEWS	*Arthur Hailey* £5.99
☐	13869 X	MATILDA'S GAME	*Denis Kilcommons* £3.99
☐	12433 8	A COLD MIND	*David Lindsey* £4.99
☐	12661 6	HEAT FROM ANOTHER SUN	*David Lindsey* £4.99
☐	13215 2	SPIRAL	*David Lindsey* £4.99
☐	13871 1	THE LUXUS	*A. W. Mykel* £4.99
☐	12417 6	THE SALAMANDRA GLASS	*A. W. Mykel* £4.99
☐	11850 8	THE WINDCHIME LEGACY	*A. W. Mykel* £4.99
☐	13771 5	RING OF RED ROSES	*Eddy Shah* £4.99
☐	13918 1	THE LUCY GHOSTS	*Eddy Shah* £4.99

All Corgi/Bantam Books are available at your bookshop or newsagent, or can be
ordered from the following address:
Corgi/Bantam Books,
Cash Sales Department,
P.O. Box 11, Falmouth, Cornwall TR10 9EN

UK and B.F.P.O. customers please send a cheque or postal order (no currency) and
allow £1.00 for postage and packing for the first book plus 50p for the second book
and 30p for each additional book to a maximum charge of £3.00 (7 books plus).

Overseas customers, including Eire, please allow £2.00 for postage and packing for
the first book plus £1.00 for the second book and 50p for each subsequent title
ordered.

NAME (Block Letters) ....

ADDRESS ....

....